MW00625916

DEEPWATER MOUNTAIN

a novel of West Virginia

by

Rebecca Cale Camhi

International Standard Book Number 0-87012-651-2
Library of Congress Control Number 00 193573
Printed in the United States of America
Copyright © 2001 by Rebecca Cale Camhi
Williamsville, NY 14221
All Rights Reserved
2001

Camera-ready material provided.

McClain Printing Company
212 Main Street
Parsons, WV 26287
http://McClainPrinting.com

For my father who can still name all
fifty-five counties of West Virginia
and for my mother, a coal miner's daughter.

AUTHOR'S NOTE

Some twenty years ago when I read Alex Haley's <u>Roots,</u> I remember a passage near the end where he described how he used to sit on his grandmother's porch as a little boy and listen to her tell the stories of his family as fireflies lit up the summer sky at twilight. When I read this, I felt like he was talking about my own childhood growing up in southern West Virginia. I recall sitting on the back porch of our little house in Glen Ferris and listening to my mother tell about the generations of Cales, Kincaids, and Woodsons. She brought the daily life of the coal camps to life in her vivid -- and often rollicking -- descriptions of living on Paint Creek during the Great Depression. Often my sister and I listened while we ate a blackberry cobbler still steaming hot from the oven swimming in creamy pools of vanilla ice cream. My mother's voice was pure silk drifting on the sultry night air amid the evening songs of crickets. The only light on those dark nights was provided courtesy of dozens of fireflies as they danced past. I come from a long line of storytellers who can mesmerize and captivate with seemingly no effort at all. So years later, when I began to think about writing a novel, I remembered the stories that I grew up with and I decided to put them together in one book set against the backdrop of the first hundred years of West Virginia's statehood.

Many of the characters in this book are based on real people -- several of the Hatfields, Mother Jones, and Eleanor Roosevelt, to name only a few. Others who may not be as famous actually lived and worked in West Virginia and were part of our family. Creedy Payne came to live with my great-grandparents when he was a boy. He was an old man living with my grandparents when I was small. Creedy came to them in just the way I have described in the novel. My uncle, Glenny Woodson, was killed in the Paint Creek mines when he was run over by a coal car. Dora Lottie is based on my maternal grandmother, and yes, she was supposed to have been born with a "caul" -- a superstition that she "heard" and "saw" things that the rest of us were unable to hear and see, a sixth sense. The character of Mr.

Shaw was based on my piano instructor, A. W. Shaw of Gauley Bridge. A band director for many years, Mr. Shaw became known across the state as "The Music Man of West Virginia". Ansel's daughter, Nellie, was Mary Ellen Wolerton, who for many years, served as principal and teacher of the Glen Ferris Elementary School, the two-room schoolhouse I attended as a little girl. Lastly, Daniel was based on two people: my grandfather, Harry Cale, and a boy I knew named Wayne Morrison. My grandfather bore a deep scar that ran the entire length of his arm. He never told anyone how he came by that scar so I supplied the battle with the mountain lion, thinking that it would finally let my grandfather off the hook after all these years. And I still remember standing in the alley in Glen Ferris and watching Wayne Morrison, young and blonde, walking toward me with a dead snake he had killed in the mountains behind our house. Between the two of them, they provided me with the perfect character for Willa May's husband.

Other characters -- Old Man Peyton, Ansel Shrewsbury, and Elroy Hicks -- were purely fictional. Ansel, however, became so real to me that in the end, he was the one character I couldn't allow to die.

Many of the events in the book were from those stories I heard growing up while others were based on West Virginia's history. My dad was a Golden Horseshoe winner, knowing more about the state's history than I will ever know. During the writing of the book, I relied on his memory of that history. I also found a treasure trove of books about West Virginia that aided me in my research of West Virginia's rich history: West Virginia: A Bicentennial History by John Alexander Williams; The West Virginia Mine Wars: An Anthology edited by David Alan Corbin; West Virginia: A History for Beginners by John Alexander Williams; Bloodletting In Appalachia: The Story of West Virginia's Four Major Mine Wars and Other Thrilling Incidents of Its Coal Fields by Howard B. Lee; New River: A Photographic Essay by Arnout Hyde Jr.; and King Coal: A Pictorial Heritage of West Virginia Coal Mining by Stan Cohen. In addition to these books, the four-part mini-series, "West Virginia" which aired on PBS, narrated by Richard Thomas, was invaluable in corroborating many of the events I had researched. My thanks to my old friend and former Secretary of Arts and Education, Stephen Haid, for that wonderful documentary. Without his efforts, it would never have been made.

Lastly, a special thanks to Alan, Liza, and Jonathan for their patience and understanding when dinner was late night after night.

Chapter One

Western Virginia

April, 1861

Something was watching him. Daniel felt the pair of eyes on him just as he could feel the weight of his tattered wool shirt on his back. Something was there all right. Without moving a muscle, his eyes scanned the new spring grass. He had killed many a rattler and copperhead on this mountain, enough to know that any sudden move on his part might be his last. His blue eyes, the color of a clear July sky, moved from left to right and back. Whatever it was that watched him so intently, it was not coiled in the grass ready to pierce his flesh with its venomous bite. Daniel's ears strained now to catch the slightest sound but he only heard the far off squawk of a blue jay somewhere down in the valley. He mentally ruled out a bear, knowing a bear would come crashing through the trees on all fours. Besides, the trees were just beginning to bud. They were still too bare yet to provide much cover for a bear.

His body tensed for attack, Daniel slowly lifted his eyes from the ground to the web of branches overhead. No sooner did he hear a warning hiss when a blur of tawny fur descended upon him. The mountain lion leapt onto Daniel's left shoulder. He tried to jump aside, but it was too late. The big cat slid down Daniel's arm, raking its sharp claws deep into his flesh and laying open Daniel's arm from his shoulder to his wrist. He cried out in agony as he looked into the snarling face of the mountain lion. It bared its glistening white fangs in a low guttural growl. As it lunged at him again, Daniel caught it with his left hand before it could sink those sharp fangs into his neck. He grasped his hunting knife in his free hand and swung it down in a shining silver arc toward the big cat's throat. He felt the knife hit home. Blood spurted from the animal as Daniel drove the knife in all the way up to the blade. Now it was the mountain lion's turn to yowl in pain. It writhed against Daniel, digging at his flesh in an attempt to free itself. Daniel managed to hold onto the hundred and fifty pound beast by the scruff of his neck. He cut a jagged line down the cat's

1

belly, feeling its warm blood soaking through his shirt and overalls. In a desperate effort to free itself, the mountain lion continued to claw blindly at him. A moment later, Daniel felt the cat's strength weakening. Then it twitched convulsively and fell limp. Its eyes, that only seconds before had been narrowed in predatory ferocity, stared blankly at him.

Daniel gulped in air as he lowered the mountain lion's slack body. His clothes were clinging to him. He felt a bit wobbly on his feet but he paid no attention to it. Once his breathing became regular, he beheld the carcass in his hand. A low whistle escaped his lips as he smiled with pride at his quarry. "Well, I'll be," he breathed. "Looks like I got me a prize for sure this time!"

He slung the dead mountain lion around his neck and started off the mountain into the valley below. He wondered why he was feeling so dizzy, unaware that the blood streaming down his left arm was his own. Having explored this mountain since he was just a boy, Daniel had suffered cuts, scrapes and snake bites in too many battles to be concerned about a few scratches. Besides, he was still marveling over how he had faced down a mountain lion and how someday, when he was an old man, he would be able to tell his grandchildren about it. It would make a mighty good story.

It took him a full hour to reach the foot of the mountain and wade across the gurgling creek that glistened like a black satin ribbon beside the dusty rutted road. The icy creek water felt good on his bare feet as he made his way across the slippery creek bed. It was midday when he came to some houses clustered on either side of the creek. By then he was staggering as much from loss of blood as from the weight of the carcass draped over his neck. Sweat ran in rivulets down his face. He tried to wipe it away but his hands were so bloody that it only made it harder to see. Through a blur, he could just make out the houses on either side of him. The dirt road beneath his feet seemed to move back and forth in an "S" shape like a black snake slithering past him. The hills on either side of the road kept closing in on him. Just five more miles and he would be home. He was beginning to feel right poorly, like the time he had eaten too much of his ma's rhubarb pie and it had all come back up. His stomach churned and again he felt everything around him swirling past like the rippling water in the creek. That was when he spotted the little girl with the long red hair, the color of a blazing fire. In her white pinafore, with the afternoon sun creating a halo around her hair, she looked like a small angel smiling up at him.

2

Willa may Kincaid stood in the front yard of her home in Page. The grass beneath her bare feet was green and soft. She spotted a young man walking her way, coming up the dirt road that ran past her house from Oak Hill down past Deepwater. He was tall and gangly, all legs like a young colt. His face was bronzed by the sun even though it was just spring. Long blonde hair streaked from the sun hung down to his shoulders. As she stood there, she couldn't help thinking that he looked as golden as the animal he was carrying. He wore bib overalls and like her, his feet were bare. When he got closer she could see blood streaming down his left arm. The sleeve of his shirt had been ripped completely off. At first she thought the blood was dripping down from a wide red gash in the mountain lion's neck, but when he got closer, she could see that his arm was laid open from his shoulder to his wrist. Deep cuts ran alongside the gash like two sets of railroad tracks, spurting blood from different spots. The blood dripping from his left hand was mixed with blood from the dead cat. In his wake was a crimson colored path.

Willa May moved closer for a better look. She had seen this young fellow before and she recollected that he was one of the Shrewsbury boys from down around Deepwater. She would have thought that he would show some sign of suffering from that arm but he was wearing the biggest grin she ever saw. Some folks might think that peculiar but Willa May understood. The Shrewsbury boy had tangled with that varmint and he'd won. He had faced down that wild cat on its own ground without any gun that she could see. All he had was a hunting knife in a leather sheath that dangled from a rope around his waist. He had beaten the beast with his own bare hands.

Some of the neighbors started to gather around, gawking like Willa May. One boy yelled, "Did you kill that thing all by yourself?"

The Shrewsbury boy grinned even wider as he nodded to the boy, showing even white teeth against his tanned face.

"Can we see?"

Willa May was amazed that everyone wanted a look at the dead carcass when it was plain to see that the young man needed help. "Bring that dead cat up here and set him on our porch so everybody can get a good look-see," she said. "Then come on in and let my mama see to that cut on your arm."

The boy seemed surprised as he looked down at his arm and the blood dripping out of him. He nodded at her and said, "Why, thank you, miss. I'd be mighty obliged."

3

Careful to take his right hand, she led him up to the porch. He winced as he reached up and put the big cat down on the top step for all to see. A fair sized crowd had gathered by then. Willa May led him around to the back of the house where here mama was washing clothes in a big washtub. Lizzy Kincaid was a small woman with the same red hair as her daughter. Like all the women in the valley she was stronger than her tiny frame belied. She looked up to see her daughter coming with a young man she thought she recognized. Her eyes went straight to the boy's bloody arm. Lizzy dropped the wet clothes in her hand along with the scrub board and rushed over to them.

"My stars!" she breathed, examining the boy's cut. "Willa May, fetch me some boiling hot water, some clean rags, and my sewing kit."

Willa May raced into the house. She heard the screen on the back door slam shut just as her mama called, "Bring this here boy a jug, too. He's goin' to need it."

Willa May scurried around the house gathering up all the things her mama had told her to get. When she came back out with the jug in one hand and the sewing basket in the other, her mama had set the boy down and he was looking mighty pale. She ran back inside and came out with a bundle of clean rags. She handed them to her mama and they started tearing off long strips for bandaging. Willa May brought out a kettle of boiling water. Lizzy took one look at the pot and told her to boil more...lots more.

When Willa May returned, Lizzy gave the injured boy some swigs off of the jug, then turned to Willa May and said, "Pull that other chair yonder over here and take hold of this boy's good hand. Hold on tight, now, you hear?"

Willa May took Daniel's right hand and squeezed it hard while her mama took the jug and poured whiskey over the gaping wound. The boy sucked in air, moaning and squeezing back on Willa May's hand until she wanted to scream. Willa May looked at the deep cut. She could see bluish tissue beneath the slit flesh. The grass under Daniel's chair was turning a pinkish color. His eyes were shut tight and he clenched his teeth in a grimace.

"Son, I'm goin' to have to start sewing you up now."

When he didn't say anything Lizzy said, "Son? You hear me?" He nodded. "Yes'm."

He had begun to let up on his hold on Willa May's hand but when Lizzy started stitching his wound, the boy clamped down on Willa

4

May's hand again. She bit down on her lip to keep from crying out, knowing that he was in even more pain.

It took Lizzy close to an hour to sew up the wounds on the boy's arm. As she came to his wrist, she found something sticking out of the cut. It was one of the big cat's claws. She dipped it in some of the hot water and shaking her head in disbelief, she dropped it in the small pocket on the bib of his overalls, knowing he would enjoy the trophy later. When she finished, she poured more whiskey over the stitches. Then she offered the boy the rest of the jug. He let go of Willa May's hand. She rubbed her hands together, trying to get some feeling back in the one he had held. She watched the Shrewsbury boy sling the jug over his right shoulder like her Pa and Uncle Jim did. He took swigs from the jug off and on while Lizzy and Willa May bandaged his arm. Willa May noticed that the ground beneath his chair had turned dark red.

"You're goin' to want to change these here bandages every day and keep that wound cleaned till you get them stitches cut out."

The boy nodded. From the glassy look in his eyes, Willa May figured that either he was lightheaded from her mama's handiwork or the jug had done its job. Maybe it was a little of both, she decided.

Lizzy said, "Willa May, this boy's in no shape to go home. Put him in Augie's bed and let him sleep it off. Your pa can take him back to his folks tomorrow."

Willa May led the boy into the house to her no-account brother's room in the back of the house. They all called Augie "that no-account Augie" because he was so lazy and irresponsible. The room was so small that aside from the cot Augie called a bed there was only a small washstand in the room. She helped the boy down onto the little bed. It was too short for him and his feet dangled over the end. As she turned to leave, he asked, "What's your name?"

"I'm Willa May Kincaid," she said.

His eyes closed, but he smiled. She thought he had drifted off so she turned again to leave. She reached the door when she heard him say, "Willa May?"

She looked back at him, wondering what he wanted now. "I'm Daniel. Daniel Shrewsbury."

"Well now, that's sort of fitting, isn't it?"

He didn't say anything but she could tell he wasn't getting the gist of what she was saying so she said, "Daniel. Like the Daniel in the Bible. He had a run-in with some lions, too."

Daniel's eyes were still closed but he smiled. She opened the door to leave when he said, "Willa May? Some day I'm goin' to marry you."

For a long time, Willa May stood frozen in the doorway looking back at Daniel. Even though she was only going on nine years old, somewhere deep inside she knew that what Daniel had said would come to pass. That she was meant to be his. Daniel had claimed two lives that day, the mountain lion's and hers.

The next morning Willa May's pa, Napoleon Kincaid -- everyone in the valley called him "Pole", excepting her mama -- hitched up his mules, Bess and Dixie, and hauled Daniel on home to his folks. Daniel's family was relieved to see him in one piece but they were accustomed to Daniel going off into the mountains by himself. They took him in without a word of warning to him, thanking Pole for his trouble. That morning as she stood waving goodbye to him, Willa May thought that she would see a lot of Daniel since he was set on marrying up with her. After all, she reasoned, it wasn't every day that someone said such a thing. She strained her eyes at every shadowy figure that appeared on the road by her house day after day until after a week, when she couldn't stand it any longer, she asked her mama, "Reckon we'll ever see that poor boy with the cut up arm again?" She tried hard to sound like she didn't care.

Lizzy looked at Willa May, knowing full well that she was more than just a mite interested. She could read her daughter like a book. Besides, she had watched Willa May peering down the road for days now. "Why, Willa May, don't you know about the war that's brewing?"

Willa May had heard her pa and some of the other menfolk jawing about "the war". Men's talk was all it was to her. "The war" was just some far away place where folks were setting to feud a spell, she figured. She had read about wars in school. They made for exciting stories but that was about all. "Sure I know about the war. Just last week Pa was saying that there was goin' to be a war for sure now that they'd fired the first shot." She didn't let on that she had no idea what he had meant.

Lizzy looked at Willa May. "Well, if you know so much about the war then you should know that every able bodied man will be goin' off

6

to take up arms. Your brother, Augie, just last night said that he'd be leaving come Saturday to join up with some other boys from northern Virginia. So I wouldn't be fixing on seeing that Shrewsbury boy again if I was you." Seeing the disappointment on Willa May's face, she reached over and put her hand on Willa May's. "Darlin', you might never see that boy again. I know that isn't what you want to hear but that's the pure and simple truth of it."

But just as Willa May had known that she would grow up to marry Daniel, she knew deep down in her soul that he would come back.

A week later, Daniel's cousin, Elroy Hicks, came by and brought Willa May a message from Daniel. Scrawny, with dirty bare feet dangling from his tattered overalls, Elroy rarely looked a person in the eye. Willa May chalked it up to what her mama called "backwardness". She thought it might be because Elroy was embarrassed about his looks then she considered that maybe he didn't have sense enough to realize how he looked. His teeth were black and rotting and he had one eye that looked inward, making him look cross-eyed. His face was smeared with dirt and he wore a constant circle around his mouth that made it no secret what he had eaten that day. His hair, the color of mud, fell in lank oily strands over his eyes.

Elroy told Willa May that Daniel was going to Ohio to join the Union army there. He said that Daniel had never held with owning slaves so he couldn't bring himself to fight with the Secesh, the Southern army. He hoped she wouldn't hold it against him for not going along with Virginia and that as he could neither read nor write, he would try to get word to her when he could to let her know he was all right. Elroy giggled, adding, "Daniel says to tell you that you're to wait for him."

Willa May swatted Elroy on the head. At twelve years old Elroy was still a runt. "Stop your laughing, you big dummy!" Willa May barked. But Elroy didn't stop. He laughed even harder. Willa May grabbed him by the front of his shirt and pulled him close. She could smell the ramps he'd had for supper on his breath. Eye to eye, Willa May threatened, "Don't you go spouting off to anybody what you just told me, you hear? If you do, I'll wring your scrawny little neck. Don't you think I can't, either!"

Elroy grew fearful. With wide eyes, he nodded vehemently and gasped, "I won't tell a soul. Cross my heart and hope to die." He looked silly standing there crossing his heart, his eyes nearly popping out of his head. Willa May let go of him. She knew he wouldn't dare break his word.

He started to run off but she called after him. Elroy stopped and turned around with a blank expression on his face. "Huh?" Willa May despaired the boy must not have a lick of sense, standing in the middle of the dirt road wearing such a silly look.

Shaking her head, she said, "Elroy, how old would you say Daniel is?" She was hoping he'd say fourteen or maybe fifteen. That way the army wouldn't take him.

Elroy scrunched up his face, thinking hard. "Daniel? Why, he turned eighteen last November. What did you want to know that for?"

"'Cause I did, that's why."

Elroy rolled his eyes and headed on down the road, leaving Willa May standing there wondering how far away Ohio was.

Daniel was as good as his word. In the fall, a Union troop was camped by Kanawha Falls and one of their scouts came looking for Willa May one Sunday. Lizzy asked him in for chicken dinner and the man ate a whole chicken by himself. Willa May thought that was more why he came calling than bringing her Daniel's message. After devouring two plates of Lizzy's home cooking, he said that Daniel was a scout, too. He was hooked up with some men over in Ohio under the command of a man named Sherman. None of Willa May's family had ever heard tell of this Sherman fellow. The messenger, whose name was Evans, said that this Sherman hailed from Lancaster, Ohio, and that he was one tough customer. Pole and Uncle Jim took all this in. They asked Evans how long he thought the war would last. Chuckling, the man replied, "Well, Mr. Kincaid, I wouldn't fret none. This war's goin' to be over pretty quick, I reckon. The North has four times as many able bodied men, more factories, and our men are better equipped." Lighting up a cigar, he puffed and nodded, "Yep. I'd say this war may not last the year."

Pole winked at Big Jim. "I hear tell that's what the Rebs are saying, too. Telling their wives to keep their vittles warm, that they'll be back to finish eating after they beat the Yanks."

Evans shook his head, wearing a serious frown. "They're wrong,

8

Mr. Kincaid. Mighty wrong."

Pole must have decided to let this drop because he said, "Are you one of them abolitionists, sir?"

"No sir, can't say as I am. But there's a lot of men in my company that are. Some say they even helped some slaves escape, helped them once they got across the Ohio River. Said they was part of that 'Underground Railroad' that got slaves north to Canada. A great many of them sing 'John Brown's Body' when we're on the march. It's almost like a hymn to them boys."

Again Pole and Big Jim exchanged looks. Pole said, "My son, Augie, seen the hanging, you know. He was right there and seen the whole thing. Said that Brown feller was all wild eyed, like some critter that's gone rabid."

Evans nodded. "I've seen the same look on some of the men in my company. Nothing more stubborn than a man with a cause. They'll defy the Devil himself, they will. And all for a cause."

Big Jim, a massive man with a bushy black beard down to his belt, spoke up. "Way I see it, a lot of them Johnny Rebs think they're fighting for a pretty good cause, too. Could make for a tough fight for you Yanks."

Evans grunted, eyeing the apple pie Lizzy had set in front of him. Shrugging, he said, "We shall see, gentlemen. We shall see."

At school Willa May pestered the schoolmaster, Mr. Shaw, every day for word of the war. She knew it was all right because she was his favorite pupil and he thought she was set on becoming a schoolmarm. It was because of Mr. Shaw that Willa May had such a thirst to read. She read everything she could get her hands on, not just the Good Book like other folks. She was way past that. Hawthorne, Malory, her favorite, and all about Robin Hood. Mr. Shaw had a fine library of his own and he let Willa May read whatever she happened to fancy. Then he talked to her about each book, always bragging on her for seeing certain things about the nature of the characters in the story or spotting what he called "fingerposts" in the plots. What she loved most about reading was that it took her places she would never see except in her imagination.

Mr. Shaw had a gimpy leg and walked with a cane. He was old enough to be Willa May's grandfather, too old to go off to war. But

9

that old man soon became her lifeline to the outside world. Since he could read, folks with newspapers and letters would bring them to Mr. Shaw to read aloud to them. He lived in Robson, just a couple of miles from Page, with his spinster sister known to all as Miss Beatrice. With their silver hair and kindly faces, they looked like twins but Mr. Shaw was five years older.

He didn't know Willa May's real reason for showing such interest in the war; he just figured she was brighter than the other girls who didn't show nearly the hankering for war talk as she did. Often Mr. Shaw's news was about something Willa May wasn't interested in but sometimes he would mention a tidbit about the Army of Northern Virginia, her brother Augie's outfit. She would run home to spill it all to her folks who hung onto her every word. It was around Easter time when Mr. Shaw told her a piece of news that made her sit up and pay attention. He said that Sherman's men had been in a scrape with some Rebs in a place called Shiloh down in Tennessee. Sherman and Grant had whupped Johnston and Beauregard pretty bad. Then old Mr. Shaw, peering through his thick spectacles and holding the newspaper right up to his nose, went on reading about something called "casualties".

"What's that?" Willa May interrupted.

"Good question, Miss Kincaid. Very good question."

Impatient for word about Daniel, Willa May just wished he would explain the word instead of going on so. At times like this, she wanted to shake the old man till his jaws flapped. "But what is it?" she persisted, knowing she wasn't showing the proper respect she'd been taught.

Mr. Shaw ignored her poor manners and said, "Casualties are the number of dead, wounded, captured, and missing."

Willa May felt a lump growing in her throat. *Oh, Lordy,* she thought. Gulping hard, she said, "Well, let's hear it."

Mr. Shaw looked back to the newspaper. His eyes scanned the page, picking up where he had left off. "Oh, yes. Here we are. Oh, dear. Over ten thousand for the South and thirteen thousand for the North."

In her mind Willa May could see her Daniel wounded and bloody like he was from the mountain lion. She prayed that some other kindhearted woman would take pity on him and tend to him like her mama did. She must have drifted off on this thought because the next thing she knew Mr. Shaw was saying, "That's as much as they're goin' to tell us for now, Miss Kincaid. But don't fret now about your brother. I'm sure he'll be fine and you'll be hearing from him soon."

Willa May nodded, her mind still seeing Daniel hurt and needing help. She thanked Mr. Shaw for sharing his news with her. She was about to leave when she asked, "Just where is Tennessee, anyway?"

Mr. Shaw hobbled over to a big book lying open on his desk and pointed with his forefinger, crooked from arthritis and shaky with age. "Right here, Miss Kincaid."

She bent over the map with him, calculating how far this Shiloh was from Page. It looked a far piece. "What's that?" she asked, pointing to a strange looking name that seemed about a mile long just below this Shiloh.

"Break it down into syllables and I think you'll see."

"Miss-iss-ipp-i," she managed.

"Exactly, Miss Kincaid. Mississippi. And if you travel to its very southern border right here," his shaky finger traced a line straight down the page, "you reach the Gulf of Mexico." Willa May stared at the blue space with "Gulf of Mexico" printed over it. Now she knew what those men back in the time of Christopher Columbus had meant when they couldn't see over the horizon and they thought it was the end of the world. She felt certain that blue space was the end of the world. Then she remembered something else, something from a story that Mr. Shaw had read to her once. "Beyond this point, there be dragons." She pictured Daniel decked out like some knight in olden days, lying at the feet of a huge fire breathing beast, its gleaming yellow eyes fixed on Daniel and poor Daniel trying to fend this giant varmint off with just a sword that wasn't much bigger than his hunting knife. She shivered.

Mr. Shaw patted her on the back. "It's not that far, my dear. Not really."

Willa May nodded, but she didn't believe it. Not for a minute.

In December folks were getting ready for Christmas, not that Christmas would be very festive that year, with everybody worried sick over loved ones off in the fighting. Lee beat Burnside at Fredericksburg and when everyone was breathing a sigh of relief over Augie being safe, word came just before the New Year that Sherman's men had been beaten back from Vicksburg. Willa May heard her pa say, "I have to hand it to that Sherman. He's one tough old cuss." As proof of that, the following summer Sherman and Grant came back and took Vicksburg.

There was a big celebration in June of 1863 when West Virginia was admitted as a state in its own right. Politicians speaking, bands playing, flags flying. Looking around her that day, Willa May saw lots of men in uniform, both blue and gray. Some from the same family. They were all proud to call themselves West Virginians that day though, no matter which side they were on. There wasn't a dry eye in the crowd when they raised the new state flag with its motto, "Mountaineers Are Always Free". Rebs and Yanks alike looked at that flag, knowing deep down in their hearts, it didn't make any difference which side they were fighting for. They were all mountaineers. They even had a moment of silence for Stonewall Jackson, who had fallen at Chancellorsville the month before. While some didn't like it because Stonewall wore gray, he was still one of them and he had made them all proud. He was a great general and a great man. Such a shame he died at the hands of his own men, folks said. Just one of those crazy things that happened in war and didn't make any sense. The crowd bowed their heads and showed their respect for one of their own. For his greatness.

It was a grand day. Willa May joined all the girls pointing and giggling at the boys slopping like pigs in the watermelon eating contest. They sniggered even more when some of the menfolk bid on their baked goods. Willa May had baked a boysenberry pie that her pa said he wasn't about to let loose of so he bid on it and ate every bite. She thought the real reason Pole bid on her pie was that he wasn't about to let loose of her yet. Since it was wartime, some girls were spoken for even before they turned twelve. She reckoned her pa didn't want her to be among them.

Each time Willa May's family heard word of a battle Augie was in her mama would send her down to Mr. Shaw's to wait for the lists of casualties. The whole valley had come to know the meaning of that word too well by then. Willa May would always find some excuse to go when she would hear about Daniel's infantry regiment being in some squabble, too. Miss Beatrice knew just when Willa May would show up and she always had a little treat for Willa May. In winter it might be a piece of hard candy and sassafras tea; in summer, a piece of fresh berry cobbler. Willa May thought it was the old woman's way of

12

preparing her for bad news if it came. Over the years, Willa May grew fond of Miss Beatrice. Quiet as she was, Miss Beatrice was a proper lady. Always tatting lace for pillowcases and dresser scarves. Even for wedding dresses for those girls who decided not to wait for their boyfriends to come home from the war but to get hitched when their men were home on leave. Miss Beatrice always smelled like fresh lemons and she kept herself and her brother's house as neat as a pin.

By the second year of the war, Willa May had become a regular fixture at their house. Whenever she finished her chores, she would head down to Robson. Sometimes the three of them would sit by the fire while it snowed outside, the wind howling at the door and they would sip their hot tea and read poetry or stories from the Good Book. In summer they would watch the fireflies blinking in the night. Mr. Shaw would play his fiddle and Miss Beatrice would sing. Stephen Foster was her favorite and she would trill like a bird to "Jeannie With The Light Brown Hair", sitting on the front porch under a starry summer sky. Times like that Willa May would feel such a peace inside that she would almost forget about Daniel camped under the same starry sky, maybe facing the Rebs the next morning.

Around the time that word came about Vicksburg, they were holding their breath for word of Augie. He was at a little place in Pennsylvania called Gettysburg. Willa May ended up staying over at Mr. Shaw's for three days and nights while they waited for the names of the dead and wounded. The lists were awfully long once they started coming through. There were so many folks waiting like Willa May that they took up all of Mr. Shaw's yard and lined up in both directions on the road as far as the eye could see. Such a sad sight. Each time a list came in, Mr. Shaw stood on his porch and read the names. There was always weeping and wailing from the crowd as he read. Poor Elroy Hicks was among the names of the wounded. Willa May felt a lump in her throat like a big rock wedged there thinking about Elroy and how he had brought her word from Daniel when the war broke out. Elroy had run off after the spring planting and lied about his age. The army took him without question. Now he had gotten both his legs blown off. She shook her head sorrowfully.

Willa May started fretting about Augie after hearing the news about Elroy. Elroy was nobody's idea of a genius but where Elroy was foolish, Augie was plain lazy. In her mind's eye she could see Augie sitting down in the middle of some bloody field, bodies lying all around him and his men in retreat. All the while Augie would be

13

saying, "Go on. Go ahead. I'll catch up in a while after I get me a little rest." Then a cannonball would land right on top of him and blow him to kingdom come. That would be just like Augie.

Willa May grew so worried thinking that Augie was going to get himself killed that she couldn't eat. Not even a piece of one of Miss Beatrice's fresh blackberry cobblers. On the third day Miss Beatrice came and sat on the porch with her. It was July and hotter than a snake's belly but Miss Beatrice never seemed to notice the heat. She always wrapped herself in a shawl, summer or winter. On that day she had on one she had crocheted in a pretty pink that reminded Willa May of dogwoods in early spring. Miss Beatrice was patting Willa May's hand when a man rode up on a lathered horse. He didn't bother getting off his horse; he just leaned over and handed Mr. Shaw one of the lists in his hand, saying this was the last of the names. Then he took off as if the Devil himself was on his heels down the road to deliver the rest of his lists.

All the folks that were still waiting drew near and Mr. Shaw started reading the list of names. Willa May held her breath waiting for that moment she was sure would come when Mr. Shaw would read, "Kincaid, Augustus" but after some thirty names, he looked up and shrugged. "That's it. That's all of them." As always, it had weighed hard on the old man as he read off the names of boys he had watched grow up. Most of them had learned their A-B-C's from Mr. Shaw. To others, he had given fiddle lessons. He wiped his eyes with a hanky as white and soft as the frothy clouds that day, his shoulders shaking from his sobbing. Miss Beatrice and Willa May got up and helped him inside. When Willa May saw that he was calmed down she said she needed to get on home and tell her mama the news. They nodded for her to go.

Willa May was relieved about Augie but she walked home with a heavy heart. So many boys and so much dying. She thought about Elroy and wondered if he was sorry that he had run off like he had. He should have been sitting down by the creek with a fishing pole or skinny dipping to get cooled off on that hot summer day. But he was lying somewhere on some cot, both his legs gone, wondering if he was going to die. Elroy wasn't even fourteen. Willa May wiped away her tears and prayed as she walked up the dusty dirt road that she'd never have to live through another war. War just plain hurt too much.

That summer left Willa May and her family exhausted from worry. Things calmed down a bit for them that fall. Chickamauga came and went, so did Chattanooga. Then it was the holidays again and Augie came home for Thanksgiving. Pa and Big Jim went up in the mountain and bagged a deer so they had venison roast and stuffing with big walnut chunks. Lizzy made her special sweet potatoes with brown sugar and tart apples stewed with cinnamon. Willa May got up at sunrise to make the biscuits for breakfast then she baked the cornbread and started in on the pumpkin pies. Before she knew it she was covered in flour. Augie came staggering in. He had been up to the still in back of the house with Pole and Big Jim. Augie saw Willa May coated in flour and swore that she had died and it was her ghost standing there. Poor Augie had been into the corn in a way she didn't think the Pilgrim fathers would have approved of. By supper time, he was out by the shed puking up his guts. Lizzy yelled out that they were about to say the prayer. Augie hollered back, "Say one for me!"

Lizzy shot icy glances at Pole and Big Jim who just shuffled their feet and looked sheepish. They were a little green around the gills themselves. Willa May snickered. A big mistake she learned as Lizzy pinched her. Trying to save some smidgen of their dignity, Lizzy pressed her lips together and said primly, "Very well, I reckon I'll have to lead the blessing over the vittles this year." She began by thanking the Lord for their fine meal and for bringing Augie home safely to them. She was in the middle of thanking the Lord for giving them Thanksgiving when someone knocked at the door.

Pole went to see who it was, trying hard not to stumble and give Lizzy more to press her lips about. Willa May could hear a man's voice but it wasn't anyone she recognized. Then Pole called, "Willa May, there's a feller here wanting to see you."

Willa May's heart leapt. She was sure it must be Daniel home on leave like Augie. She raced into the parlor to come face to face with a tall stranger. Dressed in buckskins and smelling like he hadn't had a bath in a year, the man had a black beard that curled down to his waist and long wavy black hair pulled back in a rawhide string. His feet were wrapped in rags. She reckoned he didn't own a pair of decent boots. It was starting to snow outside, little flurries whisked along the late November wind and it was pretty raw out. This fellow stood there shivering from the cold but his eyes blazed right out at Willa May. They were such a bright blue. "You Willa May Kincaid what's promised to Daniel Shrewsbury?" the man asked in a voice as rough as

15

his looks.

This took Willa May's folks by surprise because she had never told them that Daniel had asked her to wait for him. They looked at her with the same startled expression as when they saw this mountain man at their door. Willa May figured Daniel had sent this man with another message to her and no matter what kind of licking she would have to take later, she wasn't about to let this fellow go without hearing what he had come to say. "I'm Willa May," she nodded.

"The Willa May that's promised to Daniel Shrews --"

"I said I was Willa May," she interrupted, not wishing to dwell on the being promised part. "Won't you come in?" she asked, seeing that the man's teeth were starting to chatter.

Again everybody looked at her, confused and wondering what to make of all this. The man nodded a "Thank you right kindly, ma'am", at her and stepped into the parlor. Once he was inside the odor rising off him nearly knocked them all down. He had a right powerful air about him. Willa May was relieved that it wasn't one of those sweltering close days in July. The big man reached into a bag he had draped over his shoulder made out of buckskin like the rest of his clothes. He pulled out what looked like a wad of colored paper and handed it carefully to Willa May as if it contained a treasure. She felt everyone's eyes on her as she unwrapped the paper. Inside was a light blue ribbon. Willa May smiled.

The stranger said, "Daniel said to tell you he's fine and that there ribbon reminded him of the blue of your eyes and to keep on waiting for him."

"You were with Daniel?" Willa May asked.

"Yes'm. But I'm heading on home for a spell. Got to see my wife and kids and get the planting done in the spring. Then I'll head back and join up with the boys again."

"Where's home, Son?" Pole asked.

"Up on the Shenandoah, sir."

"You got another good two, maybe three days travel, then."

"Prob'ly more like three."

"Then you ought to join us for supper and get your belly filled before you set out again. We was just about to sit down and there's more than plenty to go around."

The stranger's eyes moved toward the door to the dining room. Willa May could see him sniffing a whiff of the venison and spicy apples. He looked a bit embarrassed as he licked his lips and shuffled

16

his feet. Pole clapped him on the back and said, "Aw, c'mon Son, set yourself down and dig in."

At the table, Lizzy finished her prayer, asking the Lord to bless their new friend. Here she paused, realizing she didn't know the man's name. He mumbled, "Eb, ma'am. Eb Johnson." Lizzy finished her prayer and they started passing the food around. Eb turned out to be a hearty eater, finishing off three helpings of everything, while the rest of them merely scooted their food around on their plates, unable to eat for poor Eb's stench. He thanked Lizzy at least twenty times and though he ate almost everything with his hands, sopping up gravy and sauce with his biscuits, he did seem grateful to be getting a meal. Augie finally wandered in and he and Eb talked about the war. They knew some of the same men fighting on both sides. Eb said he had done lumberjacking up around his home but once the war was over, he planned to move out west to one of the territories. Eb was a true mountain man, a loner who didn't want a lot of neighbors. Just a piece of land to keep his people going and some wilderness to lose himself in when folks and their ways got to making him feel pinned in. He was the kind of man who wanted to grow old in the mountains, taking his chances with God's creatures till one day one of them won and he lost. But he would die happy -- happier than if he settled down on a farm or worse yet, in a town.

It was getting on toward dark when Eb set off, wearing one of Pole's old jackets and some new rags tied onto his feet. He carried some hunks of venison and three slices of pumpkin pie wrapped up in his pouch. They waved goodbye from their front porch. Heading back inside Lizzy said, "Leave that door open awhile, Napoleon, and air out the house a bit." Pole stoked up the fire in the hearth and the cold November wind swept through, carrying the last of Eb with it.

Willa May tried to busy herself with cleaning up the dishes, hoping that maybe no one would think to ask about her and Daniel. Pole came in and grabbed a handful of biscuits and Lizzy brought in the last of the platters from the table, asking, "So Willa May, what's this about you and Daniel Shrewsbury? I thought you wanted to be a schoolmarm."

Before Willa May could explain, Pole, still chewing on his biscuits, demanded, "Girl, that boy ain't touched you nowhere, has he?"

Willa May whirled around. "No! Daniel's been a perfect gentleman. He just told me that day when Mama sewed up his arm that someday he was goin' to marry up with me, that's all. Then, when he went away, he sent Elroy Hicks over here to tell me and ask me to wait for him. That's all."

Lizzy and Pole looked at each other. It was clear that Lizzy wasn't going to say anything till Pole was gone but all Pole said was, "I want a talk with that boy when he comes home."

He stood up and went back into the parlor. Willa May looked at her mother, not knowing what to make of what her pa had said. "He's not goin' to hurt Daniel, is he?"

Lizzy shook her head, brushing back a strand of her auburn hair streaked now with gray and said, "No, but you're not getting married to nobody without your pa's say so."

It wasn't a "no" so Willa May figured she was still spoken for. Maybe. Next day, she combed her long red hair back and tied it with the pretty blue ribbon Daniel had sent her. When Pole saw her, he looked up from his bacon and eggs and said, "Just remember you're still my little girl till I say elsewise." Then he smiled and Willa May had to admit that she was still content to be just that...till Daniel came home.

One day that spring, Lizzy called Willa May inside. Willa May followed her mother into her parents' bedroom where Lizzy had a trunk open. Inside there was a beautiful cream colored dress covered with lace that Lizzy had wrapped in cloth. A quilt, a bit faded but still in good condition, lay beneath the gown that Lizzy pulled out. Willa May could see that the quilt was a wedding ring pattern pieced out of different hues of blue calico.

"This here's my wedding dress and my wedding quilt. I made this quilt when I was about your age and put it in my hope chest along with some other pieces of handiwork, some pillowcases that my mama had given to me so I could crochet lace trim on them. I also had some potholders and aprons I'd made out of the rest of the scraps left over after I finished my quilt. Little things but these here are all I've got left."

Willa May looked at the treasures, holding her breath. They were so pretty and fragile. Lizzy held the wedding dress up to her and pulled her over to the big oval looking glass that stood in the corner of the room. Willa May hadn't really thought about how much she had changed since Daniel had left but she saw a young woman peering back at her. Thick red hair blazed down to her waist which was narrower than she remembered. She noticed that her hips were getting round and full, more like her mama's. She had become a woman that winter. Where her chest had been flat like a boy's, now she had breasts blossoming. Her whole body was like an early spring crocus starting to bloom where once there had just been cold flat ground. Her face was changing, too. Where it had been round and childlike, now her features were more defined, as if Nature had been whittling away at it.

She looked up to see tears running down the reflection of her mama's face. Through her tears, Lizzy smiled at Willa May. Willa May felt a lump move up and lodge in her throat. For the life of her, she couldn't say a word. This seemed to be happening to her more and more often. She was shamed by it because she had never been a cry baby before and here she stood bawling like one. Lizzy must have known what she was thinking because she nodded and wiped her tears with the corner of her apron. Taking a deep breath Lizzy said, "It's nigh on time you started your own hope chest. This old war can't last much longer and when that Shrewsbury boy comes home, he's goin' to want a wife."

Speechless, Willa May watched her mother fold her wedding dress and place it back in the chest with the quilt. Lizzy handled them as tenderly as if she held a newborn baby, she cherished them so. Willa May watched her close the trunk. Then, taking Willa May by the hand, Lizzy opened one of her bureau drawers. Inside were some of Willa May's dresses that she had outgrown over the years. Lizzy pulled them out and spread them on the floor. Together, they knelt over the dresses. Lizzy sighed, "I've been saving these for when you grew up and started a hope chest of your own. Pick out the ones you want to use in your quilt and we'll start piecing it tonight."

While Willa May was busy sewing her heart piece by piece into that quilt, Daniel was in the thick of the fighting. In June, Sherman tried to move on Atlanta but he was turned back at Kennesaw Mountain. All summer word kept coming that Sherman was doing this and doing that, trying to get into Atlanta. One day in early September, a messenger rode up with the report that Sherman had at last taken Atlanta and was burning all the Confederate supplies. The entire city was in flames.

Willa May knew Daniel would be in the most danger since the war started. Every night before she went to bed she prayed that he was safe, that the Lord would bring him home to her soon. They heard that Sherman, leading some sixty thousand men, was marching from Atlanta to Savannah, laying waste to everything on the way and blocking the government up in Richmond off from its western states. From Savannah, he moved his men through North Carolina. Stories about how Sherman let his men burn folks' homes and property, taking everything that wasn't nailed down and killing all the livestock, were repeated in taverns and churches alike.

After reading an article in the newspaper about Sherman's doings, Mr. Shaw shook his head and said, "Foolish. Just foolish. And this man's supposed to be a military genius? He thinks he can break the South by breaking their spirit but what he doesn't know is folks'll remember this. It'll fester inside them till they just have to do something out of pure spite." Shaking his head once more, he mumbled again, "Foolish."

Some folks thought Sherman did what was necessary to end the war but Willa May and the rest of her family weren't sure that folks had to lose their homes and see treasured heirlooms stolen or burned. In her mind, Willa May imagined her mama crying over her wedding dress and the wedding quilt she had stored away. Her mama's heart would have been broken if somebody had burned those things. Nobody wanted the war to be over more than Willa May but she didn't want it to end this way.

That Christmas with the war all but over, Willa May was chosen to be Mary in the Christmas pageant at church. Miss Beatrice and Lizzy sewed day and night to make her a beautiful outfit to wear. As luck would have it, Clerinda Mayfield gave birth to a baby boy just a week before the play so they had a brand new baby Jesus and everyone breathed a sigh of relief not to have to use Elva Jean Huddleston's whiny three month old. For the first year of that fussy baby's life, folks could hear him coming for a good ten minutes before he got there.

The night of the play the women brought baked goods and cider and set up tables in the basement of the church while upstairs some of the men lit candles in the windows and on the blue spruce tree that the Tylers had sent that day from up on the mountain.

When Willa May took her place up at the altar there was a soft light glowing from the candles and such a hush fell over the congregation, that she just knew the Lord was smiling down on them that night. She hadn't had that peaceful a feeling come over her since before the war. She knelt there by the pretty little baby wishing she could keep that moment going forever, that they wouldn't have to make their way home through the deep snow back to the real world, a world saddened and exhausted by the fighting that just kept dragging on.

Willa May wore her pretty blue ribbon in her hair that night. She had worn it nearly every day since Eb brought it to her over a year before. She didn't want to take the chance that Daniel might show up sometime without warning and she wouldn't be wearing the gift he had taken such trouble to send to her. She wondered with the beauty and peace inside that little church that night, if she prayed extra hard that Daniel might walk through the arched doorway and right up the aisle to the altar. Her heart ached for it. It was the kind of night for just such a miracle.

Something curious did happen. After the play, several of the womenfolk made mention of how Willa May looked so natural up there holding the little Mayfield baby in her arms. About the third time it was mentioned, Pole stalked away in a huff. She realized that night that there was something about men that just didn't want their little girls to grow up.

Later that night as she lay awake in her feather bed, snug beneath layers of quilts while the wind howled outside, rattling her windows, Willa May thought back about how the women had kept saying she looked "like a little new mother". It was the first time she had given any thought to what would happen after she and Daniel were married. The thought struck her like a bolt of lightning that once they were married she wouldn't be lying there by herself. She had never thought much about her mama and her pa as husband and wife. Now she started to think really hard on it, wondering just what went on between them after they turned out the coal oil lamp in their room. She had seen her pa kiss her mama on the cheek real sweet like and sometimes when Pole had been in the jug, he would hug Lizzy to him in a big bear hug. That was all there seemed to be to it. But then how did she and Augie get in the picture?

Willa May's cousin, 'Lil Annie Morris, was expecting her first baby. She had married Denny Bob Lewis who was off fighting with their no-account Augie and the Army of Northern Virginia. They had gotten hitched when Denny Bob came home that summer. Now 'Lil Annie was as big as a mountain and looking like she might burst. Around the end of February, Big Annie, 'Lil Annie's mama, sent word that it was 'Lil Annie's time. Lizzy and Willa May had been working on Willa May's wedding quilt but when Lizzy heard the message, she packed up her sewing and fetched her bonnet and cloak. She was almost out the door when she turned and said to Willa May, "I expect it's nigh on time when you should see what you're getting yourself into. You come along with me, Willa May."

Willa May was thrilled. All her life she had heard women whispering to each other about the birthing of some baby. They would always hush whenever the little ones drew too near. Now the mystery of life was about to unfold right before her very eyes. Willa May nearly flew to Big Annie's house, her feet hardly touching the ground. Before they started up the narrow path that led to the rope bridge over the creek to Big Annie's, Willa May could hear 'Lil Annie squalling like she was dying...or worse. She stopped dead in her tracks but Lizzy grabbed her by the arm and pulled her across the swinging bridge and into the house. She had hardly had time to notice her uncle Luther pacing back and forth in the front yard, smoking his corncob pipe. But Luther was so slight -- just over five feet tall and, at best, a hundred pounds dripping wet -- that it was easy to miss him. He stopped pacing long enough to nod to them as Lizzy and Willa May swept past.

Inside, Willa May noticed there was a big kettle of water boiling over the fire in the hearth and Dessie Marie, Big Annie's oldest daughter, was sitting at the table wringing her hands and swiping at her hair which kept falling in her eyes and sticking to the rivulets of sweat running down her forehead.

"Bad?" Lizzy asked, whisking off her cloak and bonnet.

"Real bad, Aunt Lizzy," Dessie nodded.

Another long agonizing scream erupted from the tiny bedroom off of the kitchen. Willa May's eyes grew wide as she looked at the closed door of the bedroom. Lizzy grabbed her hand and pulled her toward the door to the birthing room. At first Willa May had been tickled pink to be considered old enough to witness this miracle, but now she was starting to get cold feet.

"Maybe I should stay out here and help Cousin Dessie, Mama," she said, desperate suddenly not to have to go through that closed door, not wishing to put this huge mystery behind her. She knew that same door would open for her, too, someday.

"'Lil Annie needs you more," was all Lizzy said and dragged her along.

The room was so tiny that Lizzy, Big Annie, and Willa May were squeezed in side by side with mere inches between them. Sprawled on the bed was 'Lil Annie, her big belly heaving. She was sweating and puffing like a race horse. Willa May was shocked at how red 'Lil Annie's face was as she bellowed like a cow with each pain. Big Annie positioned herself at the foot of the bed, kneeling between 'Lil Annie's widespread legs. Lizzy got on the bed behind 'Lil Annie and grasped her by her shoulders.

"Take hold of her hands," Lizzy ordered.

Willa May took 'Lil Annie's sweaty, slippery hands and squeezed as she had the day her mama sewed up Daniel's arm.

"Do you feel like you got to push, Baby?" Big Annie asked.

'Lil Annie was out of breath. She couldn't answer so she simply nodded, groaning with the start of still another contraction. She bore down on Willa May's hands until Willa May thought she would break every bone in them.

Lizzy hefted 'Lil Annie up, yelling, "Push girl, push!"

'Lil Annie pushed and pushed and pushed.

"Here comes the head," Big Annie announced.

It seemed to Willa May that the baby just slid right out of 'Lil Annie, one big bloody mess. 'Lil Annie screamed like she was being split in two. Willa May feared she was. Her eyes widened at the sight she was witnessing and for a minute, she thought she might pass out cold. Just when she thought it was all over, 'Lil Annie belted out another long scream and started carrying on like she was about to give birth all over again. This time what came out didn't look like any baby. It looked to Willa May like the innards she had seen her pa pull out at slaughtering time. She thought for sure she was going to lose her supper. Holding onto 'Lil Annie's hands, she heard the baby start to squall, too. There was a regular chorus rising from that tiny room. Dessie rushed in and took the baby as Big Annie cut a long bloody tubing connected to the baby's belly. Willa May wondered why Big Annie would cut on that poor little baby like that, but she figured that her aunt must know what she was doing. Dessie said, "Come on, Willa May. Let's go get the baby cleaned up."

Grateful to escape from the closeness of the birthing room, Willa May realized she was bathed in sweat. It felt good to take a long breath out in the kitchen. Dessie laid the baby on some cloths she had spread on the table and started washing him off. Willa May saw that it was a boy. Holding the tiny body close, Willa May thought he was the sweetest thing she had ever seen. She knew deep down in her heart that all of 'Lil Annie's suffering had been worth it.

'Lil Annie looked half dead to Willa May but she perked up when she saw the baby. Willa May handed him to her and he began feeding at 'Lil Annie's breast. 'Lil Annie beamed and said, "Go tell Pa, Willa May. Tell him I done give him a grandson."

Willa May raced outside and gave her uncle the news. For a moment, he stood silent as a preacher in prayer. Then he let out such a whoop, Willa May thought she might jump right out of her skin. He grabbed Willa May and whisked her up into the air like her pa used to when she was little. She was startled that a man as small and wiry as Luther could be so strong. Once he set her down Willa May had to run to the outhouse to see if her pantaloons were still dry.

On the way home near dawn, Willa May and Lizzy walked slowly along the dirt road. Willa May was pondering the whole event she had witnessed. "Mama," she said, "just how did that baby get inside 'Lil Annie's belly?"

"Same as with most of God's creatures, Baby," Lizzy answered. "The man plants the seed and the woman, like Mother Earth, nurtures it and brings it to full bloom." While this sounded like some of the poetry Mr. Shaw read to her, Willa May began pondering on it. She knew she must be missing something.

Two months later, the Kincaids were coming home from church when a rider galloped toward them, whooping and yelling. Pole pulled Bess and Dixie up and stopped the wagon. "What's all the fuss about?" he asked.

The rider's horse pranced beside the wagon as the rider swept his hat off and swung it up into the air. "The war's over! Lee's done surrendered. It's over! The war's over," he yelled, still whooping and putting on a real show.

Lizzy clutched her heart and said, "Thank the Lord. My boy's coming home!"

Pole shook his head and said, "Well, I'll be."

Big Jim was riding in the back of the wagon with Willa May. He pulled her to him in a bear hug, squeezing her so hard, she thought her ribs might break. Then he and Pole started whooping, too. All Willa May could think was *Daniel is coming home!*

Throughout the summer men stopped by their place -- men in blue and men in gray. All of them were ragged and exhausted from the fighting. Willa May couldn't remember when she had carried so much water up from the creek, boiling it in big kettles over open fires in the back yard so the men could have a hot bath before they continued on their way. Her family met men from Ohio, Pennsylvania, Maryland, and even New York. They took notice of one man in particular from a place called Rochester. He said he was Jewish and he wore a funny little cap underneath his army cap. When he sat down to dinner with them, he started speaking in a tongue none of them had ever heard before. He explained that was his way of praying and thanking the Lord for his meal. He was very polite and showed proper manners. He even offered to help clear the table and wash the dishes. This came as a shock to Pole and Big Jim. But it left a firm impression on Lizzy. Every chance she got, she would remind the rest of the family that Jesus was Jewish, too, and that the children of Israel were God's chosen people just like the Bible said.

Willa May was walking down the hill to the creek, buckets in each hand, one hot August day when she heard somebody call her name. She looked up. *Daniel! He's come home at last.* She could see a shadow silhouetted against the morning sun but she couldn't make out his features. "Willa May! Willa May," he called to her and started running toward her.

Lordy! It must be Daniel. Willa May dropped the buckets and started running toward the figure at the top of the hill. Tears streamed down her cheeks and all she could think was *Daniel!* Her heart pounded inside her chest and her lungs heaved from running so fast but she didn't care, she just kept running.

When she drew closer, she could see through the blur of her tears that this man wasn't Daniel. This man's hair wasn't golden like maple leaves in the fall and he wasn't nearly as tall and broad across the shoulders as her Daniel. She stopped dead in her tracks, wiping her tears away so she could see better, still hoping against hope that it was Daniel. It was then that she recognized Augie. No-account Augie, running for all he was worth, nearly flying down that dirt road toward her. He was crying, too. Something in her heart ached when she saw her brother all tattered and covered in layers of filth. She

25

started running again and hugged him to her hard, the two of them collapsing onto their knees in the middle of the road and sobbing in each other's arms. Moments later, Lizzy, Pole, and Big Jim were there. They held onto each other and cried together. For Willa May's family, the war was finally over.

Willa May kept waiting and waiting for Daniel to come home, walking down the road toward her like he had that day so many years before. She peered up the road often, searching for a sign of anyone approaching. Each time she did spot someone, it was always the wrong someone. September came and went in an Indian Summer heat. In October the leaves started to turn and she just couldn't help but think that Daniel wouldn't want to miss those fiery colors up in his mountain. He would surely want to be there to hunt squirrel and deer that fall.

One day the entire family got up earlier than usual and started peeling apples to make applebutter. Pole and Augie built a fire beneath their biggest kettle out in the yard and they stood stirring apples for hours. The Indian Summer sun that day was warmer than it had been in a couple of weeks. That false summer sun and the sweet smelling apples started drawing bees, a swarm of yellow jackets. Pole always claimed that yellow jackets were mean sons of guns anytime but by fall, when summer was stubborn and lingering on, those bees were worse than a nest of rattlesnakes. They started buzzing around Augie and being such a no-account, Augie started swiping at them, swinging his arms like a wild man till he fell down. The swarm of yellow jackets commenced to stinging him. They were even up his pant legs and inside his shirt. Pole and Big Jim tried to whisk them away but the bees stung them, too. Soon the bees were inside their overalls. All three men were screaming like they were on fire. There was nothing Lizzy and Willa May could do but watch in horror. Willa May heard her pa yell, "Get to the crick! Get to the crick!" The three men raced down the hill and across the road to the creek, throwing off clothes as they ran. By the time they ran past the house, all three were buck naked. Still the yellow jackets wouldn't let up. Lizzy and Willa May followed down the hill, picking up the men's clothes. They could hear the men screaming all the way to the creek. Three loud splashes were followed by sudden silence. As Lizzy and Willa May crossed the road, they froze. The bees swarmed in a careening arc up from the

26

creek and back toward them. Thinking they were next, Lizzy and Willa May ducked. But the black dotted arc spiraled over their heads and buzzed back up the hill, leaving them be.

Lizzy and Willa May spent the afternoon painting the welts on the men's bodies with a baking soda paste. Augie was the worst. His face was swollen and red as a beet. He looked like a bright pink cauliflower.

By the next morning, Augie's eyes were swollen shut. Lizzy hitched up Bess and Dixie and took him to see old Doc Merriam. Doc's office was down past Deepwater where the Shrewsburys lived. On the way back they heard somebody hollering at them so Lizzy pulled up the mules to see what all the fuss was about. Turned out to be Elroy Hicks. He was sitting on the front porch of his house -- he lived next door to Daniel's folks. Since Elroy had come back from the war, he was able to get around on a little scooter his pa had fashioned for him. It sat just a few inches off of the ground and it rolled on four little wheels, one at every corner. Elroy could sit on it and using two blocks of wood with handles carved in them, he could wheel around wherever he pleased. He looked pathetic. He had taken to drinking hard -- a jug before breakfast, one more to get him through the day, and one to wash down his supper. Here he was now on his little scooter, with a jug slung over one shoulder, red eyed and skinny as a scarecrow.

He wheeled himself down a ramp his pa had built and proceeded to make his way toward the road where Lizzy and Augie waited. Seeing Augie's face, he said, "What in blue blazes happened to you, Augie?"

Augie, too blind to see Elroy, turned toward Elroy's voice and said, "Damn yeller jackets near killed Pa and Big Jim and me. I had fever and chills all night and this morning I was so swoll up, my eyes done swoll over."

Elroy shook his head. "To think you survived the war with nary a scratch and now you nearly died on account of some damn yeller jackets."

"Learnt my lesson," Augie agreed. "I'll cut them bastards a wide path from now on, by God."

"Now, Augie. Don't take the Lord's name in vain. It's probably just by the mercy of the Almighty that you're still alive to tell about it," Lizzy scolded.

"That's for sure," Augie said. "Say, Elroy, when's that no-account cousin of yours coming home, the one that's been sweet talking my little sister all these years?"

"Why, ain't you heard? Daniel's been home nigh on a month now."

"What?" both Lizzy and Augie asked.

"Yep. He come home and then went off next morning up in the woods somewhere. I expect that he's holed up somewhere on the mountain. Knowing Daniel, he's all right, though. I keep telling him that some bear or some old rattler will do him in someday. But he won't listen."

Elroy could see the miffed look on Lizzy's face. Small as she was, Lizzy was a force to be reckoned with. Her blue eyes blazed now with open fury. Like Willa May, she had expected that Daniel would come home in a rush to marry Willa May, seeing as how he sure was set on it all those years. After a long silence from Lizzy and Augie, Elroy sensed the tension in the air and said a bit sheepishly, "I reckon Daniel didn't come by to see Willa May."

"No, he surely didn't," Lizzy replied coolly. All three of them knew that feuds had broken out between families over just such a thing. When a young man stated his intentions, he was honor bound to follow through with them.

"Well," Elroy grinned, shaking his head and scratching the back of his neck -- anything not to have to look Lizzy in the eye. "Daniel come back from the war, pissed all to hell at that old Sherman. Seems him and Daniel got into it one day when Daniel come back from a scouting mission. Daniel went to report to Sherman only to find Sherman's men looting and burning down the town they was staying in. Rubbed Daniel wrong, just like it did a lot of folks down South. Daniel proceeded to ask Sherman what the hell he thought he was doing letting his men act like that toward innocent folks. Well, they got into it pretty hot and heavy, shouting at each other.

Finally, Sherman looked at Daniel and said, 'Son, you're forgetting who you're talking to. I'm in command here and these here men are just following orders.'

Then Daniel looked old Sherman right back in the eye and said, 'What kind of man would order such a thing?' By this time the two of 'em was eyeball to eyeball.

Sherman said to Daniel, 'War is hell, Son.'

Daniel was real riled and he said, 'If war is hell, then you're Satan himself.' That's when Sherman had Daniel arrested for insulting an officer and Daniel spent the last six months of the war in the

28

hoosegow."

"Well, that ain't nothing to be ashamed about," Augie shrugged. "Appears to me that Daniel just said his piece, except he said it to the wrong sonofabitch, that's all."

Elroy shook his head. "You just don't get it. Daniel wasn't ashamed, he was mad. When Daniel gets riled like that, ain't no talking to him. You tell Willa May she's better off that Daniel took to the mountains. It'll take him a while to stop his fuming and make peace with himself. Believe me, you don't want to have Daniel around when he's put out. Something sets him off and he knows he can't do nothing about it so he just goes off till he can act civil again. Why, I've seen him nearly break Jed Withrow's neck once when Jed kicked Daniel's old flea bit dog, Zeke, in the ribs -- took three of us to pull Daniel off. That time he was gone three months. Just tell Willa May to sit tight. Daniel will be back when he's of a mind to."

When Lizzy and Augie arrived home, they told Willa May what Elroy had said. Willa May felt so helpless after she had been waiting all those years, thinking that the war was the only thing that was keeping Daniel away. Clearly, the war wasn't over yet for Daniel. All she could do was what Elroy had said: just sit tight.

It was in the spring when Willa May heard about Daniel again. That winter had been a harsh one, lots of nippy nights when the whole family had huddled around the fire, wrapped in quilts, and drinking hot toddies to warm their bones. Each night she went to bed fretting whether Daniel was caught in a snowdrift somewhere up on the mountain, frozen solid like a human icicle. Luckily, her family had set in good stores for the winter. Late in January a blizzard blew in and nobody could go anywhere for two weeks. At breakfast, Pole, Augie, and Big Jim licked their lips, devouring the spicy red applebutter they had made in the fall and each time they cussed the yellow jackets.

March came with the first big thaw and they had to worry about floods. There had been so much snow that now the hills behind them were like waterfalls with little creeks streaming from them. Their yard had a constant flow of water for days, trickling down to the road which looked like a huge mud pie. Then the creek rose and the road flooded with brown, rushing water carrying big tree limbs and a few dead animals. It took the men days to clean off the road and make it passable again once everything started to dry out.

Easter Sunday was a beauty of a day. Bright warm sunshine and gentle breezes promised warm weather at last. The mountains were dappled with pink and white from the dogwoods and the trees were starting to bud. There were splashes of early spring green, a soft light sage thrown in. Pole had bought Willa May a new bonnet, straw brimmed with a light blue sash that tied saucily under her chin. She felt like a princess in it. Lizzy and Willa May had worked every night for a week, sewing a new dress of light blue calico with a high collar. Augie and Big Jim had brought her a pretty cameo pin all the way from Charleston. She stood in front of her mama's big looking glass that morning, sassy as a cat with kittens, thinking she sure looked a sight. She must have, too, because when she walked out into the parlor everyone stopped their chatter and just looked at her, their jaws agape.

When they got home from church service, there was Elroy Hicks sitting on the front porch on his little scooter gaping at her, too. His mouth worked but not a sound came out. Finally his eyes welled up and one lone tear ran down his cheek. Willa May noticed that he had started getting whiskers. He had a sparse stubble on his chin and along his sideburns. "You look beauteeful, Willa May," he breathed.

Ignoring the compliment, she panted, "Elroy, how in the world did you get up here on this porch? What are you doing here, anyway?"

Elroy's face broke into a mischievous grin. "Came in through the back door. It's unlocked," he chuckled. "I came to tell you that Runt Mabe said up at the tavern last night that he done seen Daniel in town at the lumber yard. He was buying some pine planks. Old Runt asked him what the wood was for and Daniel said he was building himself a cabin."

"You mean he's never coming down out of that mountain?" Willa May was near tears.

"No! Don't you see, Willa May? He's fixing you a house to go housekeeping in. Daniel don't need no cabin. He'd just as soon live in a cave or a lean-to."

"You reckon?"

Elroy grinned again, showing a couple of black rotting teeth. "Sure enough."

Willa May was so excited she leaned over and gave Elroy a big kiss on his cheek, right where the tear had run down moments before.

30

"Thank you, Elroy. You've made me the happiest girl in this valley."

Lizzy came out onto the porch and asked Elroy if he wanted to stay for Easter dinner with them. He seemed tickled just to be asked; he didn't stop grinning all afternoon. They had a grand meal. Roast chicken, mashed potatoes and gravy, green beans they had canned the summer before with chunks of bacon in them. Pickled peaches and fresh rolls with butter and strawberry preserves they had canned. To top it off, Lizzy had made custard pie and bread pudding with lemon sauce. A splendid feast fit for a king. Pole and Augie hefted Elroy up onto a chair and for that afternoon, he looked whole again, sitting at the same height as everyone else. Willa May thought he even felt whole again even if it was just for one afternoon.

Evening came and Willa May walked Elroy down the hill. She was thanking him for bringing her word of Daniel, still wearing her new dress and where her hat had been, she had tied her long auburn hair back in the blue ribbon Daniel had sent her. There was a nip to the spring air so she had wrapped a lavender shawl around her shoulders that she had knitted that winter. As she said good-bye to Elroy, she noticed him leaning over and peering around her skirt. Wondering what he was looking at, she turned around. What she saw made her gasp, her hand raising up to her mouth. Before she knew what she was doing, she started running like the wind, dropping her pretty shawl behind her. Like when Augie had come home, tears filled her eyes. She saw him coming toward her in a filmy blur but she knew that golden mane of hair and that tall lean frame. She kept running until Daniel swept her up in his arms, swinging her around and around. She buried her face, wet with tears, in his neck and held him close. She didn't want this moment to end. Ever. He held her right back, pressing her to him, not hard like Pole or Augie, but gently like when she had held 'Lil Annie's baby boy. At last he set her down, running his rough hand down her tear stained cheek. He leaned over and kissed her forehead, a kiss so soft she hardly felt his lips against her skin. Then he kissed her closed eyelids and cupping her face, he leaned over and kissed her on the mouth, a long lingering kiss that made Willa May feel all warm down low in her belly. All the while he held her like a fine china doll. Out of breath, he pulled away and stood there silent and looking at her like he was looking at somebody new. He ran his fingertips down her hair, smiling when he saw she was wearing the ribbon he had sent. "Why, Willa May, you're a beautiful woman," he whispered. "When I left, you were like a fawn

31

in springtime, just finding your way. Now, you're full grown and graceful as a doe."

Willa May beamed up at Daniel, still not able to say a word.

He just smiled, even white teeth in an already tanned face. Shaking his head, he said again, "You're a real beauty. A real beauty." He pulled her to him and pressed her face to his chest and kissed the top of her head. Neither of them was sure how long they stood there holding each other, not wanting to let go. After all, they had waited five long years for that moment and neither was willing to let it pass.

Chapter Two

Willa May and Daniel set their wedding date in June, after Daniel
had properly asked Pole for Willa May's hand that day. The two spent
the rest of the evening on the front porch talking quietly and holding
hands, neither wanting to let go of the other. Daniel told Willa May
about the cabin he was building for them up on Gauley Mountain in
the bend of a hairpin curve in the road. He had saved all his army pay
and bought a big piece of land up there. She could tell that Daniel
loved that mountain, that he felt a part of it. Willa May wondered if
he might love it more than her. For now, though, she was content that
he had come back for her just as he had promised all those years
before. All she wanted was to look at him and hear his soft voice as
dusk settled around them, shrouding the hills in diaphanous layers of
lavender hues. Willa May cried all over again when the moon crept
high in the sky and Daniel had to go. She wanted desperately to go
with him and she would have, too, if Pole and Lizzy hadn't been there
to stop her. Promising he would visit her a spell the following
Sunday, Daniel started down the road toward his mountain. With
tears in her eyes, Willa May watched him till his silhouette blended
into the darkness.

While Daniel spent the spring building the cabin, Willa May
readied herself to set up housekeeping. She and Lizzy worked every
night on a new quilt. This time they used a log cabin design in shades
of green, the color that represented growth. At planting time, Willa
May worked in the garden, planting extra rows of corn, beans, beets,
squash, potatoes and tomatoes so when canning time came in late
summer she and Daniel would have a store set aside to see them
through the long winter months. Even Bess and Dixie could tell that
something was up, looking back at Willa May over their plow harness
with wide eyes as if to ask, "Why are you making us do all this extra
work?"

Pole helped Willa May plow up three dozen more rows than in
years past. She tended the seedlings like they were fragile lilies,

watering them and fertilizing them and watching for grubs. Lizzy teased her, saying that with all her fretting over them , the plants were too afraid *not* to grow.

Miss Beatrice surprised Willa May with a beautiful lace wedding gown she had tatted and sewn herself. It had tiny pearly buttons going down the back and a wide skirt with a long train trailing behind. Willa May burst into tears when Miss Beatrice brought it out and showed it to her. Miss Beatrice hugged Willa May and they both cried. Old Mr. Shaw said he would play his fiddle at the wedding and she asked him to play "Jeannie With The Light Brown Hair" for sure.

Daniel kept his promises and showed up every Sunday right after church. He would stay for Sunday dinner and sometimes he would join Pole, Augie, and Big Jim in a game of horseshoes in the back yard. Or if they could catch Lizzy's head turned, they would sneak up to the still Pole kept up in the woods behind the house. But Daniel never came back drunk. Willa May figured that like her, he had probably seen the jug get the better of too many men and didn't want to end up like them. It made her proud that Daniel was strong that way. At dusk when the lightning bugs started blinking like tiny cat's eyes, Daniel would set cut for the cabin and Willa May would be left standing on the porch wiping her tears as she waved good-bye.

The weeks passed quickly and just two weeks before the wedding, they were all down at Big Annie's for a picnic. 'Lil Annie's belly was swollen again with another baby on the way. Willa May helped her wash her little baby boy and put him down for his nap, cooing at him and singing, "Rock-A-Bye Baby" until he drifted off. 'Lil Annie smiled down on him and said softly so as not to wake the baby, "I just hope the one that's on the way is as good a baby as this one's been."

"'Lil Annie," Willa May started, "just how do you get a baby anyhow?"

"Glory be, girl!" 'Lil Annie sputtered, looking at Willa May like she had said something crazy.

Willa May was so startled and embarrassed that she wished she had kept her big mouth shut.

"You mean to tell me here you are almost a wife and you don't know about the birds and the bees yet?"

"I know lots about birds and bees," Willa May answered defensively.

'Lil Annie laughed and said, "Not them birds and bees, you danged fool. *The* birds and bees."

34

From the blank expression on Willa May's face, 'Lil Annie surmised that her cousin had no idea what she meant. Her tone changed from jesting to compassion. "Willa May, didn't Aunt Lizzy tell you nothin' about the ways of husbands and wives?"

Willa May shook her head. "Just that the man plants his seed and like Mother Earth, the woman brings it to fruit -- whatever that means."

'Lil Annie took her younger cousin's hands in her own. "That's a real nice way of putting it, but I'm afraid there's more to it than that."

"Like what?"

"Daniel will want to kiss you and hug you and touch you...you know, in private places."

Willa May wasn't sure that she liked the turn this conversation had taken, but she asked, "Why on earth would he want to do that?" The very idea shocked her and seemed a lot like when Augie's friend, Merle Bussey, wanted her to play doctor years before.

"After the wedding, you'll be Daniel's and he'll want to show you he loves you."

"That's how you get babies?" Willa May decided that if that was all there was to it, she reckoned she could do it if it pleased Daniel.

"Not quite. After you kiss and hug and touch each other --"

Willa May gasped. "I'm supposed to touch his private parts, too?"

"Well, he'll probably want you to," she nodded.

"Then what?" Willa May figured she had better hear the worst of this so she could decide whether she wanted to ever have any babies.

"Then he pokes himself into you."

Willa May stared at 'Lil Annie. The blank look on her face told 'Lil Annie that she still wasn't getting the full gist of what she was hearing, so she tried once more. "He pokes...he pokes his private parts into your private parts."

"Oh no he won't!" Willa May sprang up and started backing toward the door of the small room. 'Lil Annie tried to tell her that it would all be fine, that she would sort of know what to do when the time came, but Willa May wasn't buying any of that. "Daniel would never do such an awful thing like that to me. Never!" she yelled. "He loves me and he'd never ask me to do something like that."

Before 'Lil Annie could reach her, Willa May turned and ran out of the room. When she got outside Lizzy called to her to come and help her, but Willa May turned her back on everyone and headed straight for the woods, unable to face her kinfolk with such thoughts flying

around in her head. She kept walking for half a mile up into the
woods in back of Big Annie's. When she came to a little creek, she sat
down on a big boulder by the creek bank. Wrapping her arms around
herself, she rocked back and forth, trying to understand why 'Lil
Annie would tell her such a horrible thing. Why would her own
cousin want to scare her like that?

'Lil Annie told Lizzy what had happened. Lizzy told Pole and he
told Augie and Augie told Daniel. While Augie snickered about it as
he told Daniel, Daniel didn't find anything humorous about it and said
so. Worried, he followed Willa May into the woods. When he found
her, she was still sitting on the huge rock. He stopped for a moment,
unsure of just what he would say to her now that he had found her. He
had known all along that she was in many ways still a little girl. But
he had hoped that her mother had prepared her for what would be
taking place once they were man and wife. Now as he watched Willa
May stewing angrily, he guessed that was one talk Lizzy and Willa
May hadn't had. He drew a deep breath and climbed up on the rock
and sat down, being sure to distance himself an arm's length away.
He didn't want to frighten her any more than she was.

Willa May cast a sidelong glance at Daniel then hung her head,
hoping that if she didn't speak to him he would leave her be and go
back to the picnic. She never wanted to see any of her people again.
By this time she was certain that the whole thing had been their idea
of some prank, trying to give her cold feet before her wedding. Well,
she would show them. She would just run off and never come back.

"Willa May," Daniel began, sounding more than a little unsure of
himself. "I know you're awful young to be trying to be a woman.
Wasn't so long ago you was playing house and now I'm asking you to
come with me and make us a house together."

Here he paused and leaned over, trying to see Willa May's face.
She turned a quarter of a circle away from him, not saying a word.
She was mortified down to her bones that Daniel was bent on talking
to her about this.

"I'll never hurt you, Willa May. You have to believe that. I
figured you didn't know much about men and women, and I wasn't
going to push you none. I can be patient. Dang it all, I've waited five
years for you and I figure a little while longer won't hurt me none. I
just thought we'd take things slow and when you were ready,
we'd...well, we'd be together...at last."

Willa May could tell by his voice that Daniel was pained, too, about having to talk like this to her. She wanted to scream at him and tell him to find somebody else to marry and to leave her be right there on that old rock forever. Instead, she started crying. Being too much in love with Daniel, she couldn't run off. So she just sat there and sobbed, her shoulders shuddering and her lungs gasping for air. Before she knew it, Daniel had wrapped his strong arms around her and was rocking her gently. He didn't say anything. He just held her until she stopped crying and was finished hiccuping.

When he saw that she was finished, he said, "Now Willa May, we can call off the wedding if you've a mind to, but I tell you, ain't nobody else for me in this whole world but you. If you're not ready, you just say so. I'll be content to wait for you till you are."

Daniel didn't sound mad or even disappointed. Just straightforward. That was his way. But Willa May still couldn't face him; she kept her head down. Finally he reached over and lifted her chin so she had to look him in the eye once and for all. "Is that what you want? You want to call off our wedding?"

Willa May thought about Miss Beatrice and the pretty wedding gown, the quilts her mama and she had worked so hard on, and her little garden she had kept all spring. She thought about all the years she had waited for Daniel to come home and wondered if she had been just a silly little girl after all, playing at being grown up.

"No," she choked, feeling the tears welling up in her eyes again. "I don't want to call off the wedding. But -- but --"

"But what?"

"I'm scared," she blurted, bursting out in fresh sobs.

"I know you are. I know." Daniel cradled her in his arms, holding her to him. "But you've got to know I mean it when I say I won't ever hurt you, Willa May. I promise. Ain't I always stood by my word?"

She couldn't argue with that. Daniel was probably the most honest man she ever knew. If he said he was going to do something, then come hell or high water, he would do it. He had kept his word through an entire war so she figured he meant to keep it this time, too.

She was crying too hard to speak. She just nodded and leaned into him. He held her tighter until she calmed down.

"We'd best be getting back now," he said, after he saw she was over her tears. He helped her down off the rock and before they started back, he stopped and looked down at her one last time. "We're goin' to be all right. You'll see."

Willa May had never known anyone that she could put her faith in like she could Daniel. Five years before, he had won her heart. That day he won her trust.

Something old, something new, something borrowed, something blue. Like the saying, Willa May was decked out like a princess on her wedding day. She wore her grandmother's veil, brought over from Scotland two generations before. Her "something new" was the wedding dress Miss Beatrice had made for her. Since 'Lil Annie had the same size foot, she borrowed the satin shoes she had worn on her wedding day. Luther had laid out drunk in Charleston one Friday night and hadn't come home all night. This was just before 'Lil Annie's wedding, so he showed up at Big Annie's with the shoes as a peace offering the following night. The "something blue" was Willa May's blue ribbon that she had worn all the years while Daniel had been off to war. She dressed in her mama's and pa's room. Standing back to look at herself once she had finished, she could see Lizzy and Miss Beatrice behind her in the looking glass. They were both crying and declaring how pretty she looked.

Pole took her to the church in their old wagon and even it looked beautiful, decorated in swags of pink roses and little purple pansies the womenfolk had woven for her at sunup that morning. Even Bess and Dixie were dressed up with little straw hats that bore bands of the same roses and pansies. Neighbors lined up along either side of the dusty road to the church and called out good wishes and blessings to Willa May and her bridegroom. She felt just like a queen going to her coronation. Never again in her life did she feel as special as on that day.

Inside the church Mr. Shaw played "The Wedding March" on his fiddle, trying to keep it from squeaking out any sour notes, with his arthritis so bad. Daniel and Augie, their best man, waited for her and Pole by Preacher Willis at the altar. Everyone stood up as Pole walked Willa May down the aisle. She noticed her pa wiping a stray tear on the way. Daniel's eyes locked on Willa May and he smiled. He told her later that he had been about to burst with pride that he could call her his, she looked so beautiful. Daniel looked handsome, too. With some of his money he had left over from building their cabin, he had gone to Charleston and bought a Sunday suit, a white shirt, a tie, and some decent shoes. His skin glowed like amber from working out in the sun every day, setting off his sparkling blue eyes. Willa May saw a blue topaz ring once in Charleston in a store window. She would have given anything to have had that ring. It was the same color as Daniel's eyes. His long, sun streaked hair which he usually wore loose was combed back neatly and tied at the nape of his neck. When Daniel had gone off to war, he had been a gangly boy, and he had come home a man, all filled out with strong, rippling muscles from years of hard work. He would never lose his wild mountain man look about him, but he was a fine specimen of a man all the same. Looking at him, Willa May was glad she hadn't been foolish enough to call off the wedding.

When Pole and Willa May reached the altar, Daniel took Willa May's hand and Preacher Willis started in with the "I do's". After the ceremony, everyone gathered outside where all the families had brought a dish for the occasion: Miss Beatrice's lemon layer cake, Big Annie's chicken and dumplings, and Mrs. Shrewsbury's baked beans. The list went on and on. All this was topped off with the triple layered wedding cake with strawberry filling that Ernestine Hibbs had made with graceful swans formed out of sugar -- the most glorious cake Willa May had ever seen.

As the cake was being served, Mr. Shaw took up his fiddle once more and started playing "Camptown Races" and folks swept up their partners and kicked up their heels. The day was bright and sunny and everyone danced until the sun was a bright orange ball in a deep mauve sky peeping over the slope of mountain behind the church. Daniel, who had been clapping and stomping to the music, leaned over and told Willa May that it was time for them to set out for their little cabin. Willa May wished she could have made that celebration continue. But in her heart, she knew Daniel was right. It was time to say their good-byes and head toward their new home. When she hugged her mama, Lizzy started to cry. She hugged her pa next and just as she started to turn and look for Augie, Pole pulled her back to him for one last hug, knowing it was the last time he could call her his. When she had hugged Augie, Willa May turned and took Daniel's hand. As they raced for their buckboard wagon, everyone crowded around them and threw rice and rose petals at them, calling, "Good luck" and "God speed".

Daniel lifted Willa May up into his wagon, a wedding gift from his family, and she held on tightly to his arm as they started off together. They leaned in close to each other and talked and laughed about the good time they had that day, both of them holding on to the memories already.

By the time they reached their cabin, a crescent moon had crept up into a star studded sky that twinkled over them like a velvet blanket. Daniel lifted Willa May down from the wagon and carrying her in his arms, unlatched the heavy wood door. He stepped over the threshold. Until then Willa May hadn't seen the cabin, but even in the glow of the night sky, she could see that Daniel had done a fine job. He kissed her and set her down. He lit some candles around the big square room, and in the candles' glow, she spotted some furniture. A long trestle table with benches was close by the hearth and there were two wooden rockers, a step stool she could use for milking, a bureau with an oval looking glass over it. Then she saw a ladder that led up to a loft near the high, peaked ceiling. She didn't have to be told that the bed they would share was up that ladder. Daniel, seeing her looking that way, grew nervous and said, "I'd best go out and unhitch the team."

Willa May looked away and nodded, knowing he was trying to give her time to get herself ready. From the worried look that came over Daniel's face, Willa May knew he was anxious over what he might find when he came back, but she was determined to prove that she was a woman in every way. She braced herself and watched Daniel go back outside. She started unbuttoning all the little pearl buttons Miss Beatrice had sewn on her dress, but her hands began to shake and it took a lot longer than she thought. Eyeing the big wooden door, she prayed that she would be able to get out of the dress that imprisoned her and slip into the bed up in the loft before Daniel came back. The more she rushed, the worse her hands shook and the tiny buttons kept slipping out of her fingers. Willa May never heard Daniel come in -- her back was to the door -- but suddenly she felt another pair of hands at her back.

"Here, let me help," he said.

Startled, Willa May thought she might just die right there. But Daniel leaned down and gently pressed his lips to the back of her bare neck. She had managed somehow to get the top buttons unfastened and the back of her neck lay exposed; her long auburn hair tumbled in tendrils over her shoulders. The feather soft touch of his lips against her neck sent ripples flowing through her, ripples she had never felt before. Slowly he kept kissing her bare flesh while he unbuttoned the remaining pearl buttons. By the time he slipped her dress down to her waist, Willa May was leaning against him, nearly woozy from the ripples she felt with each new kiss. Her dress fell onto the bare wood floor around her ankles and Daniel, still lightly kissing her neck and shoulders, put his arms around her. She couldn't take it any longer. Turning in his arms and standing on tiptoe, Willa May kissed Daniel back. Without realizing exactly what she was doing, she started helping Daniel out of his jacket. Then she unfastened his tie and unbuttoned his shirt. All the while, Daniel was kissing her and tugging at her chemise. She felt his bare chest against the soft flesh of her breasts and she marveled at the hardness of his muscles and the strength they held. She felt so small and weak next to him. Then she felt his breath, warm on her ear as he whispered, "Come up to bed with me, Willa May."

Without any further prompting, Willa May led the way up the ladder to the feather tick up in the loft. As she sank into its warm softness, Daniel leaned over her, lowering his body onto her and kissing her sweetly. He had an unmistakable power that she was sure he was trying his best to keep in tow. Daniel started caressing her and touching her like 'Lil Annie had said he would. But now it didn't seem so frightening and she remembered how 'Lil Annie had told her everything would come naturally. She had said that Willa May would know what to do when the time came. 'Lil Annie was right. Those ripples started flushing through her veins with each new kiss and soon she and Daniel were holding onto each other harder. Their breath was coming faster and their hands started roaming, exploring each other until soon Willa May felt Daniel inside of her. All her fears and doubts fell away like the last lingering leaves in fall fluttering to the ground.

Afterward they clung to each other, unwilling to let go. Willa May rested her head against Daniel's chest, listening to the steady beat of his heart until she fell asleep, knowing she had found a new happiness to share with her new husband.

That summer was a golden dream for them. Together, they worked on their place. They milked the cow at dawn and fed the chickens. Daniel sawed wood for the winter and cleared land to be planted the following spring. Willa May picked berries and smoked bees out of their hives to steal their honeycombs. They took long walks together

41

to view the spectacular gorge with its mountains spread out like a picture before them. Come evening, Willa May picked up her sewing or read to Daniel. He couldn't read or write. Willa May offered to teach him, but Daniel shrugged and said, "What for?" Willa May figured Daniel felt he knew all he needed in his world. Besides, he had her to read to him now. They soon had a routine -- first a chapter from the Good Book and then a chapter or verses from a book of Willa May's choosing. Through the summer months, she introduced Daniel to all the great writers, from Shakespeare to Walt Whitman. Daniel particularly liked <u>Leaves of Grass</u>. One evening, she read how Whitman, alone in mountains of his own, hunted and made camp for the night. He told how he cooked his kill over an open fire and fell asleep on a bed of leaves with just his dog for company. Daniel sighed, listening intently, as he rocked to and fro in his rocker on the front porch. The cool night air settled over them, bringing relief from the heat of the day while the shadows from the surrounding hills grew longer, blending finally with the darkness. "That feller -- that Mr. Whitman -- he spins the power of words like no other."

Willa May felt this showed a deep reflection on Daniel's part, but then she figured that if Daniel had been a writer, his words would have come out like Mr. Whitman's. She discovered that her husband possessed a poetic spirit; there was more to him than muscle and good instincts. He saw majesty in each flower, beauty in the soaring of a bird on the wing, and wonderment in the pattern of a snake's skin. He was in harmony with it all. He just never had the schooling that other folks had. But those same folks couldn't identify an animal from its tracks, nor track the animal through the woods like Daniel. He could always sense when something was amiss in his woods, he was so attuned to every living thing.

Mr. Twain became another of Daniel's favorites. He often said that Mr. Twain must have been some old rascal to be able to make a body chuckle like he could. The first time Willa May read "The Celebrated Jumping Frog of Calaveras County", Daniel slapped his knee, chortling over it and begging her to read it again. Years later when <u>The Adventures of Huckleberry Finn</u> was published, Daniel kept her up reading half the night three nights in a row until she finished it.

Willa May borrowed these books from Mr. Shaw and Miss Beatrice. She would finish one and Daniel would ride over to Robson and come back with another. He always brought some confection that Miss Beatrice had made or a new lace dresser scarf or pillowcases she had tatted for them. Mr. Shaw would slip Daniel some peach brandy on occasion, too. In return, Willa May always tried to remember their birthdays and holidays with a little something special to repay them for these small kindnesses: fruit cakes at Christmas; Divinity at Easter; and Mr. Shaw's favorite, chocolate layer cake, for birthdays. Mr. Shaw and Miss Beatrice were good friends and they provided Willa May and Daniel with a window to the world beyond the mountains. Willa May felt obliged to them for that even more than for their gifts.

Often as they worked together, Daniel would remark on whatever book they were reading. It seemed to make the work go faster. There was plenty of work to do, too. No sooner would they get the day's chores done than the rooster would crow and they would have to start in all over again. The weeks passed blissfully and before they knew it, September had come and they started setting in the stores of all the canned foods they had harvested from Willa May's little garden. Willa May was so proud of the jars of food. She counted them and rearranged them on the shelves that Daniel had put up for her. Daniel teased her, saying that she dusted them off every day like they contained gold instead of vittles.

One Friday they rode over to Lizzy's and after lunch, they picked apples from her orchard till sundown. Early the next morning they started making applebutter. This time Daniel tended the kettle while Pole and Big Jim watched from a distance, not taking any chances after their experience the previous fall. Willa May noticed that Augie hadn't come home the night before and she asked Lizzy about it. Lizzy just shook her head, mumbling, "That no-account Augie". Outside, Willa May asked Pole about Augie and got the same reply. He stalked away in a huff toward the barn. She turned to Big Jim, but he tried to avoid her as well. She told him that she wasn't going to be put off. After all Augie was her brother and even though she no longer lived there, she still had a right to know about her own kin.

Big Jim scratched his head and nodded. "I reckon you do at that. Well, since the war, Augie ain't been able to hold down a job. Him and Elroy Hicks took up together and spend the day in the jug, talking about the war. I'm afeared that if Augie don't straighten up and fly right, he'll end up a drunken no-good panhandler and nobody will hire him."

That night Daniel and Willa May stayed over at Lizzy's and Pole's, then went to church the following morning. They were happy to see all the folks they knew. Since the church was too far away for them, they had to make do with an extra reading from the Good Book most Sundays. Sometimes Lizzy, Pole, and Big Jim visited on Sunday afternoons and stayed for dinner. Everybody welcomed them back at church and asked how they were getting along. They asked, too, if Daniel and Willa May had a little one on the way yet, a question that embarrassed them both. They were still just getting used to each other and this kind of prying made them feel like folks were wanting to know just what they had been up to together. Willa May blushed a bright crimson every time someone asked them and she noticed that Daniel pretended to be consumed in the scenes depicted in the stained glass windows all of a sudden. When 'Lil Annie asked them -- she must have been about the fifth person to ask -- Willa May couldn't take it any longer. "Mind your own business." Willa May acted as snooty as she could manage. 'Lil Annie merely jabbed Denny Bob in the ribs. They twittered, winking and grinning knowingly at each other. "Besides," Willa May went on, "looks to me like you got a lot of business there to watch, Missy." Willa May gestured toward 'Lil Annie's big belly.

'Lil Annie laughed again and patted the huge swell under her breasts. She nodded. "Just a little longer. Ain't that right, darlin'?"

Denny Bob grinned, looking every bit the proud papa and nodded, seemingly turning shy now that the tables were turned on them. To Willa May, they looked as lovey-dovey as they had when they had gotten married two years before. It did her heart good to see two people so in love. She determined to start right away on trying to have a baby, too.

After the service, everyone went to Lizzy's and Pole's for a cookout. Daniel and Big Jim set up a spit and built a fire under it. They roasted one of Luther's pigs. Meanwhile, the women husked corn and wrapped the ears to roast over the fire. Miss Beatrice and Mr. Shaw arrived, bringing stewed apples, cornbread still warm from the stove, and rhubarb pie. Big Annie and Willa May peeled potatoes and boiled them with cabbage and carrots right out of the garden. Lizzy and 'Lil Annie were up to their elbows in flour, making dough for apple and raspberry pies.

They ate and ate till their bellies ached. The menfolk all had second and third helpings of everything. Everyone laughed watching

'Lil Annie's baby, 'Lil Luther, sucking on a roasting ear and smacking his little lips. He let out a belch so loud that it sounded like it had erupted from a grown man. Uncle Luther clapped Denny Bob on the shoulder and declared, "That's my little boy!" He was so proud of his namesake, he bragged on anything the toddler did. Willa May watched her uncle cooing and cuddling the baby, wondering what it would be like when she brought home a grandson for her own pa. It sharpened her decision to get busy making some babies.

"Daniel! Daniel!" Big Annie yelled, pulling Willa May back to the real world. They turned to see Big Annie running for all she was worth up the hill beside the house. This was a rare sight, considering that Big Annie had earned her name from being the biggest woman in the valley. She was huffing and puffing, her face flushed and wet with rivulets of sweat. "A snake," she gasped, holding onto her sides as she heaved her huge body with every gasp. "A big old -- rattler!" Big Annie extended her arms wide, showing them the size of it.

Daniel stood up. "Where?"

Big Annie pointed, still trying to catch her breath. "Down -- yonder -- in the front yard. Next to the rose bushes."

Without a word, Daniel rushed off to the barn and got Pole's hoe. Everyone followed him down to the front yard, keeping their distance and watching the grass for any sudden movement. Daniel spotted it first. He had a sharper eye after all the years he had spent up in his mountains. "Stay back," he ordered, raising the hoe over his shoulder. Gripping it tightly with both hands, he started toward the snake. The rattlesnake coiled and reared its head. Its rattlers were shaking and it started hissing, its seed shaped eyes focused on Daniel. Willa May held tightly to her pa's hand. Glancing at her, Pole wrapped one arm around her and pulled her to him. It was a real face-off. Daniel and the snake eyed each other to see which would make the first move. It seemed to Willa May that they were both frozen in time, waiting for the other to strike. The snake snapped at Daniel, lunging fangs first the entire length of its body. Everyone gasped. Daniel leapt to one side as he swung Pole's hoe. The blade of the hoe slashed the air in a downward arc. Daniel struck the snake in its middle. Hissing, the snake struck again, missing Daniel's leg by less than an inch. Willa May cringed and screamed, not wanting to watch and not daring to turn away. Pole patted her shoulder as they looked on. With sinewy arms, Daniel swung the hoe again and sliced off the snake's head. The snake lay in three pieces, still writhing and flopping on the grass,

45

spewing blood from every wound. Nobody dared to move till they saw the remains of the snake grow still. Each one feared that somehow the serpent would rear up and strike yet again. Daniel was the first to move, slowly lowering the hoe. He stood over the bloody mess, cautiously nudging it with the sharp blade of the hoe. Raising the hoe one last time, he chopped off the rattlers. He picked up the dripping trophy, then turned and grinned at Willa May. Holding the rattlers out to her, he said, "Here, Willa May, go put these here rattlers in the wagon for me."

Willa May stared at Daniel, her eyes wide, unable to say a word. Daniel laughed and shook his head. She realized then that he had only been teasing. Without warning, he tossed the rattlers to Big Jim who caught them more out of reflex than any desire to handle the bloody mess. "Never mind, darlin'. Jim here will put them away for me." Pole and Luther guffawed at the surprise registered on poor Jim's face as he stared down at the rattlers. Still chuckling to himself, Daniel strode off toward the barn leaving the rest of them staring at Big Jim, grateful it had been him and not one of them who had caught the rattlers.

That fall Willa May worked extra hard on becoming a mother. She found out that setting on it was a far cry from actually becoming one. By that time, she and Daniel had adjusted to being together as husband and wife. She could even admit that she looked forward to the few precious moments when they could set the world aside and be together, just the two of them. Only trouble was, it didn't appear to be getting her any nearer to having a baby of her own.

One frosty Sunday evening early in November, they were at her mama's when Luther rode up in his wagon, hell-bent. He called, "Lizzy! Lizzy! Come quick!"

Everyone rushed out to the porch, wondering what was wrong. "What is it, Lute?" Lizzy hollered back.

"'Lil Annie's time is come and she's in real trouble this time."

Lizzy pulled off her apron and tossed it to Pole. Turning to Daniel, she said, "I'd like Willa May to help me, so if you have to head home, I'll have Napoleon fetch her on home tomorrow."

Daniel was already shaking his head, his blue eyes growing dark as he realized how serious the situation was. He said, "I reckon we can

46

stay over the night, Lizzy."

Lizzy, sparing no words for anything else, grabbed Willa May and pulled her inside to fetch their bonnets and capes. They hurried down the hill to where Luther had already turned the wagon around. His mules looked exhausted, lathered up and panting for each breath that rose in smoky clouds from their flared nostrils. When Luther cracked his reins down on them, they took off like race horses on the Fourth of July, kicking up dark clouds in their wake.

When they arrived, Dessie was there again, swollen with child, and frazzled from helping with her sister's labor. She helped Lizzy off with her bonnet and cape saying, "Baby's feet first, Aunt Lizzy. Mama's been working with it, but 'Lil Annie's done for. She passed out just a minute ago and Mama says if we can't get the baby turned soon, they'll both be goners."

"Hush that talk," Lizzy scoffed.

Willa May noted how her uncle's face had turned ashen when he heard this. 'Lil Annie was Luther's favorite and everyone in that room knew he couldn't stand it if something happened to her.

"No Dessie," Lizzy continued, "you just set yourself down awhile and get some rest. You look like you need it. Willa May, make your uncle and your cousin some fresh coffee and boil lots of water while you're at it."

Willa May started to nod, but Lizzy had already whirled around and headed for the small room where 'Lil Annie had given birth to Baby Luther. For a minute Willa May was swept back to that night, recollecting how 'Lil Annie had screamed and screamed, trying to have that baby. Then it struck her. There were no screams this time. The silence all around them seemed like a bad omen and she felt a chill shudder up her spine. Hoping that Luther and Dessie weren't thinking the same thing, she set about the kitchen making a fresh pot of coffee and boiling a big kettle of water over the fire.

Each of them had finished three cups of the coffee by the time Lizzy came out. They had been fidgeting with their coffee cups, tapping their fingers on the table top. Every now and then they looked toward the door where 'Lil Annie was trying to give birth. The look on Lizzy's face now as she stepped through the doorway, pulling the door closed behind her told them that she bore bad news. Before she could say a word, Luther fell to his knees on the bare wood floor, grabbed his head, and burst into tears. "Oh, Lord. Oh, Lord, my baby's gone."

47

Dessie jumped up, crying, and raced toward the door where Lizzy stood. Lizzy took Dessie in her arms and wouldn't allow her to go any further. She spoke in a calm voice. "Your mama wants some time alone with your baby sister." Dessie looked at Lizzy, shaking her head as if she didn't grasp what Lizzy was saying, but Willa May and Lizzy both knew she understood. She just couldn't abide it. 'Lil Annie, all of sixteen years old, was gone. It struck Willa May that 'Lil Annie was only a year and a half older than she was. Memories leapt into Willa May's mind. She thought of the two of them picking raspberries when they were little and eating all that they picked. They had gotten sick off those juicy ripe berries, their bellies aching and both of them crying and puking red all day. She remembered how they had dared each other to dive off the cliff by their favorite swimming hole and neither of them was brave enough to do it. Together, they had waited for their men to come home to them from far off places where they never should have had to go. Now this.

Luther was still on his knees, crying to the Lord. Dessie was leaning against the wall, holding herself and crying, too. Lizzy, with one silent tear running down her cheek, bent over Luther and wrapped her arms around him, rocking him silently in her arms. Willa May's knees felt buttery. She couldn't stay in that kitchen another minute knowing her dear cousin and the best friend of her childhood was lying dead in the next room. She raced out of the house and into the cold November night. She stopped only for a second, looking around her and wondering what in the world she was going to do out there at that time of the night. Deep down inside, though, she knew. She set out for home where someone waited for her who could rock her and hold her till she was all cried out, too.

Setting out, she ran up the road toward her mama's house, tears streaming down her cold face with only the silvery light of the half moon to show her the way. She ran until her sides ached and she had to stagger awhile to get her wind back. Holding onto her ribs, she rushed on. Big Annie's place was about four and a half miles from her mama's house. It took her well over an hour to get home. When she reached their front yard, she started screaming, crying out as she struggled toward the porch steps. She knew she must have sounded like she had gone mad. Before she reached the bottom step, Daniel, Pole and Big Jim were all there, coming down the steps as fast as their bare feet could carry them. Daniel, in just his overalls, picked her up, and cradling her in his arms, carried her up the steps. She knew she wasn't making much sense; she was out of breath and sobbing. Daniel carried her into the parlor and set her down next to the hearth where the embers were still warm. Pole stoked the fire, seeing that Willa May's teeth were chattering even though she was soaked with sweat.

Daniel rubbed her arms and shoulders, trying to warm her cold skin. "Go fetch me a quilt for her," he said to Big Jim. When Jim brought the quilt, Daniel wrapped Willa May in it and kept rubbing her arms and shoulders until she stopped shivering and her breathing grew normal.

Pole couldn't bear it any longer. Rubbing the back of his neck, he said, "Willa May, what in the world's got into you?"

"It -- it's 'Lil Annie," Willa May gasped. "Sh -- she's dead." Willa May started sobbing again.

Daniel held her close. Pole looked at Big Jim who sighed deeply, shaking his head. He stood up and left the parlor, coming back with some cups and one of Pole's jugs. "Here, Willa May. Drink this." Willa May shook her head and turned away, but he pushed the cup at her, saying, "Drink it. It'll keep you from getting sick now, you year?"

She took the cup and sipped the fiery clear whiskey they called "White Lightning". After the first swallow, she knew why it was called that. Her heart ached, her sides ached, and her legs and feet ached. But the liquor did its trick, taking hold of her and soothing her hurt insides. She was still sobbing and hiccuping between sips. She took another drink from the cup, feeling all lit up inside, like somebody had put a lantern down in there that glowed as warm as July sunshine. She was so exhausted that she didn't even finish the cup before she drifted off to sleep.

The next morning she woke up in Daniel's arms. He was still sleeping, his head next to hers. She could hear his breathing coming slow and even. Suddenly she wondered where Denny Bob had been the night before when 'Lil Annie lay there dying. She reminded herself to ask Lizzy about it later. As she lay there, feeling Daniel's hands on her body, she wondered if maybe she had been too eager to start having babies. She certainly wasn't ready to die. Just the thought of giving birth now put fear in her like she had never known before. She began to wonder if there was some trick to not getting in the family way, recalling the few married women in the valley she knew who had never had any babies. "Barren" was the word she had heard as she grew up whenever these women were spoken of in sad, pity filled tones. It was like some sort of curse: barren. It didn't appear to be much of a curse now. But what, she wondered, did a body have to do to become barren?

Daniel stirred, his hand fondling her breast. He would be awake any minute and for the first time since they had married, she didn't want to let him make love to her for fear that this would be the time she would get the baby she thought she had wanted. Her mind started to race, trying to think of a way to get out of bed without waking Daniel. She knew he wouldn't understand why she had turned cold to his touch. She knew, too, that he would still expect her to do her "wifely duty" as she had heard the womenfolk call it.

While Willa May was busy thinking of how to get out of Daniel's arms, she didn't realize that he was lying there watching her. She looked up, trying to stay as still as she could, to see him looking at her with such a sad expression on his face that she almost reached up and pulled him to her. But she didn't. She just lay there, looking back at him, not wanting to leave and not wanting to stay. It was Daniel who got out of bed. He kissed Willa May softly on her cheek and pulled on his shirt and overalls. Carrying his socks and shoes, he slipped out of their room without so much as a look back.

Willa May watched the door close, wishing she had never been thinking what she had been thinking. She knew that Daniel had somehow read her thoughts. She had hurt him deeply and she didn't know what to do. Too frightened to be a wife and too frightened not to be, she felt a double loss -- first 'Lil Annie and now Daniel. *Oh Lord, I never meant to lose him, too.*

Willa May decided to stay over at her folks' place until the funeral. Daniel had to go back to the cabin and tend to the livestock so he kissed her on the cheek, not on the mouth, she noticed. He set off that morning. "I'll be back for you the day of the funeral," he told her.

Watching him from the road where she had been standing the day she had seen him coming toward her with the slain mountain lion, Willa May couldn't bear to see him go. She worried that Daniel might not think he had much to come back for now. Maybe he would just set off into the mountains like he had done last winter. Panic took hold of her and before she knew what she was doing, Willa May chased after the wagon. "Daniel!" she called.

Daniel reined in the mules and turned to Willa May as she ran up alongside the wagon out of breath. Now that she was there, she couldn't think of what to say. She wanted to say, "Please don't go, Daniel. Because if you do, I'm afraid I won't ever see you again." But she knew that would sound foolish, like a baby crying after its mama. She just stood looking up at him, not knowing what to say.

Daniel saw the desperation in Willa May's eyes. He sprang down from the wagon and hugged her harder than her pa's bear hugs when she was little. She clung right back to him, knowing she could never turn him away again, not if it meant that horrible empty feeling she had been carrying inside her all morning since he left their bed. As much as she feared being with child, she feared losing Daniel's love more. Just as Daniel had read her thoughts in bed that morning, he knew just what she was thinking now. He lifted her chin and looked down in her eyes with his smiling blue eyes. He bent down and kissed her, pulling her up off her feet.

When he set her back down, she finally found her voice and pleaded, "Don't leave me here. I can't stand it when I'm not with you. Please don't leave me. Don't ever leave me."

Daniel ran his fingers through her long hair and whispered in a husky voice, "Why, Willa May, don't you know by now that I could never leave you, no matter what?"

"But I was so scared after this morning --"

"Hush now, Girl. I reckon I understand about this morning," he said. "After 'Lil Annie dying and all. Tell you the truth, it scared me some, too."

"It did?"

Daniel nodded and laid her head against his chest. "Ain't much in this world scares me, darlin', but the thought of losing my Willa May scares the hell out of me."

Willa May knew that what Daniel was saying came hard for him. He was never the kind of man to sweet talk a girl. He didn't mince many words with other people, either. She put her arms around his neck and pulled his face toward hers. She kissed him, a long lingering kiss. The sweetest kiss she could ever remember. Daniel's breath was coming hard when they parted.

"I best be goin' or else we'll have to find some bushes somewhere to sneak behind if you keep kissing me like that," he said.

Willa May giggled and they hugged again. Daniel got back up on his wagon. Looking down at her, he said, "I'll be back for the funeral...and to take you home with me come Thursday. I promise.

Don't I always keep my promises?"

She could see the twinkle was back in his eyes now as Daniel looked at her. She felt a relief like a drowning man when he finds his hold and knows he's been saved. Nodding her head, she winked up at him and asked saucily, "You won't forget me, will you?"

"Forget you? Hell, Girl, after that there kiss, I won't be able to think of nothing else but you."

"You'd better not," she teased.

He grinned at her then picked up the reins and called out to the mules. Looking back over his shoulder, he waved his hat and called, "See you on Thursday."

"I'll be ready," she answered. She watched him till he was out of sight.

The funeral was held in the little white Baptist church in Page. Everyone was fit to be tied that nobody had been able to find Denny Bob. Lizzy and Pole were mad, too, because no one knew where that no-account Augie had gotten himself off to, either. Lizzy had stayed up for two nights with Big Annie, helping with the wake. Willa May never liked wakes much. Seemed to her to be just an excuse for the menfolk to drink and make extra work for the women. They had to cook and clean up after all the folks who had come to sit up with the dead. Pole and Willa May went up to Big Annie's both nights, staying till way in the morning hours. Big Jim went looking for Augie, thinking to find him in some tavern or taken up with some woman. As dog tired as Willa May was each night coming home, she knew that her mama was even more exhausted. Lizzy had dark circles under her eyes and the strain of helping Big Annie and Luther hold it together through their grieving showed in the deep furrows around her mouth and across her forehead. In her heart, Willa May knew that some of the strain was Augie's doing, too. What a time for him to pick to go off somewhere and lay up drunk.

Willa May sat in the third pew with her folks, Daniel, and Big Jim, right behind Big Annie, Luther, their children and spouses, and their grandchildren. As enormous a woman as Big Annie was, she had a big heart to match and that huge heart was broken. Luther wrapped his skinny arm around Big Annie's wide girth, trying to comfort her. She sobbed and cried out, "My baby's gone. The Lord's done took my precious baby," over and over. It hurt Willa May anew to hear her going on like this. Poor Luther was trying his best to keep himself under control, but finally he broke down and bawled like a baby. He and Big Annie sat wrapped in each other's arms, crying their hearts out. There wasn't a dry eye in the church. Even Preacher Willis had to stop his preaching and wiped his eyes with his hanky. Choking back tears, he forged on, talking about how 'Lil Annie was with the angels now and how she had been an angel to everyone on earth when she was living.

In the middle of his eulogy, the church door swung open with a loud bang. In staggered Denny Bob, drunk as a lord, with Augie trailing behind him. Elroy Hicks rolled in behind them. Denny Bob, looking like he had been dragged there by a team of wild horses, stumbled toward the plain wood coffin at the foot of the altar. He bumped into the sides of several pews and nearly knocked himself down. All the while, he was crying and shrieking, "My darlin'! My darlin'! Don't take my darlin' away! When he had almost reached the coffin, he lurched forward and fell on top of it. The coffin crashed to the floor with Denny Bob sprawled on top of it. Big Annie screamed and fainted, toppling over in her pew. Everyone jumped to their feet, gasping in horror.

Seeing Big Annie's limp body, Luther thought she had passed on from shock over this outrage and leapt on top of Denny Bob, grabbing him by the throat and throttling him. Luther's two boys tried to pull Luther off of Denny Bob while Pole, Big Jim, and Daniel scrambled to the coffin. It was overturned and lying face down. They set it back on the long table it had been resting on and turned to help Luther's sons who were tangled with Luther and Denny Bob. Pulling Luther off of Denny Bob proved to be more difficult than any of them would have thought. As slight a man as he was, Luther was crazy with grief and the shock of seeing Big Annie passed out. Now he was taking it all out on Denny Bob whose face was turning from scarlet to purple.

It took all five men to get Luther up. Still kicking and fighting, he tried to break free. Preacher Willis, his face chalk white, shouted at the top of his voice. "Stop it. Stop it, I say. In the name of Jesus, stop this right now!" On hearing the name of Jesus being called on, everyone stood stock still, reckoning that the hand of the Lord would swoop right down into the little church and flatten them all. Holding his hand up for silence, Preacher Willis ordered, "All of you sit down and show proper respect for the dead, by God."

Luther shrugged his loose suit back into place and went to Big Annie's side. Lizzy and Dessie were fanning her and rubbing her hands. She came to, looked up at Luther, and started bawling anew. Lizzy and Dessie, seeing that Big Annie was all right, returned to their places. Augie had slunk in and sat down next to Willa May. Lizzy gave him a look that Willa May recollected from childhood. It was her "Just wait till I get you home" look. Augie gulped and looked sheepish as he hung his head. Elroy rolled himself over by their pew and did the same. Denny Bob, terrified of Luther, came back and seated himself next to Daniel.

Willa May was afraid that the fussing and fighting would start up again outside the church, but she was relieved when everyone came out quietly. The funeral proceeded in an orderly fashion as if nothing had happened. With grim faces, the congregation headed for the graveyard. It seemed like nothing more was going to take place until they lowered 'Lil Annie into her grave. Denny Bob started howling and wailing, sounding like a coyote. He tried to throw himself into the deep hole with her, but Augie and Big Jim held onto him. Denny Bob kept fighting them off and just as he got a few feet closer to the grave, they would grab him again. This went on for a few minutes, all of them watching wide eyed, wondering what they would do if Denny Bob managed to jump down into the gaping grave. Suddenly, in the middle of his screeching and fighting, Daniel turned and hurled his fist, knocking Denny Bob out cold. Augie and Jim held Denny Bob's sagging body to keep him from falling on top of the lowered coffin. Willa May thought she would have just dropped the no good sonofabitch right there on the ground. When the service was finally over, Augie and Big Jim hauled Denny Bob over to Pole's wagon and loaded him onto the back. He didn't come around for two more hours.

They rode home in silence. Lizzy and Pole left in their wagon with Augie and Denny Bob in the back. Big Jim rode with Daniel and Willa May. Back at the house, Lizzy and Willa May started cooking supper while the menfolk sat in the parlor. As Willa May set the table, she noticed that there wasn't much of the usual men talk going on in the other room. She wondered when the dam would break loose inside her mama and her pa and come gushing out at Augie. He had caused them all a lot of worry and disgrace, laying out drunk when his cousin was dying and his family needed him.

Everyone sat down to dinner and Lizzy said the blessing, asking the Lord to watch over 'Lil Annie and to forgive all good-for-nothing sinners -- here she looked pointedly at Augie -- and to bless the vittles they were about to eat. As they started to pass the steaming platters and bowls of food, Pole fixed Augie with a look and said, "When you're done eating, I want you to pack your things and leave."

Augie started whining. "What did I do? How was I supposed to know that 'Lil Annie was dead, for Chrissake?"

Before Pole could reply, Lizzy stood up and slapped Augie full in the face. The sound of it seemed magnified in the silence of the room. Lizzy's face reddened with rage and Willa May could see that she was seething with fury. "You're a disgrace to this family and a disgrace to the good Lord who put you here. Now get out of my sight and never darken my door again."

Augie shoved back his chair and threw down his napkin. He stood up, looking from his mama to his pa and back again. Willa May thought he would beg them to let him stay and promise, like he had done a thousand times lately, that he would straighten himself up. Instead he said bitterly, "Fine, damn it. If that's the way you all feel, then the hell with you all."

Pole, Big Jim, and Daniel stood as one, just waiting for Augie to say another word. But Augie strode out of the room, through the parlor, and slammed out the front door. Willa May figured they hadn't seen the last of him. Men like Augie had a way of draining the sap right out of the people that cared about them, always wheedling away at them.

The men sat back down as though nothing had happened and started passing the bowls of steaming food to each other again. Willa May had been feeling a bit queasy in her stomach all day, but when Daniel passed her the fried chicken she took one whiff of the meat and ran out to the outhouse. When she emerged not feeling a whole lot better, Daniel was waiting for her. "Are you all right, Willa May?"

She shook her head. "I feel awful. My stomach is churning and I can't bear the smell of the food. I know Mama worked real hard on it, but I don't think I could eat a bite."

"You reckon you're just upset over 'Lil Annie and all that hullabaloo at the funeral?"

Lizzy had come out to see about Willa May, too. She joined them just as Willa May said, "I don't know what's wrong with me. I wake up feeling like I'm goin' to be sick right on the sheets. I can't eat anything without feeling that same sickly feeling."

Daniel put his arm around her and looked at Lizzy. "Reckon we better stay over till she's over it?"

Lizzy smiled knowingly. "Not unless you can stay nine months, Son."

They looked at Lizzy, too stunned to say anything. She laughed. "Why, don't you two know? There ain't nothing wrong with Willa May. She's just being a woman, that's all. And now, Son, she's about to give you your firstborn."

Pole and Big Jim had followed them outside and when Pole heard this, he let out a whoop and clapped Daniel on the back, ruffling his blonde hair. "Well, I'll be! I'm goin' to be a grandpa, Jim," he cried. Then he hugged Willa May so tightly that she started to feel a little desperate again. He finally let go of her and threw his arm around Daniel's shoulder, saying, "This calls for a little celebration. Let's go up to the still, boys."

"But what about your supper?" Lizzy cried.

Pole waved her off. "Supper can wait. I don't get a new grandchild every day, Lizzy."

Willa May watched the men head up the hill to the woods where the still stood, and then feeling even more desperate, she headed back to the outhouse.

Chapter Three

Their first winter together was a harsh one. Snow started coming down on Christmas Eve when they were over at Willa May's folks' place, planning to go to the Christmas pageant. Daniel paid a call on his folks in Deepwater and came back around sunset. As he stomped snow off his boots and brushed more off of his coat, he said, "Snowed about ten inches this last hour, I'd say." He moved over by the fire to warm his hands and dry off.

"Reckon they'll call off the pageant?" Lizzy asked, peering out the window at the storm brewing outside.

"Nope," Daniel spoke up. "I saw Preacher Willis heading to the church on my way back. He said that folks would be disappointed if they didn't have a pageant. Besides, snow started too late to get word out that it had been canceled."

"Preacher Willis just may have to put some people up for the night, too, if this keeps up," Lizzy declared, still watching the sheet of white snow billowing in the night air.

"You figure Old Man Peyton will make it this year?" Willa May asked.

Pole chuckled softly and shook his head. "I have an idea that if anybody can make it, it'll be that old buzzard."

Old Man Peyton was a hermit who lived in a cave somewhere up on the mountain. He only came around on Christmas Eve. Every year he played Father Christmas, looking every bit the part. With a long white beard down to his belt and long silver hair to his shoulders, he wore an old bearskin coat that came down to the top of his buckskin boots. Nobody knew how old he was, but some said he was the illegitimate son of Johnny Chapman. Others said he was the first white settler in the valley. One Christmas Eve night when he had gone out to chop down a spruce for his family, he came back to find his wife and three children scalped by the Shawnee. Some said that was why he only came around on Christmas Eve, that he was looking for his dead family. Willa May liked to think that even if his family had been killed like folks said that he came around on Christmas Eve because that was the season of peace and goodwill toward men. Why, even the meanest folks showed a kind heart at the Christmas season. Maybe it was for that reason that Old Man Peyton chose that day of all the days in the year to rejoin the civilized world. Maybe he had seen so much that was vile in the nature of man that he would only favor the world with his company on the only day when true goodness was abounding. She only knew that his eyes held a gentleness in them when he would smile at the little ones each year and hand them their Christmas pokes, like the gentleness in the eyes of a deer. He didn't seem exactly trustful of those around him, but not meaning them any harm, either. A spry old soul, he never seemed to age. The old man had always looked as old as the hills since Willa May had been one of the little ones who received a poke from his withered hands. In return, he got a poke for himself with some pieces of hard candy, a few black walnuts, and an apple. Like the young ones who believed he was truly Father Christmas, he would open his poke and pop one of the pieces of candy in his mouth the moment the poke was handed to him. From the expression on his face, the way he closed his eyes and looked so content, Willa May figured that he savored the contents of that poke even more than the youngsters. No, Christmas wouldn't be Christmas without their very own Father Christmas.

"You know," Daniel was saying, "I used to run across Old Man Peyton up by his cave sometimes. Scared me to death the first time I saw him. He came up on me from behind, so quiet, I never heard him coming."

All of them knew that Daniel had such keen senses that for him to be caught off guard would indeed be unusual. They knew how attuned he was to every living thing in his mountains. Willa May thought he could even hear a snake slithering on its belly in the summer grass. But maybe he didn't hear it as much as he felt it. Folks they knew were always surprised when Daniel would say, "Better see who's at the door," long before the rest of them heard any footsteps. It was eerie.

Pole and Big Jim shook their heads, unable to fathom how anyone could surprise Daniel. Lizzy said, "You've seen his cave? What's it like?"

"Nice and dry. Big, too."

"No, that's not what I meant," Lizzy frowned. "How does he live? What does his cave look like?"

"Oh. Well, he's a right finicky old rascal. He's collected some old worn out pieces of furniture over the years. There's a big oak table and a couple of old chairs with legs broke on them. He sleeps on a pallet with lots of hides to keep him warm in cold weather. In summer, he's always out gathering berries and keeps himself a little garden of sorts."

"Well, I'll be." Lizzy shook her head in disbelief. "If he lives just like the rest of us, then why doesn't he live with people around him?"

"He's done been up there by himself for so long, I reckon he can't tolerate folks much. He was always good to me, though, whenever I'd come around. Always offered me food and a place to sleep." Looking a bit sheepish, Daniel added, "That's where I holed up when I came back from the war."

Seeing the sudden interest on everyone's faces, he went on. "I just about froze up there in a lean-to I'd built in the fall. Got snowbound. Almost buried alive one night in a storm. I managed to crawl out, but I was too cold and too tuckered out to go on. So I just curled up in the snow and that's how Old Man Peyton found me."

"How did he get you back to his cave?" Big Jim asked, leaning forward.

"He had snowshoes. He went back to the cave and got an old sled. Somehow he managed to tie me onto it and pulled me back to his cave. Took care of me most of a month, feeding me homemade remedies he had concocted out of plants he collected. When I finally came around, he said that if I was goin' to be a mountain man, I'd better learn the ways of mountain men. He took me under his wing and showed me all he knew about plants, medicines, and surviving on my own. I reckon I owe that old man my life."

Mesmerized by Daniel's tale, they had forgotten about getting to church. The clock on the mantle chimed six o'clock and Lizzy exclaimed, "Goodness sakes! We had better get goin' if we're goin'."

Daniel looked at Willa May and said, "Darlin', are you sure you want to risk goin' out in the storm? It could get mighty wicked."

"Daniel Shrewsbury! I'll have you know I've never missed Christmas service and I'm not about to start now. Just take some extra quilts in the wagon and I'll be fine."

She knew that Daniel was concerned, that he would have rather she had stayed home safe and warm, but she just couldn't bear the thought of not sharing in all the excitement. She was determined to go, snow or no snow.

They made it to the church, but Willa May wasn't quite sure how.

"Wicked" was a good word for the way the snow and wind blasted against them, forcing them to huddle close together for warmth. Now and then, Daniel climbed down and cleared the mules' nostrils of snow and ice that collected in them and threatened to suffocate the poor beasts. They had several layers of quilts and some hides spread over them inside the wagon. Willa May reckoned that was how they kept from freezing. It was almost eight o'clock by the time they reached the church, but they weren't late. Most of the other folks that had ventured out were just arriving, too.

The snow was up over Willa May's knees so Daniel carried her into the church. After he saw her settled in their pew, he went back out to unharness the mules and put them in Lowell Upton's barn in the nearby field. Willa May looked around to see who else had made it. Big Annie and Luther, their children, and grandchildren were there. Miss Beatrice and Mrs. Hibbs were sitting together in their usual places up front where they could hear better. Daniel's folks weren't there, though, and neither was Old Man Peyton. The snow must have been too much for him, she thought. Daniel came back in, covered with snow -- it was even down his boots and his collar. A half-hour later, when it looked like everybody who was coming was there, the pageant got under way. Mr. Shaw played "O Little Town Of Bethlehem" on his fiddle and everyone stood to sing. Willa May looked around at the candles in the frosted windows and then up at Daniel, feeling a wonderful sense of peace. Even though they could hear the old North wind howling and shaking the timbers of the little church above the sound of the hymn singing, she was glad that she had insisted on coming.

When the pageant ended, Preacher Willis stood up at the altar and said, "Now I know we usually ask Old Man Peyton to be Father Christmas, but seeing as how he hasn't been able to make it --"

The arched door of the church banged open suddenly, and everyone in the congregation jumped. Like everyone else, Willa May turned in her pew to see the old hermit walking with a staff that looked like it came right out of the Good Book. Bent with age, he held the stick with an iron grip. He managed to get the door closed and started up the aisle. Decked out in his old bearskin coat and boots wrapped in extra rags for warmth, he marched to the front pew and took a seat. Covered with snow, he looked every bit like a ghost.

Father Christmas arrived after all. Everyone smiled -- especially the little ones -- knowing that Christmas would still go on in spite of the raging blizzard outside. Right away, Old Man Peyton passed out the pokes to the youngsters and took his own over to a corner next to the long needled pine the church ladies had decorated with cranberries and ginger cookies. As always, he searched for a piece of hard candy first. Finding it, he settled back, relishing its sweetness while the rest of the grownups drank cups of mulled cider and devoured the fruitcakes the womenfolk had baked.

Willa May made her way over to where the old man was sitting and perched herself on the edge of the pew beside him. "I want to thank you for saving my Daniel's life last winter. He told us this evening about how you took care of him and nursed him back to health. He means the world to me and I don't know what I would've done if he had died up on his mountain."

The old man watched her closely, his soft brown eyes taking in every word. "Well, I reckon it was worth it," he teased. "Especially seeing as how you're carrying Daniel's child now."

"Why, how did you know that?" she gasped. She wasn't showing yet and they had only told Daniel's folks.

It was the old hermit's turn to show surprise. His bushy white eyebrows shot up. "Why, I knew the minute I saw you here tonight. Child, you're just glowing with happiness. Don't take no genius to figure it out from there now, does it?"

Blushing as red as a candy apple, Willa May murmured, "No, I reckon not. Do you think anyone else knows?"

"Don't matter none if they do or they don't. This is yours and Daniel's joy. Ain't nobody else got to have a say in it. You just take care of yourself and that there baby growing inside you. Give that husband of yours the happiness he deserves. He loves you like no other. Always remember that."

Willa May wanted to talk some more, to find out how this old man had come to be what he was. She got such a strange feeling that he somehow knew what the future held in store for her and Daniel. All these things were spinning in her head, swirling like dried leaves swept along in a fall wind. Daniel came over just then, shaking hands with the old hermit and asking, "How have you been this year, Mordecai?"

Willa May stared at Daniel, surprised to hear him call the old man by his first name. She had never heard anyone call him anything but Old Man Peyton all her life. From the grin on Daniel's face, you would have thought he was talking to his kin, not some old recluse nobody really knew.

Old Man Peyton's mustache curled up at the ends as he smiled back at Daniel. "Been a lot less busy this winter without some young pup to watch over."

"Did you get any deer this fall?"

"Yep. Sure did. Got me a big doe and I been eating some of the best venison I done ever et in my life. What about you?"

"Got me a deer, some squirrel, and a 'possum, too. Been meaning to make Willa May here some of that stew you showed me how to make."

Old Man Peyton nodded. "That's mighty good eating, all right. And she could use some fattening up. She's a mighty scrawny little thing. Strong wind would carry her away, you don't watch out."

Willa May felt herself blushing profusely, not used to such talk from a virtual stranger.

"Reckon she'll be fat and sassy soon enough now," Daniel replied.

Willa May blushed even more hearing that.

Old Man Peyton clapped Daniel on the shoulder. "Just take real good care of her and help her get that baby born so you'll have somebody to take hunting with you, you hear?"

Daniel looked at Willa May and answered softly, "Oh, I plan to take extra good care of my Willa May. I guarantee you that."

The old man stood up and said, "Well, it's goin' to take me till morning to get back up the mountain, so I reckon I best get started."

"You're not goin' back out in that storm, are you?" Willa May asked, alarmed for the old man's safety.

"Missy, you been around long as I have, you done seen a lot worse than this." Shaking hands with Daniel again, he said, "Good luck to you, Son. If that there baby's a boy, you name him Mordecai, you hear?"

Daniel laughed and watched his friend stash his Christmas poke inside his bearskin coat. He picked up his staff and headed for the church door. The rest of the congregation seemed as dismayed as Willa May that the old man would attempt such a foolish thing as to hike back up the mountain in such a terrible storm. They looked on in silence as he opened the heavy arched door. He was immediately blown backward from the blast of frigid wind that greeted him. Hunching his shoulders, he forced his way through the door, shutting it with a loud bang.

Watching the old hermit's struggle, Preacher Willis stood up and announced to his flock that anyone who wanted to stay the night was welcomed to do just that and make their way home in the morning. Willa May's family decided it might be wise to wait out the storm. They stayed up late, talking in hushed voices so as not to disturb the children who were sleeping like little angels on pallets next to the Christmas tree. One by one, folks stretched out on the hard wooden pews and drifted off. Daniel sat up talking to Pole and Big Jim. Seeing that Willa May was getting sleepy, he let her rest her head in his lap. Outside, the wind gusted and howled all night.

The next morning the menfolk got up at dawn and shoveled a path from the church out to the road. From there, it was each man for himself. It took Willa May's family a long time to get home. Daniel and Pole had to cover the road with their coats and some of the quilts to get the wagon wheels through the deep snow. Big Jim held the reins while Pole and Daniel positioned themselves in back of the wheels. They pushed and heaved as hard as Bess and Dixie. Fortunately, the snow had stopped and the wind had died down. Otherwise, Willa May thought they all might have frozen on that trip home.

When they finally made it back to Lizzy's and Pole's, the women headed straight for the kitchen to make a big turkey dinner. The men, too worn out from battling the snow covered road, rested in the parlor. Together, the women set the food out on the table, using Lizzy's finest tablecloth and her best dishes. When all was ready, they called for the menfolk, but they didn't come. Looking into the parlor, they found all three men snoring by the fire. Reluctant to wake them, but knowing the men were starved after the long struggle to get home, Willa May nudged each one. She doubted that any of them tasted the turkey that day. They were simply too exhausted.

Daniel and Willa May managed to get home the next day. Daniel went out to feed the livestock right away, giving them extra feed. Willa May set about making supper, getting the biscuits started and stoking up a good fire for cooking. Daniel came back in, rubbing his hands from the cold. "Willa May, forget them biscuits. It's too danged cold in here to fret about getting food on the table. Let's you and me go up to the loft and let the fire start to heat this place up."

"I suppose you got an idea as to how to keep us warm while we're up there in that loft, too?" Willa May teased.

Daniel's blue eyes glistened. "Yep. I got a pretty fair idea, at that."

"Seems to me it was that idea that got me this baby."

"Sure enough? I don't rightly recollect how you got that there baby. Why don't you show me? Maybe then it'll come back to me."

"You go on up and get the bed covers warmed up for me. I'll be up directly, as soon as I finish these biscuits I'm making." Willa May smiled to herself as she went back to the floured table top and started rolling out a ball of dough.

When she finished making the biscuits and had cleaned up the floury mess she had made, she climbed up to the loft and hopped in the cot, clothes and all. Daniel, already undressed, wrapped himself around her until she got warm. Kissing her, he helped her off with her clothes. He smiled down at her and said, "Merry Christmas, darlin'." Willa May reached up and pulled him to her, happy to be back in their little cabin, just the two of them. They made love and Daniel held her close afterward. It was then that she felt a strange sensation inside her belly like delicate butterfly wings fluttering inside her. She had been asking Daniel about his winter with Old Man Peyton when the feeling started. She stopped in the middle of what she was saying and pressed her hand to the warm soft flesh of her belly. There it was again.

Daniel sat up. "What is it? What's wrong, Willa May?"

She could hear the fear in his voice and she took his hand in hers and placed it where the butterfly wings still fluttered. "Here," she whispered, smiling up at him. "Feel it?"

She watched as Daniel's worried frown turned to a knowing smile. "That's him?"

"Or her."

Daniel's hand massaged the warm flesh of her stomach slowly, gently. Kissing her again, he whispered in his husky voice, "I love you, Willa May." They made love again, not caring if they ever got out of their warm bed.

By February, Daniel teased Willa May that she was starting to look like she had swallowed a pumpkin. Her stomach was round and growing bigger every day. She constantly had to let out the waist on her dresses to make room for the baby who, at this point, didn't feel like butterfly wings fluttering, but more like a little mule kicking around inside her. The snow had been mounding up, sometimes covering the door, so Daniel had to slide down from the window next to their cot in the loft and dig out the door and windows below. The roads were piled high so that no wagons or horses could get through. Willa May hadn't seen her folks since Christmas. She prayed that they were all right and that soon the snow would let up so they could get over to see them.

Daniel worked inside that winter, building a cradle out of pine and a high chair to match. Willa May busied herself crocheting baby clothes and making a new quilt. This one was in the Baby Blocks pattern in pink and blue scraps that Lizzy and Mrs. Shrewsbury had given her. Even though it was cold outside, they were cozy in their little cabin, building a nesting place for the life they were about to welcome. Willa May was grateful that the bad weather would be behind them by the time the baby arrived. The thought of giving birth without another woman -- she wanted her mama -- to help was too much for either Daniel or Willa May to bear. Daniel let on like he was sure everything would turn out all right when her time came, but she often caught him watching her when he was pretending to be working on the cradle. At those times, she knew he was thinking of how it had been with 'Lil Annie. He looked so grave.

Lizzy told Willa May that she wouldn't get another baby while she nursed this one and Willa May was relieved when she heard this. She fretted over whether she would make a good mother, constantly worrying about what to do if the little thing took sick. What if she didn't know what to do for it? More than once when these fears took hold of her, she found herself wishing she was back home, still waiting for Daniel to come home from the war. But it was too late for that, she told herself, way too late.

In March, they got a thaw and like the year before, their yard turned into a rushing creek from the snow melting out of the mountains behind them. Daniel looked out at it from the door one day and said, "It's sure to be flooding down in the valley. Just wish the road was dry so I could get over and see to our kinfolk. They may be in a heap of trouble with all this water."

It was Easter by the time the road dried up enough to get a wagon over it. Willa May woke up that day, bursting with excitement about seeing her folks and getting out of the little cabin again. Daniel felt the same way. They talked and laughed all the way to Page. When she could see her mama's and pa's house, Willa May started to worry that she would find someone sick...or worse. But the house was still standing, so that was something, she reckoned. They pulled the wagon in and rode up the hill to the house. Daniel was just helping her down when Lizzy hurried out, smiling to see them. They were hugging when Pole and Big Jim came out and joined them, exclaiming that she looked like she was going to give birth to a barrel. The men shook Daniel's hand and clapped him on the back when Willa May saw someone else come out of the house, someone too small to be Augie. At first she thought it was an old man, bent with age. As he drew closer, she saw that it was a boy around ten or eleven years old. She could see, too, why she had mistaken him for an old man. He was a hunchback. His right shoulder stuck out from his back like a peddler's pack. She saw he was having a bit of trouble walking as well. His legs were bowed out like pictures she had seen in school of big monkeys called apes. Looking back at her mama, she wondered who this boy was and what he was doing there.

Lizzy said, "Oh, that's right. You all haven't met our Creedy yet." She called to the boy who stood shyly by the house, his head bent like he might be studying the grass. "Come on over here, Creedy," she called.

Willa May glanced at Daniel. He looked as surprised and confused as she was. The boy made it over to them and shook hands with them as Lizzy introduced him. She said that Creedy had come to live with her and Pole to help out around the place. The boy, with carrot colored hair and freckles, looked too frail to be much help to anyone. Willa May decided to let it pass, aiming to ask her mama more when she could get Lizzy alone. She said, "You found some good folks to take up with, Creedy. They'll treat you just fine." She thought she saw a glimmer of a smile pass over Creedy's face as he nodded, still too shy to speak.

It wasn't until supper was over and the menfolk went out to the yard for a game of horseshoes that Willa May found out more about this strange newcomer. She and Lizzy cleared the table as Lizzy told her that she and Daniel had no sooner left at Christmas time when she spotted a man driving a wagon down the road, cussing and fuming at his mules. Lizzy recognized the man. Zeke Payne, a gruff character known to be a drunk and a troublemaker. Spotting the frail, crippled boy in the back of the wagon, Lizzy asked, "Where are you taking that youngun?"

In a surly tone and showing no manners at all, the man hollered back, "To the poor farm, if it's any of your business."

Knowing full well that a place as hard as the poor farm would be the end of a boy so crippled, Lizzy yelled, "Oh, no you're not. You just leave that boy here with me and my husband. We'll see to him and he can help us around our place in return."

Without a word, his pa shoved Creedy out onto the snow covered ground like he was nothing more than a feed bag. Turning his wagon around, Zeke Payne called back over his shoulder, "You want him, you got him. The hell with you all." He left the boy sprawled in the snow at Lizzy's feet.

She described to Willa May how Creedy and his folks lived in a shack back in the hollow by Deepwater. His pa, meaner than a snake, was said to beat his wife and anyone else within arm's reach whenever he was drinking, which was almost all the time. "He must have beat that poor woman when she was carrying Creedy and he was born all crippled up like that," Lizzy added in a sorrowful tone.

Willa May shuddered, thinking about the suffering that Creedy's mother must have taken at the hands of his pa. She knew that any woman in the family way would instinctively do her best to protect the baby growing inside her. "Is Creedy's mind all right, Mama?"

"Far as I can see. I reckon the good Lord took pity on him, seeing that he was goin' to be a hunchbac'· and gave him a good mind. Wouldn't have surprised me none that a man like Zeke Payne would kill a baby that wasn't right in the head just as easy as you or I would snuff out a candle."

"Is Creedy really able to be of much help to you?"

"As much as I need. I figure he'll be a real help once we start working out in the garden. Besides, it's right nice just having the company now that you and Augie are gone. I missed having somebody to look after and fuss over and Lord knows Creedy could use some of both. So I guess you could say we're made for each other."

For Willa May, Creedy became a member of the Kincaid family that day, like a cousin come to live with Lizzy and Pole. She could see that Lizzy was right: they needed each other.

That spring, as Daniel and Willa May were busy with the planting, a family of ex-slaves came down the road by their cabin. Daniel was out plowing and Willa May was in the middle of her laundering when she looked up to see the biggest man she had ever seen. He looked pained to be asking, but he stood there with his hat in his huge hands, looking Willa May in the eye. "Ma'am, do you think you can spare some water for my wife and children?"

She followed his eyes to see a slender woman dressed in calico and wearing a bright red scarf wrapped around her head like a cap, a boy around ten years old, and a little girl who didn't look to be much more than eight. They were a sorry looking lot, dusty from their walking and way too thin to suit Willa May, especially the little ones.

She glanced back to the field where Daniel had stopped his mule and was heading toward her. As he came upon them, he exclaimed, "Joe Turner! That you?" Wiping his hands on his overalls, Daniel reached out to shake the big man's hand, pumping it hard like he was genuinely glad to see him.

The big black man grinned and clapped Daniel on the back as he shook Daniel's hand. "Well, mercy sakes. If it ain't Sergeant Daniel Shrewsbury, the best galldern scout in Sherman's army."

"Not no more," Daniel said. "I ain't a soldier now. Just plain old Daniel Shrewsbury. Oh, and this here's my wife, Willa May."

Joe Turner looked at Willa May, still smiling broadly. "Well, I reckon I done heard about you, Missy, only a hundred times or more."

Willa May could feel the red blush working its way up from her collar. She held out her hand and said, "I don't know what all Daniel's told you, but I'm real pleased to make your acquaintance, Mr. Turner."

The man's eyebrows rose slightly. He obviously wasn't used to white folks calling him "mister" and being so polite to him. Daniel spoke up, "Joe, here, is the best blacksmith I reckon I ever did see. He joined up with our outfit in 'sixty-three and tended to everybody's horses. Did a mighty fine job, too, I might add." Turning back to Joe, he asked, "What in the world brings you to this neck of the woods?"

"We was headed north, back to Ohio, but now I ain't so sure. These here are pretty parts, these here mountains you was always goin' on so much about. I was aiming to buy me some land up in Ohio and start my own place. Sure do like these here hills, though."

"So why don't you settle down here?"

"You reckon I could get somebody to sell me some of this here land?"

Daniel thought on it a minute. "Reckon I would, if you have a

68

mind to buy it from me."

Again Joe Turner's eyebrows shot up. This time he said, his eyes scanning the field behind them, "Reckon I'd be of a mind to do just that."

"How much did you want to spend?"

Joe Turner said, "I got what the army gave me. We spent a little of it to get this far, but I got a good part of it left."

Daniel turned serious then. "Won't be easy, Joe. Folks ain't used to seeing ex-slaves owning land yet. But I reckon that if you got the money, I'd be willing to sell you a piece of my land. Why don't you come on in and rest a spell. We can dicker over the price over some biscuits and gravy."

Another big smile spread across Joe Turner's face and he motioned for his family to join him as he followed Daniel and Willa May into their cabin. Once inside, he introduced his people. His wife was named Sarah and his children were Isaiah and Dicey. Sarah stood a whole head taller than Willa May with a very straight posture, almost queenly. She had a noble way about her, dignified. Her voice was soft and quiet. Listening to her, Willa May thought that Sarah seemed soothing to be around. She asked right away if she could help and Willa May showed her where everything was. Soon the two women were setting the table and fixing the meal like they had been friends for years. Willa May liked having a woman around and she got the feeling Sarah liked her, too. She could tell that Sarah liked being in a house again by the way she moved around the place, admiring this and that, taking joy in little things like the dainty design on Willa May's dishes. She remarked on the shelves that Daniel had built for Willa May and the little herb plants in the windows.

The children were famished. They gulped down their biscuits and sopped up their gravy before Sarah and Willa May could get seated. Willa May offered them more, but Sarah spoke up quickly. "We don't want to put you out no more. It was real kind of you to feed us, but we don't want to seem like we ain't got no manners, asking for more."

"Nonsense," Willa May said. "Those younguns are still hungry and there's plenty more."

The little ones looked hopeful, but Sarah put an end to it. "Thank you kindly, Miss, but they done had plenty already."

The women set about cleaning up after everyone was finished. The children played outside while Daniel and Joe Turner made their deal. Willa May watched Daniel take Joe's money. He asked her to put it in writing that he had sold ten acres of his property to one Joe Turner on the twentieth of April in the year of our Lord, eighteen hundred and sixty-seven. When she had finished copying down everything Daniel told her, he signed his "X" on it next to where Willa May had written his name. When Joe Turner saw her start to add his name, he said, "I can sign for myself, ma'am." He proceeded to scrawl out his name in a fancy hand. Willa May could see that he was proud about being able to read and write, but he wasn't boastful. He just seemed pleased and honored by it.

Once Joe Turner signed the paper, Daniel shook his hand and gave him directions and landmarks so he could find the land he had just purchased. "If you need anything, you all come on back here and we'll be glad to help if we can. I'll help you build yourself a cabin once I get done with my plowing," Daniel added. They stood in their yard and watched the four Turners heading down the road to their home. They were fairly dancing, they were so excited. Willa May and Daniel had offered to let them stay over at their place till they could get some supplies and set up for themselves, but they were eager to see their new land and wouldn't hear of staying any longer. Willa May wrapped up some biscuits, some boiled eggs, and some licorice sticks for the children and gave them to Sarah. She thanked Willa May over and over with tears brimming in her eyes.

"Nice folks," Willa May said, watching them walking up the road.

"They're good people, Willa May. Some folks'll curse me for what I've done today, but I reckon it's my land and I can do with it what I damn well please."

"What do you mean?"

"Some folks hereabouts ain't goin' to like it that I sold land to coloreds. But I've seen what it was like for them poor folks, seen plenty during the war. This here feller's the most honest and hard working man I ever did see. When you come right down to it, that's all that should matter. I just hope he gets a fair chance."

"Why wouldn't he?" she asked. To Willa May's way of thinking, the war was over and President Lincoln himself had said that colored folks weren't to be slaves anymore. There was land being sold out west to immigrants and ex-slaves so she couldn't get the gist of what Daniel was saying.

A look came over Daniel like he knew something, but he didn't know just how to put it into words. She didn't think he knew that she had figured out when he was holding back on her, but after living together, just the two of them, she was starting to know his looks. She certainly knew this one. "Let's just say some folks don't want to see no ex-slaves getting a fair chance and leave it at that."

She wanted to know who Daniel was talking about. She hadn't heard anybody saying such things. Daniel had already headed back toward his mule to start plowing again. Still, it nagged at her -- not what he had said, exactly, but how he had said it. He was being so mysterious like he had a secret he wasn't telling her.

Joe and Sarah proved to be good neighbors. While Daniel helped them clear some land and cut down trees for their cabin, Sarah and Dicey helped Willa May with her gardening and her housework. She was ever so grateful since by that time, she was getting so big, she couldn't see her feet. She found she had to stop and sit every now and then. Her back ached all the time. When the hot weather set in, she thought she might roast in the hot sun, carrying around all that extra weight. Daniel was worried about her, too. He would make supper even though she knew he was dead tired when he came home from working all day at the Turners'. Try as she might, he wouldn't let her do another thing once he came home. Her time was getting near and she was glad to have Sarah nearby if she couldn't get to her mama's.

As it turned out, she needn't have worried about getting to Page. Lizzy and Creedy came to stay around the middle of May. Lizzy insisted that Willa May needed their help and she wasn't about to have her giving birth in the middle of a cornfield all by herself. Now she had Sarah, Dicey, her mama, and Creedy doing all the work, not letting her lift a hand. Willa May had to admit that she was beginning to feel like a princess again with all this extra attention. She had heard all her life that all good things came to an end so she figured her princess days were numbered.

On the twenty-eighth of May, Willa May got up feeling fine. She was starting to feel rested, better than she had felt all spring since the planting. She ate a hearty breakfast of bacon, eggs, gravy, biscuits, and coffee. Shortly before noon, as Lizzy and Sarah started cooking lunch, she began to feel little twinges down low in her belly, just unpleasant enough to be annoying. She was sopping her biscuits in the chicken and dumplings that Lizzy had made when she felt another of these twinges. Willa May rubbed her belly, thinking maybe she had eaten too much and she was in for a case of indigestion. Lizzy eyed her rubbing her swollen belly and looking at Sarah, said, "You feeling some pains, Willa May?"

"No, Mama," she answered, innocently. "I just have the belly ache from all this good food you've cooked up."

Lizzy and Sarah looked knowingly at each other. "Willa May, I have an idea that's no simple old belly ache you've having."

"Oh, Mama," Willa May scoffed, thinking she should know her own body better than anybody else. "I'm telling you, it's just a belly ache. That's all."

That evening when Daniel came home, Willa May was starting to feel more than little twinges. It felt like somebody had put her belly between two logs and was pressing down hard on her then letting up. This feeling of being mashed to pieces was coming on her more often and lasting a little longer each time. She was trying to be brave, not wanting to scare Daniel because she knew he had never seen a baby being born. As she sat down at the supper table, she got half-way down to her chair when another one of those pressing pains struck. Her belly felt like it was going to explode, she hurt so. A moan, low at first, then mounting to a full bodied scream erupted from within her as she grasped the table. Her knuckles turned white from gripping it so hard.

Daniel jumped up from his chair and helped her sit down. She could feel the pain easing a bit and she heard her mama say, "Daniel, we've got to get her to bed."

Daniel scooped Willa May up in his arms and set her down on the cot. He had brought it down from the loft a few months before when she found it difficult to climb up and down the ladder. He had no sooner set her down when another pain took hold. She grabbed her belly, turning onto her side and screamed with the pain as the pressure inside her abdomen grew unbearable. Gradually, it eased off.

Sarah and Dicey were still there. They had planned to eat supper with Willa May and Daniel and take the leftovers back to Joe and Isaiah. Now Sarah looked at Daniel and said, "I can't leave Willa May now, Daniel, so you're goin' to have to take word to Joe and get their supper to them."

Daniel was torn, wanting to stay with Willa May. Lizzy said, "Go ahead, Daniel. She's got hours yet and you've got plenty of time to get back before that baby makes it into the world."

Hours? How was she supposed to suffer these horrible pains for hours? They were nearly killing her as it was. Willa May prayed that her mama was wrong or that she was just saying that to Daniel so he would go on to Joe's. That had to be it. Her mama just didn't want to scare Daniel and she was letting on like it would be hours, that he had all kinds of time. Willa May knew better. She knew that her baby was going to pop out of her any moment now. Maybe with the next pain. Or the one after that. It couldn't be long, not when she was already in more pain than she could ever have imagined.

Sarah somehow managed to get Daniel on his way. He went out the door, still looking back at Willa May. Even in her pain, she could see that he was loathe to leave her. She saw something else, too. There was a look of complete helplessness in Daniel's eyes. That was something Willa May had never seen before. He was always so sure of himself, so strong and determined. Now he couldn't do anything to help her and the thought was more than he could bear. In the end, he left.

When Daniel got back, Willa May was bathed in a sweat and her throat was hoarse from screaming. Sarah had placed a butcher knife under her cot, saying she had always heard that it cut the pain. Willa May didn't believe it, not for a minute. The pains were coming about every two minutes now. She would just catch her breath and start to relax when she felt the horrible pressure building inside her for what seemed the thousandth time. She started crying, begging for it to stop, to *please* just stop.

Daniel got behind her, bracing her shoulders. Sarah stood beside her and wiped her face as Lizzy positioned herself between Willa May's legs. After what seemed like hours of screaming and clamping down on Daniel's and Sarah's hands, Lizzy said, "I can see the head. Willa May, I want you to push with your next pain. Push! You hear?"

Willa May nodded weakly, wondering where she was supposed to find the strength to push. She just wanted to go to sleep, to have it all over so she could sleep for days. She felt that all too familiar squeezing inside her belly and she groaned, knowing another terrible wrenching pain was coming. Grabbing Sarah's hands, she held on while Lizzy ordered Daniel, "Help her lean forward while she pushes. Lift her shoulders like she's goin' to sit up, you hear?" Daniel nodded as Willa May's groan turned into a full-fledged blood curdling scream. Through it all, she could feel Daniel pushing her up and she heard her mama saying, "Push, Willa May. Push hard." She bore down as hard as she could, thinking she would surely pass out from the pain. But she didn't. She just kept pushing for all she was worth. Finally the pain passed and she heard Lizzy say, "We're almost there. Next time, push as long and as hard as you can, Willa May."

"I am pushing as hard as I can!" Willa May hollered.

Sarah dabbed her face with a cold cloth and Lizzy said, "I know, darlin', but you're almost there. Just remember -- push!"

Willa May started to get mad. After all, she had been the one lying there in that relentless pain for hours. How could they think she wasn't doing her part when it was *her* that this was happening to? Her belly was sore from aching and her back felt like somebody had tried to split it with an ax. She was so tired, she could drop. There they all stood, telling her to push.

Another pain seized her and again Daniel lifted her forward and Lizzy told her to push. She squeezed her eyes shut and pushed and pushed, her screams elevating with the pain. Lizzy cried, "I've got it. The head's come through. Keep pushing, Willa May, we're almost there!"

The next pain seemed to last an eternity with Daniel holding her up and her mama yelling at her to push. Again, she bore down and pushed with all her might. She thought that if a woman could have that kind of strength in her arms and shoulders, it might have been a woman who knocked down the walls of Jericho. When the pain eased up, Lizzy held up the baby, covered in blood and still connected by its birth cord. They could see it was a girl. Willa May had a little princess of her own.

Sarah took the baby once the cord was cut and washed her off. She brought her back to Willa May. The baby was squalling louder than Willa May had, but Daniel and Willa May thought she was a real beauty. Daniel held Willa May and she held the baby and cried with joy. Willa May put the baby to her breast and she quieted down once she started nursing. The baby had a full head of red hair, the same copper color as Willa May's. She had Daniel's big sparkling blue eyes.

Lizzy and Sarah looked on. Sarah asked, "What are you goin' to name her?"

"Eliza Josephine. For her grandmamas," Willa May said. "But we'll call her Josie for short."

This brought tears to Lizzy's eyes. Looking at her, Willa May could see her mama was almost as exhausted as she was. Lizzy took the baby from Willa May after she finished feeding her and leaned over and kissed Willa May on the cheek. "Thank you for my namesake. She's the prettiest little baby I've ever seen. Now you get your rest. You're goin' to need it."

Truer words were never spoken, Willa May discovered. She could never seem to get enough rest. Up night and day with feedings, teething, and fevers, she found that Josie would recover from one ailment only to start in with something else. What time she wasn't holding her or feeding her, she was washing diapers and baby clothes. What time she wasn't doing that, she was tending the garden, canning, baking, cleaning, or chopping firewood. Her life was no longer her own. She was enslaved to a tiny tyrant who ruled the roost from the moment she arrived. Josie was the shining light of her daddy's day. Daniel cooed at her and played with her from the time he hit the door in the evening after a day of helping Joe with his cabin. After hours of attention, he would wear her down and she would drift off...for a few short hours. He couldn't bear it if Josie was sickly or when she carried a fever from her teething. He stayed up with Willa May, rocking her and trying to make her feel better. There were many mornings when the two of them dragged themselves out of bed with dark circles ringing their eyes from being up half the night with the baby.

Without Sarah, Willa May didn't know what she would have done. It was Sarah who told her to rub a little moonshine on Josie's sore red gums to numb them so she could get to sleep at night. Once, when Josie had caught cold and was running a terrible fever, Daniel went to fetch Sarah in the middle of the night. Never one to say no, she rushed back with Daniel, out of breath, but she knew just what to do. They bathed Josie in cold water for hours till the fever broke. Exhausted from crying, Josie finally slept for the first time in two nights. Frantic from worry, Willa May and Daniel were ever so grateful to Sarah.

They came to depend on Joe and Sarah like they were kin. The Turners knew they could ask Willa May and Daniel for anything in return. Willa May thought that was the way neighbors should be. By Josie's first birthday, though, people in the valley had grown resentful that there was a colored family living in their midst. Daniel had been right. These people didn't care that Joe and Sarah were honest and hard working. They didn't care that Joe and Sarah had two small children. They only saw that Joe's and Sarah's skin was black, not white like theirs. To them, that was all that mattered.

Around the middle of July a year after Josie was born, Willa May and Daniel woke one night to a soft pecking at the door. It sounded like a small animal was out there, digging to get in. When it kept up, Daniel crawled out of bed to see what was out there. He unlatched the shutter on the window by the door. Opening it cautiously, he peered out into the darkness of their porch. Willa May stayed in bed up in the loft. She heard Daniel ask in a soft whisper, "Joe? That you?"

She heard the door open and footsteps below. Curious, Willa May got up to find all four Turners in the cabin. Daniel and Joe were still whispering and she wondered why Daniel didn't light a lamp. Daniel came back up to the loft and pulled on his overalls, whispering to her that Joe and Sarah were staying with them the rest of the night.

"Why? What's happened?" she asked.

Daniel motioned for her to be still. He went back down the ladder and crouched by a window. Willa May heard him slide one of his hunting rifles down from the wall pegs followed by some clicking sounds that told her he was loading the gun. Aside from the faint clicks, she couldn't hear another sound.

Fifteen, maybe twenty minutes passed in that utter stillness. In the distance, she heard horses coming slowly, quietly outside followed by muffled voices. She couldn't make out what they were saying, but she knew Daniel was straining to hear them, too. The whole thing terrified her. She could hear the thumping of her heart inside her chest like a bass drum in the Fourth of July parade. Straining harder to hear what the voices were saying, she sat frozen in their bed. Moments later, everything grew still again. Then came a sudden flash of bright light from outside. She heard horses galloping away. Scrambling out of bed, she hurried down the ladder to see what on earth was happening. Daniel and Joe stood at the door. When she reached the bottom rung of the ladder, Willa May turned to see the two men silhouetted in the doorway against a blazing orange light. Daniel told Joe to get back out of sight and for God's sake, not to show his face. With his rifle gripped in his hands, he stepped outside. For the first time, Willa May could see beyond him to the blinding light. She gasped as she stared in disbelief at the flaming wooden cross in their yard.

She ran outside, not caring that she was clad only in her nightgown and stood in the cool grass next to Daniel. Looking up at the orange and red blaze shooting smoke into the night sky, she asked, "What is it? Why did somebody set fire to a cross right here in our yard, Daniel?"

Daniel's eyes scanned the darkness beyond the cross, searching for the slightest movement, his rifle raised and ready. "Get back inside, Willa May."

"But Daniel --"

"Go on! Get back in the house."

She rushed back into the cabin. In the darkness, she felt Joe pull her over beside Sarah and their little ones in the corner of the cabin. He placed himself in front of the two women. In the light from outside, Willa May saw the silvery flash of one of her butcher knives in Joe's right hand. Sarah held her children with one hand and Willa May with her other. "Stay back, Willa May. Let the men handle this," she whispered. Scared out of her wits, Willa May was grateful that the baby was sleeping through all this. She didn't know what she would have done if Josie was having one of her fretful nights.

After what seemed like hours, the fire died away in their yard, leaving the stark black remains of a charred cross that even in daylight looked frightening and evil. Daniel came back in after he had completed a search around the property. "They're gone," he reported.

"Who? Who were those men?" Willa May demanded.

"Klan," Joe spat.

"Who?" she persisted, not understanding.

"I'll tell you later," Daniel said. "For right now, you go on back to bed, Willa May. Sarah, you and the kids take some quilts and get some rest, too. Joe and me'll stay up in case they come back."

In case they come back? Willa May wondered what they would come back for, but she reckoned she didn't want to know. She went up to bed, but she couldn't sleep. Trying to make sense out of what had happened, she guessed that somebody must be mad at Joe. For what, she didn't know. But they surely knew how to put fear in a person's soul, that she did know.

After Joe and Sarah left the following morning, taking one of Daniel's rifles with them, Willa May confronted Daniel and asked him just what had taken place the night before. He looked like he didn't want to talk about it, but she looked him in the eye and said, "Whoever burned that cross in our yard won't be goin' away any time soon, I reckon. So I think I've got a right to know if me and mine are in danger."

Daniel sighed heavily. "I didn't want to scare you more than you were is all. The men that burned that cross know exactly who they're dealing with, though, so I don't figure we're in any real danger. Besides, they just meant to scare us a little."

"Scare us a little? Who were those men, Daniel?"

"Down South, they're called 'The Invisible Empire' or 'The Ku Klux Klan'."

"I've never heard of them. Who are they?"

"Till now I thought they were just in the South, but I reckon some of the folks around here that don't much cotton to having Joe for a neighbor thought they'd pull some of the tactics the Klan's become famous for. The Klan rides around scaring ex-slaves and anyone who tries to help them. They wear white robes and hoods and they burn crosses to warn folks to keep colored folk in their place...like they was before the war, with no rights and no way to get them."

"Those men who did this to us -- they belong to this Klan?"

"Naw. I think maybe they just want us to think that they're Klan. To let us know they don't want us helping Joe and Sarah no more. They just got a chip on their shoulder and they think they can scare Joe and Sarah away by acting like they're Klan."

Willa May thought that Daniel was holding something back. She wondered if he had guessed who some of the voices she had heard last night belonged to. She reached up and turned Daniel's face toward her. "Daniel, who was that out in our yard last night?"

Daniel held her by her shoulders and looked down at her. "Let's just say I think maybe I recognized some of them men and leave it at that. Just rest assured that they won't do us no real harm. You and Josie are safe. Remember that. They wouldn't dare hurt either of you because they know they'd have me to reckon with. And they sure don't want that."

Willa May decided that she would have to leave it in Daniel's hands and trust him to protect her and their baby, but she certainly didn't want to see those men come back. She didn't want to think of what could happen to her family or to the Turners. Still, it didn't settle well with her that Daniel had guessed who the men were and he wasn't telling her. She thought he was treating her like a child and she resented it.

That Sunday, they went over to Page to see Lizzy and Pole. It was a hot July day so they spread a quilt on the grass in the shade of a weeping willow in the back yard. Daniel and Pole set up a spit over an open fire and they roasted three chickens. Big Jim had made Creedy a bow and was teaching him archery. Jim had never cared for guns, wouldn't fire one if his life depended on it. But come fall, he would go up in the mountains with his bow and arrows, looking like an Indian. Over the years, Jim had become an expert with that bow. He always brought back a deer or a 'possum. Daniel was taking in all that Jim was showing Creedy. Willa May could see that Daniel was going to start on a bow of his own once they got home.

They had decided not to say anything to their folks about what had happened. They didn't want to upset them and have them fretting over them, wondering if they were safe. They spent the afternoon talking over all the news. Luther was in jail for bootlegging again. Big Annie was staying over at Dessie's and helping her with her brood. Dessie was expecting her fifth baby come fall. Mr. Shaw had been down with his arthritis all spring, but he had been to church that morning, Lizzy said. Willa May asked about Augie, but Lizzy and Pole merely grunted. Pole spat a stream of brown tobacco juice on the grass. They never did say what Augie was doing or where he was staying. She noticed that Daniel had turned away from Big Jim and Creedy at the mention of Augie's name, but Josie started fussing and Willa May took her inside to change and feed her.

They had a delicious picnic with the roasted chicken, green beans, fried green tomatoes, and fresh peach pie. It took their minds off of their troubles and Willa May was glad that they had made the trip. Their nerves had been on edge all week after the cross burning and just being with their kin and knowing that the world hadn't turned topsy-turvy after all was just what they had needed.

At sunset, they started for home. Lizzy gave them some leftover pie and some of her peach preserves she had put up that week to take home with them. They laughed and talked all the way home, the swaying of the wagon lulling the baby to sleep. Now that Josie was taking her milk from a cup, Willa May had taken her off the breast and just as Lizzy had told her, she had started in with the morning sickness again. Holding onto Daniel's arm and watching the big red-orange sun setting behind the mountains, she looked up at him and said, "Reckon you're goin' to have to build another room onto the cabin before winter."

Daniel laughed. "I done built two cabins in two years, our and Joe's. Why would I want to build onto --"

He stopped short and looked down at her. His look turned tender and his voice grew soft and gentle like when they were in bed at night. "Willa May, are you saying what I think you're saying?"

Blushing, she nodded.

Daniel stopped the wagon and set the reins down. He turned to her and kissed her, long and sweet. "I love you more than I ever loved anybody in my life, Willa May."

She smiled up at him, her eyes glistening. She loved him, too. She knew deep in her heart that like the knights she used to read about back in school, he would fight all the demons of hell to protect her and their babies. It made those men who burned that cross in their yard seem silly and bothersome now. "The perfect end to the perfect day," she told herself, nestled in the arms of the man she loved. They rode the rest of the way home in joyous silence, just happy to be belonging to each other and sharing a life together.

They pulled up to the cabin under a starry sky. Willa May handed Daniel the baby who was still asleep, then he helped her down. He carried in the food that Lizzy had given them and said he was going to put the mules down and feed the livestock. Taking her in his arms, he said, "When I come back, maybe we can pick up from that kiss on the way home." He kissed her again and turned to go, a devilish grin across his face.

Willa May busied herself putting the jars of preserves away on the shelves and straightening up the cabin when Daniel burst through the door, grabbing her and Josie, and putting out the light. He pushed them back into a corner by the hearth. She heard him take down his rifle and thought of the night those men had burned the cross in their yard. She wondered if they were back, fear filling her insides.

"What is it? What's goin' on?" she whispered. Her throat was so dry from fright that her words came out in a rasp.

"They were here while we were gone. Must've been watching us. Damn!"

"How do you know they were here? What did they do?"

"They killed all the livestock. Slit their throats and let them bleed to death. They even killed all the chickens."

Willa May sucked in air, shocked that somebody would do such a thing. Those animals were all they had. She felt that somehow those

80

animals were only the next step in this wily game of cat and mouse. "You think they're still here?"

"I can't tell. But I ain't taking no chances."

Huddled in the darkness, they strained to hear the slightest noise above the croaking of the frogs outside. They remained crouched there for more than an hour. Daniel had his gun cocked and Willa May held their sleeping baby in her arms, neither of them daring to breathe. From outside, they heard something. The mules in the barn brayed like they did when someone was approaching them. Daniel jumped up before Willa May could stop him and rushed toward the door, saying, "By God, they ain't goin' to kill no more of my animals!"

He was out the door before Willa May could cry, "Daniel! Come back. Don't leave us here alone!" In her mind, she screamed it over and over as she sat there clutching her precious baby to her and wondering if she would see Daniel alive again. Paralyzed with fright, she waited with tears streaming down her face.

It seemed like a lifetime until she heard footsteps coming toward the cabin. She wanted to get up and get one of Daniel's rifles down or at the very least, to scream for help, but she couldn't move. The footsteps came up on the wood porch and through the open door. A sigh of relief gushed from her when she saw it was Daniel. Then she saw two more figures -- Isaiah and little Dicey. Isaiah had sprouted that winter and stood almost as tall as Daniel. He was holding Dicey to him and she could hear the little girl sobbing softly. She was just as terrified as Willa May. Willa May got up, stiff in her joints from sitting for so long. Holding Josie to her, she rushed over to where the three of them stood. "What are you doing here so late, Isaiah?"

It was Daniel who answered. "Them men have been to see them. Joe shoved Isaiah and Dicey out through their root cellar and they got away. I'm goin' back with Isaiah to help. Keep Dicey here with you and don't light any lamps, you hear?"

"But what if those men come back here?"

Daniel crossed the room in four quick strides and pulled down one of his shotguns. He took some bullets from the top drawer of their bureau and loaded them. Coming back to where she was standing, he said, "Here, take this."

Willa May handed the baby to Dicey who was still crying softly, her eyes wide with fear. She took the shotgun in her hands. It was so heavy, she almost fell over with it. "What do I do with it? I can't fire this thing."

81

Daniel pulled a chair over and placed it in front of her. He rested the shotgun across the seat of the chair and said, "If anyone but me or Isaiah comes through that door, just pull the trigger. Believe me, there won't be enough of the bastard left to do you no harm."

She nodded, knowing it was up to her to protect her baby and their property while Daniel was gone. She owed it to Joe and Sarah to protect Dicey, too, as if she were her own. Daniel took Isaiah by the arm and said, "Here, Son, use this if you have to. Don't let them take you if you can help it." He put his army pistol in Isaiah's hand. Isaiah, looking like the man-boy he was, nodded bravely, knowing like Willa May that it was up to him. They started to leave then Daniel turned around and pulled her close. Kissing her one last time, he said, "I'll be back. I'll give you a signal so you'll know it's me. If you hear a whippoorwill call three times, it'll be us. Anybody else comes up on that there porch without you hearing that call, shoot to kill, you hear?" Without waiting for a reply, he turned back to Isaiah. Then they were gone.

Willa May closed the door and barred it. She took Dicey by the hand, went back to where the shotgun laid across the chair and settled themselves down to wait. About three hours later, she thought she heard something outside. She got up on her knees and waited, not daring to breathe, but she didn't hear anything more. Slowly, gradually, she started to breathe again. Looking at Dicey and Josie, she was glad to see that Dicey had fallen off to sleep. Dicey lay on the floor with Josie curled up in her blankets beside her. *Poor little thing must have cried herself to sleep, she was so tuckered out from all this scary business.* Watching Dicey sleep, Willa May wondered how those crazy men could ever intend to harm a small child like that. It was beyond her reasoning. This thought had barely crossed her mind when she heard a whippoorwill call, then another, and still another. Relief flooded through her as she got up to unlatch the door. A minute later, Daniel and Isaiah were back inside. Daniel shut the door and barred it again.

"Where are Joe and Sarah?" Willa May asked.

Daniel looked at her. His face was smudged here and there with dirt. He looked at her so long and so hard, she wondered if he had heard her right. She turned to Isaiah, but he looked away. Daniel said, "Them men done burned Joe's cabin. They tied Joe and Sarah to two crosses in the yard and burned them to death." He paused, taking a deep breath. "Isaiah and me just finished burying them over by the gorge."

Willa May was stunned. She felt her knees buckle under her. Daniel caught her and held her by her shoulders. "There's nothing we can do for them, Willa May. But I can save Isaiah and Dicey. We owe Joe and Sarah that much."

She nodded, still unable to speak.

"I'm heading out right now. We just came back to get Dicey and some provisions."

"Where are you taking them?"

"I ain't telling you. You'll be safer if you don't know. All you need to know is that I'm taking them to where they'll be safe. I'll be gone a couple of days. In the morning, I want you to hitch up the mules and hightail it back to your Pa's house. Don't stay another night here alone, you hear?"

She nodded again, knowing Daniel was telling her that the men who knew them so well would do them harm after all. He just didn't want to give them the chance.

"Get us some grub to take with us. Enough for two or three days. Then get back over to that shotgun after we leave." She did as she was told, grateful she didn't have to think about what she was doing. She handed Daniel a small sack filled with biscuits from that morning, the leftover pie her mama had given them, and some tomatoes and raw potatoes she had picked that morning from their garden. Daniel handed the sack to Isaiah and went over to pick up Dicey. He wrapped their wedding quilt around the little girl, then headed for the door. Looking back, he said, "Remember what I told you. Get over to your Pa's at first light."

Willa May nodded once more and latched the door after he left. She took her position behind the shotgun again. Josie was still sound asleep behind her.

She must have nodded off sometime after Daniel had left because the next thing she heard was a grating sound like wood scraping against wood. In her grogginess, it took her a minute to realize that it was someone lifting the latch from outside the door. By the time that thought cleared her mind, heavy footsteps were coming across the doorway. Willa May looked up to see men in feedbag robes and hoods carrying torches. She scrambled toward the shotgun, but they saw her. One of them grabbed her and pulled her, kicking and screaming, out the door to where they were burning another cross in the yard. Josie woke up and started wailing. Hearing her cries, Willa May screamed for her baby, but it was no use. Two of the men had hold of her arms, squeezing her flesh and digging their fingers in until it hurt. She saw one of them carry Josie out. At first, she thought he was bringing her baby to her. But he stopped a few feet away from her. Another man in a hood held a pistol up to Josie's little head. Willa May screamed like a wild woman, struggling to free herself and get to her child. Another man strode up and slapped her so hard, he knocked her off her feet. She would have been knocked to the ground, but for the two men holding her. "Shut up!" the man snarled. "Stop your screaming or we'll give you something to really scream about, you nigger-lovin' bitch."

She was crying, but she stopped screaming for fear of what they might do to Josie. She was sure that these men were bent on harming them this time no matter what Daniel had said about them.

"Where's that man of yours?" he yelled at her.

"I -- I don't know," she sobbed.

He whirled around, his robe swirling around his legs. "Shoot it," he told the man holding the gun to Josie's head.

"No! No, please don't hurt my baby!" she pleaded. "Please! Don't hurt my baby!"

The man turned back to her and slammed his fist into her belly. Willa May doubled over, unable to breathe. He hit her again as she hung between the two men holding her. A third pain, down low in her stomach, erupted. Something warm filled her pantaloons and ran down her legs. She knew it was blood. The man had killed the baby growing inside her with those blows to her stomach. He grabbed her by her neck and jerked her head up so she was forced to look at him. He tightened his grip, nearly strangling her. "Where's Daniel?"

"He -- he took the k-- kids," she gasped, struggling for air.

"Took 'em where?" he shouted.

She shook her head as best she could. "He -- he wouldn't -- tell me. Just s-- said he'd -- be gone two, thr-- three days."

The man squeezed her neck tighter and she started to choke. "When did he leave?" His face was so close to hers she could feel the warmth of his breath on her through the opening in his hood.

"An hour or -- so. I -- I don't know. I f-- fell asleep."

She didn't see that the man was holding a gun until she saw him raise his hand. She thought he meant to slap her again. The one holding Josie yelled, "No! Don't --" In that split second, Willa May recognized this one's voice. She looked toward him and started to say,

"Augie?" But the butt of a pistol crashed against her head and everything around her went black.

When Willa May came around, she was back in her old bed at her mama's. She wondered why everything looked fuzzy, then she realized she only had one eye open. She reached up to touch the other one and heard a deep, low moan when she felt the swollen, bruised flesh. For a moment, she wondered if she had been dreaming. She thought that maybe marrying Daniel, bearing Josie, and the men in their robes had all been one long dream. The shiner she was sporting let her know that none of it had been a dream. Her head throbbed relentlessly and her belly was sore, too. She remembered the men holding her and the blows to her belly. She knew that she had lost her baby. Josie! Were was Josie? She tried to sit up, but the pain inside her head made her dizzy and the room whirled around her in a blur. A familiar blackness settled over her.

The next time she came around, Daniel was beside her. He looked terrible. His eyes were red-rimmed as if he had been crying and dark circles outlined them in his face. She could see from his beard that it had been several days since he had shaved. He leaned over and kissed her softly on the lips. "Welcome back," he whispered.

"Josie?"

"She's safe."

She sighed with relief.

"They found her beside you the next morning, screaming and putting up a fuss to be fed." He tried to smile, but both of them knew there wasn't any reason to smile.

Tears came to her eyes. She said, "I lost our baby." She sobbed, the tears gushing forth like a geyser. Daniel held her and let her cry herself out.

Lizzy came in, knocking softly on the door first. She brought Willa May a hot toddy and told Daniel to see to it that she drank it all. Lizzy said, "It'll help ease her pain and quieten her down some."

Daniel took the mug from Lizzy and held it for Willa May to sip. It was hot soothing tea laced with some of Mr. Shaw's brandy.

When Willa May was calm again, she asked Daniel what happened after they knocked her out. It took him a few minutes before he could speak of it. Looking away, he said, "Elroy came here the next

morning. He'd been laying out drunk again. He told your Pa and Jim
that he had been out at the tavern down in Deepwater. He'd heard
some men come in real late, saying as how they was thirsty. Elroy'd
been drinking hard, but through the liquor, he could make out that the
men had been to our place. They was bragging and carrying on,
saying that there weren't goin' to be no more niggers living high on
the hog around here no more. Elroy made it here, like I said, and told
your Pa. Him and Big Jim made tracks for our cabin. When they
found you, you were out cold on the ground with the baby tied to you.
They'd done burned another cross in our yard. They burned the cabin
and the barn, too. All that was left was the charred cross beside you."

Her heart sank. "They burned us out?"

Daniel couldn't answer her. He simply nodded. There was a look
in his eyes that she didn't like. A cold, steely look. She knew this
thing wasn't over, not by a long shot. "Daniel," she begged, "please
don't go stirring up more trouble. If they come back again, they might
kill us all."

He turned to her with that cold, determined look in his eyes. "They
already killed three people -- Joe, Sarah, and...our -- our baby. They
nearly killed you, too. By God, they're goin' to pay and pay dearly."
Tears sprang to Daniel's eyes when he spoke of their lost baby. It was
then that Willa May realized that he had probably been there by her
side for hours -- maybe days -- crying over what those men had done
to them and feeling guilty that he hadn't been there to take care of
them. She realized something else. Daniel meant what he had said.
He wasn't going to rest until every last one of those men were made to
pay for what they had done.

"What about Isaiah and Dicey?" she asked, trying to turn Daniel's
thoughts from his vengeance.

"They're safe. Remember Eb?"

Memories of that Thanksgiving when the tall mountain man
brought her the blue ribbon Daniel had sent her for her hair came
flooding back. She nodded, smiling at how none of them could bear
the smell of poor old Eb.

"I took them to Eb and he said he'd see to it that they got to
Pennsylvania. To some Quaker folks who had helped runaways before
the war. They'd get Isaiah and Dicey to Canada."

Remembering that Thanksgiving when Eb showed up, Willa May
recalled how Augie was so drunk he couldn't eat. Another memory
struck her full force -- she remembered that just before the man had

knocked her out, she had recognized Augie's voice. He was pleading with them not to hurt her any more. He was wearing one of those white feedsack robes and holding her Josie.

Daniel was looking at her peculiarly. "What's wrong? What were you thinking just now?"

She knew if Daniel found out that Augie had been with those men, he would kill Augie for sure. How could she let him do that when it would only end up hurting her mama and her pa? If she could have gotten her hands on that no-account Augie, she would have beaten him senseless for doing such a horrible thing to his own flesh and blood. No, she couldn't tell Daniel. But she would never forget -- or forgive -- it, either.

While Willa May was healing, they stayed with Lizzy and Pole. Willa May found out that she had a concussion, according to Doc Merriam. She was several days getting her balance back and her vision cleared. As for the miscarriage, Doc said there was no permanent damage and she could still bear all the babies she wanted. That made her smile for the first time since she had held Josie. But Daniel never smiled. He just went about everything, helping Big Jim and Creedy, without taking any pleasure in the things he had always loved like chopping wood and working in the garden. There was a set expression, a frown, on his face. The only time he seemed his old self was when he was holding Josie and cuddling her. Or when he held Willa May to him at night in her old bed. Sometimes even after they had made love, he would get up and pace the floor like a caged animal wanting to break free. She knew at those times that he was thinking about getting his revenge.

It was Elroy Hicks who spilled the names of some of the men to Daniel. Daniel got it out of him after he took Elroy a jug and pretended to get drunk with him. But Daniel had stayed sober, sober and waiting. Waiting for the minute he could get Elroy to babble about that night at the tavern when those men came in bragging about how they had been to their place. Elroy had been drinking that night, but he wasn't so drunk as to not know who was there. Daniel pumped moonshine into him till Elroy, drunk as a lord and talking out of his head, told Daniel everything he wanted to know.

Daniel didn't eat his supper the next night, he just played with his food. Willa May watched him, knowing that something had to be bothering him because her man was one hearty eater. He started pacing after supper when they all sat on the front porch and the lightning bugs started their nightly show. Lizzy and Pole knew that something was up, too, as they watched him walk the length of the porch. When it grew dark, Willa May went in to put Josie down for the night. It was a hot August night when the air felt stifling and close. Josie fussed a bit in her little bed, but she finally drifted off. Willa May went back out to the porch where her pa and Big Jim were already into one of their jugs. Creedy was helping Lizzy wind some yarn for her knitting and Daniel was still pacing. She stood in the doorway and thought how he looked like a trapped animal again, just looking for a chance to break loose. Even the way he moved was cat-like, every muscle and every sinew moving with an easy flowing grace that could lash out with a fierceness that would have amazed the rest of her folks. She had witnessed his quickness all too often in their time together. In times of trouble, over the time they were man and wife, she had come to see this wild savage side of Daniel and realize that all those years up in his mountains, he'd had to reach back inside himself to this wild state to survive in that untamed world. Like the bear and the mountain lion, he was a hunter with keen instincts that other folks had lost living in a more civilized world. Watching this creature side of Daniel, Willa May sensed that there was something stirring him, riling him, and turning him into the deadly killer he could be. He could stalk his victim and bring that victim down with no mercy, no sense of right and wrong, no laws that bind man, nor any feeling of compassion. Just pure killer instinct.

She wasn't surprised when Daniel said to her as everybody started inside for the night, "I reckon I'll take me a little walk tonight. I'm feeling a mite restless."

She thought her folks figured this "restlessness" was just an unsettled feeling from all that they had been through and for Daniel, there was still a feeling of helplessness. She knew better. Daniel was far from helpless. The others dismissed his "restlessness", thinking it was just something he would have to work through for himself, but Willa May realized that he was going to take action this night. All this pacing was just his way of passing time until he could get down to his real aim. She fretted, not wanting to lose her husband over some feud he felt he had to right. She knew, though, that he was honor bound to do whatever he was planning to do.

She kissed him and said, "Be careful out by yourself."

Daniel looked her in the eye, surprised. He realized that she knew what he was about to do. He nodded and started down the steps.

The others went in to bed and a little while later, Willa May could hear her pa's snoring and Jim's answering snore. She must have finally fallen off herself because it seemed a long time later when she heard her uncle Luther's voice outside. "Pole! Pole, come quick. He's goin' to kill Augie! You hear me? Pole? Pole!"

Everyone jumped out of bed and Pole, in his nightshirt, ran out onto the front porch. "Lute? That you? What're you hollering about?"

"Get your gun, Pole! He's goin' to kill Augie," Luther squawked.

"Who? Who's goin' to kill Augie?"

"Daniel! He's beating Augie's head against the wall. Hurry!"

Pole turned to Willa May. "You know anything about this?"

"Augie was one of the men who burned us out." She didn't mince words, knowing that her pa was bound by blood to avenge Augie's death if Daniel did kill him.

"Shit!" Pole muttered. "The damned fool!" Pole and Big Jim rushed inside and pulled on their overalls, then Pole grabbed his shotgun. They nearly flew down the steps to where Luther was waiting by the road. Lizzy and Willa May watched them till they were out of sight, heading toward Deepwater. Lizzy turned to Willa May. "What's all this about Augie being with the men that attacked you?"

Willa May told her everything she remembered. Lizzy shook her head and said, "C'mon then. We might as well stay up. I'll make us some coffee."

Creedy woke up and the three of them waited and waited. It seemed like it would take all night for them to break up the fight between Daniel and Augie. The question on all their minds was whether they could get there before Daniel beat Augie to death. When they came back, they had Daniel tied up in the back of Luther's wagon. Daniel had a mean looking welt on the side of his head, but otherwise, he appeared to be all right. He was still wound up and wanting to fight anybody near him. Willa May ran over and untied him. As she worked at the rope, Pole said, "Now Daniel, I think of you like my own flesh and blood. But you've got to understand, Son, I couldn't let you kill my boy. I know he's a no good sonofabitch, but he's still my boy. Just be satisfied that he's out of your life for good."

Willa May pulled the ropes off Daniel and he stood there rubbing his wrists. After a minute, he looked at Pole and said, "I'll let Augie go this time, but if I ever see his face again, I'll do just what I said I'd do." He turned and stalked off up the hill to the house.

"What in the world happened?" Lizzy asked.

"Oh, we got there in time to save Augie's sorry ass," Pole sighed. "Daniel had beat him to a pulp. He was bleeding all over and Daniel was knocking his head into the wall over and over like Lute said. We finally pulled Daniel off of Augie -- took all three of us, too. That boy's stronger than a mule. Before Augie passed out, Daniel shook his finger in his face, with us holding him back as best we could. He told Augie that he'd better get clean out of the state. The only reason he was letting him live was that he was kin, but if he ever saw Augie again, he'd kill him with his bare hands. Then he yelled to all the men standing there in the tavern that he knew who was there at his cabin that night and he was goin' to hunt each one of them down like they was dogs."

Luther looked at Willa May and asked, "Will he do it?"

"Wouldn't you?" she asked. "They killed our baby and burned our house. You'd better believe Daniel's not goin' to forgive and forget something like that. None of you would, either."

Pole looked at her and said, "I just hope the next time your husband decides to sell off some of his land, he'll think twice about the consequences." He turned to Big Jim and added, "I reckon Daniel's goin' to need some help."

Big Jim nodded. The two of them started up the hill. Luther spat tobacco juice onto the road and rubbed his hands together. "Damn! I ain't been in a good feud for years, but by God, this is blood. All of us has got to stick together. Hell, what have we got if we ain't got each other? Right?" He followed Pole and Big Jim up to the house.

Lizzy, Creedy, and Willa May stood looking at each other, each one knowing that Hell had come to the hills.

Chapter Four

It was decided that they would make their strike on All Hallows Eve. Creedy had come up with the idea, saying, "If they can disguise themselves so nobody knows who they are, why can't we?" Laughing at this, Big Annie thought of a way to distract the men. She suggested dressing Luther up like a woman. Since Luther was so frail and small, she reasoned that he could pass for a woman with the right getup, especially once it grew dark.

Daniel had gotten it out of Elroy who four of the hooded men were. It turned out one of them was Denny Bob, 'Lil Annie's husband. After 'Lil Annie died, he had taken up with a woman over in Mullens with five children, all said to be fathered by different men. What time Denny Bob wasn't drunk at some tavern with Augie and Elroy, he was shacked up with this woman. Big Annie and Luther had heard that the woman had already had one child by Denny Bob and another one was on the way. Angry and heartbroken, they had taken 'Lil Luther to raise as their own. Denny Bob never bothered to visit the child. The family surmised that the loving looks he had given 'Lil Annie had been merely an act. Big Annie told Willa May and Lizzy that they were told that Denny Bob was out cavorting with this Mullens woman the night 'Lil Annie died. The woman was sleeping with Denny Bob and Augie both...at the same time. Lizzy shook her head, saying, "You know, Big Annie, that we raised Augie better. I thought he had more sense."

Big Annie patted Lizzy's hand, seeing how ashamed Lizzy was of what Augie had done. "He's just a man, Lizzy. And you know when it comes to bedding a woman, they all think with their peckers and not the brains the good Lord gave them."

"Still," Lizzy sighed, "it's no excuse. Bedding a woman is one thing, but bedding her right alongside another man is an entirely different thing. We both know that. I reckon I ought to be glad that Daniel ran Augie off before his pa could hear such a thing. Napoleon will be downright mortified when I tell him, but he should know what a low-down skunk Augie's become. He'd better never show his face around here ever again because if Daniel doesn't kill him, Napoleon surely will after hearing this."

Big Annie grumbled, "Reckon it's good enough for him. Our mama always did say, 'If you make your bed, then you've just got to lay in it'."

Willa May had never heard of two men bedding a woman together and she was shocked that Augie would stoop to such a thing. What in the world was he thinking about? They were both raised the same way, believing in sin, shame and knowing that the worst you could do was to disgrace yourself and your own kin. Yet that was exactly what he had done. He was a fool and a traitor to his own blood. From that time on, he would never mean more to her than a blade of grass. As far as she was concerned, she didn't have a brother.

As for Denny Bob, she would feel a certain pleasure in seeing that he got his just desserts, for 'Lil Annie's sake and her own. She figured that if it was Augie holding their little Josie that night, then the one holding his gun to her head must have been Denny Bob. The thought made her want to scratch his eyes out; it just burned her to think that her kin -- even if it was by marriage -- could do such a thing.

The other two men, Daniel had discovered, were Buster Holcomb, a deacon in their church who ran a store over in Deepwater and Lyle Hendershot, the county sheriff's deputy. No wonder the law had done nothing about finding out who raided their house that night, Willa May thought. Soon they would meet up with another kind of law.

Big Jim said right from the start that he didn't hold with killing. He would help, but he wouldn't do any of the shooting. "I don't want to see this turn into a blood war like them Hatfields and McCoys over at Tug Fork. Them folks'll be killing each other off into the next century. Let's just get it over now and have done with it."

Pole nodded in agreement.

Daniel said, "None of you has got to do any of the shooting. I'll do that myself."

It was decided that Pole would set fire to the barn on Lyle Hendershot's place and Big Jim would burn down Buster Holcomb's store. Meanwhile, Luther would play a little trick on his son-in-law come Beggar's Night.

Daniel wouldn't let Willa May go with them that night. He didn't want her to be in any further danger. She helped Big Annie and her mama dress up her uncle Luther. They put a corset on him and used some of Lizzy's quilt filling to make him look like he had a big bosom. Then they put one of Lizzy's old faded dresses on him. They made up his face like a low woman, smearing blackberry juice on his cheeks and lips. He put on one of Lizzy's sun bonnets to cover his short hair. Standing back, they looked him over. Big Annie laughed, "Why, Luther, you make a right pretty woman. Maybe you could use this getup next time you go bootlegging. I bet the law would never figure out that they was looking for a woman."

Luther grinned at his reflection in the mirror, happy that they had thought up this disguise and seeing how he could put it to future use. "I may never have to go to jail again," he cackled.

The plan called for Big Annie's boy, Shep, to go sparking the Mullens woman and offer to buy her a drink at the tavern. Once she was out of the house, Luther would go up and knock on the door. When Denny Bob came to see who it was, Luther would start sashaying around on the porch, playing coy, and lure him to the barn. Big Annie and Lizzy would be hiding behind the outhouse to take Luther back home in Luther's wagon and Daniel would wait inside the barn for Denny Bob. It sounded like a flawless plan, but it depended on Shep luring the Mullens woman out of the house and Luther making a good enough offer to get Denny Bob's attention. Neither task proved very difficult. The Mullens woman took one look at Shep, who was a fine specimen of a man even at eighteen, and rushed out tying the strings of her bonnet. They watched her rub against Shep's young strong body till they were out of sight.

Then it was Luther's turn. Lizzy and Big Annie took their posts by the outhouse while Daniel stole into the barn. Luther waited for everyone to get into position and then climbed the steps onto the porch. He knocked on the door, but no one answered. He knocked again, harder. Still no one came. Muttering under his breath, Luther started banging his fists on the door till a few minutes later, Denny Bob opened it. "Shit fire," Denny Bob whined. His hair was disheveled and he held onto the top of his head like it was threatening to explode. "What do you want, woman? You trying to wake the dead or what?"

Luther started swaying his body back and forth, careful not to let Denny Bob see his face too well. He spoke in a girlish voice. "It's Beggars Night and I've come begging for some of your sweet kisses, big boy. Why don't you come on out to the barn with me and you can

93

show me how it's done."

Denny Bob stopped rubbing his head and looked Luther up and down. Slowly, a grin spread across his face. He licked his lips, ran his fingers through his hair in a feeble attempt to sweep it off his face, and smiled. "I reckon I don't mind if I do, sweetheart."

Luther started playing hard to get and raced off the porch, giggling. Turning back toward Denny Bob, he unbuttoned the top buttons of his dress and teased, "Last one to the barn has to pull the other's pants down!" He took off across the yard toward the outhouse and the barn.

Denny Bob hollered, "Hey, wait for me, darlin'!"

When Luther reached the outhouse, he rounded the corner in back and Big Annie grabbed him. She pushed him behind her. Denny Bob must have spotted Luther as he scurried behind the outhouse and followed in hot pursuit. Just as Denny Bob raced hell-bent around the back of the outhouse, Big Annie reared back and flattened him with one blow from her big meaty fist. Denny Bob was raised off his feet and fell flat on his back in the dirt. He was out cold.

"Oh, no! Now what?" Lizzy could see that their plan was going differently than they had calculated.

Big Annie pulled a butcher knife from a pack she had secretly left there and said, "I've been waiting to do this ever since we put 'Lil Annie in the ground." Lizzy and Luther looked on in horror as Big Annie unfastened Denny Bob's pants and pulled them down around his knees. Hastily, she set about putting her knife to use.

Inside the barn, Daniel realized that something had gone wrong and came out to the outhouse. By that time, Big Annie had made sure that Denny Bob would never father another baby. Daniel was the first to find his voice. "You all had better get goin'. No telling when some younguns will be coming around. They might see you."

Without a word, Luther helped Lizzy and Big Annie up into his wagon and headed back to Lizzy's. Nobody said a word on the way home.

That same night as the wind stirred the last dry leaves on the trees and witches and goblins came knocking at doors, Lyle Hendershot's barn went up in flames. All his livestock mysteriously disappeared. While neighbors fought to put out the fire at the Hendershot place, the general store in Deepwater was blown up, the roof shooting straight up in the air twenty feet or more according to folks who witnessed it. People ran for cover as windows in nearby houses shattered from the force of the explosion. As for Denny Bob, nobody found him till the next morning when the Mullens woman came home singing happily to herself from her night with Shep. She discovered him lying in a pool of his own blood with a gaping wound where his private parts had been.

Nobody saw Lyle Hendershot or Buster Holcomb after their places were wiped out. Word spread throughout the valley that some men bearing an old war grudge had taken Lyle and Buster up in the mountains to a secret hideout and hung them. Posses searched the hills for two weeks, but never found any trace of either man. With no clues to go on, the men were given up for dead.

Daniel never told Willa May what happened to the two men. That winter he started acting like his old self again. He stopped his pacing and laughed and joked with the menfolk once more. He said he couldn't wait for spring so he could get started on a new cabin for them. Nobody questioned the new horses, mules, and cows that showed up at Daniel's folks' and the Kincaids' places.

With the money that Daniel still had from what Joe Turner had given him, he bought supplies to build another cabin, a bigger and finer cabin than their first. He wanted to build it up on the hill, but Willa May put her foot down. She didn't want to hike up such a steep hill every time she carried water up from the well Daniel had dug. The well was down by the road about a hundred yards from where they ended up building. Pole and Big Jim helped Daniel build the new cabin and plowed a big garden in front of it so Daniel and Willa May would have food to get them through the next winter.

Daniel used the rest of their money to buy some second hand furniture in Charleston -- a big brass bed that Willa May had been wanting and a dining table made out of mahogany. He also bought a settee covered in dark red velvet. Willa May didn't ask where it came from, afraid that maybe it had belonged in a house for low women. Daniel purchased a mahogany bureau with a marble top and an oval mirror that had leaves carved around the frame. While they stayed with Lizzy and Pole, Daniel made a bed for Josie and some chairs to sit by the hearth during the long winter months.

As Doc Merriam had predicted, Willa May was still able to conceive more babies. Around the new year she started in with morning sickness again. Doc said she was due around the end of

July or beginning of August. It was not a very good time to be off her feet, what with the gardening and canning. But Willa May learned that babies came whenever they pleased. There was no rushing them or delaying them. Daniel beamed with happiness when Willa May broke the news to him. He was still too new to fatherhood to recognize the first signs.

Lizzy and Pole gave them a new set of dishes for Christmas and the Shrewsburys gave them a new wagon. Daniel didn't appreciate it when his pa said, "Just see that this one don't get burned up." Both her folks and Daniel's folks knew how close they had come to getting killed. As a result, they were always saying such things as if Daniel and Willa May didn't have sense enough to know how lucky they were. Willa May watched Daniel bristle every time anything was said, but he kept his temper in check and showed proper respect for his elders. That was the way both of them had been raised. Neither of them ever showed any disrespect to their elders.

All winter and through the spring, Lizzy and Willa May sewed and knitted. Willa May didn't have anything left from her hope chest. Her wedding quilt was with Isaiah and Dicey and the rest of her things that she had worked so hard on were nothing more than ashes now. She remembered how she had felt such pity for folks down South when Sherman looted and burned their places. Now she knew how it felt to be in their shoes. The new quilt, she decided, would be another log cabin design. This one would be in shades of brown, gold, and red because it would be fall before they were really settled in again. Lizzy made Josie a new quilt, an Irish chain pattern in shades of rose and ivory. Josie would have a new bed and a new quilt when they moved into their new cabin...and a new baby brother or sister. It was all so exciting that Willa May couldn't wait to get moved in.

Miss Beatrice made them new pillowcases and dresser scarves. The thing that thrilled Willa May most was the beautiful lace tablecloth she made for their new table. Willa May knew Miss Beatrice must have spent hours, day after day, tatting the delicate lace cloth. When they moved in, they invited everyone over for a Sunday picnic. Willa May put the new lace tablecloth on their fancy mahogany table. She was so happy that she just stood looking at it through tears of joy. Lizzy and Miss Beatrice hugged her, trying to console her. Willa May said, "I'm not crying because I'm sad. I'm just plumb tickled to have something so pretty."

They moved in near the middle of July. Daniel still had some work to do inside the cabin to finish it, but Willa May wanted to have their baby in their new home. She could see that Daniel was happy to be back on his own without having to be lectured any more on being careful in the future. Lizzy and Creedy stayed with them, helping out around the house. They had a hard time keeping up with Josie who was walking everywhere, seemingly headed in four directions at once. Creedy was good with her, playing "Pat-A-Cake" and taking her for little walks around the cabin to keep her occupied. Josie dearly loved Creedy. She had been saying mama, dada, Jo, and calling Lizzy and Pole "nana" and "pa-paw". Now she added a new name to her vocabulary: "Kee-tee", which was as close to "Creedy" as she could manage.

Willa May was just settling into the new place when, on August first, she started in labor around sunup. By dinnertime, they had a baby boy named Daniel. He had Daniel's golden hair, big blue eyes, and something new -- dimples. He was a fat little fellow, weighing almost nine pounds when they took him the following week to Doc Merriam's. Doc said that 'Lil Daniel was just about the healthiest baby he had ever seen. 'Lil Daniel's pa beamed with pride.

Over the next three years, Willa May gave birth to two more babies -- Hattie Sue and Walt Whitman -- both strong, big babies like 'Lil Daniel. In the spring of seventy-one, she was expecting her fifth. To make ends meet, Daniel went to work building the Chesapeake and Ohio railroad. He was gone all week, staying over at the campsite and working sometimes up to eighteen hours a day in good weather. He came home on week-ends, getting home so late on Friday nights that Willa May would already have the kids in their beds and be drifting off in her rocker by the hearth. These hard times showed in Daniel's eyes. Those blue eyes, that once glistened like the stars in the heavens, had deep circles under them and tiny red lines. Willa May knew this was a sign of fatigue. Daniel was working night and day to feed his family and all his hard work was taking its toll. For all the hours he spent working, though, he was bringing home just enough pay to feed them. Besides the six of them, he had the livestock to feed. A flash flood that spring had just about wiped them out. Luckily, their cabin was still standing, but the barn was gone and the crops were ruined. They had lost two of their cows and all the hogs and chickens. They were scraping bottom when Daniel came home from Fayetteville talking about the railroad needing men. That was in May. By August when Willa May was about six months along with their newest baby, Daniel came home one Friday night, excited about a race he had witnessed that day between one of the men working with him and a machine.

"What kind of race was it?" Willa May asked, trying not to yawn. Daniel seemed tickled telling about it. This was the first sign of life she had seen in him since he had started working there.

"Now you listen up, girl, and I'll tell you," he said, grinning like he was about to tell the world's funniest joke. "We've been building this tunnel for the railroad. One of the men -- this big feller, bigger than Joe Turner -- well, he's been digging so fast, ain't nobody can keep up with him."

"What's this feller's name?" Willa May interrupted.

"Henry. John Henry," Daniel answered, dismissing this as unimportant to the story. "Anyway, old John Henry was digging so fast that some of the fellers took to betting on just how fast he could finish that there tunnel."

"You didn't bet, did you?" She didn't like the way this story was heading and she figured that maybe Daniel was buttering her up to tell her he had lost all his wages on some bet. She was all set to remind him about a fool and his money.

"Will you let me tell the story, Willa May?" he sighed. "I know better than to bet good money on some fool race. This ain't that no-account Augie you're talking to."

She decided to shut up and let Daniel tell the rest of his story, especially when she heard Augie's name. She didn't need to be reminded of that low-down dirty skunk.

"So every day, some of the men would bet on how far this here John Henry could dig. Pretty soon word spread and folks started coming over from Fayetteville just to see him and place their own bets. I don't reckon the foremen liked it much, but we all figured they was placing their own bets on the side. Next thing you know, word done spread all the way to Charleston about John Henry. Folks started showing up in their fancy carriages, bringing picnic dinners with them to eat while they waited for word of the digging inside the tunnel. Must've been one of them fellers in the fancy carriages that got the idea to have old John Henry race this here steam drill."

"You mean that drill was supposed to drill right through the

98

mountain?" she gasped.

"Naw." Daniel shook his head. "You ain't getting my meaning at all. The drill doesn't drill through the mountain. It digs the holes in the ground so we can put dynamite in them and blast our way through."

"And what about that John Henry? Does he dig his way through?"

"Girl, I'm telling you, John Henry pounds these big spikes into the ground and we put dynamite in them holes, too. To blast our way through."

"Oh," she said, acting like she understood.

"So today, they brung that drill and placed it on one side of the mountain. John Henry went to the other end and the race was on. And don't you know, along about sundown, old John Henry beat that danged steam drill."

"Well, I declare," Willa May said, trying to sound like she was truly amazed. Truth of it was she was so worn out from chasing her babies around the house all day that she really didn't care which one had won.

Daniel must have thought she sounded convincing enough, because he nodded and crossed his arms over his chest, grinning with satisfaction. "Ain't that something?"

"I reckon it sure enough is," she agreed, stifling another yawn.

Daniel leaned over and patted her knee -- what part wasn't covered by her big belly -- and said, "Yesiree, that's something to tell our grandchildren about, all right." He frowned as he looked at her belly. "Willa May, honey, don't take this the wrong way now, but I don't recollect you being so big this far along with the other babies."

She patted her huge belly and sighed, "I know. You'd think with running after the other four all day that I'd be downright puny, but I'm as big as a mountain. And it's not like I've been birthing little babies before. Maybe this one is just extra healthy and fat."

Daniel gave her a long look, a fretful husband look. Seeing this, she added, "I'm feeling fine, so you needn't worry about me. I'll be all right. You just worry about how we're going to feed this passel of babies you keep fathering, Daniel Shrewsbury."

Daniel grinned. Slyly, he added, "Since you're feeling all right, maybe you might be up to reminding me how we get them babies again."

"Maybe I will," she said, " so long as you don't expect me to race you to the bed. I'm not in much condition for races, so if it's races you like, you've come to the wrong place."

Two weeks later Willa May was working out in the yard on a Friday morning. She was scrubbing the porch and tidying up a bit after a storm the night before. The little ones were playing "Ring-Around-The-Rosy" in the yard. Bending over on her hands and knees, she didn't see the stranger coming up on her. It scared her when he said, "You look like you could use some help there, missy."

She spun around as fast as her cumbersome belly would allow to find this man standing almost right over her. He was grinning at her in a way she didn't like. As quickly as she could, she scrambled onto her feet. The stranger leaned over to help her. She felt his hand under her arm, brushing against her breast ever so lightly as if it had been an accident. To Willa May, his touch had been too familiar and she suspected that he wanted to keep on touching her all over. She pulled away and reached for the broom that was leaning against the wall of the cabin. She held it between herself and the man, ready to clout him on the head if need be. "Thank you, but I can manage just fine on my own," she said.

She took a closer look at the man now. She noticed he had a hunting knife tucked into a small leather sheath that hung from his belt. He was wearing a faded Confederate uniform and big boots made out of skins. He was trying to look like a mountain man, but something inside Willa May told her he wasn't any mountain man. He had a wild look in his eyes and he smiled too much to suit her. It was like he was up to something and he thought he could pull the wool over her eyes.

He looked past her into the cabin, those wild eyes darting all around and taking in everything. "Where's your man? Pretty little thing like you has got to have a man around to look after her...and keep her busy." At that, he looked down at her swollen belly and then back up at Willa May. He winked knowingly.

She started to say that Daniel was up in the woods behind the cabin, sawing down some trees for firewood, but Josie came up onto the porch just then and said, "Pa's away working on the railroad."

The stranger's smile turned to a leer. "So you're here all by yourself then."

Without waiting another second, Willa May raised the broom and

100

started whacking the man over the head, yelling, "Get away from here! Go on. Git!"

The stranger covered his head as best he could with both hands. She half expected him to try and wrestle the broom out of her hands. He clearly had the advantage, with her in her condition. Surprisingly, he started backing off the porch and saying, "Okay, okay. I'm goin'. Just stop hitting me."

She gave him one last solid crack against his head and a couple more to his shoulders as he turned to run. "Josie, get the babies inside," she yelled. Josie ran to gather all the little ones who stood gaping at their mama whupping the stranger with her broom. They held onto each other's hand as they climbed the steep steps to the porch. Each one knew by the tone of her voice that they had better do what they were told.

"Get in the house!" Willa May ordered. Josie herded them into the cabin. Not taking her eyes off of the stranger who was in full retreat, Willa May backed into the cabin. Staying between the stranger and her babies, she held her broom at the ready. Once inside, she slammed the door shut and barred it. Then she ran to each of the windows and barred the shutters from inside, still gripping the broom in case he tried to surprise her.

Luckily, the cabin was cool inside. They spent the rest of the day locked in like prisoners. Willa May had no idea where the stranger had gone, but she wasn't taking any chances that he would come back and threaten her and her little ones with the long, sharp knife he wore. She pulled down Daniel's shotgun and dragged it across the room to the bureau where Daniel kept the bullets. Her hands shook so that she dropped the first four bullets she tried to pick up. She managed to load the shotgun and position it on a chair like Daniel had shown her the night he left with Isaiah and Dicey.

The babies started to cry, they were so frightened. As best she could, she calmed them down and told Josie to sing to them quietly. She hoped that would make them stop crying. They sat there through the afternoon hours, waiting for any sign of the stranger. Willa May's nerves were so frazzled, she thought she heard footsteps all around the place as if the house was surrounded. Every time a leaf stirred or a bird screeched, she jumped. Watching her, the little ones jumped, too.

Sundown came and she set out some leftover biscuits for the babies and some bacon she had fried that morning. She opened a jar of applesauce for them and they busied themselves cleaning up their

101

plates. Still, Willa May felt edgy. She thought that the stranger had given up too quickly. From the cagey look about him, she believed deep down that they weren't quit of him yet. She figured he would wait for nightfall, like a fox fixing to raid the henhouse. She chewed on a cold biscuit as she hunkered down over the shotgun, waiting for him to make his move. Nightfall found her still there, her belly begging for more food and her joints stiff from sitting for so long. The babies had played a little after their supper then, one by one, they had drifted off to sleep. She picked them up and put them to bed, changing diapers and cleaning them up as best she could. They were running low on water, but Willa May wasn't about to set foot outside the cabin in the dark to get to the well.

She huddled once more behind the shotgun and prayed that Daniel would get home soon. But time seemed to be standing still, giving the stranger the advantage. In her mind, Willa May could see Daniel coming home to find his family killed, each of their throats slit by that big hunting knife the stranger carried. Stories about scalawags lurking around were circulating more and more since the war. They were mostly drifters who would show up asking for work or handouts. Some would steal a person blind. She recalled the stories she had heard growing up about Old Man Peyton finding his family scalped by Indians on Christmas Eve. This frightened her even more. "Please, Lord, please don't let that happen to us," she prayed.

It seemed to Willa May like a lifetime had passed when she thought she heard something -- something that made her blood run cold. Wood scraping against wood. Suddenly, she was back in their first cabin. She was trying to wake up as hooded men carrying torches raced in and surrounded her. She couldn't let that happen again.

Her eyes had adjusted to the darkness of the cabin by then. She saw the bar across the door raising slowly, very slowly. The grating of the wood bar against the door sounded like the shrieking of a pack of demons. A thousand thoughts raced through her mind. What if it was Daniel? What if the shotgun misfired and the stranger got in? What if he wasn't alone? What if...but before she could finish that thought, the door burst open and a man stood silhouetted against the moonlight. The man was too tall and skinny to be Daniel. Not wasting another second, she pulled the trigger on the shotgun. There was a loud crack and a flash of bright light burst across the room at him. The blast knocked her backward, off her knees. She protected the baby she was carrying as well as she could, still not taking her eyes off that dark shape in the doorway. Her first thought was that she had missed. The shape stood there for fifteen, maybe twenty seconds. "Oh, no," she heard herself gasp. Before she could get her bloated body back to the shotgun, the black shape started through the door, heading straight for her. Five steps into the room, he fell to the floor with a loud thud. Willa May sat frozen, thinking he was going to stand up and come for her and the babies if she dared to move. She hardly breathed. From the empty blaring silence inside her head, she heard the babies wailing and screaming as if from a long distance. She started to get up and run to them when another shape appeared in the doorway. Clamping her hand over her mouth, she tried to stifle the scream that worked up from her gut and charged into her throat. The dark figure in the door raced toward her. Unable to contain the scream any longer, she heard herself shrieking again and again.

The figure grabbed her by her shoulders and she started scratching and clawing like a trapped she-bear. Through her panic, she heard Daniel's voice. "Willa May! Willa May, it's me. Daniel. It's Daniel."

She stopped fighting him and threw her arms around his neck, sobbing. Daniel held her to him. When he was able to get her calmed down, she told him what had happened. He said that he had heard the shot as he was coming down the road and had bolted for the cabin. Seeing that she was still shaken, he helped her up and told her to see to the babies. Lighting a coal oil lamp, Daniel knelt over the dead man and rolled him over. It was the stranger from that morning. In his right hand, he still clutched his long, gleaming hunting knife.

"Do you know him?" she asked Daniel.

"No, can't say as I've ever seen the varmint before." Daniel shook his head. "But I'd say you had every right to shoot the bastard. I don't think he'd have thought twice about using that knife on you."

"What are we goin' to do? Will I have to go to jail?" Willa May was starting to fret over just where her bad deed would lead.

"They ain't goin' to do nothing to you," Daniel said, looking her straight in the eye. "They ain't goin' to do nothing because they ain't never goin' to find out, you hear?"

She nodded, too upset to argue. "Get him out of here. Just get him out of here," she pleaded.

"I'll be back directly. Are you all right?"

She nodded again, desperate for the stranger to be gone.

Daniel dragged the body out of the cabin. In the moonlight, he dug a grave down by the gorge close to where he and Isaiah had buried Joe and Sarah. Willa May waited for him, unable to forget how terrified she had been when that dark shape appeared in their doorway and she was the only thing between him and her babies. To have something to do -- anything, oh Lord -- she started scrubbing the blood stains off of the floor. It didn't help. Bent over on all fours, she couldn't shake the memory of how she had been scrubbing the porch when the stranger came upon her that morning. When Daniel came home, he made her a cup of hot tea and a decent meal. Willa May began to feel better. Daniel held her till hours later, near sunup, she was able to drift off to sleep.

Willa May was not comfortable about keeping the shooting a secret like Daniel had said. Nightmares about someone finding the grave and the law coming after her haunted her dreams. She would wake up, crying out in her sleep and drenched with sweat. Daniel decided to quit his job to be home with his family where he could protect them. He held her every night until she could fall asleep. She had grown afraid of going to bed, for fear of having one of her terrible dreams.

Two weeks later on a Sunday, they rode over to her folks' place for dinner. It was growing crisp outdoors, the first hint of fall. Lizzy made a big ham dinner with mashed potatoes, corn, pickled peaches, and to top it off, a pumpkin pie. It felt good to Willa May to be back among her kin. For the first time since the shooting, she started to relax. She worried about Josie most of all. Josie had woken up that night, hearing the shotgun blast. She had seen the dead man, watching in wide eyed silence. When she brought it up a few days later, talking about the man Mommy had shot, Daniel told her it had all been a bad dream and that nothing like that had happened. Willa May worried that Josie would slip and say something about it when they were around other folks, but Josie must have caught on to what had taken place and known instinctively that she wasn't supposed to say anything about it. Somehow, that worried Willa May even more.

She was beginning to relax, ready to take a bite of the pumpkin pie that Lizzy had baked when Big Jim said, "You all hear about that family over in Bluefield that was killed? A woman and her eight younguns. All with their throats slit clean open."

Looking hard at Willa May, Daniel asked, "Did they catch the murdering varmint that done it?"

"Nope. But they got a description of some straggler dressed in a Secesh uniform that was picking up odd jobs around town and carrying a big old hunting knife. Seems he disappeared the day that woman and her younguns was found dead."

Willa May held her fork in her hand, frozen between her plate and her mouth. Visions of that stranger coming up on their porch, smiling, and all the while looking for just the right moment to attack them played in her head.

"Do you like this pie, Willa May?" Lizzy asked.

Snapping out of her daydream, she gobbled the bite of pie. "Sure do, Mama," she replied, hoping she sounded convincing. She noticed her pa out of the corner of her eye fixing her with a long look. Daniel must have seen him, too, because he said, looking at Pole now, "Well, I don't figure that rascal will be causing nobody else no harm."

Pole turned to Daniel who looked directly into Pole's eyes. Pole gave Daniel the slightest nod.

Daniel never went back to work on the railroad. No amount of pleading on Willa May's part could convince him to go back. The following Monday, when she saw that he wasn't going to leave, she asked, "What will we live on if you don't go back?"

He sighed, not liking it that she was nagging at him. "I can't go back, Willa May. Not after what happened. Not with so many men roaming the countryside these days. You know as well as I do that feller won't be the last to show up here. Ain't none of them worth the clothes on their backs." Taking her by her shoulders, Daniel looked down at her with his tired eyes and said, "You got lucky this time. Do you really want to take the chance that it'll happen again?"

Put that way, Willa May was forced to agree with him. She shook her head. "No, I don't ever want to be that scared again." Tears welled in her eyes as she recalled how afraid she had been for herself and the babies. Daniel pulled her close and whispered softly in her ear, "And I don't want you to be afraid like that again."

She still wondered what in the world they would do. "What'll happen to us, Daniel?"

"Ain't nothing goin' to happen to us that we don't want to happen. You hear what I'm saying?"

"But how are we goin' to live?"

"I got me an idea. If your uncle Luther likes it, I reckon we'll be business partners."

"Bootlegging?" she asked, surprised that Daniel would even think of such a thing.

"Ain't nothing wrong with giving folks what they want."

"But it's dangerous," she argued. "And look at how many times Luther's been thrown in jail."

Daniel looked away, recalling the time when Sherman had him thrown in jail. His voice was cold as ice when he answered, "Ain't nobody goin' to lock me up again. Nobody."

Daniel hitched up his horse, a big gray he called Traveller after Robert E. Lee's famous horse, and rode over to Big Annie's to strike up a deal with Luther. Before the war, they had always called running whiskey moonshining. But during the war, when peddlers began hiding bottles of whiskey inside their bootlegs and selling it to Union troops, folks began calling whiskey runners bootleggers. Now Daniel was going to be like those men, taking the same risks of getting caught. Risks that scared Willa May to the marrow. Daniel was set on it, though, and when he was set on something, there was no talking to him. It was no use suggesting to him that he could go into the mines. There was just as much danger, if not more, what with cave-ins and poisonous fumes. Besides, Daniel wouldn't last one day inside a mine. He loved being outdoors too much and could never be cooped up like that and Willa May knew it.

Daniel's idea proved too enticing for Luther to turn down. Since Daniel and Willa May were so isolated up in the hills, Daniel reasoned that it would be safer to put Luther's stills up in the woods behind their cabin. While Luther was in charge of making the whiskey, Daniel would make barrels for transporting it. Barrels with false bottoms that they could fill part way with grain. If the law stopped them, they could trick them by opening the barrels and showing the sheriff all that grain. Daniel couldn't read or write, but he had a creative mind. Not only did he team up with Luther, but he stopped by Elroy Hicks' place. Finding Elroy already in the jug before noon, Daniel took his jug away. Even with both legs gone and drunker than a skunk, Elroy put up quite a fight for his jug. When Daniel finally managed to wrestle it away, he brewed a pot of strong coffee and forced it down Elroy. Once Elroy was clear in the head, Daniel explained his plan to go into the bootlegging business with Luther. He told Elroy how they were going to deliver the goods under the guise of taking grain into Charleston. Daniel knew that Elroy, with his drinking habit, would know every tavern keeper in the valley. He thought Elroy could sway them into buying their whiskey from him and Luther. He offered to take Elroy on, letting him ride shotgun on their deliveries. Daniel figured that the law would never suspect a farmer and a cripple of being bootleggers. Daniel proved to be right. Elroy was happy as a pig in mud to be useful to somebody once more. Daniel brought Elroy home with him and built Elroy a little place of his own that summer, just a few yards from their cabin. It had two ramps leading off the porch and furniture that looked to Willa May to be made for a small child, but everything was designed to be easy for Elroy to reach. She was glad to have Elroy close by. He could talk a blue streak, but he had a good heart. Elroy was so happy, happier than she had ever expected to see him again. He loved the children, especially 'Lil Daniel. He loved to watch 'Lil Daniel running barefoot in the yard. Shaking his head, he'd say, "Just like his pa, that boy. Just like his pa." One day he turned to Willa May with a serious look and said in a warning tone, "Will May, you're goin' to have a hard time keeping that one home. He's so much like Daniel, he'll probably run off into these here woods one day and come back three weeks later dragging a dead bear behind him."

She stopped scrubbing her laundry and set the washboard down, drying her reddened hands. She looked over to where 'Lil Daniel was chasing after their rooster, his little bare feet black with dirt and his strong little legs already so much like Daniel's. "You're probably right, Elroy. But till then, he's still my baby and I plan to keep him close by me as long as I can." Even Elroy understood that.

Willa May had made a new quilt for the baby she was expecting, this time a flying geese pattern in blues because she wanted another boy. For each baby, she had made a different pattern, sewing as much love and tenderness into each stitch as she could. 'Lil Daniel's was a Bear's Paw in red and white, Hattie Sue's was a Shoo Fly in gold, brown and ivory. Walt Whitman's was a Bow Tie pattern in shades of purple. The new baby's quilt was finished and just waiting for a baby to cover.

Daniel was up in the woods that fall, cutting down trees for making barrels. The first snowflakes were falling and Elroy was sitting by the hearth, soaking up the warmth from the fire. It was almost noon when Willa May felt the first pain, that familiar feeling like some huge hands were reaching inside her belly and squeezing her insides together like an accordion. She set down her skillet -- she had been making gravy for the biscuits -- and howled like a she-wolf. It nearly scared poor Elroy out of his wits. He wheeled himself over and looked up at her, his eyes nearly popping out of his head. "What's wrong, Willa May?"

Gripping the table, she held her swollen belly. Between gritted teeth, she said, "Get Daniel."

Elroy's head swiveled around as he looked over his shoulder at the door, then swiveled back to peer up at Willa May. "But I can't, Willa May. He's up in them woods and I can't get up there, not on these wheels." His voice was shrill with desperation.

"Then take the babies over to your place and watch them. I'm goin' to have this baby any second, the way it feels." Another sharp pain bent her double. Turning pale, Elroy wheeled himself around and told Josie to round up the babies and follow him to his place.

Willa May had three more pains while they were getting out of the cabin. She could hear their voices outside. Josie asked what was ailing Mommy and Elroy, trying his best not to break under pressure, told her that her mommy just had a bad bellyache from eating so much gravy that morning. *Just like a man,* Willa May thought, rolling her eyes. The next pain drove her down to the floor and her water broke, making a small puddle on her clean wood floor. On her hands and knees, she wiped up the planks, stopping for the next four pains. She crawled over to their bureau and took out some clean sheets from the bottom drawer. She spread them doubled over on the floor. Stopping long enough for another pain, she pulled off her pantaloons and hitching up her skirt, she squatted over the clean sheets. The pains were so sharp now that she felt the urge to push. She strained to bear down, huffing and puffing between the pains, howling with every new one. Moments later, she felt the head come through and caught hold of it with her hands. She had barely reached for it when another hard, bearing down pain brought the shoulders through and the baby slipped out into her hands, slippery as a fish. She didn't have a knife handy so she reached up to the top drawer of the bureau for her hair cutting scissors. She cut the birthing cord and tied it. As she pulled herself up to clean off the baby, she bent double again with another sharp pain. Wondering what was happening, she felt a strong urge to push again. Out came a second head. Willa May was so surprised, she couldn't think clearly. The next pain brought her out of her shock and she placed the second baby, another boy, next to his brother on the soft sheet and set about cutting his cord.

Wet with sweat, she was a bloody mess, but she brought both babies over, squalling and wriggling, to the copper lined sink and washed them both. She wrapped them in flannel blankets. Setting them down, she cleaned herself up as best she could. Everything around her started spinning in a swirl, like a cyclone was loose inside the cabin. She felt herself being swallowed in darkness. When she came to, she was in their bed. Daniel was wiping her face and neck with a cool cloth. She tried to sit up, saying, "The babies --" but Daniel pushed her back and shushed her, saying that the babies were fine, just hungry.

Daniel brought them to her and they started to nurse, hungry as two little bear cubs. Both of them had her red hair and they looked exactly alike. They were smaller than the babies she was used to having, but they looked healthy enough to Willa May. After a week of nursing, they were well on their way to being fat. She named them Glenny and Garnet. To their pa, they were the most beautiful babies in the world. He was so proud, it reminded Willa May of when Josie was born. He would hold the two babies, one in each arm. He cuddled them and talked to them, saying how they were going to grow up to be great mountain men.

Mr. Shaw died the following spring. It was on Easter Sunday and Daniel and Willa May were in church. Their twins were being baptized and after the ceremony, the congregation stood to sing, "Rock of Ages". Mr. Shaw, as always, was playing his fiddle despite the arthritis that made his hands look like gnarled branches. They finished the last verse of the hymn and started to sit down when Mr. Shaw, moving slower than the rest because of his gimpy leg, pitched forward onto the altar by Preacher Willis. Preacher Willis jumped back as if someone had shot him. He gaped at the still body at his feet. Miss Beatrice screamed and stood up, shaky on her feet, looking around for help. Daniel and Pole got to the altar first. Daniel rolled Mr. Shaw over and put his head down to the old man's chest, listening for a heartbeat. Several seconds passed while the rest of the congregation stood in silence, watching. Daniel looked up at Pole and the preacher and shook his head. Miss Beatrice screamed again and had to be helped back into her pew. Lizzy and Big Annie fanned her to keep her from fainting. She looked so small and frail, resting her silver haired head on Lizzy's shoulder. Preacher Willis asked for some men to come up and carry Mr. Shaw's body. Six more men came forward, including Luther and Shep. They carried Mr. Shaw out of the church. Lizzy and Big Annie helped Miss Beatrice down the long aisle and out the door. Creedy and Willa May followed, bringing her babies in tow. Elroy wheeled out behind them. Outside, Daniel brought his wagon around and the men loaded Mr. Shaw's limp body onto the back. Pole brought his wagon and helped Miss Beatrice and Lizzy up onto the seat. Daniel lifted Willa May and the kids onto the back. They took Mr. Shaw home where Lizzy and Big Annie helped Miss Beatrice to lay him out. Willa May and the babies stayed over at her folks' until after the funeral. Together, with Big Annie and Dessie, she cooked, baked, and worked night and day to keep up with all the folks who came to pay their respects and sit up with the body. There were plenty of jugs being passed around each night and Miss Beatrice offered everybody a little taste of Mr. Shaw's favorite peach brandy that he made every year. Willa May never saw so many people come to a funeral as when Mr. Shaw was buried. He had taught just about every person from Page to Deepwater and they all showed up to pay their last respects to a man who, as anyone would have agreed, was a far better person than the rest of them. He had done more than just teach them their letters and numbers. He had shown them what great music and literature were. He had always taken the time to keep in touch -- like when he sent books over to Daniel and Willa May once they were married -- in hopes of making their daily living a little bit lighter. Willa May was going to miss the old man.

That summer Miss Beatrice sold their place and moved to Richmond where she still had family. Before she left, she put all of Mr. Shaw's books in crates and had them sent over to Willa May's folks. She said that Mr. Shaw would have wanted Willa May to have them. Daniel built some bookcases to hold the precious books. First editions of The Scarlet Letter, Moby Dick, and Poe's poems were among them, writing that Willa May treasured.

Because of the books she had inherited and Mr. Shaw's passing, Willa May decided it was time for Josie and 'Lil Daniel to start their schooling. She was determined that all her children would know how to read, write, and cipher, so she started teaching them herself that fall, tending the twins and holding a book at the same time. Josie took to learning just as Willa May had. 'Lil Daniel, though, would stare outside, watching a blue jay flutter past the door or a cloud floating up in the sky. He couldn't have cared less about his A B C's and his

110

numbers, not that he wasn't smart. When he wasn't staring outside, he could read and cipher as well as his mother. He and his pa clung to every word as she read from Robert Louis Stevenson and Mark Twain. After she had finished one of those books, 'Lil Daniel looked up at Willa May and said in a dreamy voice, "Mommy, someday I'm goin' to see all them places, too." Deep down, Willa May knew that he would. Her little boy was growing up faster than she liked and she knew that each sunrise brought her closer to the day he would set off on his own adventure. She just thanked the Lord each night that it wasn't that day.

Over the next eight years, Willa May gave birth to five more babies, bringing her brood up to eleven -- Effie Lee, James Houston, Harry Joe, Blanchie May, and Ethan Allen. It was the spring of 1880 and she was due with her twelfth. That spring was a beauty. It reminded her of the spring she had first seen Daniel. The hills were speckled like robin's eggs with pinks and purples, first from the dogwoods and then the mountain laurels that city folk called rhododendron. She would stroll with the children over to the gorge each day and take in the beauty of the hills, feeling certain that no artist had ever captured that much grandeur in a painting.

As they stood there, she told her babies how the mountains they were looking at were older than anybody could remember, going back before men came into the world. Except for 'Lil Daniel and Walt Whitman, she didn't think any of them believed her. They all thought their mommy was telling them a story she had made up. But 'Lil Daniel and Walt Whitman both nodded and gazed out at the hills like they knew that something so majestic had to have come first. Like in the Bible, in Genesis, in the beginning when the Lord reached down and created the heavens, the earth, the seas, and the mountains.

Willa May told them about the Indians who had settled there, how they built mounds for burying their dead. Even they were gone now, replaced by the Shawnee, and then by the first settlers themselves. She told them about George Washington, their first President, coming through those hills with a surveying party. How her family, the Kincaids, came there by way of Scotland and Ireland to make a new home for themselves in a wild and vast country. When Walt Whitman asked her who the first Kincaids were, Willa May answered, "I'm not

111

sure, Son, but my pa says there were Kincaids in Scotland before the time of Robert, the Earl of Bruce. Now that's a far piece back in time." Again, the others nodded, thinking it was just a made up story, but the two boys' faces were set like they were studying, taking it all in.

'Lil Daniel looked at her one day and said, "Someday, I'm goin' to be like them first settlers, Mommy. I'm goin' to be the first to go into a brand new territory and watch it grow. Why, someday, I'm goin' to see that there Pacific Ocean you showed us on that map, too."

He said it with such conviction that she knew he meant every word. She looked at him, seeing a boy of eleven years standing on the threshold of manhood. Already, he loved to go up in the woods with his pa, hunting and learning the ways of mountain men as Daniel had learned them from Old Man Peyton years before. Daniel said that 'Lil Daniel could already track as well as he could. Big Jim had taught him how to shoot with a bow. Back in the fall, at Thanksgiving, they had enjoyed a fine wild turkey that 'Lil Daniel brought down with his bow, a fact that his pa reminded them of throughout the evening. His aim with a rifle was even better. Time and again, he would go up into the woods that fall by himself and bring back squirrel and 'possum. They had some mighty good meals thanks to 'Lil Daniel. He was turning into quite a mountain man.

June was long and dry, hotter than any June Will May could remember. She was overdue already with her twelfth. One Monday, she started the wash, filling the tub with kettles of steaming hot water and scrubbing sheets and clothes on her washboard, then rinsing everything in cold water brought up from the well. She started hanging the sheets on the line and was pinning one up when she heard a low rumble close by, too close to suit her. Peeking around the edge of the sheet in her hands, she saw a black bear reared up on its hind legs, pawing the air and baring his teeth with each growl. The bear was no more than an arm's length away. Willa May screamed and tried to make a run for the cabin. The bear gave out a roar that seemed to rattle the ground beneath her. He charged through the clean sheets on all fours, heading right for Willa May. In her condition, she couldn't really run. She scooted along as fast as she could, holding onto her huge belly and screaming like a wild woman with every step.

She had just rounded the corner of the cabin when the bear tackled her from behind. She plunged to the ground, trying to protect her unborn baby as best she could. She fell with a solid thud that sounded like a door slamming shut. It made her teeth rattle. The bear fell on her, clawing her back and ripping through her dress.

She was still shrieking and the bear was roaring thunderously when she felt its muzzle close to her neck, its breath warm against her bare skin. Willa May knew she was going to die. She started praying that the good Lord would let it be over with quick. An ear splitting blast that seemed to echo for a full minute exploded above her head. The bear stopped raking her back and gave a deep growl. Its huge body crashed to the ground beside her. As he lay there, a deep sigh escaped from his open mouth.

Willa May looked up to see smoke floating off onto the air like morning mist on the river. Through the smoke, she could make out the barrel end of Daniel's shotgun, and behind that, 'Lil Daniel. He was still holding the gun up to his shoulder, ready to fire again if the monstrous beast moved. Moments passed and the bear still lay there, stone dead. Slowly, 'Lil Daniel lowered the shotgun and came to kneel over her. "Mommy? You all right, Mommy?"

"Help me up, Son," she groaned. Her back stung in a hundred places where the bear's sharp claws had ripped her flesh. She knew she would carry the scars from the bear for the rest of her life.

'Lil Daniel set his gun down and with both hands, hoisted her up and helped her inside, but not before she took one last look at the black bear. 'Lil Daniel's aim had been true. He had gotten the bear right between the eyes, leaving a dark hole over his snout, trickling bright red blood over his open mouth and onto the ground.

Inside, Josie, who had been watching the babies, rushed over to Willa May. She gasped in horror when she saw Willa May's back shredded and bleeding. "Mommy," she cried, "what happened?"

"Bear," Willa May answered. "Now help me get myself cleaned up. Boil some water and clean out these wounds for me. My back feels like it's on fire."

Josie sent the little ones out to play and told Hattie Sue to watch them. She carefully peeled what was left of Willa May's dress off her back and set to cleaning out each wound, first with soap and water then with whiskey. That made Willa May scream almost as much as the bear's clawing. Josie bandaged her up as best she could and helped her change into clean clothes. Willa May sat down, desperately needing to rest. She had Josie make some tea with the rest of the hot water. She started to fret about her unborn baby.

A week went by and she never felt the baby move again. She went into labor the following Monday and Daniel, just as worried as she was, delivered their little girl, stillborn. They named her Mary Kate. Daniel buried her next to Joe and Sarah where she could always see the mountain laurels in bloom.

Chapter Five

That winter Daniel and Willa May took their children over to her folks' place to go to church on Christmas Eve. Old Man Peyton had been dead for five years. At least that was what people up and down the valley had surmised since nobody had seen the old recluse in all that time and it wasn't very likely that he would miss playing Father Christmas, he had loved it so. When word spread that nobody had seen him, Daniel went up into the mountains to look for him. He came back a few days later saying that Old Man Peyton's cave looked like it hadn't been kept up in months. That wasn't like the old man at all -- he was very finicky about his surroundings. Daniel searched all over the mountain for him, but never found any sign of him. If the old man had died up there, animals would have made off with the carcass, leaving no evidence of his fate. Christmas wasn't the same for Willa May. To her, Old Man Peyton had really been Father Christmas.

She couldn't deny her children all the excitement of the Christmas pageant each year so they bundled themselves up and scooted in close to each other in the back of the wagon and made the trip over to Page. Her folks were doing fine, just looking older. Her mama had gray hair now. Pa and Big Jim weren't up to as much heavy work around the place as they had once done. Creedy was a young man, red haired and freckled, sporting a red beard and mustache. Over the years, he had taken to Lizzy and Willa May supposed he was like a son to her mama now that Augie was gone. It made her feel better to know that Creedy was there for her folks, even with his deformity and its handicaps. He was a great comfort to Lizzy and he worked hard in the garden every year.

Big Annie and Luther were at church that night with 'Lil Luther who was turning into quite a young man himself. He was already a head taller than Luther and just as ornery. At fifteen, he was telling his grandpa just what was needed to improve their bootleg whiskey. The bootlegging business had proved profitable for Luther and Daniel. With Elroy's drinking past, the tavern keepers trusted Elroy to know a good jug of moonshine. Daniel gave them all a discount at first just to get them to do business with him. Soon everybody in the valley from Fayetteville to Charleston was buying from Daniel and Luther. Luther was working his stills night and day to keep up with all the business. Luckily they never lacked for buyers. Once the law and the revenuers got wind of Daniel being in the bootlegging business, they often stopped him as he made his deliveries. Daniel would open the grain end of one of his barrels and the sheriff would stand there shaking his head and shrugging his shoulders, unable to figure out just how Daniel was doing it, but knowing that Daniel had gotten the better of him. One time a revenuer had Daniel open all the barrels in the wagon. When he didn't come up with any whiskey, he had Daniel unload the wagon. The revenuer proceeded to examine every crack and crevice in the wagon, trying to find a hiding place for the whiskey he knew was there. Settling himself down on one of the barrels, he said, "I know you're guilty as sin, Shrewsbury, but I'll be hogtied and whupped if I can prove it." Elroy crowed, laughing from his seat on the wagon and getting a mean look from the revenuer. Even Daniel had to snicker about it whenever he told the story.

Daniel and Willa May were faring all right, making enough to get by and then some. Until that Christmas. There were some new faces at church, signs of more folks settling in the area, coming to work in the mines or for the timber mills. With them came some new houses and new customs...and new sickness. None of the people in church that night knew it until it was too late, but one of those new faces was carrying smallpox.

Around mid-January, Glenny and Garnet came down with a high fever, followed by Harry Joe and Blanchie May. Three days later, they each broke out in a rash on their faces, hands, and even on the soles of their feet. Daniel and Willa May stayed with them around the clock, washing them with cool cloths and trying to get them to keep down some water or some broth. Willa May couldn't understand how she and Daniel kept from getting sick, too. As soon as she saw the rashes on the children, she sent the others over to Elroy's and told them not to come back to the house till she came for them, thinking it might be the measles. Elroy promised he would watch out for them. Josie and 'Lil Daniel were big enough to know how to take care of the little ones. Once the rash showed up it was only a matter of days until the pox set in, covering each child with seeping yellow puss sometimes mixed with blood and bringing with it another high fever. They lost

116

Garnet on the thirteenth of January, his little body crusted with sores. Blanchie May died the following morning. Harry Joe passed on two days later. All Willa May and Daniel could do was to hold each other and cry.

The night Harry Joe died Willa May feared Daniel came close to losing his mind. They were both ready to drop from exhaustion, from hours and hours of tending the babies and from the feeling of helplessness as they stood by and watched each of them die. Dark rings circled their swollen, red rimmed eyes and neither of them had been able to eat much. Late that night Willa May fell asleep next to Glenny who was still feverish, but starting to show signs of being almost through the worst. When Harry Joe died, Willa May fell to her knees and begged the Lord to spare her last, crying and screaming on the cold wood floor. Daniel, fighting tears of his own, picked her up and held her until she could calm down. "We ain't got time for that, not with Glenny needing us," he said. Willa May knew he was right, so she took up her vigil beside Glenny's bed and stayed by him until she could no longer stay awake.

Hearing a loud crash, she woke up to find Daniel hacking away at Harry Joe's empty bed with his ax. She rushed over and grabbed Daniel's upraised arms. "Daniel? What in tarna--"

But Daniel shook himself free and kept chopping away at the bed until it lay in splinters all over the floor. While he was chopping up the bed, she looked around the room and saw that he had thrown all three feather ticks from their three dead babies into the fire along with the sheets. He started throwing the pieces of Harry Joe's bed in on top of them. One by one, he went about his work in dreadful silence, tossing each and every piece of the beds into the blazing fire. When he was finished, he carried each of their dead children out, wrapped in the quilts Willa May had made when they were born. He carried them up into the hills and buried them. At daybreak, Daniel came back, still silent and set on his task. Willa May had seen a picture in a book when she was a young girl. It showed the Grim Reaper, ominous and unyielding. She thought that Daniel looked just like that picture. She tried to talk to him again, but it was no use. With a glazed look in his eyes, he merely shook her off. He set about scrubbing down the walls, the floor, every stick of furniture, drawers and all, with lye soap and ammonia. He never uttered a word as he worked. What really frightened Willa May was when he started filling the washtub with handfuls of snow and ice he carried in reddened hands. When the tub was nearly full, he started toward Glenny who lay soaked with sweat from his high fever. Delirious, the boy was talking out of his mind. "Daniel, no! No!" Willa May screamed, trying to block his path. Daniel pushed her aside and picked little Glenny up in his arms. Tenderly, he placed Glenny in the tub and filled it up to the brim with more snow. "You're goin' to kill him," Willa May yelled. "You're goin' to kill him for sure!" She tried to run to Glenny and get him out of the tub, but Daniel pushed her back. She could see that he wasn't going to let her near their little boy, no matter how much she argued or fought him. With her arms wrapped around herself, she rocked back and forth. And prayed.

Daniel mixed some roots and herbs and boiled them in a big kettle. All the while he chanted strange words Willa May thought might be Indian words. He swayed back and forth, squatted by the fire as if he were under some strange spell. Staring into the fire, he seemed to see into another world. When the kettle started steaming, he took some of the mixture and cooled it in a bowl then he forced it down Glenny's throat, spoon by spoon. Willa May figured the concoction was something Old Man Peyton had shown Daniel. He kept the kettle steaming and continued his chanting without so much as a look in her direction. He kept up this ritual all day and into the night. Willa May watched him, waiting for some sign that he knew her. She wondered if Daniel was off in that other world he saw in the flames, somewhere far away from her and the rest of his kin, reaching down into that savage side of himself. Looking at Glenny, still mumbling and crying out in his delirium, she thought he might be there with Daniel. By the next morning, Glenny's fever was gone and he had stopped his gibberish. He was white and ghostly looking, scabbed over everywhere. He opened his eyes and asked in a hoarse whisper, "Mommy?"

Willa May ran over to where Daniel had laid him on his bed and took his thin little hand in hers. "I'm here, baby. Mommy's right here."

Before she could look up, she heard the door to the cabin shut behind her. Turning around, her eyes searched the cabin for Daniel, but he was nowhere to be found. She ran to the door. By the time she got out to the porch, she could see him heading up into the hills with his favorite dog, Roscoe.

It took Glenny all that spring to get back on his feet again. The fever had left its mark; he was never quite right in the mind again. He still did his chores and worked around the farm, but he was a lot slower than the others. It was the same with reading and writing. Walt Whitman, Willa May's best pupil, took him under his wing and worked hours on end with Glenny, helping him learn to read and print his name.

Daniel came home after the dogwoods had lost their blooms and the mountain laurels were just starting to color the hillsides. Willa May had to tell him that they both had lost family members that winter from the smallpox. Daniel's mamma and pa, her pa and Big Jim. All through the hills, all the way down to Paint Creek and Cabin Creek, they heard of folks dying that winter from the spread of the horrible disease. Willa May wasn't sure how Daniel would take the news about his folks. She thought he might just turn around and head back into the mountains, but he didn't. He simply nodded and asked where they were buried. That Sunday they went to church and both of them visited their dead, placing fresh flowers on their graves.

Willa May wanted her mama and Creedy to come live with her and Daniel, but Lizzy wouldn't hear of it, saying that she couldn't take the isolation of living up in the hills like them. As often as she could, Willa May sent Josie and 'Lil Daniel over to help her. 'Lil Daniel was a strapping young man now, as tall as his pa. He was strong with broad shoulders and hard muscles down his arms. His sun streaked golden hair and his sparkling blue eyes brought comments from everyone that he was the spitting image of Daniel. Like his pa, he moved with a sinewy animal grace.

Josie had grown up, too. Her blazing red hair tumbled, full and shiny as a copper penny, to her waist. Tall and slender, she moved with a quiet dignity, reminding Willa May of Sarah Turner. It was downright queenly. But Josie was so quiet that it troubled Willa May. Willa May could never guess what notions were churning in Josie's head. The older she grew, the less she shared of herself. She couldn't abide hearing the little ones say "ain't" and was always correcting their grammar. Willa May wondered if maybe she had taught Josie too well. Sometimes the little ones would tease Josie, calling her "Princess". She would stand up straight as a rod and glare down at them, saying, "At least I act like I've got some sense, which is more than I can say for any of you."

119

Willa May sent Josie and 'Lil Daniel over to Lizzy's late that spring to help with the plowing and cleaning. They came home a few weeks later and the family had just sat down at the dinner table when suddenly 'Lil Daniel started snickering. Willa May saw Josie casting an angry look at him.

Looking at 'Lil Daniel, Willa May asked, "What's got into you, Son?"

"Nothing, Mommy, just something that happened while we were at Grandma's, that's all." Here, he broke out laughing and nearly choked on his food.

Everyone else at the table was wanting to know what was so funny. They all looked at 'Lil Daniel, waiting for him to tell them. He looked across at Josie and, seeing the warning look in her eyes, tried to sober up. But as soon as he looked away, he started laughing again. Willa May thought she could put an end to all this by asking, "Are you goin' to let the rest of us in on it or not?"

It took 'Lil Daniel a few minutes before he could stop his snickering long enough to get his story out. He told them how one hot, sultry day while they were at Lizzy's, Josie had gone out to the outhouse. Always a dreamer, talking about the rich folks Willa May read about in books, Josie dreamed of being one of those fine rich ladies herself. Lost in one of her daydreams, she never noticed the two copperheads she passed on her way out to the outhouse. No sooner did she get into the outhouse and pulled down her pantaloons when she spied the two copperheads slithering straight toward the outhouse. 'Lil Daniel was helping Creedy plow up the garden when they heard screaming and shrieking -- a real fuss -- coming from the outhouse. Recognizing Josie's voice, 'Lil Daniel called, "Josie? What in tarnation are you carrying on about?"

"Snakes! Come kill them, Daniel. Hurry!"

'Lil Daniel raced over to the outhouse and spotted the two copperheads, matching S shapes parting the smooth grass. Inside the outhouse, Josie was standing on the seat of the wooden toilet. She jumped up and down, beating at the walls, nearly overturning the outhouse. 'Lil Daniel told Josie to stay put while he fetched a hoe from the shed. He took off for the hoe and got back just in the nick of time. The two snakes were coiled in front of the outhouse door, hissing at Creedy who was keeping a safe distance. He could see that Creedy had distracted them from going right into the outhouse. Josie was still screaming and setting up a ruckus inside, nearly shaking the outhouse apart. 'Lil Daniel raised the hoe and attacked the snakes, but by then Josie had wet down her legs and all over her pantaloons.

"Okay, Josie, you can go now," 'Lil Daniel yelled to her, picking up the dead snakes.

Instead of waiting for Creedy and 'Lil Daniel to leave, Josie charged out of the outhouse, headed toward the house. When the boys saw the dark telltale shadow on the back of Josie's skirt, they both hooted with laughter. Humiliated and shaken, Josie marched red-faced into the house.

As 'Lil Daniel told the story, Willa May could see that Josie was growing angrier. Willa May joined with the others in laughing at 'Lil Daniel's tale, just the same. He had made it sound so funny. When Josie saw everyone laughing, she stood up in tears and raced out of the cabin. Some of the bigger boys like Ethan Allen and James Houston laughed all the harder.

"Hush up your laughing," Willa May scolded, following Josie.

Josie was already down to the road by the time Willa May found her in the darkness. She had reached the overlook by the gorge and stood gazing out at the mountains. When Josie heard Willa May approaching, she looked up. Willa May could see that she was crying. Between her sobs, Josie said, "If you came over here to make me go back, I'm not goin'. I won't go back into that cabin again, Mommy. Never!"

Willa May felt a pang of guilt for laughing at 'Lil Daniel's story. "I'm sorry we all laughed. We weren't really laughing at you, Josie, we were laughing at the pickle you were in. Not at you."

"Don't you see, Mommy? It's not just that. It's...living here."

"I reckon I don't see. What's wrong with living here?"

"Ha!" she sniffed, extending both arms in a gesture of helplessness. "What's *wrong* with living here? Mommy, you're not dumb. You read us books all the time. Books that tell us about folks goin' to places and doing things we never get to do. I don't want to spend the rest of my life like you, tied to some shanty and giving birth to a new baby every year. I want to be somebody. I want to have nice things and live in a real house with pretty rugs instead of dirty wood floors. I want to see those big cities where folks ride in fancy carriages instead of an old whiskey wagon. I don't want to be like you, never having anything and working hard just to get nothing more!"

Every word Josie said cut Willa May to the bone. She tried to put her arms around her daughter and hold her. She was afraid if she didn't hold onto her now, she would lose Josie forever. Josie pulled back from her, backing away. An empty feeling filled Willa May's heart as Josie turned her back to her. "Go on back, Mommy. There's nothing you can say to me that'll change the way I feel. Just go on back to your bootlegger and your mountain ways." She spat out the last sentence as if somehow it all disgusted her. Willa May was stung. She couldn't think of anything to say, so she turned and headed back. Back to a life she loved and Josie hated.

Before Willa May went back in the cabin, she tried to wipe away her tears so Daniel wouldn't see them. Part of her understood what Josie wanted, the part that recalled wanting to be a teacher and spend her life immersed in books. Another part thought it was just a dreamer's notion. She looked at their cabin and Elroy's little place nestled against the hillside. The frogs and the crickets were singing and the fireflies were speckling the night air with their tiny yellow lanterns. To her, this was the only place she wanted to be. For Josie, it was the very place she didn't want to be. They had given her all the love they had and taught her the best they knew how and yet somehow it wasn't enough. Josie was fourteen, the same age Willa May was when Daniel took her for his bride. Maybe if she had the right man, Willa May thought, she would see that their life wasn't so bad, not nearly as bad as some. She remembered how she had caught 'Lil Luther watching Josie just that day when she came back home. He was just about the right age to marry and set up housekeeping. With his dark hair and dark eyes, he was a fine looking young man. He was already in business for himself, doing most of the work up at the stills, so he was able to provide for a family. Maybe Josie just needed to settle down. Then she would see how silly her dreamer's notions were.

The next day Willa May saw 'Lil Luther ride up and watched as he talked men talk with Daniel and Elroy. As he turned to set off for the stills, she called him over. "You know, 'Lil Luther, I was just saying yesterday to our Josie what a fine looking young man you're turning into."

He blushed crimson and turned his attention to his boots. But he wasn't so shy that it stopped him from asking, "What did Josie say?"

"Oh, she agreed with me."

"She did? Josie?" He said it as if he couldn't believe it.

"Uh-huh."

"Well, I'll be."

"Don't let me keep you from your work, Son. Just thought I'd tell you how impressed some of us womenfolk are with you."

He shuffled his feet in the dirt some more and said, "Well, thank you kindly, Willa May. Tell Josie I might stop by later to see her."

Willa May didn't tell Josie anything. True as his word, 'Lil Luther stopped by that evening. He came in and sat down to supper with them -- fried chicken, fresh tomatoes right out of the garden, corn, turnips, and biscuits with gravy. When they finished eating, 'Lil Luther watched Josie as she started on the supper dishes. He squirmed in his chair for a good while. Willa May hoped Daniel wouldn't ask him if he had the stomach ache from his dinner, but finally 'Lil Luther said, "Josie, could I talk to you outside?"

Josie's expression showed that she wondered what in the world 'Lil Luther would have to say to her in private, but she set down her washcloth. Wiping her hands on her apron, she followed 'Lil Luther out to the porch. They were only out there a few minutes, speaking in low voices when Willa May heard Josie say, "No! And don't ever ask me again, Luther. I have my sights set higher than you could ever dream of being." She flew through the open door and over to Willa May. "Don't ever do something like that again," she seethed. "I reckon I can find my own beaus for myself without any help from you. Besides, I'm not about to settle for some low-down bootlegger like Luther."

When she got to "low-down bootlegger," Daniel stood up. Josie finished what she had to say then Daniel spun her around by her shoulders. Shaking his finger at her, he warned, "You ever speak to your mama like that again, Girl, and I'll take you over my knee, you hear? You ain't so big that you can't be brought down a notch or two and I'm the one to do it. You got that?"

Josie knew that Daniel meant every word. He had been raised to respect his elders and he expected the same respect from his own children. If he had said such words, his pa would have warned him that he was getting too big for his britches and Daniel would have met up with the end of a willow switch or a fist. Josie knew she had overstepped the boundary. Hanging her head, she nodded.

"I didn't hear your answer," Daniel bellowed, sounding like a cranky old bear.

"Yessir," Josie managed to say in a small voice.

That night in bed, Daniel asked Willa May about the scene Josie made. When she told him what she had done, he said, "Better that she

123

gets them fool notions out of her head." He turned over and went to sleep, but Willa May couldn't sleep. She was fretting too much over what was going on inside Josie's head and feeling an empty aching inside her heart again. She must have lain awake for hours. Sometime before sunup, she drifted off.

When the rooster crowed, she got up to make the biscuits and start the fire. Usually Josie and 'Lil Daniel would get up to do their chores. That morning 'Lil Daniel was already up. Willa May glanced over at the figure huddled under the quilts in Josie's bed and told 'Lil Daniel to go wake up his sister. She had turned her attention back to her biscuits, flouring the table top, when 'Lil Daniel said, "Mommy, Josie's not here."

Looking up, Willa May saw that 'Lil Daniel had pulled back the covers on Josie's bed, exposing some pillows and rolled up sheets on the mattress. Daniel came into the room and looked down at the empty bed. His face filled with fury. "She can't have gone far. I'll go after her." Pulling down his shotgun, he started for the door.

"No," Willa May protested, grabbing Daniel by his arm. She thought he would shake her off and go anyway, angry as he was, but he didn't. "Let her go, Daniel. It's time. If she needs us, she knows where we are. She can always come home, but she's got to want to come back. We can't force her to keep living here. Just let her go."

Daniel stood frozen, looking down at Willa May, wanting to go bring their baby back. Gradually, the thunderous look in his eyes cleared. Willa May could see that he knew it was best to let Josie go. When he pulled away from Willa May, he set off into the mountains and didn't come back for the rest of the summer. Elroy, 'Lil Luther, and 'Lil Daniel kept the business going through the summer months. Elroy said that Daniel would be back when he got over losing Josie. When he came back that October, Willa May was in the family way again. Daniel never spoke of Josie, but Willa May knew he would never recover from losing her.

Two years later, Willa May saw Josie again. They all rode to Charleston in the wagon for the big Fourth of July celebration. As they rode by the river leading into the city, Willa May admired the beautiful mansions that faced the road. She saw some ladies in fancy dresses and big straw hats sitting in front of one of the homes. They were sipping iced tea. A man in a black suit and white gloves was serving them cake on china dishes. Willa May spotted Josie right away. Her red hair, cascading over her shoulders, glistened in the sunlight. She was dressed in a pretty pink dress with lace ruffles. Josie looked up from her conversation and seeing the familiar wagon, rushed inside the wide double doors of the splendid house. Willa May had seen the fear in her eyes, though, before she turned away. Daniel was too busy driving the team and missed the lovely lawn party altogether. Willa May decided not to mention it.

'Lil Daniel, sitting up front next to his pa, saw Josie, too. He glanced back at Willa May, ready to say something, but she shook her head in warning. 'Lil Daniel looked back at the big mansion until they drove out of sight.

A year later Willa May learned that Josie had married a wealthy young man, the son of a mine owner. She had changed her name to Elizabeth Josephs and made up a story about being stranded when her family had died, forcing her to take work to make a living. Having been such a daydreamer, she apparently had daydreamed herself all the way to riches. Lucky for her, Willa May thought, that some foolish man had fallen for her lies. Now she was living what Daniel would call high on the hog, with expensive dresses and servants to wait on her.

When Daniel heard about it, he grumbled something Willa May couldn't make out and went hunting with 'Lil Daniel. To him, Josie was the same as dead. He claimed that she had disowned her blood kin. Willa May was glad that he hadn't seen her that day in front of her big house with her fine lady friends. If he had seen her turn away like Willa May had, he would have stopped right then and there and called her a traitor to her own family.

Daniel started taking 'Lil Daniel everywhere with him. 'Lil Daniel shadowed his pa night and day. They were kindred spirits, one with nature and one with each other. 'Lil Daniel listened for hours while Daniel spun tales about his war years, scouting for Sherman, telling the family about all the places he had seen. The same dreamy eyed look Willa May had seen on Josie's face when she listened to stories about society folks would appear on ' Lil Daniel's face. In her heart, Willa May knew it wouldn't be long till 'Lil Daniel would break free and go out into the world. Daniel never saw where his war talk was leading. He thought that 'Lil Daniel would always be right beside him.

That year Daniel and Elroy started taking 'Lil Daniel along on their delivery trips into the valley. Whenever they stopped at a tavern, they picked up bits and pieces of news from the outside world. 'Lil

Daniel always came home excited about some Indian uprising or talk of gunslingers out west. He would be so full of talk that he couldn't talk about anything else till the next trip.

On one of their stops at the Stockton Inn in Glen Ferris, 'Lil Daniel heard a soldier on his way home from a fort out west telling about fighting the Apaches and an Indian chief who was causing them all kinds of trouble. The Indian went by the name of Geronimo.

"Did you catch that old Geronimo?" 'Lil Daniel asked.

"Nope. That old cuss is a slippery rascal. Every time we thought we had him, he'd just slip right through our hands. Give us a run for our money, he did."

"You ain't goin' to let him get away, are you?"

"Can't. Orders are to catch him and bring him in, dead or alive. Trouble is we need us a good scout to track him down. When I go back --"

"You're goin' back? When?"

"I got two weeks leave, Son. Then I have to report back to my commanding officer. We're all goin' to set out again and see if we can't find that snake-in-the-grass once and for all."

'Lil Daniel mulled over what the soldier said, then asked, "What do you have to do to become a scout for the army?"

The soldier looked 'Lil Daniel up and down, saying, "You're a mite young to be joining up, aren't you, now?"

"How old do you have to be?"

"Eighteen, Son."

"Well, I'm goin' to turn eighteen next week, sir," 'Lil Daniel said. He had just turned seventeen three months before.

"You say you're good at tracking, do you?"

"My pa says I'm the best in these here parts, so I reckon I'm pretty fair at that."

"In that case, Son, I'd say you'd best be hightailing yourself out there and joining up."

'Lil Daniel came home that night fired up about Geronimo. Daniel took all he could stand. Looking into his boy's eyes, he said, "I've lost six babies. I'll be damned if I'm goin' to lose another one." He shoved back from the supper table and strode out the door, madder than a hornet.

'Lil Daniel looked at Willa May and said, "Why doesn't Pa understand? He fought in the army. Why can't I?"

That familiar empty aching started up inside Willa May's heart.

Seeing the hurt look on her oldest boy, she knew that no matter what his pa said, he was set on going. "You heard what your pa said. He needs you too much around here."

"He don't need me. He's got Elroy and 'Lil Luther. And Walt Whitman's as old as I was when Pa started taking me on deliveries."

"Don't argue with your elders, young man!" It was all she could think to say. She wanted to hold him to her and tell him she never wanted him to leave. Instead she got up and helped Hattie Sue and Effie Lee with the supper dishes.

With a baby on the way, Willa May would have thought that it would be easier to let one of the older ones go. But it wasn't. That night in bed, Daniel wrapped his arm around her and ran his hand over the swell of her belly. "Why is it such a joy to bring a baby into the world and such misery to see them grown?" he asked.

She turned to face him. He had tears in his eyes. She hadn't seen Daniel cry since that night when Harry Joe had died. Here he was, about to lose another one, and no more able to face it than he was then. Putting her hand on his whiskered face, she kissed him gently and said, "You know 'Lil Daniel's got to go. His time has come. Like when the last leaves fall off of the trees, there comes a time, Daniel. Now is 'Lil Daniel's time. Let him go with your blessing. It'll mean the world to him."

Daniel, unable to say anything, buried his face against her neck. She could feel his wet tears. She held him close like she had wanted to hold their boy that evening. They made love that night as they had when they were young and new to each other. Dawn came and Daniel got up with the first rooster crow. When 'Lil Daniel got up, Daniel said, "I expect you'd better eat a hearty breakfast if you're goin' to set off today to join up with the army."

A look of surprise gave way to a broad grin on 'Lil Daniel's face. Like the good boy he was, he hugged his pa and his mama. "Thank you. I'll make you proud. Just wait and see!"

Willa May cried all day after 'Lil Daniel left. As always, Daniel headed up to the mountains. Even Elroy sat looking like he had lost his last friend in the world. 'Lil Daniel had always been his favorite. Through Willa May and Daniel, Elroy was learning what it was like to have children, dealing with the every day scrapes and bruises. Now and then, bigger problems pulled heavy on their hearts. By that night, Elroy had found a jug and was drunk for the first time since he had come to live with them.

When Willa May was ready to go to bed, she noticed a light still on in Elroy's place, so she put a shawl around her shoulders and went over to see about him. She found him passed out on the floor, lying in his own vomit. His jug was turned over, spilling out white lightning that had pooled with his mess. In her condition -- she was a good five months along -- it took her awhile, but she managed to drag Elroy over to his little cot and get him cleaned off then she covered him with a quilt. She scrubbed the floor and put out the light. As she opened the door to leave, Elroy mumbled, "I'll never see him again. Oh Lord, I'll never see that boy again."

A chill raced up her spine. The omen hung in the air. She wanted to shake Elroy for going on like that, but she knew he was too drunk to know what he was saying. Still, the curse seemed to take a life of its own. It spread through the room, casting a dark shadow over her. Ever since she had been a little girl hanging onto her mama's apron, she could recall hearing horrible stories about Indian uprisings. Folks called them murdering savages and told about entire families being massacred. Standing in the doorway, listening to Elroy's ramblings, every bad thing she had ever heard came back to her. She shuddered. It rattled her entire body as she thought about those things happening to her own boy. Tears welled in her eyes as she closed the door. She stood on the porch with her arms wrapped around herself, wishing it was Daniel's arms that were holding her, needing to take comfort in his big, strong arms. She was mad at Daniel for going off like he always did, thinking he was the only one who couldn't face what was happening and leaving her to face it all on her own somehow. Damn men! For all their swaggering talk, they were nothing but weak cowards in the end. Daniel was off in the hills somewhere and Elroy was lying inside, drowned in his whiskey. She wanted to shake them both till their teeth rattled.

Grumbling all the way back to the cabin, she continued fuming while she climbed into bed. Usually she could work off her anger, but not this time. She even surprised herself when she got up still in a huff the next morning. Out of meanness, she went over to Elroy's and banged loudly on the door, yelling at the top of her lungs for him to get up and come to breakfast. "Okay, okay," he screamed through the door. "I'm coming, damn it!"

When he rolled into the cabin and she saw how green he looked, she still banged and clanged her pots and pans as loudly as she could. Poor Elroy grabbed his head in his hands and cried, "Willa May, do you have to make so much gallderned racket? I never knew cooking to be so noisy!"

Walt Whitman lifted Elroy up to the table in his armchair as Willa May slammed his plate down in front of him. The biscuits flew up a good four inches and came back down, splattering in his gravy.

"You want breakfast, there it is," she said.

Elroy and Walt Whitman shot looks at each other as if to say, "What's got into her?" But Willa May kept on slamming things, sending food flying everywhere -- biscuits rolled across the floor and gravy splattered onto the table. Watching her, the little ones grew quiet. Willa May knew they were afraid, but she couldn't bring herself to stop. She served them all and then sat down, too. Looking at everyone's wide eyed stares, she said, "Well, what are you all looking at?"

The more courageous ones mumbled, "Nothing, Mommy." They set about eating what food was still on their plates. The rest just started gulping huge mouthfuls of food. It was the quickest meal Willa May had ever seen her family eat. They all finished their food and made excuses to go outside, either to start their chores or offer to do some of hers. Willa May reckoned the children thought that might bring her out of her foul mood, but it didn't. Only Elroy stayed inside with her. She had to hand it to Elroy; he was braver than she would have been if she were in his place. She finished her breakfast, eating so fast that she gave herself indigestion. She got up to do the dishes. All the while, Elroy just watched her, not saying a word. She turned her back to him and started scrubbing the plates like they were caked in dried mud. She wondered that she didn't scrub the design off of them.

Meekly, Elroy said, "I'm sorry, Willa May, for getting drunk on you like I done. That is what you're mad about, ain't it?"

She had reached over to pick up the skillet she had used for frying the bacon. For a second, she stood frozen, thinking that she would explode, she was so mad. Suddenly, she threw the skillet across the room, spraying bacon grease in all directions. Spinning around, she cried, "No! That's not what I'm so danged mad about. I'm mad because every time something happens that Daniel can't handle, he goes off into the mountains and leaves me to do the handling for him. What kind of man would do such a thing? Don't I have feelings, too?"

Elroy gaped at her. Her question hung there between them as they stared silently at each other. At first, she thought that Elroy was too afraid to answer. His mouth opened as if he were going to say something, then it shut again. Moments passed as he sat there staring at her. Thinking that maybe she was losing her mind, Willa May collapsed into a chair and started crying. Elroy stayed with her through her sobbing until she could talk again. He never said a word; he just waited for her to calm down. She figured that if she had started throwing things again, he would have called for one of the boys to come in and give him some help. But she didn't throw anything, she just sobbed into her hands. When she was finished, she sat up straight and dabbed her eyes with her apron. "I'm sorry, Elroy, to take all this out on you, but there are times when I just can't understand how Daniel can leave me like he does."

Elroy didn't answer right away. After several minutes, he said, "You know, I never reckoned Daniel to ever marry when we was growing up together. He was always so wild like some buck, full of spirit. Even though Daniel was good to his folks, I don't really think he ever cared real deep about nobody till he met you. I remember when he came home that day after he killed that old mountain lion. He told me about meeting you and I knew who you were and forgive me for saying so, but for the life of me, I couldn't figure out what it was that had set off such a spark in Daniel. To me, you were just a scrawny little girl. But Daniel saw something right off that took me years to see."

By this time, Elroy had gotten her attention. "What's that?" she asked.

"Of all the men and women I've ever known, you're the toughest, Willa May."

"Ha!" she laughed. "Here I've sat, bawling my eyes out and you're telling me I'm tough?"

Elroy didn't blink an eye; he just looked right at her and nodded. "Yep. You got spunk, Willa May. Don't you know that by now? Daniel's got to be wild and free. He always will. But you've got something he don't: courage. Not the kind of courage to face down a rattler that's ready to strike; I'm not talking about that kind of courage. I'm talking about the kind of courage it takes to face the worst kind of trouble there is and have the guts to keep on goin' afterward. Call it a strong will or determination or whatever you dang well please, but you've got that...and Daniel don't. That's why Daniel goes off like he does. He doesn't want you to see his weak side. He'll only come back when he can face things again. I used to think he only

130

went off when he was mad at the world over something he couldn't help. But after all these years of seeing him with you and the younguns, I know different. Being mad as an old bear is just his way of covering up because he just can't deal with the pain of it. That's why he needs you like he does. I think he knew that from the first time he met you. He told me all about how you took care of him. A man like Daniel will always need a strong woman to take care of him. See...he's got you to turn to like I got my whiskey to turn to. Don't keep me near as warm at night, but it helps me make it through."

Willa May stared at Elroy, stunned to hear him talking with so much sense -- more than she had ever credited him for having. What he was saying not only made sense, but in her heart, she knew it was true. At first she felt better. She felt she had come to see Daniel in a way she had never seen him before. Then she looked at Elroy and said, "But who do I turn to, Elroy?"

That fall when Daniel came back, Willa May was still mad. She gave him a cool reception when he showed up, carrying a dead 'possum for supper. He tried to hand her the dead carcass, smiling like he expected her to throw her arms around him and go on about how glad she was that he was home. But she wouldn't take the bloody carcass. Turning her back to him, she said, "If you want that thing for supper, go skin it yourself. I've got other things to do."

He went over to Elroy's and sat on the porch, the two of them jawing while Daniel skinned the 'possum. Occasionally he glanced over at their cabin, so she figured Elroy was telling Daniel how she had felt about him leaving this time. When he brought the 'possum over to the cabin for her to cook, he didn't apologize or try to talk to her, which burned her all the more. He simply turned around and headed back to Elroy's. He stayed there till Hattie Sue told him supper was ready. The children were thrilled that their pa was back, asking him a hundred questions at the supper table. Meanwhile, Elroy kept glancing at Willa May who had grown very quiet. Too quiet. Daniel acted like his old self, as though nothing was wrong. He acted like he hadn't been gone for the last four months, like he had been there with her every day keeping up the garden and tending to the children. The longer she sat there thinking about it, the angrier Willa May grew. Hattie Sue and Effie Lee cleared the table. She started to get up when

Daniel said, "You know, I feel like a good game of cards. How about it, Elroy?" Elroy nodded, looking up at Willa May. "Walt Whitman, you and James Houston can sit in on the game, too. You remember what I taught you about poker, don't you?" Walt Whitman and James Houston nodded, happy to be included in the game.

Willa May couldn't stand it any longer. She reached under the table and with all her strength, she turned it over, scaring everyone out of their senses. "Poker!" she screamed. "Daniel Shrewsbury, if you think you're goin' to waltz in here after being gone for four long months -- four months of hard work for the rest of us -- and just sit there playing --" Before she could finish, a sharp pain wrenched her insides and she bent double. Daniel picked her up in his arms. She tried her best to fight him off, holding her swollen belly while she kicked and squirmed for him to set her down. But Daniel was too strong for her. He set her down on their bed and said, "Stop being silly, Willa May, and let me help you."

Still holding her belly with one hand, she reached up with her free hand and slapped him as hard as she could. "Don't you go calling me silly!" she shrieked. "You're the one who's silly, goin' off in the mountains to sulk like a baby."

Daniel looked stung, not just from being slapped, but from how fiercely she had turned on him. She had another pain and she held her belly with both hands, turning onto her side. Daniel leaned over her and tried to help her, but she pushed his hands away and wouldn't let him touch her. She lay there groaning through another pain when Daniel called for Hattie Sue and Effie Lee. Both girls looked fearful, but they stayed with her for the next few hours while her labor grew steadily worse. She knew they didn't know what to do once her time came. When she couldn't bear the pain any longer, Willa May told them to get their pa even though she still didn't want him to touch her. But she knew if the baby was to get there, he would definitely have to touch her. She gave in against her will.

Daniel didn't improve the situation. When he came back into their room, he said, "So, are you ready to be reasonable then?"

Through gritted teeth, she said, "Just get this baby that you put in me here and we'll talk about who's 'reasonable' after."

He had been smiling, thinking he was teasing her. His smile faded. For the first time since he had come home, he looked worried. Willa May could see that he was just beginning to understand the depth of her anger.

For the next three hours, Daniel stayed by her side. She could hear the clock on the mantel over the fireplace chiming twelve midnight when their baby came in the world. A little girl. Daniel, holding her up when she came through, said, "What's this?" He pointed to something that was covering her eyes. An extra piece of afterbirth. Weakly, Willa May lifted her head and when she saw what Daniel was pointing at, she gasped.

"What's wrong? Is she all right?" Willa May could hear the worry in Daniel's voice.

"Well, I declare," she breathed. "I've heard of it, but this is the first time I ever saw it."

"What? What is it?"

"Cut the cord and I'll tell you," she moaned. Daniel did as he was told, tying the cord, wrapping the baby up, and handing her to Willa May. "It's what some of the old timers call 'being born with a caul', an extra layer of afterbirth over the eyes."

"Will she be all right? It don't have nothing to do with her sight, does it?"

"It's supposed to mean that she'll be able to see things that other folks can't."

Daniel looked at her, mystified. "What kinds of things?"

"Oh, it's probably nothing more than superstition, but it's supposed to be a sign of seeing things that are goin' to happen before they happen."

Daniel's look turned fretful. "Look her over and make sure she's all right. If you want me to, I'll hitch up the wagon and take her over to Doc Merriam."

Willa May unwrapped the blanket around their baby. She was crying at the top of her lungs, wanting food and warmth, but she looked to be just fine. Willa May told Daniel not to worry. He looked worried all the same. Willa May got the idea that maybe it was best to let him worry. Maybe then he would feel obliged to stay with her and help her with this new baby.

They named her Dora Lottie. With red hair and gray eyes the color of a winter sky, she was much smaller than their other babies. A good little baby, she hardly ever cried and rarely got sick. But Daniel worried about her from the night she was born. That, more than anything else, was why Willa May thought Daniel didn't take off again, not even when the letter came the next spring addressed to both of them saying that 'Lil Daniel had been killed by the Indians in a skirmish. Inside the letter was a picture of 'Lil Daniel dressed in his army uniform, grinning as though he was having the time of his life. Now the army was telling them he was gone, just like that. The letter didn't say where he was buried, just that he had been wounded and died from his wounds. The army thought his family would rest easy knowing he had died fighting for his country, but Willa May didn't care. All she wanted was her boy back. Her heart was broken, knowing she would never lay eyes on him again. Part of her wondered if in his last moments on this earth he had wished he had never gone out west. She wondered if he was thinking of how pretty the hills were in spring with the dogwoods in bloom, or if he was wondering how upset they would all be. Lord, how she wanted to hold him to her.

She knew it was hard for Daniel, but he didn't turn and go off into the hills like she expected when she finished reading the letter aloud, wiping her tears away so she could see to read. He just sat down in his chair on the porch and stared silently at the garden the whole afternoon. She wanted to say something to comfort him, but she was so heartsick that she couldn't find the words to say. Elroy rolled himself over that evening around sundown. Willa May had started supper, but she didn't figure that Daniel would be up to eating. She guessed Elroy had figured the same thing when she saw the jug he had brought. Together, the two men sat on the porch, watching the sun sink lower into the lavender and gray sky. They passed the jug to each other, the letter still folded in Daniel's hand.

Before she went to bed, Willa May placed the picture of 'Lil Daniel in the family Bible. In it, she had recorded the births and deaths of all her babies. Now, next to 'Lil Daniel's birth date, she marked the date of his death.

In 'eighty-six, two things happened that caused them to sit up and take notice. With the beginning of the American Federation of Labor, there was talk right away of a union for all the mine workers. The mine owners, hearing of it, did everything in their power to keep the miners from unionizing. Their grip on the miners reminded Daniel of the slavery he had fought to end just twenty years before. It wasn't long before the Knights of Labor and the American Federation of Labor decided to join forces and create the United Mine Workers. Through union members, miners throughout the state heard talk of strikes and ways of getting better working conditions and better living conditions for their families. From the start, Daniel thought it was a battle the miners could never win. Mine owners hired Pinkerton men, outsiders from Bluefield. Things were rough. They grew rougher with these hired bullies who used any means to force the miners back to work. In retaliation, the miners used force of their own. Daniel heard about a secret society called the Molly Maguires. The Molly Maguires weren't afraid to use violence against the mine owners and their hired thugs. Just ten years before, some members of the Molly Maguires in Pennsylvania had been sent to the gallows for standing up for their rights. Willa May read in a newspaper Daniel brought home from his deliveries that the name "Molly Maguire" came from Ireland where Irish miners had banded together to resist feudal owners.

While miners throughout the valley were affected by this, Daniel brought home another piece of news that had more personal meaning to them. Geronimo had surrendered. Willa May was glad that the army had finally forced the Apaches to give up, ending twenty years of bloody fighting, but it didn't matter to Daniel. Nothing was going to bring 'Lil Daniel back. Still, Willa May felt that 'Lil Daniel could rest easy knowing that they had ended up capturing Geronimo.

On the day that Daniel told her about Geronimo, he handed Willa May a letter addressed to her. He said it had been waiting at the Stockton Tavern for him when he stopped there on his way home. Wondering who on earth would be writing to her, Willa May opened the envelope written in a fancy hand to find a hundred dollars inside. Nothing else, just the money. She counted it, exclaiming, "Well, I'll be! There's a hundred dollars in this envelope. Who in the world would be sending me mon--" She stopped short, knowing the answer before she even finished. Josie. It had to be. Nobody else they knew had that kind of money.

"Send it back," Daniel grumbled, realizing, too, who the money was from.

Before she could reply, Daniel stormed out of the cabin. Willa May knew he meant for her to send the money back and that was his final word on the matter, but as she held the crisp bills in her hand, she decided she would put it to good use. With or without Daniel's say so. For years, she had watched Walt Whitman grow into an intelligent boy, smarter than anyone she had ever known, with the exception of Mr. Shaw. She determined right then and there to put the money back for Walt Whitman, for when he decided what path he would take in life.

After that, steady as rain, Willa May received a hundred dollars in the mail every month for two years. As far as Daniel knew, she was sending the money back month after month. Willa May assumed that he thought it was the same hundred dollars being passed back and forth all those months. She didn't tell him any differently. A year later, Walt Whitman came to her and said he had an itch to go to school and become a teacher. By that time, Willa May had a fair sized bundle saved.

When she told Daniel that Walt Whitman wanted to go to college, he snorted, saying, "Where in tarnation does that boy think I'm goin' to get the money to send him off to some highfalutin college?"

"You don't have to get the money, Daniel Shrewsbury. I've already got it."

He looked at her for a long time, not saying anything. With a grunt, he finally said, "I reckon you've been holding back that money that Josie's been sending you, ain't you, Willa May?"

"What's wrong with Josie wanting to send her little brother to college?"

Daniel didn't answer; he just sat there looking at her. She knew he was trying to hold his temper with her for not doing as he had asked, but she didn't care. It was for one of her babies and that made it all right as far as she could see. Daniel sighed deeply, scooted his chair back, and walked out. Since he never said not to use the money, Willa May told Walt Whitman he should start making plans to go to college that fall. She handed him the money she had saved. He looked at the wad of bills in his hand and then at his mama, surprise written all over his face. "Mommy," he cried, "I can't take all this money from you. What if you need it for the little ones?"

She closed his hands around the bundle of cash and said, "Hush now, you hear? This is money I've been saving back a long time. If the others had needed it, I would've spent it by now. So you take this money and make us all proud of you now and no more arguing about it. My mind is made up."

That summer before Walt Whitman went off to school, Willa May gave birth to another set of twins, Asa and Ansel. Walt Whitman served as best man in his sister, Hattie Sue's wedding to 'Lil Luther. Although by now 'Lil Luther stood even taller than Daniel, everyone still called him 'Lil Luther. Willa May thought that Hattie Sue had done well for herself, marrying a young fellow the likes of 'Lil Luther.

He had his own business and he had already built himself a fine house close to Lizzy's place. Hattie Sue was so thrilled, she even got her folks caught up in all her excitement. She and Willa May sewed and sewed that spring, making her wedding quilt. Willa May regretted that her wedding dress had been destroyed in their first cabin. She would have let Hattie Sue wear it. When she saw her daughter in the lace and satin dress that Daniel brought back from one of his trips into Charleston, though, she had to admit it was the perfect dress for Hattie Sue. Hattie Sue insisted on wearing the veil Willa May had worn. Luckily, Willa May had given it back to Lizzy after her wedding and there it had stayed tucked away in Lizzy's trunk all those years. Hattie Sue looked so beautiful that Willa May burst into tears at the sight of her. Her little girl was grown up.

Willa May cried through the entire wedding ceremony, sitting with Daniel, Lizzy, and Creedy in the front pew at their church. Not all her tears were over Hattie Sue getting married. For the first time, she began to feel that she and Daniel were getting old. At thirty-five, she had brought fifteen babies into the world and had seen five of them die. She was getting as protective as a she-bear about the rest, wanting to make sure that they had everything she could possibly give them. She and Daniel weren't rich, she knew that. But she wanted her children to have every chance they deserved.

Seeing her tears, Daniel leaned over and said, "Ain't you supposed to be happy at weddings?"

She nodded, trying to smile through her tears. "It's just that it doesn't seem that long since we were the ones standing up there saying I do."

"I know. But it ain't been all that bad, has it?" He grinned at her and winked, that familiar sparkle lighting up his eyes just as they had the day they met.

She shook her head. "No, I wouldn't trade my life with you for anything."

"That's a relief."

She knew he was set on teasing her out of her tears. "Why is that?"

"'Cause I'd hate to think I'd have to hog-tie you to stick around for the next forty years with me."

"You know better than that, Daniel Shrewsbury!"

The preacher told 'Lil Luther he could kiss the bride. Before Willa May knew it, the couple was rushing down the aisle and through the church door. After Daniel helped Lizzy up, he turned back to Willa

May and pulled her to him. In front of everyone there, he kissed her
fully on the lips as if they had been the ones just pronounced man and
wife. He was still kissing her when she heard the folks around them
clapping their hands and cheering. When Daniel finally let her go,
she glowed as red as an apple in autumn, embarrassed that he would
do such a thing in front of everyone they knew. Daniel merely grinned
his devilish grin like he was eighteen again and she was his new bride.

Two months later near the end of August, Willa May was picking
corn for supper when she looked up to see Hattie Sue walking up the
road to their place. She shaded her eyes with one hand to block out
the afternoon sun. When she did, she saw a huge black and purple
welt over Hattie Sue's eye. Putting the ear of corn with the others she
held in her apron, she started toward the road. Hattie Sue's face was
red from the heat and her dress was sticking to her in dark, wet
patches across her front. But it was the black eye that held Willa
May's attention.

"Lord, what on earth's happened to you? Who did this to you,
baby?" She started to put her arms around Hattie Sue to hug her, but
Hattie Sue winced and pulled away. Willa May wondered what other
bruises Hattie Sue was hiding under her clothes.

Hattie Sue's lower lip quivered. Through the tears streaming down
her face, she said, "Mommy, I want to come home!"

"Did 'Lil Luther do this to you?"

She nodded, covering her face with her hands. Willa May knew
that Daniel would beat the stuffing out of 'Lil Luther, maybe even kill
him for doing this. A big knot floated up from her belly and lodged in
her throat. She could feel her heart hammering inside her chest like
the hammering sound Daniel made when he was making his barrels.
She didn't want this to be happening. Lord, how she didn't want this.

"Hattie Sue, this is still your home and always will be. You know
that, darlin'." She started to take her daughter's arm when the ears of
corn she held in her apron tumbled onto the ground. They both bent
over to pick up the dozen or more ears, bumping their heads.
Laughing at their own clumsiness, they picked up the corn together.
"You're welcome to stay as long as you want, baby, that's if we don't'
knock ourselves senseless just trying to get in the house."

Willa May thought that Hattie Sue could use some lighthearted teasing. Hattie Sue chuckled and nodded. Turning quiet again, she said, "Thank you, Mommy. I knew I could count on you."

Seeing Hattie Sue so serious, Willa May thought she should be honest with her. "You know, I can't promise you you'll have a husband after your pa sees that shiner."

"I know. I done thought of that. But I couldn't let him keep on beating me, not when I'm carrying his baby inside me."

"You mean to tell me that he beat you knowing your condition?" Now Willa May wanted to kill 'Lil Luther herself.

Hattie Sue nodded. "He's done beat me every week since we been married. That's not the worst of it. Once he's through beating me, he...he makes me do things."

Willa May wasn't sure she wanted to know what Hattie Sue meant, but she asked, "What kind of things?"

"Once, he made me take my clothes off and he made me crawl on my hands and knees with a rope around my neck the rest of the day."

Willa May stared at her daughter, wondering what had gotten into 'Lil Luther to make him do such a thing. She wanted to tear him limb from limb for humiliating her little girl like that.

"Another time, he tied me to the bed and wouldn't let me up for three days. Not even to go out to the outhouse. So I just laid there in my own mess, begging him to let me up. Every time I asked him to untie me, he hit me again."

Willa May raised her hand. "Don't tell me any more. I don't think I can bear to hear it. Just come on into the house and I'll get you some cold buttermilk. We'll wait for your pa to get home."

When they reached the cabin, James Houston and Ethan Allen were cutting wood beside the house. James Houston saw them coming first. He smiled, seeing his sister, then he spotted the shiner she bore. He slung his ax aside and headed straight for them. At fourteen, he stood a head taller than Willa May with strong, wide shoulders. "'Lil Luther do this to you?" he asked, glowering like the steel gray of the sky before a storm.

"Your sister's come home to stay," Willa May said, trying to keep her boy from going off to do a man's job. "Your pa will deal with 'Lil Luther when he gets home, I expect. Right now, you and Ethan Allen can finish picking some more corn for supper and shuck it for me."

James Houston didn't budge. He stared at his sister's black eye. Willa May grew afraid that he was going to go off right then to hunt down 'Lil Luther and she couldn't have that. "Go on now and give your sister some peace. She looks like she could use it, don't you think?"

Slowly, James Houston moved out of their way and let them pass. Once she pushed Hattie Sue past him, Willa May heard him say to Ethan Allen, "You heard Mommy. Let's get that there corn and finish chopping this wood. Pa might want us to go with him."

Inside the cabin, Willa May tried to busy herself fixing supper. She poured a glass of buttermilk for Hattie Sue who sat down at the table and crumbled some cornbread left over from lunch into the buttermilk. "There's some beans still warm in yonder pot if you want some," Willa May said, gesturing toward a pot with her floury hands. While Willa May rolled the biscuits, Hattie Sue finished off two bowls of beans and another piece of cornbread along with a second cup of buttermilk. "I can see that you haven't gotten the morning sickness yet," she noted.

"I had it once a few days ago, but so far, it ain't been bad."

"It will be so enjoy those vittles while you can. Once you get the sickness, you won't even want to look at food."

Willa May heard Daniel and Elroy pull up outside in the wagon, back from their weekly deliveries. Daniel had taken Glenny with him. Glenny loved to go along. He liked seeing new places and new people. Folks were always good to him, seeing right off that he wasn't right in the head. Glenny never made any enemies. Everyone loved him. With his pa and his brothers always with him, he never had to contend with any teasing from other youngsters. Nobody would dare say anything in front of the Shrewsbury men.

Glenny came in, smiling from his adventure that day, and sat down at the table with Hattie Sue. Elroy rolled in, calling, "Willa May, you got anything cold to drink? I'm dry as cotton!"

Elroy had pulled up by the table and had just noticed Hattie Sue when Daniel came through the door, followed by James Houston and Ethan Allen. Daniel smiled and said, "Why, Hattie Sue, what in the world --"

Daniel stopped in his tracks when Hattie Sue turned her face toward him and he saw the shiner she was sporting. His words turned from pleasant surprise to a short, clipped demand. "Who did that to you?" His smile changed to a dark glower.

Hattie Sue didn't say a word. She just started bawling. Elroy looked up at Willa May, shaking his head, knowing as she did that Daniel wasn't going to let whoever did this to his little girl live to tell

140

about it.

"Hattie Sue, I asked you who did that to you."

"It was 'Lil Luther, Pa," James Houston spoke up, eager to seek revenge.

Without a word, Daniel went straight to his gun rack and pulled down his shotgun. He was loading it when Willa May said, "You're not goin' to kill him, are you? They'll hang you for a murderer, Daniel. Don't go killing 'Lil Luther over this."

Daniel glanced at her, a look that chilled her through and through on that hot August day. Then he was out the door. James Houston and Ethan Allen followed close behind.

"Elroy, do something," Willa May pleaded. "Tell him not to go and kill that boy. Tell him!"

Elroy shook his head. "Willa May, you know as well as I do that there ain't no telling Daniel nothing. Especially when it comes to something like this. Truth be told, 'Lil Luther deserves whatever he gets for this."

Hattie Sue sobbed harder, scared and sorry that she had brought this on them. Effie Lee came in from watching the little ones and sat down beside Hattie Sue. She patted Hattie Sue gently, trying to give her sister some comfort.

Daniel and the boys didn't get back until nearly noon the following day. When Daniel came in, Willa May saw that his shirt was torn in three or four places and one sleeve was hanging by a thread. He was black and blue across his belly and ribs with one long angry scratch down his right cheek. "Set yourself down and let me tend to those bruises," she said. While Daniel took off what was left of his shirt, Willa May looked the boys over, but they appeared to be all right.

As she tended to Daniel, Willa May asked James Houston what had happened, knowing that she would never hear it from Daniel. James Houston looked from her to his pa, not knowing if he should say anything.

"I asked you what happened and I want to know right now," she repeated.

Shuffling from one foot to his other, James Houston said, "We found that stinking polecat, 'Lil Luther, in bed with that Mullens who-- uh, woman. Pa dragged him outside at gunpoint and once we were out there, Pa threw down his gun and said, 'I'm goin' to give you just as much of a chance as you gave my little girl.' He knocked 'Lil Luther flat on his back, leaving 'Lil Luther with a black eye of his own. Then 'Lil Luther stood up and tried to hit Pa, but he just left that there scratch. Pa belted 'Lil Luther right in the middle, making him double over. Then Pa knocked 'Lil Luther down again and this time he kicked him in the ribs when 'Lil Luther passed out." Here, James Houston paused, grinning broadly, "Pa done beat that no good sonofabitch to a bloody pulp."

Willa May looked down at Daniel and raised his face, forcing him to look at her. "Did you kill him?"

Daniel pulled away. "He was still breathing when we left."

"What are you goin' to do about the business now that there's bad blood between him and us?"

Daniel sighed wearily. He didn't appreciate her asking all these questions. "Fool woman questions," he called them. "I rode over to see Luther and Big Annie. I told them what I done. When they heard what 'Lil Luther did to Hattie Sue, they said I did the right thing and that 'Lil Luther needed to learn a lesson. They said they wouldn't be holding no grudge over it. Far as I'm concerned, my partner is your uncle. Always has been. Not that low-down piece of shit they call their grandson. So I reckon that means we're still in business."

Willa May breathed a sigh of relief. Relief that Daniel didn't kill 'Lil Luther, although, she knew deep down that he had wanted to. Relief that Daniel wasn't going to hang because of some no-account, good for nothing bastard like 'Lil Luther. Relief that there wasn't going to be any feud breaking out between them and her kin.

"In that case, Grandpa, I reckon you might as well sit right there and let me fix you some vittles."

"Who are you calling grandpa? I might have twenty plus years on that no good 'Lil Luther, but I whupped him, didn't I?"

She grinned down at Daniel. "Yep. I'd say you whupped him good, too...Grandpa."

She could see that Daniel was getting irritable about this grandpa business. He looked at her and grumbled, "Girl, I'd like to know why you think you can call me an old grandpa when I done beat a snot nosed sonofabitch half my age. I'd just like to know."

"'Cause you are a grandpa...or at least you're goin' to be."

Daniel looked at her a full minute, letting what she had said sink in. He turned from her to Hattie Sue who was standing beside James Houston. Hattie Sue looked at her pa and nodded.

"Damn!" Daniel slammed his fist down on the table. "If I'd known that, I would've killed the little bastard and got it over with."

Chapter Six

Hattie Sue stayed with them all winter, growing bigger every day it seemed. In January, Willa May started getting the morning sickness, too. Hattie Sue couldn't have been happier, what with her and her mama both having babies. But after fifteen others, Willa May didn't quite share her excitement. Every time Hattie Sue's baby moved, she gasped in delight and smiled as if it were the first time she had felt the baby move. Sickly as Willa May felt, she tried to understand Hattie Sue's wonderment about it all, trying to remember back when she was carrying Josie. For the life of her, she couldn't help getting exasperated now and then with the way Hattie Sue carried on.

Her exasperation grew into guilt that she wasn't as excited as she had been the first time. Each new life was a miracle in itself and not to be taken lightly, she reminded herself. But after bringing up her food all day and being too nauseous to stand, she just couldn't make herself feel that same wonderment. Some days she didn't get out of bed, she was so sick. Daniel was used to her morning sickness and didn't fret as much as he once had. It seemed to Willa May that everybody else was going about their business and she was the only one who couldn't. It was purely aggravating.

Hattie Sue was around seven months along when Willa May reached her third month. She was beginning to feel a bit better with each passing day. They sat down one day to work on her baby's quilt, a log cabin pattern in pinks and blues, when Willa May felt a strange sensation come over her, all hot and cold at the same time. Feeling like she was going to lose her lunch, she said, "Hattie Sue, you'd better help me over to bed. I'm feeling poorly again." They were half way across the room when Willa May felt a sharp pain down low in her belly followed by a warm, wetness in the seat of her pantaloons. The room spun around her, growing dark. "Mommy, are you all right?" she heard Hattie Sue say from a great distance. She sank deeper into the darkness rising around her.

She woke up in their bed and found Daniel was next to her. "What

143

happened?" she asked, wondering why she felt so weak.

"You lost the baby, Willa May."

She was surprised that after fifteen babies she would miscarry now. Thinking of how miserable she had felt and how much Hattie Sue's excitement had annoyed her, she wondered if she was to blame. Maybe she hadn't wanted this baby enough. She turned away from Daniel and wept, wishing she could take it all back and give Daniel another healthy baby. Daniel lay down beside her and took her in his arms. He held her all night.

The following week Daniel was still worried about her, claiming she looked too pale. He insisted on taking her to the doctor, but Willa May didn't want to go. What could the doctor do now? Daniel was set on it, though, so she went. Old Doc Merriam had died with the smallpox the year their babies had died. He had treated so many of the people in the valley who were dying from the disease that he caught it himself. Since his death, his son, Young Doc had taken over. She didn't feel as comfortable in Young Doc's care, but she followed him into the examining room.

After examining her, he said, "Mrs. Shrewsbury --" (Old Doc had always called her "Willa May".) -- "after having so many babies, I think your body has come to a point where it won't be able to carry another baby to full term."

"Are you saying I can't have any more babies?" Her heart was broken just thinking about it.

"Probably not. Besides, you have ten healthy children and I should think that would keep you plenty busy."

"Can't you do something to make it so I can have more babies?"

"Not really. The best thing would be for you to try not to get pregnant again. With each miscarriage, you'll be endangering your own health."

She stared at the young man and wondered if he had children of his own. She wondered if he knew any of the joy that babies bring into a person's life. Here he was, trying to take that joy away from her.

When she came out of the examining room, Daniel asked her what the doctor had said as he helped her into the wagon.

"Nothing useful," she answered, deciding that maybe this young doctor didn't know as much as he thought he did.

Daniel looked at her and asked, "What's that supposed to mean?"

"Just what I said. Nothing useful."

When she didn't say anything more, Daniel turned his attention to the mules and they headed home.

Hattie Sue went into labor near the end of April. Since it was her first, she was in labor almost twenty hours before the baby decided it was time to make his entrance. Daniel paced the floor for hours while Effie Lee and Willa May tended to Hattie Sue. The pain grew to the point that she couldn't stand it. Hattie Sue screamed with each new pain. Daniel couldn't bear it so he sought escape at Elroy's. When Willa May went to tell him he had a grandson, he and Elroy were halfway through a jug. They finished it in celebration of the new baby, but not before Willa May sat down and helped herself to a swig, too. She figured she had done all the work so she should reap some of the reward. She could tell it shocked Daniel to see her taking a drink of whiskey, but he didn't say anything. Like her, he must have thought she deserved it.

Hattie Sue named her baby Ernest Roy. Over eight pounds, he was a big baby. He was the very picture of 'Lil Luther with coal black hair and brown eyes just like 'Lil Luther's. Every time Willa May looked at the baby, she couldn't help but think of 'Lil Luther. She never mentioned it to Hattie Sue. Nor did Hattie Sue ever remark on the resemblance. But Willa May was sure Hattie Sue must have noticed it.

Ernest Roy was four weeks old when Walt Whitman came home on summer break from college. He was making good grades and picking up extra work at the general store, doing the bookkeeping. The whole family was glad to see him again. They went on about his mustache, a big handlebar mustache like the famous western hero, Wyatt Earp, wore. In Willa May's eyes, he looked so much like her pa, she couldn't believe it. She only wished that her pa had lived to see what a fine young man her boy had become. And smart. Why, he talked endlessly about the things he had learned in history and literature classes, sounding so educated. Folks might say he had changed, but Willa May could see he had grown. Education had done that for him. True, he even sounded different from the rest of the family, what with his schooling. But he never looked down on his kin like Josie. As a gift, he brought Willa May a book of poems by Miss Emily Dickinson and a copy of <u>Great Expectations</u>. Laughing at the title, she said, "And that's just what we've got for you, Son, mighty great expectations."

He chuckled along with her. Walt Whitman was so easy going and good natured. He said, "Mommy, wait till you read some of those poems. You're going to just love Miss Dickinson's style."

Opening the precious book, Willa May said, "Show me some right now."

Together, they read twenty or more poems, sharing in the beauty of such writing. When they finally looked up from the book, the sun was setting and Willa May realized she had forgotten all about supper. Daniel had been sitting back, watching them and listening to each poem. He leaned forward in his chair and said, "That's all right, darlin'. It was worth it just to hear the two of you so fired up over them poems." Turning to Hattie Sue and Effie Lee, he said, "Girls, help your mama get supper on."

Later that night, they sat out on the porch and listened to Walt Whitman read from the other book about a young Englishman named Pip. Willa May could tell that it was going to be one humdinger of a story. Even Elroy started coming by each evening just to hear Walt Whitman read another chapter.

Listening to their boy's voice in the warm summer night and watching the lightning bugs pierce the darkness with spots of yellow light, Willa May wished that summer could go on forever. It was so good to have her family whole again. She knew it would never really be whole again, not with Josie gone. But she had come to accept that Josie was where she wanted to be and was happy there, living in her big house and wearing her lace dresses. On those summer nights, she liked to think that her five babies they had lost were there with them, too, in spirit. With Walt Whitman home again, she almost expected 'Lil Daniel to come through the door right behind Walt Whitman. Her heart filled with a hollow emptiness when she remembered that 'Lil Daniel was never going to come home again. But those moments of sorrow passed. Mostly, she just enjoyed the stillness of the hills around her and the quiet company of being together those warm, wonderful nights. She savored the peacefulness she felt.

While Walt Whitman attended Marshall College, he got the idea that he might want to teach at one of the colleges around the state. It seemed they were constantly hearing about new colleges being built. Concord and then Glenville back in 'seventy-two followed by Salem and Morris Harvey. West Virginia State opened three years later, finished just as Walt Whitman was about to graduate. There was a university in Morgantown that had sprung up during the war, along with some smaller colleges that sprang up in the years following the war. Like Willa May, folks were pining for a good education, wanting their children to have every opportunity they hadn't had. She and Daniel were so proud of Walt Whitman that they made the trip -- two days in their wagon -- all the way to Huntington to see their boy get his diploma. Lizzy and Creedy made the trip with them and Elroy came along, too. Lizzy shook her head and said, "Well, I declare. I never thought I'd live to see the day when one of my own flesh and blood graduated from a real fine college like this."

Even Daniel was all smiles that day in a brand new store bought suit, nearly dancing down the street as they walked into the college chapel where the graduation ceremony was held. Willa May spotted Walt Whitman in the third row right away. He was wearing a black robe just like a preacher. He had a funny looking flat hat on his head with a black tassel that looked like the kind folks used to tie back fancy curtains. At the end of the ceremony, the young men gave everyone a shock when they all stood up and tossed their funny looking hats high into the air. They let out a whoop that could be heard on the outskirts of town.

Elroy and Daniel started whooping along with the boys, drawing the attention of everyone around them. Next thing Willa May knew, Daniel swung her up in the air. She held onto the pretty new hat she had bought just for the occasion. Creedy giggled to see them acting so foolishly. Willa May knew they must have looked a sight, but she didn't give a hoot. They were just so proud; they were bursting at their seams.

After the ceremony, they attended a fancy tea the college had set up at the home of the president. Looking at the tall white pillars lining the broad verandah of the mansion, Willa May was reminded of Josie and her big house. She only wished that Josie could have been there to see her baby brother get his degree that day. Maybe then she wouldn't feel so ashamed of them. Maybe, too, Josie would see that they were doing all they could to give their babies a good start in life. Willa May thought of writing to tell Josie about Walt Whitman's graduation and ask her to go since it had been her money that had made it all possible. But Daniel put his foot down, saying that if Josie wanted to know how they were getting by, she knew where she could find them. No amount of arguing on Willa May's part would convince him otherwise.

At the tea, there were long tables set out with crisp white tablecloths and laden with cookies, little cakes, fruit tarts, and big silver bowls filled with ripe red strawberries. Several colored men in black suits made their way through the crowd, pouring coffee and tea from elegant silver pots. Biting into one of the strawberries, Lizzy leaned over and whispered gleefully, "I'll never forget this day as long as I live."

Willa May smiled back and said, "Me neither, Mama. This is a moment I'll cherish forever. I only wish Pa and Big Jim could be here to see this."

Lizzy nodded, looking sad as she remembered her Napoleon. "They wouldn't have missed this for the world, Willa May. It sure would have been nice to have all our loved ones gathered here to see this."

"You know, Mama, I know this is goin' to sound right foolish, but I like to think that Pa and Big Jim are here today, along with 'Lil Daniel and my other babies. Here in spirit, if you know what I'm saying."

Walt Whitman had joined them and heard what she had said. "Mommy, I know what you mean. I was packing away my things, getting ready to come home, and I found a letter that 'Lil Daniel had written to me, saying how much he missed us all. It's funny, I'd completely forgotten about that letter. When I read it, it was like hearing 'Lil Daniel right there next to me saying he still missed us and wished he could be here with us. So maybe you're right about all our kin being here, even if it's only in spirit."

Willa May stood on tiptoe and gave Walt Whitman a kiss on his cheek. "Thank you, Son, I'm glad you told me that. Makes me feel like they really are here."

Lizzy smiled and nodded, sharing the same sentiment. Elroy rolled his way through the crowd over to them and asked Willa May to fetch him some chocolate cake. Some of the people nearby stared at Elroy and Creedy, looking uncomfortable with the two disabled men in their midst. Willa May wanted to tell them they could just stop staring, that each in his own way was a hero. Both faced things the rest of them didn't have to think about, being whole and healthy. A woman dressed in an expensive looking peach colored dress glared at Elroy disapprovingly as he sat a few feet away, eating his chocolate cake and having the time of his life. Willa May returned her long stare. The woman saw Willa May watching her and looked away abruptly, but not before she had the good grace to look embarrassed at being caught.

Nothing seemed to faze Walt Whitman, though. He was simply

glad to have his family with him on his special day. Elroy, finishing off his cake, looked up at Walt Whitman and said, "So, what're you goin' to do now that you finished your schooling, Son?"

"Well, sir," he began. Walt Whitman always addressed Elroy with respect, telling Willa May once that to him, Elroy was the closest thing he knew to a war hero, aside from his own pa. "I've been writing some articles for the local paper and I got a letter the other day from that MacCorkle fellow who's running for governor."

"You don't say." Willa May gasped. "But I thought you wanted to be a teacher."

Walt Whitman nodded. "I plan to teach eventually, but it seems that MacCorkle would like for me to write some speeches for his campaign. He sent me a list of several issues he wants to address. Anyway, if he likes my speeches, he might hire me."

"You mean you're goin' to be telling him what to say about things?" Elroy didn't quite get the gist of it.

"Not exactly, sir. He's told me how he stands on these issues and I'm supposed to put it all down in a way that will make the voters respond to him with their votes come election day."

With his face screwed up, Elroy said, "You mean he can't just come right out and say how he feels and be done with it?"

Walt Whitman laughed. "If all politicians said how they really felt, nobody would vote for them."

"Ain't that a little bit like cheating?"

"No, Uncle Elroy." Walt Whitman grinned. "That's a little bit like politics."

Everyone laughed, except for Elroy who was still thinking hard on this new piece of knowledge. Daniel joined them in listening to Walt Whitman's plans. He clapped his boy on the back and said, "Best of luck to you, Son, if that's what you want to do with your life. Speaking for myself, I don't have much use for politicians and all their fancy talk. Just as soon they leave me be. But if you think this MacCorkle can do some good, then you owe it to yourself and to the people across the state to do your best for him."

Willa May looked at Daniel, thinking that this was the most she had ever heard him say about any subject other than hunting and farming since they had been married. Reading her thoughts, Daniel said, "Well, now, enough of my preachifying for the day. Let's all go get some supper. We've had a mighty big day and come morning, we've got a long trip back."

At their hotel, they sat down to a big steak dinner topped off with homemade boysenberry cobbler with whipped cream. That night in their room, Daniel put his arms around Willa May in bed. As he kissed her neck, he said, "I've got to hand it to you, Willa May. I guess you were right about keeping all that money Josie sent you and putting it to such good use. That boy of ours made me powerful proud here today. Powerful proud."

On the way home, Willa May listened to Daniel pointing out to Walt Whitman where the timber men were cutting down trees. Shaking his head, he said it was a sin and a shame what those timber companies were doing to the mountains. After the war was over, there was plenty of forest land everywhere. Wherever Willa May looked now, she saw nothing but blackened stumps of trees. The hills had been stripped, parched by fires, then plowed up by the railroads that were cropping up all over the state. These railroad and timber companies who were ravaging the forests were owned by men who didn't even live in West Virginia. Looking at the mountains, Daniel grew angry. When they reached Gauley Bridge and saw the river clogged with lumber for the timber mills, Daniel was mad as an old wet hen. "I'll be damned if they're goin' to cut my trees down for their gallderned mills!" he spat. "Any sonofabitch that touches even one tree on my property will meet up with the barrel end of my shotgun."

Willa May had to agree with Daniel. She was amazed at the ugly blackened hillsides they were passing. Living up on their mountain, they hadn't been affected by the big boom of business around the state: railroads, timber mills, coal mines. That seemed far away to them like the names they heard being dropped about -- Camden, Davis, Elkins, and Huntington. To Willa May and Daniel, they were merely names.

In July, Willa May was helping Hattie Sue with Ernest Roy's bath when she heard a knock at the door. She opened it to find a stranger dressed in a tight fitting suit. The suit was made of a large beige and brown check fabric that made the man look like a checkerboard. With a round face and a potbelly that threatened to pop the buttons right off his starched shirt, he politely introduced himself. He immediately inquired whether she did much sewing. Willa May laughed, "I'm a woman, aren't I? I do a pile of sewing. Mending, quilting, and making almost all the clothes we wear."

The man smiled broadly and said, "Well, Mrs..."

"Shrewsbury."

"Well then, Mrs. Shrewsbury, I believe I've got the very thing for you. Just looky here at this wonderful machine." He swept his arm in a grandiose gesture toward his wagon standing in front of the house.

Willa May glanced at Hattie Sue who shrugged, a curious look on her face. Willa May shrugged, too, and followed the man out the door to his wagon. Hattie Sue trailed close behind with Ernest Roy in her arms. The man helped them both up onto the back of his wagon and uncovered a shiny black sewing machine with elaborate curlicues painted on it in silver. In just seconds, the man had the machine threaded and ready. He showed Willa May how it worked by pressing his foot on a pedal at the base of the machine and making the needle go up and down so fast she couldn't even count the stitches. Taking the material out from under the needle, he showed her the lovely even stitches it had made. Willa May took the material and gave it a tug to see if the stitches would unravel. It seemed way too fast to do real sewing. To her surprise, the material held. She showed it to Hattie Sue who was just as amazed. Willa May thought about how much easier it would be if she had this remarkable machine and how much more time she would have to do other chores. "Show me how it works," she said.

She sat down on a little stool with a velvet cushion and the man proceeded to show her how to thread the machine. Once she had that accomplished, he put some material under a metal plate and locked it in place, then he dropped a lever and lowered the needle right over the material. "Now," he said, "press real gentle on the foot pedal down there and give this here wheel a little turn."

Willa May did what he said, but apparently not gently enough. The needle flew up and down so fast, it became a blur. With a little squeal of surprise, she pulled her foot off the pedal and jumped back from the machine. The needle came to a dead stop. "Lordy," she cried, "what did I do?"

The salesman chuckled and said, "No harm done." He gestured with both hands to calm her down. "Just takes a real light touch. You'll get it. Try again."

Afraid that she would press too hard again, she tried once more. This time the needle started off with a low whir. The salesman showed her how to feed the material evenly and keep it straight so that

151

her stitches would look even. Pulling out the material she had sewn, she could see where her first stitches -- the fast ones -- were and where they evened out and looked almost as good as the salesman's. Willa May showed it to Hattie Sue who said, "Oh, Mommy. Just think how much this here machine would help you."

Willa May nodded. "Yes, it surely would, but how much does this wondrous contraption cost, Mister?"

Chuckling again, the salesman thumbed his bright green suspenders and rocked back on his heels. "Just fifty-nine ninety-nine, Mrs. Shrewsbury. A dandy bargain. I'm sure you'll agree."

"Seems a right fair price, all right, but I don't have fifty-nine ninety-nine."

The man cleared his throat like he had something caught in it that wouldn't come or go. "Is your man about?"

"Why?" Willa May wondered if maybe this sewing machine salesman might be a sneaking revenuer just trying to trick her.

"Oh, I just thought maybe him and me could come to some terms about this marvelous machine and I could just leave it here with you today."

She looked up at the sun and saw that it was almost straight above them. "He should be home for lunch directly, if you're of a mind to wait."

"What's for lunch?" He grinned, looking like a fox that had just spotted dinner in the hen house.

"Beans, turnips, cornbread, poke greens, and rice pudding."

The salesman rubbed his belly and licked his lips. "Why, I ain't had rice pudding in a coon's age."

"Then I reckon you'll want to stay and sit down to eat with us, too."

"Well now, I thank you kindly for your warm hospitality," he beamed.

He sat out on the porch, sipping some cool buttermilk and swiping a big white hanky across his sweaty face every now and then. Daniel and the boys came down from the woods around noon and Willa May told him about the wonderful sewing machine. The salesman introduced himself, pumping Daniel's hand like he was pumping for water. He told Daniel how much Willa May deserved this fantastic machine. She could see that Daniel didn't want to seem downright rude, but this chatty little man was getting on his nerves. Daniel turned to her and said, "Willa May, do you really want this thing?"

152

Before she could answer, Hattie Sue said, "Oh Pa, it'd be such a help to Mommy. She'd have more time to spend doing other things."

Daniel looked from Hattie Sue to Willa May. She shrugged. "Only trouble is the machine costs fifty-nine ninety-nine. We haven't got that kind of money to waste on such a luxury."

Daniel could see the problem right away. Willa May knew that he was torn over what to say. He didn't want to deny her something that she really wanted, knowing she never asked for anything, but he still couldn't afford it. The salesman spoke up. "Well now, Mr. Shrewsbury, I think we can reach an agreement, if you're running low on cash at the moment."

"How's that?" Willa May could hear the suspicion in Daniel's voice.

"How much of this land do you own?"

"Enough and then some, I reckon."

"Well, you could sign over some of it to me...in payment for this miraculous machine. It'll be a magnificent gift for your lovely wife."

Daniel looked at the man. He didn't say a word, just kept staring. Willa May knew he was just about at the end of his rope with this weasel and she figured it was just because of her wanting the machine that he didn't pick the man up and throw him out on the seat of his checkered pants.

The salesman couldn't read Daniel like Willa May could and it was almost his undoing. He made the mistake of saying, "So what do you say, Mr. Shrewsbury? Your land for this machine."

"You know, Mister, I recollect now that I've been hearing about this sewing machine salesman who's been taking folks' land in trade for his machines. Making quite a name for yourself, I'd say. Take a look at this land. Now it's goin' to be here when you're rotting in a pine box, but this machine might last ten years, if we're lucky. I'm telling you right now, ain't no way I'm goin' to give up my land. Land's a precious thing. That machine, while it might do all the things you say it can, still ain't nothing but screws and bolts. So you're wasting my time and yours if you think you can gyp me out of my land."

Daniel had been moving a step at a time toward the salesman, forcing him to back up with every sentence. They were almost to the door. Willa May expected Daniel to spin the portly little man around and give him a kick in the seat of his pants that would send him head first out the door. But Walt Whitman said, "Pa, you don't have to give this man any land. And Mommy, I'd consider it an honor if you'd let me buy this sewing machine for you."

"But Son, how are you goin' to buy something so dear?" Willa May asked.

"I told you I had a job keeping records for a store while I was at school. And I set aside a little nest egg."

"I can't let you spend your savings on me."

"Mommy, there'll be plenty left over. Please, I really want to do this for you."

Willa May shook her head. "No. Never."

"Fine. Then I'll buy it for myself."

"What? What on earth would you do with a sewing machine, Walt Whitman?"

"Why, I'd give it to you," he grinned.

"Well, I won't take it. I won't let you spend your money on me. You'll need it if you get that job working for that MacCorkle fellow."

"But that's just it. I won't need it if I get the job. They'll be paying me plenty and I won't need any of this money. Please? Won't you let me do this one thing for you?"

She looked to Daniel, hoping he would tell Walt Whitman to hush and keep his hard earned money for himself. But Daniel shrugged and said, "I reckon it'd be mighty poor manners for you to turn down a fine gift from your boy, Willa May."

"Mommy, please, let Walt Whitman do this one thing for you. He really wants to and you know you want that sewing machine. Please?" Hattie Sue begged.

Everyone looked at Willa May, waiting for her to say something. The salesman looked at her with outright desperation. With a sigh, she gave in. "Oh, all right. But you've got to promise me, Walt Whitman, that from now on you'll spend all your money you earn on yourself. No more fancy gifts for your mama. You hear?"

Walt Whitman put his arms around her and kissed her cheek. "I promise, Mommy."

That evening Willa May put on a show with her new sewing machine. Even Daniel had to admit it was nothing short of a miracle. When she had finished her sewing demonstration, she hugged Walt Whitman again, thanking him.

Daniel heard a few months later that the sewing machine salesman was making a killing off poor people across the state. He owned huge holdings of land, growing rich off of it. Luckily for the salesman,

Daniel didn't let him have any of his land because all he would have gotten was what he could eat as he lay face down in it.

In August, Daniel insisted on taking Willa May to a state fair being held in Charleston. She could have thought of a thousand things she needed to do instead, but Daniel was set on it. She gave in, figuring it was probably more for menfolk than for women. Daniel was eager to enter his hog, Hannibal, in a livestock contest to see who owned the biggest hog in the state. Hannibal wasn't only big; he was mean, too. He would just as soon bite a chunk out of any of them as to look at them. The youngsters were too terrified to get near him, but Hannibal had decided that he liked Elroy. Willa May felt maybe it was because Elroy, sitting on his little wheeled cart, was nearly the same height as Hannibal. She thought Hannibal probably liked it that he could look Elroy in the eye. Whatever the reason, the mammoth hog wouldn't let anyone else near him but Elroy. For Elroy, he behaved so politely that he seemed as tame as Daniel's hound dog, Roscoe.

Hannibal was black and white with a huge pink snout and a grunt so deep and nasty that it sounded like it was coming from a grizzly. Willa May had seen many a hog in her day, but Hannibal was the biggest by far. Elroy and the boys kept going on and on about Hannibal. It sounded to Willa May like they were jawing about the whale that swallowed old Jonah in the Good Book. All their talk gave Daniel the idea to enter him at the fair. He came back from his deliveries with a poster that someone had nailed to a tree on their property. When Willa May read the poster to Daniel, the boys begged Daniel right away to enter Hannibal.

Looking at James Houston who was carrying on the loudest, Daniel said, "Now, Son, tell me just how in blue blazes I'm supposed to get that mean sonofabitch all the way to Charleston without him killing one of us or tearing my wagon apart?"

Walt Whitman spoke up. "Pa, I don't think you'd have any problem if you put Elroy in the back of the wagon. Then you could tie Hannibal in back where he could see Elroy. He'd think he was following Elroy. And we all know how Hannibal likes Elroy."

Daniel rubbed his whiskery chin. After a minute or two, he nodded, "Yep. Walt Whitman, you might just have something there. If Hannibal thinks he's following Elroy, it might just work, at that."

Seeing how this conversation was headed, Elroy said, "Well, I can't just sit back there on the end of the wagon by myself. If you hit a rut, I could end up riding Hannibal all the way to Charleston!"

Everyone burst out laughing at the thought of Elroy riding into the fair on Hannibal's back, screaming and hollering. Elroy didn't laugh at all. He was deadly serious. Elroy didn't trust Hannibal quite the way Hannibal trusted him. The problem was that nobody else wanted to take the chance of falling off right in Hannibal's face, either, so the room grew quiet again.

Walt Whitman came up with a solution. "Pa, why don't you sit in the back with Elroy and I can drive the team? Mommy and Hattie Sue can sit up front with me."

Even Daniel squirmed in his chair at the thought of coming that close to Hannibal. After a minute of thinking on it, though, he said, "You're right, Walt Whitman. It's the only way."

Three weeks later on a Sunday morning, they got up at sunrise and packed up the back of the wagon with some food to eat on the way. They packed some jars of preserves that Hattie Sue and Willa May had made: elderberry, blackberry, and raspberry. Hattie Sue had baked her favorite cake -- blackberry jam cake with caramel icing -- to enter in the baking contest. Hattie Sue hugged and kissed Ernest Roy at least twenty times before she finally relinquished him to Effie Lee to watch while they were gone. It was the first time Hattie Sue had left her baby and she cried like she was leaving him for good as they pulled away from the cabin. It upset Walt Whitman to see her carry on so. Willa May didn't dare to look back at Daniel, knowing he couldn't take tears from his womenfolk. She thought she heard him clear his throat a couple of times before they got down off the mountain into Gauley Bridge. Trying to get Hattie Sue's mind off her baby, Willa May said, "Seems like every time we come down off the mountain, this little old town has some new building or house that wasn't here before."

Walt Whitman picked up on her idea. "Mommy, I'd say in another ten years, this whole valley will start to build up in a way we never dreamed."

"Why do you say that?" Willa May had lived her entire life on that mountain and she couldn't imagine the sweeping change that Walt Whitman was describing.

"There are going to be lots of people wanting the coal and lumber we've got here. That means workers to bring out the coal and cut down the trees. And all those workers are going to have to have some place to live. There's even more happening every day in the rest of the world: new inventions, new discoveries in science and medicine. Why, I read last spring about two brothers who say they think they can build a flying machine."

"No!" Willa May gasped. After a moment, she laughed, saying, "What kind of fools think they can fly?"

"It's going to happen, Mommy, just wait and see."

Daniel had been listening in the back of the wagon and said, "You ain't goin' to catch me in no flying machine. I'll just do my traveling on the ground, if it's all the same, thank you. But Elroy, here, might want to try flying. Ain't that right, Elroy?"

Elroy wouldn't take his eyes off of Hannibal who seemed content to gaze right back at him. He said, "I'm with Daniel. If the good Lord had meant for a man to fly, He would've made us all with wings."

Hattie Sue surprised everyone, saying, "Walt Whitman, if you ever see one of them flying machines, would you take me to see it, too?"

"Sure will, Sis. But I have to say I never would have taken you for such an adventurer."

"Oh, it ain't for me. It's for Ernest Roy. I want my boy to have a chance to see things and do things, so he'll see that there's a whole big world out there just waiting for folks to change it and shape it for what's to come."

Everyone stared at Hattie Sue. Her voice was filled with all the hopes and dreams a young mother could hold in her heart for her child. It was the first time that it really struck Willa May that her daughter was a grown woman, a mother like her and her mama before her. Hattie Sue wasn't her little girl any more. She made up her mind then and there to start treating her daughter more like her friend than one of her babies, to start seeing her as an equal.

Hearing his sister pouring out her feelings, Walt Whitman was stirred, too. His admiration for his sister shone on his face when he looked at Hattie Sue and said, "I promise I'll help you see to it that Ernest Roy gets all the chances you want for him. Remember, you can always turn to me, Sis."

Willa May felt tears stinging her eyes. They sounded so serious; it pierced her heart. Lying in bed with Daniel that night she grew teary all over again. Daniel said, "Now Girl, what's gotten into you, carrying on like this? It's only right that Walt Whitman would look out for his sister. That's what family's all about. Just means we've done a good job raising them, that's all. That ain't something to cry about."

But that morning, when Walt Whitman caught her dabbing at her eyes, he turned his attention back to the team and called back to his pa, "How's Hannibal doing back there?"

As if the beast knew they were talking about him, Hannibal grunted a loud reply. It sounded like the earth was giving way under them. Elroy said, "Can you pick it up a tad, Walt Whitman? Old Hannibal's looking like he could charge this here wagon any minute."

"Do you want to stop and let him rest a bit?"

"Hell, no," Elroy called. "Better just get us there so we can shut him up in a pen and be done with it!"

Walt Whitman grinned, detecting more than a hint of terror in Elroy's voice. He laughed and said to Willa May in a low voice, "Sounds like Hannibal's got a case of unrequited love."

"If you mean it's a lost cause, I'm afraid you're right. Your pa says Elroy won't show it, but he's mortally afraid of that old hog."

They giggled, hoping Elroy wouldn't hear them in the back. "I expect you're right, there," Walt Whitman agreed.

By the time they got to Charleston, Elroy was in bad need of a drink. Once the men got Hannibal settled into a pen, they went off in search of a tavern. Willa May and Hattie Sue began looking for the booths for the baking contest and the judging of the preserves. Both of them were surprised to see such a crowd of people, some bringing livestock while others brought a variety of baked goods to enter in the contests. After Willa May and Hattie Sue left off the cake and preserves, they strolled by the nearby stands. They came upon a quilt display. Looking at all the beautiful quilts, Willa May felt like she was in quilters' heaven. There were quilts appliqued with flowers, two Sun Bonnet Sue patterns, and one that was called a picture album quilt with each square showing some happening in that woman's life. There were patchwork quilts: Tree of Life, Schoolhouse, Flower Basket, Nine Patch, Star of Bethlehem, and Drunkard's Path. There were also some Crazy Quilts in precious velvets and satins. One quilt caught Willa May's eye. She had never seen anything like it before. Across a black field was a large scarlet diamond inside a dark blue square. The pattern was bold and daring. When Willa May asked one of the judges about it, the woman told her that it was made by an Amish woman.

"Who?" Willa May asked, never having heard of these "Amish" before.

The woman explained. "They're a religious group. Call themselves 'Plain People'. They wear only dark colors. But, as you can see, quilts are a sort of outlet where the women can use color."

"What do you call this design?"

"Diamond In A Square, same as it looks."

"You reckon I could see it up close?" she asked. "I promise I won't get anything on it, I just want to see the quilting stitches up close."

The woman seemed reluctant, but she let Willa May past the tables lined up in front of the quilts hanging around the tent. When she got up to the quilt, Willa May was amazed at the fine, neat stitches and all the fancy designs the stitching made -- feathers, hearts, flowers -- black stitches against the black material. Stepping back to appraise it further, she said to Hattie Sue, "I've got to make a quilt just like this one. For 'Lil Daniel."

Hattie Sue looked puzzled. Unable to take her eyes off the quilt, Willa May said, "This quilt says everything I feel when I'm reminded of our 'Lil Daniel -- the black reminds me of our grieving, the blues and reds remind me of the daring boy we raised. The way they stand out against the black background reminds me of how courageous 'Lil Daniel was. He always dreamed of goin' on some grand adventure. I just have to make this. It'll be like a memorial to my boy." She said the words with such fierce determination that Hattie Sue knew her mama was bound to do this one thing or die trying.

Willa May turned back to the woman. "Where can I find the woman who sewed this quilt?"

"She said they were goin' to have their lunch. You might try over in that big field yonder, past the livestock pens. You'll know them by the way they're dressed."

They found a group of men and women dressed in solemn colors, the men with long beards and the women wearing black bonnets. The group was resting on some quilts under a shady oak tree. They had food set out and were eating together. When Hattie Sue and Willa May came upon them, they stopped talking, looking at the two strangers in their midst.

"A woman over by the quilt stand said that I could find the woman who made that Diamond In A Square quilt -- the one that's hanging up for the contest -- over here with you folks." The small cluster remained silent, staring with grave faces at Willa May and Hattie Sue. For a moment, Willa May wondered if she was breaking some rule of theirs by speaking to them. She offered an apology for interrupting their meal. She turned to leave when a young woman said, "I made that quilt."

Willa May watched as a woman around Hattie Sue's age stood up. She came over to them. "What can I do for thee?"

"I want to make a quilt like that one. For my boy. He died fighting Geronimo some years back and when I saw that quilt of yours, it reminded me of him."

The Amish woman nodded. A look of understanding passed between the two women. They came from different worlds, but being women, they both knew the heartaches being a woman carried. "How can I help thee?"

"I've made quilts for years, but I've never put so much stitching in them. Yours was so beautiful. I don't know if I can make such pretty designs with my stitching."

"Allow me to give thee some of my patterns."

Willa May shook her head. "I can't take your patterns. You'll be needing them."

"Please. Take them. I can make more. It's a gift the good Lord has blessed me with. Please let me give thee some."

Willa May relented, nodding politely. "I thank you kindly, Miss."

The woman walked over to one of the wagons and came back with some folded papers. "Thou may have these. I will pray that thy quilt is all thou wishes it to be."

"Thank you. That's mighty kind of you. I'm ever so grateful."

The young Amish woman said nothing more; she just turned and went back to her people. Willa May and Hattie Sue made their way back to the cake booth to wait for the judging to start. Hattie Sue's cake won a blue ribbon and Willa May's elderberry preserves came in first place for the preserves tasting. Even Hannibal made Daniel proud, taking the prize for the biggest hog in the state. While Willa May had a good time and was happy for Hattie Sue and Daniel, she couldn't wait to get home and start on her quilt for 'Lil Daniel, her memorial quilt.

Late in August, Hattie Sue took Ernest Roy and went with Glenny over to Lizzy's to help with the canning. The days were long and hot. The sun blazed like a scorching white ball of flame hanging over their heads. Willa May fretted about her mama working in the garden in that kind of heat and she told Creedy how worried she was. Creedy nodded, fretful too, and said, "I know, I know. No matter what I say, though, she's bound and determined to get out there and do her part." It came as a relief to Willa May when the kids offered to stay a spell and help out. Lizzy was tickled pink to have little Ernest Roy to spoil.

Willa May was expecting again, suffering morning sickness morning, noon, and night. She found herself wishing that Hattie Sue was home again, she felt so poorly. Effie Lee was a big girl, though, and she did Willa May's chores whenever she saw that her mama was sick. One day as they were canning, putting up corn and beets for the winter, Willa May started feeling hot and cold at the same time. The room began to swirl around her. She remembered feeling the same way when she lost her last baby. Frightened, she said, "Help me to my bed, Effie Lee. Then go fetch your pa."

"What's wrong, Mommy?" Willa May detected a tinge of fear in Effie Lee's voice as she wiped her hands on her apron, then helped her to the bed.

"Just fetch your pa. Now!" she cried as she felt a sharp pain in her groin.

Effie Lee turned and ran outside to get Daniel. By the time Daniel got to her, Willa May could feel warm sticky blood coming through her skirt. "It's happening again," she moaned. Her breath was coming hard between pains and the awful sickly feeling that continued to sweep over her. "I'm losing our baby."

Daniel said to Effie Lee, "Get James Houston and Walt Whitman to hitch up the team. Quick!"

Effie Lee rushed out the door. In a few minutes, Walt Whitman came in and said, "We're ready, Pa."

"Come here and carry the mattress out and lay it down in the back of the wagon."

Daniel lifted Willa May in his arms and carried her outside. Walt Whitman followed behind. He tossed the feather mattress in the wagon. Daniel lay Willa May on it as gently as he could, then he climbed in beside her. Looking up at the boys, he said, "Get down the mountain as fast as you can and we'll take your ma to the doctor down in Gauley Bridge."

The wagon took off. Even in her pain, Willa May could tell they were nearly flying, swinging around bends in the road. She was jostled about as they bumped along over deep ruts. Willa May clutched her stomach. When they pulled up in front of the doctor's office, Daniel jumped down and carried her inside. He rushed up to the nurse seated behind a big desk. Willa May left a crimson trail from all the blood she was losing.

"Come this way," the nurse ordered. Daniel followed her into a room with a cot against a wall. He placed Willa May on the cot. "I'll get the doctor," the nurse said. The last thing Willa May remembered was seeing the nurse rush out the door.

When she came to, she was still on the cot. Her insides felt sore. She started to sit up when a deep voice said, "Don't move. Just lie still, Mrs. Shrewsbury, and keep your legs elevated." She looked over at the doctor. He had gray hair and wore a white shirt with the sleeves rolled up. He peered through small, round spectacles as he wrote something. The doctor sat in front of a table just a few feet away from her cot. Scattered about on the table were jars and bottles of medicines and some shiny metal instruments.

"I lost my baby, didn't I?"

"Yes, you did." His chair was mounted on little wheels and he rolled around to look at her over the top of his glasses. "And you're damned lucky you didn't bleed to death."

Willa May turned her head toward the wall. She didn't want to hear this. She was too scared that this doctor was going to tell her what Young Doc Merriam had already said -- that she wasn't going to have any more babies.

"Do you know how worried your husband is, Mrs. Shrewsbury?"

When she didn't answer, he said, "I told him how lucky he is that you didn't die trying to carry another baby full term."

"You had no right scaring Daniel like that," she cried, knowing Daniel wouldn't want to try to have more children if he had heard such a thing.

"Do you want to die, Mrs. Shrewsbury? Because if you do, you're doing just what it'll take to kill yourself. Now Mr. Shrewsbury tells me you have a big family...ten children? I should think you'd want to live to see them grow up and have children of their own."

"I do!" Willa May cried, turning back to the doctor.

"Then why are you risking your life trying to have more children?"

"What else can I do?"

"That's what I'm going to talk to you about. I've already talked to your husband and he understands how important it's going to be that you follow my instructions. No slip-ups. No carelessness. Do you understand?"

Willa May nodded, tears streaming down her face. She knew that this doctor was going to tell her she couldn't be the wife to Daniel that she had always been. Her heart was breaking with each word he spoke.

When the doctor finished, he went to get Daniel. Willa May couldn't look at him, knowing that he knew what that doctor had been telling her. She stared at the wall, an ugly color of green, wishing for the second time in her life that Daniel would just leave and let her be. For the life of her, she couldn't look him in the face. Years ago, when she wished he would leave her alone, she had been afraid he would think she was still a little girl, not woman enough to marry. Now she was afraid he would think she was old and used up. Not woman enough to be desirable. Daniel waited until she could accept his being there. Hesitantly, he spoke to her in a way that would tell her he understood.

"If it's another woman you want, Daniel, I understand," Willa May sniffed, wiping at her tears.

"Girl, why on earth would I want someone else when it's always been you that I've wanted."

"Because I can't be the wife to you that I've always been. I'm not a woman any more," she blurted with a new rush of tears.

Daniel sat down on the cot beside her and took her chin in his hands. He turned her face toward him. "Willa May, you're more woman than any woman I've ever known. And what's more, you're my wife and always will be. Ain't no other woman could ever take your place, so you hush up this silly talk about not being a woman, you hear?" He leaned over and kissed her tenderly on her lips. She put her arms around his neck and held him to her, wishing she could turn back the hands of time, back to their first years when they were learning their way with each other. But she knew that time had a way of changing things they couldn't help. She didn't want to take the chance of dying and leaving Daniel behind. She wanted too much to keep on being with him and their children. When he sat up, Daniel looked her in the eye and said, "Promise me you'll do what that there doctor said to do. I can bear a lot of things, but I can't bear to think of losing you."

"I promise," she said.

Daniel nodded. "Doctor says we can take you home if you feel up to it, but you're not to get up and do no work for a full week."

Willa May agreed. Daniel lifted her and carried her out to their wagon. Walt Whitman and James Houston were there waiting for them. Willa May thought they looked like two old men with their worried faces and their grim silence.

By the time they pulled up to the cabin, the moon was high in the sky and the children were all in bed. Elroy was still sitting up on his porch. He wheeled himself over to them as Daniel got down from the wagon. "Is she goin' to be all right?" Elroy tried to sound sober, but Willa May could hear a slight slur in his words and she knew he had been into a jug.

Daniel leaned over and picked her up. Looking her in the eye, he said, "She's never been better." Elroy and the boys gave Daniel a peculiar look, but Willa May knew what he meant. She smiled up at him, loving him more than she ever thought possible.

At the end of a week, she was starting to get around again, doing some of the cooking and helping the little ones with their baths. One evening, as she was bathing Dora Lottie in the round tin tub, the child splashed and played gleefully. Suddenly she sat up straight and gazed at the wall. Later, when Willa May tried to describe it to Daniel, she said it was like Dora Lottie was waiting for something, listening to a voice Willa May couldn't hear. "Baby?" Willa May said uneasily. Dora Lottie didn't reply. Her eyes grew wide as she stared intently at the wall. Frightened, Willa May said louder, "Dora? Dora Lottie?" Dora Lottie sat mesmerized with big saucer eyes. When she still didn't answer, Willa May rushed to fetch Daniel. She had just reached the door when, behind her, Dora Lottie gasped loudly, crying, "Glenny!"

Willa May hadn't thought about Glenny and Hattie Sue since she had come home from the doctor's office. Now, looking at her little girl, she felt an overwhelming sense that something was wrong. She knew intuitively that something had happened to Glenny. Chills ran through her as she raced through the door, screaming, "Daniel! Daniel!"

She saw Daniel racing toward her and pulled him inside. He looked from Willa May to Dora Lottie who still sat transfixed. Looking back at Willa May, he saw that her face was chalky white. "What? What's wrong?"

"It's Glenny. Something's happened to Glenny!" she cried, pounding on Daniel's chest.

Daniel grabbed her by her shoulders and shook her. "Willa May, get hold of yourself. What are you saying?"

She told him what had happened with Dora Lottie. Daniel rushed over to where their baby sat splashing merrily now. Standing over the tub, Daniel looked from the little girl back to Willa May. She knew he was thinking that the whole thing was crazy -- "Crazy as a bedbug," he would say -- but that ominous feeling that something was amiss was still ripe inside her. "Please, Daniel. Just go see if he's all right. Please," she begged.

Not knowing what to make of all this, Daniel shook his head. Then rubbing the back of his neck, he said, "Okay, okay. I'll ride over right now. I'll take Walt Whitman with me. Just stop your fretting. You don't need to have a setback, you hear?"

Willa May nodded, feeling a flood of relief rush through her knowing that Daniel was going to see about Glenny. The two rode off, Daniel on his big gray and Walt Whitman on a chestnut mare with four white stockings and a little star over her eyes. Elroy watched them with Willa May as they disappeared in the darkness. "I'll stay up with you, Willa May, if you want."

"Thank you, Elroy. I'd like that," she said, never taking her eyes off of the two shadowy figures retreating into the night.

"I'm staying up, too, Mommy," James Houston spoke up.

"All right, but you've got to do extra chores come morning, what with your pa and your brother gone."

James Houston nodded. "I wouldn't sleep anyway."

Once they put the children to bed, they sat up on the porch, watching and waiting. Around midnight, Elroy rolled over to his cabin and brought back a jug. Willa May went inside and brought out some leftover cornbread and bacon. They ate, drank, watched, and waited some more. It was nearly three o'clock when Walt Whitman came riding up at a gallop. Willa May ran to him as he jumped down from the chestnut. "What is it? What's happened?"

"It's all right, Mommy. Glenny's goin' to be all right," Walt Whitman breathed.

"What happened?" she repeated.

Walt Whitman drew a long breath and said, "That damned 'Lil Luther. He came over to grandma's drunk and wanting to see Ernest Roy. Grandma was already in bed, thank goodness. So was Ernest Roy. When Hattie Sue wouldn't get the baby, 'Lil Luther started slapping her. Glenny jumped up and went for 'Lil Luther, but 'Lil Luther picked up a butcher knife and stabbed Glenny."

"Oh no!" Willa May gasped, nearly out of her mind with worry.

165

James Houston, seeing her sway on her feet, put his big arms around her. She tried to push him off, but he was too strong. He stood there, solid as a wall, holding her up.

Walt Whitman saw her swaying and said, "He's going to be all right, Mommy. Pa took him to Young Doc and he's got some stitches, but he's going to be fine."

"What about Hattie Sue? And the baby?"

"They're fine. As soon as 'Lil Luther stabbed Glenny, I guess he knew he'd gone too far. He dropped the knife and took off."

"Your pa. Where's your pa?" Willa May cried, knowing full well that Daniel would kill 'Lil Luther, for sure, if he found him.

"Pa's looking for 'Lil Luther."

"Take me to Glenny," she said. "Right now."

Walt Whitman looked from Willa May to Elroy and then to James Houston. He didn't want her to get any more upset than she was. Nor did he want to take the chance that the ride to Lizzy's would be too much for her after her miscarriage. But Willa May wasn't going to let her boy wake up hurt and frightened without her there. "I want you to take me to Glenny and I want to go now," she insisted.

"You've got to take her," James Houston said.

"Go ahead, Walt Whitman," Elroy agreed. "Glenny will be wanting his mama, I expect. We'll watch out for everything here. And tell Daniel if he finds that bastard, 'Lil Luther, I said to skin that sonofabitch alive!"

Willa May ran inside and stuffed some clothes into a bag then came back out. "I'm ready," she said. James Houston had hitched up the wagon and had it waiting. Walt Whitman tied his horse to the back of the wagon and helped his mama up. All Willa May could think of was getting to Glenny as fast as she could.

Chapter Seven

Daniel hunted 'Lil Luther across the state and into Kentucky where the boy had kin. After three weeks, Daniel came home. He told them that 'Lil Luther had holed up with some of his cousins. They had tried to surround Daniel and trap him, but Daniel was too clever for them. He headed up into the hills and hid, sleeping inside the hollow trunk of a sycamore tree. After five days, 'Lil Luther and his kin figured they had seen the last of Daniel and headed home. Daniel took them by surprise, racing out of the hills and blasting away with his rifle in one hand and his Colt .45 in the other. He winged most of them, taking careful aim when he came upon 'Lil Luther staggering around the corner of the cabin. He blasted one of 'Lil Luther's knees to kingdom come. 'Lil Luther fell to the ground, writhing in agony as he held his bloody leg. Reining in his horse, Daniel shot him in the shoulder. The big gray pranced beside 'Lil Luther who lay screaming in a pool of blood. Daniel glared down the long barrel of his rifle at him. "If I ever see your face again, I'll shoot you dead."

The law chased Daniel across the state line into West Virginia. When the sheriff heard Daniel's side of the story, he saw the whole thing as self-defense. He had heard 'Lil Luther's kinfolk boasting about how they had scared off a man who had come looking for them. The sheriff warned Daniel, "You'd better stay on your side of the state line, Shrewsbury. Next time, them boys will be ready for you."

Daniel looked him right back in the eye and said, "As long as that polecat, 'Lil Luther, stays put, them boys won't have to worry about me again. But if he comes near my family again, ain't nobody who can keep me from killing him."

The sheriff looked at Daniel long and hard. Giving a slight nod, he turned and headed back for Kentucky. When Daniel got home, he asked Willa May, "How's Glenny?"

"Mighty sore. 'Lil Luther got him low in the ribs. Young Doc says that was what saved him. He's inside. Go on in and see him."

Seeing his pa, Glenny tried to sit up, but Daniel motioned for him

167

to stay put. Daniel ruffled Glenny's red curly hair and asked, "How you feeling, Son?"

"Okay, I reckon," Glenny said. He looked afraid as if he thought his pa would be mad at him for causing so much trouble.

Willa May patted Glenny on the shoulder and said, "It's all right, honey. Your pa's mad at 'Lil Luther for hurting you and your sister. He's not mad at you."

Glenny looked up at Daniel. Smiling, Daniel said, "You just get well now, you hear?"

Happy that he wasn't in any trouble, Glenny smiled his childlike smile and said, "I will, Pa."

Willa May fixed Daniel a plate of leftover beans and turnips. She poured him some coffee -- black, the way he liked it. "How's Hattie Sue and Ernest Roy?" he asked as Willa May sat down at the table with him.

"They're fine. Hattie Sue had a bruise or two, but she was more upset over Glenny than anything. She's still with Mama. I sent James Houston and Walt Whitman over with them, just in case."

Daniel nodded. "I reckon I'll have to ride over to see Luther and Big Annie tomorrow. To let them know what I done. They won't like it much, I expect. But I mean to let them know that if 'Lil Luther comes around again, it'll be the last time."

Not since the trouble with Augie had Willa May felt so torn over her kinfolk. They had known 'Lil Luther since he was a baby. Why, she had been right there the night he was born. Her uncle doted over the boy, loving him even more because of 'Lil Annie dying, leaving him with no mama. It would be hard on both Big Annie and Luther for Daniel to tell them what he had to say. Lizzy would be right in the middle of it, torn between her loyalty to Big Annie and Luther and her love for Willa May and Daniel. Willa May wished that her pa and Big Jim were still alive. Maybe they would have been able to keep the lid from blowing off the powder keg that Daniel was going to lay at her family's doorstep come morning. She knew that Daniel was right in wanting to protect his family from further harm. Who was to say that 'Lil Luther wouldn't cross over the border with his kin, wanting vengeance of his own now? She shivered just thinking about it. She found herself wishing that Daniel had put an end to 'Lil Luther once and for all. But she knew as well as Daniel that if Daniel had killed 'Lil Luther, it would have devastated Big Annie and Luther.

Watching her mulling over this, Daniel took her hand in his and said, "I never wanted this, you know that. And that's what I aim to tell Big Annie and Luther. They have to see that 'Lil Luther brought this on himself. I couldn't let him cut my boy and get away with it. How would I live with myself if I did that?"

She clutched Daniel's hand. "I know what you're saying. I feel the same way. It's just that I don't want this to come between us. Remember when you got in that fight with Augie and was beating his head in and Pa, Big Jim, and Luther had to pull you off of Augie?"

Daniel nodded.

"When you said that you were going to get back at those men who burned us out, Luther saw that Pa and Big Jim were set on helping you. Luther agreed to go in on it, too. He said, 'What else have we got if we don't stand up for each other?'"

"I remember."

"I just wonder if he'll still feel the same after tomorrow."

Daniel didn't say anything. He sat there holding Willa May's hand, both of them dreading what they were honor bound to do. Both of them knowing that folks would come and go in their lives, but they weren't blood. And blood was what mattered. It was all that mattered.

Daniel left at sunrise the next morning, first to see Big Annie and Luther to get squared with them, then to stop by Lizzy's to see Hattie Sue and Ernest Roy. Riding up to Big Annie's and Luther's, Daniel was no sooner off of his horse when Luther came out the front door with a big wad of chewing tobacco clenched in his jaw. Luther knew why Daniel had come. Word had gotten around about 'Lil Luther stabbing Glenny. Word had it, too, that Daniel had gone off hunting for 'Lil Luther. Luther came down the front steps slowly, his eyes focused in front of him so as not to acknowledge Daniel's presence.

"Morning, Luther," Daniel said, seeing that Luther was waiting for him to be the first to break the silence between them. Daniel sensed that Luther was waiting for him to say he had killed 'Lil Luther.

Luther spat a stream of brown tobacco juice. Nodding, he mumbled, "Morning."

"I've come to tell you I tracked 'Lil Luther over into Kentucky. Staying with some of your kinfolk over there. They knew I had followed 'Lil Luther and they were waiting for me, laying a trap for me. I hightailed it up into the hills when I saw them boys and stayed up there watching them for a few days."

Here, Daniel stopped and looked at Luther. Luther stared out at the road, pokerfaced. "I've come to tell you, Luther, that I rode down into their camp and wounded some of them boys."

"Did you hit 'Lil Luther?" Luther asked, still staring straight ahead.

"Yeah, I did. I shot him in the knee and then in the shoulder. He'll probably walk with a cane the rest of his days, but he's still alive. Before I left, I told him that if he comes around again, I aim to kill him."

Luther was quiet for a long time. Finally he spewed another brown stream and looked at Daniel. "You did what you had to do, Daniel. I know that. Big Annie knows it, too. But I want you to know that if you kill that boy, I'm goin' to be coming for you. I can't let that kind of thing go."

"Fair enough." Daniel nodded. "Would you tell Big Annie we're all awful sorry that it had to come to this? But, like you said, I couldn't let it go."

Luther gave Daniel a brief nod and went back to staring at the road. Daniel turned and mounted his big gray. He dipped his hat to Luther and rode back up the road to Lizzy's. Hattie Sue was glad to see her pa, but Daniel could see that she was sorry that he hadn't killed 'Lil Luther. He guessed that after all the beatings and humiliation she had suffered, she wanted 'Lil Luther dead and gone so he couldn't be a threat to her and Ernest Roy again. She asked Daniel if she could stay with Lizzy for the winter.

"You're a free woman, Hattie Sue. It's your decision. If that's what you want and Lizzy's up to having you, then that's all that matters."

Hattie Sue looked happier than he had seen her since she came back home. She asked if one of the boys could bring her things to her. "Tell Mommy I'll miss her, Pa, but I just want to be on my own for a while."

In September, Walt Whitman left for Charleston to work for the candidate for governor. Hattie Sue and Ernest Roy stayed over at Lizzy's. James Houston announced a few days later that he had hired on at the Paint Creek mine. In January, Ethan Allen decided to go into the mines, too. Spring came and Effie Lee married a Hughes boy from Deepwater and Walt Whitman brought home a girlfriend he had met in Charleston. He announced they were going to be married in June. It seemed to Willa May that things were happening so fast her head was spinning, trying to keep up with all their children's comings and goings.

Shortly before Walt Whitman's wedding, Willa May took Asa and Ansel to see Young Doc. Both boys had the croop. Hattie Sue was sitting in the waiting room with Ernest Roy. "What's wrong with the baby?" Willa May asked, taking a seat beside Hattie Sue.

"He's had a runny nose and a cough for the last week. It's not any better."

Willa May had barely sat down when they heard a long, shrill scream come from inside the examining room. Hattie Sue leaned over and whispered, "Ellie Carson's having her baby. Sounds like she's having a bad time."

Willa May nodded as another scream filled the waiting room. It was still echoing off the walls when the door opened. Young Doc rushed out into the waiting room. "Hold out your hands," he ordered.

Everyone in the room stared at him like he had spoken in some foreign tongue. He yelled, "Everybody. Hold out your hands so I can see them!" He circled the room, looking at each person's hands. Shaking his head, he mumbled to himself under his breath. When he came to Hattie Sue, he took her hands in his, examining them closely as he turned them over. "Come with me," he said and turned on his heel.

Hattie Sue looked from Young Doc to Willa May, wondering like the rest of the waiting patients, what Young Doc wanted. He reached the door and turned around, looking back at Hattie Sue. "What are you waiting for? Come on."

Hattie Sue rushed across the room and through the door that Young Doc held for her. From inside the examining room, Willa May heard another pain filled scream. It dawned on Willa May that maybe Ellie Carson's baby was turned the wrong way. Young Doc might need someone with small hands to reach in and turn the baby around. The next five minutes seemed like five hours. The screaming grew worse. Everyone in the waiting room sat so quietly, it seemed like they were at a funeral. At last, they heard one final cry of agony that made Willa May's insides ache as she remembered the kind of pain that brought on such a scream. This was followed by a loud, high pitched cry of a baby and the people in the waiting room sighed with relief. Moments later, Hattie Sue came out of the examining room, beaming. She told

Willa May that the baby had indeed been turned around. Young Doc had instructed her on how to shift the baby so it could be born.

"Is Ellie all right?" Willa May asked.

"Yep. Couldn't be better." Hattie Sue just couldn't stop grinning.

It was a while before Young Doc started seeing his other patients. Hattie Sue and Willa May waited and waited. They were the last ones Young Doc saw that day. When he called in Hattie Sue, he said, "Young lady, I have to thank you again for helping me out today."

"Oh, that's all right," Hattie Sue blushed. "It's something I'll always remember."

"You know, I've been thinking, Hattie Sue. You really did a marvelous job. And I have to say, I am a little shorthanded around here. The more I've thought about it this afternoon, the more I've come to feel that I could use someone like you to help out full time."

"What?" Hattie Sue's voice was filled with surprise.

"That's right. I'd like you to come to work for me. I've got more patients than I can handle, as you've seen today. And there are all kinds of emergencies each week when I could use a spare pair of hands. I'd be willing to train you if you're willing to give it a try."

"But what about my baby?"

"You've been living with your grandmother, haven't you? Could she watch Ernest Roy for you when you're at work?"

Hattie Sue couldn't think, everything was happening so fast. "I reckon so. I'd have to ask her."

"Fine. Let me know what you decide. Just remember, I really do need someone to help out here. You'll get training and you'll be earning your own living. If you decide you want the job, I could use you as soon as possible."

Hattie Sue thought for a minute, trying to take in all that Young Doc was saying. "Could I get word to you tomorrow?"

Young Doc smiled. "That would be fine. Just fine."

The next day, Hattie Sue had a job.

In the fall of ninety-two, William A. MacCorkle was voted the next governor of West Virginia. Willa May and Daniel were proud, knowing that Walt Whitman had played a role in the new governor's election. But a multitude of problems awaited the newly elected governor. People throughout the state had been swindled by timber companies and mine owners. Thinking to make a little money, folks had sold off timber rights and mineral rights. They believed that they still owned their land, but they soon discovered that the companies could march their crews in and take over their property like they owned it. When a few of them took the companies to court, they were vexed when they learned that the slick, big city lawyers who worked for these companies had made certain that their clients could do whatever they pleased to get to the precious timber and coal on their property. Across the state, folks were fuming. Whole mountains were shaved clean, leaving nothing but stumps. Horrible floods gushed out of the blackened hillsides each spring. Worse, though, the place Willa May had always believed to be heaven on earth had become ugly and barren. A wasteland. It sickened her to see it. Daniel cussed and paced almost every night, shaking his fists. He claimed it was a sin and a shame that folks had been tricked into giving up their land to a bunch of two-timing thieves who raped and ravaged the land, making it unfit for even the animals that had once lived there in bountiful number. Daniel worked himself into such a lather that it made Willa May want to cry. He dearly loved those hills. For him, it was like watching a loved one die by inches from a cancer that ate away everything that was whole and good, spreading decay day by day.

Some so-called experts tried to sugar coat it, claiming that the state was experiencing an economic boom. Through all of this, nobody seemed to see that all the money was pouring out of the state. It went to companies owned by rich men who were getting richer by swindling honest, hard working people. When the boom theory fizzled, everyone's hopes sank. They had all learned a bitter lesson.

Not only were folks upset about losing their land, but it seemed that more and more often, they heard about mine cave-ins, flash floods, or epidemics sweeping down on them like the four horsemen in the Good Book. Every time they heard about these things, Willa May and Daniel breathed a long heavy sigh of relief that their own flesh and blood were safe and untouched by these cruel and fickle spells cast down upon them. Willa May held her breath, wondering when it would be their turn to bear the cross of bad news, knowing their luck couldn't hold out forever. She worried constantly for her family's safety.

After Walt Whitman married Miss Annie Catherine Harless, a school teacher from Charleston, James Houston eloped with a girl from Ingram Branch by the name of Nila Rae Miller. Both James

Houston and Ethan Allen were eking out a living in the Paint Creek mine, living in company owned houses and forced to buy from the company owned store since they were paid in scrip. Each payday, the company totaled up each miner's debts, rent, groceries, and medical expenses -- even the doctor was on the company payroll. Whatever a miner had coming to him after these deductions, he received in scrip. Scrip could either be tokens or paper that said a miner was allowed credit for a certain amount. The scrip system served to keep the miner indebted to the mining company. Nine times out of ten, a miner ended up owing the mine owner more work. Miners were like vassals obligated to a feudal lord, sinking deeper in debt and making it impossible to leave. The mine owners raked in profits and grew fat off of the hard work of the miners they hoodwinked. Some complained that it wasn't any better than slavery. The shacks the miners lived in weren't any better than the shoddy slave quarters used on plantations. They were lined up in rows along a dirt road while above them, on a hill, the fine houses built for the mine foreman's family, the doctor and the store owner looked down on them.

Daniel pleaded with the boys to come back home. They could build themselves homes on his property and help Daniel with the business and work his land. But the boys saw themselves as grown men, out from under their pa's thumb. Blind men was what Daniel called them. He would have told them to their faces, but Willa May reminded him that they had to learn for themselves. Daniel couldn't live their lives for them. When he saw the conditions that his brothers were forced to live in and work in, Walt Whitman agreed they would be better off back up on the mountain farming. Neither one of the boys would give up. Willa May thought she had accepted their decision when Glenny got it in his head to go into the mines. She and Daniel both tried to talk him out of it. They told him that it was far too dangerous work for a person with his limitations. Glenny's lower lip jutted out in a pout. He hung his head, saying, "I reckon I can go work with the boys if I want." Seeing that they weren't getting through that streak of Shrewsbury stubbornness, Elroy said, "Now, Glenny, you don't want to go into them mines. It's dark and scary down in them shafts. Cold and damp, too. What time you ain't scared to death, you'll be fighting off a cold and working when you're so sick, you could drop."

Glenny scuffed his boot across the wood floor and said, "I reckon I can be a miner if I want."

He looked so pitiful, wanting to do men's work like his brothers, but acting like the little boy he was in his mind. That was what finally made Daniel give in. He hated for Glenny to be hurt over something; it was always so much more painful when it was Glenny who was hurting. "Okay, Son, I tell you what. We'll ride over to see James Houston tomorrow. If he says you can work next to him, I'll let you do this." Seeing Glenny's face light up when he heard this, Daniel added, "I ain't saying I'm happy about it, though." But Glenny was happy. He was tickled pink.

Daniel and Glenny left early the next morning. Glenny took all his clothes and belongings in case he got hired on. Standing beside Elroy, Willa May watched them go. Her heart ached with every step they took. When they were out of sight, Elroy looked up at her, his forehead wrinkled with worry. "Willa May, I got a bad feeling about this."

"Me too, Elroy. But what can we do? If we say no, he might just run off like Josie did and we haven't seen her in all these years. Either way, we lose him. I don't want to drive Glenny away. He's not smart, but he's smart enough to know what he wants. Short of tying him up, how can we keep him here?"

Elroy shrugged, knowing she was right, and like Willa May, hating the being right part. Dora Lottie was playing in the yard and heard what they said. She came over to them and looked down the road where her pa and Glenny had just been. When Willa May saw the worried frown on Dora Lottie's face, she felt suddenly cold. She remembered the night when Dora Lottie had screamed Glenny's name, looking like she was worlds away. A shudder worked its way up Willa May's spine.

A year had passed since 'Lil Luther stabbed Glenny. Asa and Ansel were growing into big boys, going off hunting with their pa. The two of them were so close, it was like they lived in their own little world. Sometimes they didn't even have to speak to know what the other was thinking; they just sensed it. The pair was so identical Elroy could never tell them apart. Even Daniel slipped now and again and called Asa "Ansel" and Ansel "Asa". The twins giggled and squealed like little piglets, tickled that they had tricked their pa. Watching them racing around the yard and playing together, they reminded Willa May of 'Lil Daniel. So blonde they were almost golden with

175

hardy little bodies that promised to be strong with lots of muscle when they turned into men. Watching them at those times, a voice inside her would say, "Not these two, Lord. I'm not giving up these two to go off and get killed."

Dora Lottie was as sweet as the boys were ornery. All summer, she brought Willa May wildflowers that she picked. Willa May put them in a jar of water and placed them in the center of the table. She thought they perked up the place even if they were just Queen Anne's Lace, honeysuckle blossoms, and some dandelions. She always bragged on the flowers when everyone gathered around the table for supper. Daniel would add, "You know, Willa May, I don't think I've ever seen such beautiful flowers. They're a picture, sure enough." Dora Lottie would beam, freckles scooting across her face to make way for all her pearly white teeth.

One night in late August, they sat on the porch reading Oliver Twist, a copy that Walt Whitman had brought them. Everyone was caught up in poor Oliver's troubles. The twins were overjoyed with the passel of buddies that Oliver had taken up with, especially The Artful Dodger. They hated Fagin, saying they would like to meet up with him and show him a thing or two Shrewsbury style. It was hard to get the twins to bed, they carried on so about the book. Willa May finally got them quieted down around eleven. Elroy took a nip from his jug with Daniel as they talked over plans to build a new still to keep up with the demands of the taverns they supplied. When they finished their discussion, Elroy rolled himself home and Daniel came in for the night. Climbing into bed, he reached for Willa May and pulled her to him and they made love. It was a safe night by her calculations. As Daniel started snoring, Willa May heard a knock on the door. It woke Daniel and he crawled out of bed, mumbling, "Who in tarnation could be waking us up at this hour?" Willa May was curious, too, wondering what calamity had struck now. She made a mental count of her children. When she got to Hattie Sue, she thought of her mama and whispered, "Oh, Lord, please don't let it be Mama." But her mind was already enumerating all the things that could take her mama away from her.

Daniel hurried downstairs and opened the door. Willa May was climbing down the steps, wrapping her shawl around her shoulders when she heard Creedy's voice. "You'd better come quick, Daniel. Lizzy needs you."

Willa May rushed to the door and stood just behind Daniel.

"What's happened? Is Mama okay?" she asked, still praying that everything was all right, but knowing it wasn't when she saw the blood on Creedy's face...and the bruises. She caught her breath, "What's happened to you Creedy? Who did this to you?"

"It was 'Lil Luther, Willa May," he said, looking more stooped than usual and so frail. Panting for breath from the long walk, he struggled to tell them what had happened. "He came in on us, drunk as a lord and cussing and screaming like he was out of his mind. Lizzy was already in bed and so was Ernest Roy. Hattie Sue was reading the Good Book to me and we were having some cold buttermilk out at the kitchen table when 'Lil Luther busted through the back door. I tried to keep him off of Hattie Sue, but he kept hitting me and knocked me out."

Creedy sounded so pitiful, Willa May said, "It's okay, Creedy. We know you did your best. What about Hattie Sue, the baby, and Mama?"

"They're okay...well, Hattie Sue's awful upset, crying and all."

Daniel spoke up. "Did 'Lil Luther hurt Hattie Sue?"

Creedy started backing away, afraid to tell Daniel what had happened. In a more urgent voice, Daniel repeated, "Creedy, is Hattie Sue all right? What did 'Lil Luther do to her? That sonofabitch didn't stab her this time, did he?"

"No. No, he didn't stab her. Nothing like that."

"What? What did he do?" Willa May cried, growing more frightened with every word.

"He...well, he--" Creedy couldn't say any more.

A look came over Daniel, a look that Willa May hadn't seen since the men came and burned them out, beating her and killing their unborn baby. He almost barked at poor Creedy, "Where's 'Lil Luther now?" Willa May knew that Daniel meant to kill 'Lil Luther this time, kill him in a way that would make him suffer.

"That's just it!" cried Creedy. "He's dead. Lizzy's done blowed him to kingdom come with Pole's shotgun."

A scream raced up from Willa May's gut past her throat and out of her mouth. She could see her mama, old and feeble in her white nightgown, holding the big old gun her pa had used so often. It was almost as big as Lizzy. Willa May knew that Lizzy must have been terrified. "Just let me get dressed," she breathed.

Daniel caught her by her shoulders as she turned away. "Hold on, Willa May. I'd better take Creedy and go see about 'em myself. You stay here with the babies."

"But Mama's goin' to need me. And Hattie Sue. What are you goin' to do about Hattie Sue? She'll need her mama."

Daniel thought it over and nodded. "We'll get Elroy to come over and watch the younguns. You get dressed."

They left ten minutes later. Elroy kept telling Daniel to keep his head, not knowing that Lizzy had shot 'Lil Luther. When they reached her mama's, Lizzy was putting cold cloths on Hattie Sue's face. Daniel lifted the cloths and looked at Hattie Sue. Willa May heard his breath rush out as if he had taken a blow to his gut. His jaw clenched and his face took on that killer look Willa May hadn't seen since the night he nearly beat Augie to death. It was a dark, thunderous expression. Hattie Sue's face was beaten to a pulp, both her eyes were swollen shut and turning a dark purple color. The right side of her jaw stuck out like she had a bad case of the mumps. Wondering what other wounds Hattie Sue bore, Willa May pushed Daniel and Creedy out of the room, telling Daniel to see to Creedy's cuts and bruises while she and her mama tended Hattie Sue.

Lizzy pulled the covers back from Hattie Sue's battered body. What Willa May saw made her turn away. She started shaking; she wanted to kill 'Lil Luther herself. She wanted to slit his throat and cut off his privates for what he had done to her daughter. Hattie Sue's breasts were bleeding from where 'Lil Luther had bitten into her soft white flesh. She bore teeth marks all over her body -- on her belly, on the back of her legs, and on her buttocks. She was bruised everywhere, big black and purple splotches ringing every bite. Lizzy said by the time she had woken up and knew what was happening, 'Lil Luther had already had his way with Hattie Sue. When she came in on them, 'Lil Luther had forced Hattie Sue down on her knees in front of him at gunpoint.

Willa May held up her hands, "Please, Mama, no more. Don't tell me any more." Her mind was swirling with hatred and desire for revenge. "I'm just glad you killed him," she said, putting her arm around Lizzy's frail, bony shoulders. "I hate to think what he would've done if you had missed."

Lizzy, wiping away her tears, nodded. Both women knew that 'Lil Luther would have killed Lizzy and Creedy both, crazy drunk like he was. Lizzy asked, "What are we goin' to do about 'Lil Luther? What will I tell Big Annie and Lute? It'll kill them. They'll hate me for the rest of their days. I don't know if I could live with that. They're all

I've got except for you, Daniel, and Creedy."

She sounded so pitiful, Willa May didn't know what to say. She wanted to tell her that Big Annie and Luther would just have to face the truth. That 'Lil Luther was a bad seed, nothing more than a ruthless rapist. But she didn't say that, knowing it wouldn't help and it would only make her mama more upset.

They washed Hattie Sue and gave her a glass of Daniel's moonshine. Daniel was pacing the kitchen floor when they came out. Wearing a bandage around his head, Creedy sat at the table having a drink of whiskey. His forlorn look told them how guilty he felt over letting Lizzy and Hattie Sue down. Willa May patted his shoulder and said, "Creedy, don't feel bad. You did all you could. Nobody could ask for more."

Creedy shook his head sadly, unable to speak.

Daniel asked, "How's Hattie Sue? Is she goin' to be all right?"

Willa May didn't want to tell him about what he hadn't seen on Hattie Sue, but he was her pa and he had the right to know. None of them had thought of what they would do about 'Lil Luther. That would be for Daniel to decide. "Come sit out on the porch with me," she said, pouring Daniel some of his own moonshine.

He looked at her questioningly. Willa May looked him directly in the eye. She could see the dawning realization on his face that what she had to tell him, he needed to hear in private, sitting down with a strong drink. He followed Willa May out to the porch. She told him about the cuts and bruises he hadn't seen when he saw Hattie Sue. Daniel slammed his fist into a post supporting the roof over the porch. He wailed like a wounded animal. Turning his back to her, he stood shaking with rage, his hand a bloody, limp mess. Willa May wrapped her arms around him to keep him from doing more harm to himself. She expected him to push her away, but he let out another cry, a helpless sound from down deep in his chest that rose up like it had burst right out of his heart. That cry seemed to erupt from Daniel with all the pain and fury she had ever heard. Willa May wrapped her arms around him tighter, holding on for dear life. She was afraid that Daniel might revert completely into a wild, savage state with this new suffering. When he finally stopped screaming, Daniel held onto her. She could hear the panting of his breath. Willa May clung tightly, her head pressed to his chest. She held onto Daniel even tighter to keep him from turning into the untamed animal she knew he carried inside himself. Daniel, in turn, held onto her so tightly she thought he might

179

crack her ribs.

"What do we do now?" she asked. "Do we tell the law about 'Lil Luther and hope they believe Mama? She shot him in the back, you know. Do we put Hattie Sue through all that shame with everybody knowing what 'Lil Luther did to her? What about Big Annie and Uncle Luther? Do we tell them what went on here tonight?"

Through a clenched jaw, Daniel looked straight ahead into the darkness of that August night. "I'll take Creedy with me up behind the house and bury 'Lil Luther. Won't nobody know nothing. It'll be like he took off somewheres and never came back. I ain't putting my girl through more pain and that's that. Tell Lizzy what we decided and I'll warn Creedy not to ever say nothing about what he saw here. He's a good man. We can count on him."

With that, he looked at Willa May and said, "You want me to go get Young Doc for Hattie Sue?"

"No," she shook her head. "She probably won't want him to know about this, she's grown right fond of Young Doc since she's been working for him. She'd be mortified if he knew about this."

Daniel nodded then held her to him for a long while. When he finally let go of her, he said, "I'd best see to 'Lil Luther now."

The next morning Daniel got up early and rode over to tell Young Doc that Hattie Sue was sick and wouldn't be coming to work for a few days. They thought that might satisfy him, but two days later, Young Doc showed up at Lizzy's door, carrying his medical bag and saying he wanted to look in on Hattie Sue. When he saw the looks being exchanged around the room and the bandage on Daniel's hand, he said, "Hattie Sue isn't sick, is she? There's something you're not telling me."

Willa May stood up. "You know that Hattie Sue was married?"

"Yes..."

"And you recall last year when he came here and stabbed our Glenny?"

"My God," Young Doc gasped. "That bastard didn't stab Hattie Sue?"

"No," she answered, not sure how to tell him just what 'Lil Luther had done. "He didn't stab her--"

"Let me see her. Now!" Before Willa May could stop him, Young Doc was already half way across the room, set on seeing Hattie Sue whether they liked it or not.

"It's the room on your left," she said as he rushed past her on his way back toward the two bedrooms off of the parlor. She followed him into the darkened room and watched as he looked down on Hattie Sue's battered face, swollen and splotched dark purple. "My God," he breathed. He bent down, taking Hattie Sue's hand. Ever so gently, he said, "Hattie Sue, it's me. Doc. I'm going to take care of you. Don't worry about a thing, we're going to have you back on your feet in no time. I need you too much at the office to have you lying here in bed, young lady."

Willa May knew that Young Doc was trying to calm himself down while making Hattie Sue better by saying these things. She was grateful for his gentleness. Then he pulled back the covers, preparing to examine his patient. When he saw the bite marks and bruises on her body, Young Doc looked up at Willa May, his face turning a ghostly white. Being a doctor, though, he set about tending to the wounds. When he was finished, he gave Hattie Sue a shot so she could rest. He led Willa May back out to the parlor. Looking from her to Daniel, then to Lizzy, and finally to Creedy, he sighed wearily. "Okay. Tell me right now what the hell went on here."

Willa May told him everything. Even where they had buried 'Lil Luther. She feared he might say something about getting the law and reporting them, but he sat down and said, "You did the right thing. There's no help for young Luther and why put Hattie Sue through further humiliation? Certainly Eliza doesn't need the trauma of further retribution from the law or from her relatives." He said all this as if he were trying to convince himself that it was the right thing after all. Looking at Willa May, he grew quiet. Finally, he asked, "Have you considered what you'll do if Hattie Sue is pregnant?"

Indeed, she hadn't. No one had. Stunned, Willa May looked from Young Doc to Daniel. What *would* they do? Daniel looked as thunderstruck as Willa May. Then they both got mad at 'Lil Luther all over again, wishing he were still alive so they could kill him again. It seemed to Willa May that shooting him had been too good for him and far too quick. With this new problem, she wanted to see 'Lil Luther die a slow, suffering death.

Seeing how angry they were, Young Doc said, "Well, we don't know that she is pregnant. We can face that bridge when we come to it, I suppose."

But Hattie Sue was pregnant. Just when she was back on her feet again, able to go back to work and start to put what had happened past her, she started in with the morning sickness. No one in the family

181

knew what to do. Young Doc offered to help her get rid of the baby if that was what she wanted, but Hattie Sue shook her head and said it wasn't the baby's fault. While the rest of them were wondering what kind of story to make up, knowing that folks hadn't seen 'Lil Luther back, the answer sprang up for them. Gossip spread throughout the valley as soon as Hattie Sue started to show. Rumor had it that she and Young Doc shared more than just a working relationship. Willa May felt certain that Young Doc knew what was being said behind his back, but he never did anything to deny the whispers that were spreading faster than mold on old bread. It was then that Willa May knew Young Doc was in love with Hattie Sue.

Hattie Sue's baby was born late in May the following spring. She named him Claude Daniel for Young Doc whose name, they discovered, was Claude and for her pa. When neighbors heard the baby was named Claude, they nodded to each other knowingly, as if this sealed their speculations that the baby belonged to Young Doc. But Claude Daniel wasn't the only grandchild who arrived that spring. Walt Whitman's wife, Annie Catherine, gave birth to a fine little boy, too. They named him Thomas Lee, a big baby with snapping brown eyes. James Houston and his wife had a little girl they named Ivy Jean. Come Sundays when all the children came to visit, Willa May and Daniel had all they could do to keep up with the three babies, crying to be fed, changed, or held. Daniel and Elroy sat out on the porch every Sunday after the company left, swigging from a jug and watching the fireflies dance on the night air. They laughed and talked about all the cute things the babies had done that day. Daniel was so tickled at being a grandpa, but Willa May found herself wishing that she could still give Daniel children and she often felt depressed over it.

After one Sunday visit, she finished putting their youngest ones to bed, resorting to threats to get Asa and Ansel to go to sleep. She went to bed, feeling a familiar heaviness weighing at her heart over not being able to have more babies. Daniel came to bed early and caught her crying. He almost had to drag it out of her, but when she finally told him what was wrong, he pulled her to him and kissed her like they were young again and just married. "You done give me all the younguns I'd ever want, Willa May. So why are you carrying on so?" His voice was soft and tender.

"I don't know," she sniffed. "I just wish that I could call those babies my own, I reckon. To see you looking at me in that special way you always did whenever we'd have a new baby and you'd watch it nursing at my breast. I could always see the love in your eyes at those times."

"But I love you now. More than ever. Don't you know that?"

"Do you?" she asked, needing to hear it even if she knew it deep down in her heart.

"You know I do," he said, nuzzling her neck and wrapping his arms around her. Then he turned her toward him and kissed her again, long and sweet. She held onto him, wishing they were young again. Yet she couldn't turn back the clock; she knew that this was a different time for them. They were standing at an open door looking in on this new time and all the new joys it held. She felt whole again, thinking about it. Daniel held her to him all night, he could be so tender. She started to believe that growing old with him was like holding onto a bottle of fine wine -- not the homemade blackberry wine they were used to -- watching it age and knowing it was still growing into something more perfect with each year.

Daniel and Willa May were looking forward to Thanksgiving that year. All the children were coming home, except for Josie. Friday was a gray November day when the wind whisked the dried leaves this way and that like it was playing a game of chase. Daniel and Elroy were up in the woods hunting with Asa and Ansel, hoping to bring home a deer. Willa May set a bowl of vegetable soup on the table for Dora Lottie's lunch when Willa May saw Dora Lottie's back go ramrod straight. The little girl stared wide eyed at the far wall. Without a word, she sat in a daze, lost in another world. Willa May felt a chill shudder up her spine, remembering when Dora Lottie had done the same thing the night 'Lil Luther stabbed Glenny. Willa May's heart raced and she thought it might leap right out of her chest onto the floor. A feeling of dread washed over her followed by an overpowering sense of desperation.

"What is it, Dora Lottie? Tell Mommy what's wrong." She repeated the plea again and again, feeling more distressed each time. But Dora Lottie sat so still in stony silence, her eyes transfixed. Willa May was going mad with fear each passing second, wondering what was wrong with her little girl -- and worse, what Dora Lottie might tell her was wrong with one of her other babies.

Without a word, Dora Lottie slumped over, her whole body going limp. Her eyes fluttered and rolled back in their sockets. Willa May was afraid she would pass out. "Dora Lottie?" Willa May cried, but Dora Lottie still didn't hear her. A minute passed and the little girl heaved a long, weary sigh. Her eyes stopped fluttering and she looked at Willa May. She seemed disoriented, blinking three, four times and looking away. Willa May gave her a few moments to clear her head.

"Dora Lottie?" she tried again.

The girl looked up at Willa May with tears in her eyes. Her tears frightened Willa May more than the spell she had experienced. Willa May knew that her little girl was crying over something that had already taken place, something she couldn't prevent. Willa May felt instinctively that it was something she didn't want to hear. In her sweet child's voice, Dora Lottie said, "Better get Pa, Mommy."

Willa May had no idea where Daniel was hunting. Her mind raced, trying to figure out a way to warn him. She looked to Daniel's gun rack and saw that his rifle was gone. Below the empty rack was the double-barreled shotgun she had used the night she shot the stranger years before. She rushed over and pulled down the heavy shotgun. Dragging it across the floor, she found some bullets and loaded it. Then she hauled it outside and raised it into the air, nearly falling over from the weight of it. She shot ten times into the sky, as fast as she could reload. Her eyes scanned the horseshoe shape of the hill, searching for any sign of Daniel. She berated herself for foolishly expecting Daniel to come running out of the woods as soon as she stopped firing. She reloaded again and again, firing off ten more shots. Each blast made her ears ring and nearly knocked her off her feet. Still no Daniel. She thought it best to wait five minutes before firing the next ten shots. Wet tears coursed down her cheeks. She was shaking, not knowing what Dora Lottie had seen, but knowing that it must have been really bad.

In twenty minutes, after firing off ten shots at five minute intervals, Daniel ran out of the woods on her right, hollering, "What are you shooting for?"

Dropping the shotgun, Willa May raced toward Daniel. As she drew close, he could see her tears and the look of fear imprinted on her face. He pulled her to him and asked, "What's wrong? What's happened? Are you hurt?" His voice was fraught with alarm.

"No," she shook her head. "It's not me. Dora Lottie's had another one of her spells."

"Is she okay?" he asked, looking toward the cabin.

"Seems to be. She wouldn't tell me what was wrong, just said I'd better get you. I'm awful worried, Daniel."

Daniel nodded and rushed toward the cabin with Willa May on his heels. Inside, he knelt beside Dora Lottie and put his arms around her. "What's the matter, Baby?"

Dora Lottie wrapped her arms around Daniel's neck and started sobbing. Daniel looked up at Willa May who shrugged helplessly, unable to tell him anything beyond what she had already. Daniel held Dora Lottie close until she seemed to let up and her sobs turned to hiccups. Gently, he said, "Dora Lottie, tell Pa what happened."

"I -- I seen it, Pa. I s-- seen it."

"What'd you see, Darlin'?"

"It -- it was dark. Black as night. Th-- then I seen something big in the dark and heard a l--loud rumbling sound like a train coming th-- through. And that's when I heard the man scream."

"What man?"

Dora Lottie looked from Daniel to Willa May. She didn't want to tell them who it was she heard screaming.

She was still looking up at them when Daniel repeated, "What man, Dora Lottie?"

"It -- it was J-- James Houston!" she blurted, sobbing again.

Daniel's eyes met Willa May's. Both of them knew what the other was thinking: *cave-in*. Willa May raised her hand to cover the scream she felt lurching up into her mouth. Daniel picked up Dora Lottie and handed her to her mama, saying, "I'm riding over to Paint Creek. You stay here and take care of Dora Lottie. The boys should be back soon with Elroy."

Before Willa May could say a word, Daniel turned on his heel and headed out the door. Minutes later, she heard the clip-clop of his horse as he headed away from the cabin. She sat down and hugged Dora Lottie. Silently, she prayed that what the child saw in her spell wasn't true.

The boys came back a short time later with Elroy. They had bagged the deer they had wanted. They strung the carcass up to a maple tree by the house and slit its throat. Elroy wheeled himself in and swung himself into a chair. Willa May fixed him a bowl of vegetable soup still warm on the stove. "What was all the shooting about, Willa May? Where's Daniel?"

She looked at Dora Lottie and said, "Why don't you go out and see the deer your brothers brought back for our Thanksgiving dinner?"

185

Like the good little girl she was, Dora Lottie nodded and went outside. Willa May poured herself a cup of sassafras tea, taking little comfort in its spicy aroma, but needing to hold onto something so her hands would stop shaking. Watching her, Elroy saw that something was amiss. He waited for her to speak in her own good time. When she had told him everything, Elroy put his hand on her own trembling hands and said, "Now, Willa May, we both know that James Houston is as strong as an ox and quick as a cat. If there was ever anybody that would be safe down in them mines, it's him."

"Thank you, Elroy. I needed to hear something to soothe my fears."

"It's the God's honest truth, Willa May, and we both know it. I figure Daniel will come back and tell us that James Houston's just fine, not a hair on his head harmed."

Daniel came home a little after midnight. Elroy was sitting up with Willa May when they heard Daniel's horse coming up the road. This time, though, the clip-clop of the horse's hooves sounded slow and heavy. A few minutes later, Daniel came through the door. His pale face was a mask of pain. At that moment, he looked ninety-five instead of fifty-five. His whole body was stooped so unlike the strong, able-bodied man Willa May knew. His blue eyes were red rimmed and swollen.

Willa May stood up, facing him from across the room, feeling the cold breeze that swept in behind Daniel. She didn't have to ask if something was wrong. "James Houston?" Her tiny voice sounded as if it came from a long distance away.

Daniel shook his head slowly and ran his hand over his eyes. She thought he was going to cry. His voice trembled as he said, "No. It was Glenny."

"Cave-in?" she asked, hearing how tight and shrill her voice had become.

Daniel shook his head again and turned away. Moments later, when he was able to speak again, Willa May could tell he was crying. "Coal car hit him. Cut him in half. James Houston said --"

But Willa May didn't hear the rest. She passed out right where she was standing. She came to in her bed. Daniel was leaning over her. Elroy rolled over with a jug and poured her a glass of white lightning. Handing it to her, he said, "Here, Willa May. Drink this. You're goin' to need it."

She took the glass and sipped, feeling the fiery liquid as it journeyed down her throat and warmed her insides. She had come to feel that dying was harder on the living, harder because the living were left to find some way to go on without the ones they loved.

She sipped at the glass and had another. The three of them sat up through the night. Together, they did in the jug. Through tears of grief, they clung to each other. Daniel said that James Houston was only a few feet away from Glenny when it happened, but he couldn't get to Glenny in time to save him. When James Houston saw Glenny lying there, cut in two, the other miners had to pull him, screaming and fighting, out of the mine. Willa May thought it must have been one of those screams that Dora Lottie had heard in her vision. Daniel had stayed with James Houston and his wife till he thought James Houston was all right. He begged James Houston not to blame himself, saying that they had tried to warn Glenny about the dangers of mining. Daniel said that James Houston looked at him through his tears, saying, "Pa, you weren't there. You didn't see what that coal car done to our Glenny." Then he broke down, sobbing anew.

On his way home, Daniel had stopped in Deepwater and Page to tell Big Annie and Lizzy what had happened. Lizzy asked for Glenny's body to be brought to her house to be laid out. She sent Creedy to tell the preacher -- Preacher Caldwell it was now -- that they would want to have the funeral at the Baptist church where all their kin were buried. Willa May was grateful to her mama for taking on this burden of planning everything. She felt too numb to do anything.

They rode over to Lizzy's the next day. Glenny's body had been carted up there by some of the miners. Ethan Allen brought Glenny's good Sunday suit. Lizzy and Hattie Sue washed him and dressed him. Daniel went to the undertaker after he left Willa May and the children off at Lizzy's and brought back a coffin. Willa May placed Glenny's baby quilt in with him, covering his mangled body as best she could. Then she realized that Lizzy had parted his hair on the wrong side, so Hattie Sue helped her comb his hair. Then the people came.

For the next two days, folks called on them day and night, bearing plates of food. All of them tried to say something to ease the family's pain. The men went outside and pulled on a jug together, cussing about the damn mines and fuming over their working conditions. Hattie Sue, Effie Lee, Big Annie, Dessie, Lizzy and Willa May took turns washing dishes and sitting with all those who had come to mourn and pay their respects. By the time Glenny was buried, they were all exhausted. There wasn't a dry eye in the church when

Preacher Caldwell gave the eulogy. Everyone had loved Glenny, he was so sweet. James Houston took it worse than any of them had imagined. He came to the wake and to the funeral with red, swollen eyes. Unshaven and disheveled, he looked like he hadn't slept a wink. Willa May felt sorry for his wife, Nila Rae. She was so young. James Houston was taking this so hard that Willa May wondered how much suffering his young wife had witnessed in the days since the accident. As they left the church, James Houston was one of the pallbearers. Willa May stopped him as he rose with the others to shoulder Glenny's coffin. She asked him to walk with her instead. Luther took James Houston's place at the coffin. Willa May held onto James Houston's big callused hand and said, "Son, you've got to stop blaming yourself for something that wasn't any of your doing. Glenny was a grown man, even if he had a little boy's mind. He died hard, but he couldn't live any other way. None of us could keep him from goin' into the mines. He had to find out for himself what it was all about. So don't spend the rest of your life asking yourself, 'What if...?' I've spent my life doing that very thing, so I know what I'm talking about."

James Houston gave her a puzzled look. Willa May smiled through her tears, saying, "Don't you think that I've spent many a night wondering if we hadn't gone to that Christmas pageant years ago if my babies would be here today, alive and well?"

"But Mommy, that wasn't your fault. You had no way of knowing that they would catch the smallpox that night and die," he argued.

"No more than you could've known that coal car was goin' to come roaring down out of the mine shaft with Glenny in the way."

She looked hard at her boy, her big strong boy. She thought he was beginning to realize that he really wasn't to blame for his brother's death. "I want to think," she went on, "that 'Lil Daniel is up in heaven looking over your brothers and sisters. That he's with Glenny right now and they're watching over us, too. I bet if Glenny could say so, he would tell you that he was proud to die like a man, earning his own way in the world, not living like the child he was trapped in."

Tears streamed down James Houston's whiskery face, a face already lined from hard work and hard times. But through his tears, he looked at her and nodded, managing to say, "Thank you, Mommy. I think I understand better now."

They buried Glenny next to Pole and Big Jim, just below where 'Lil Annie rested. It still gnawed at Willa May that they never got to bury

'Lil Daniel, that he was somewhere out west where they could never be with him again. After the burying, they went back to Lizzy's and had supper, not that any of them felt much like eating. An emptiness settled around them, soft as a cloud, as they spoke in quiet voices. Willa May felt that emptiness become so solid that she could have reached out and touched it. As soon as they cleared the dishes, the family started to disperse. Willa May and Daniel hugged and kissed all the grown children and their babies and waved them off. Finally, it was time for Willa May and Daniel to head home, too. She hugged her mama and thanked her for all she had done, for seeing them through one more hard and bitter time. She hugged Hattie Sue, holding her close and wishing she could do the same with all her babies. She yearned to hold each of them one more time. Daniel cleared his throat. Willa May knew he was trying hard not to break down. She let him lift her up onto the wagon with Elroy, the twins, and Dora Lottie. They headed home, too sad to speak, too empty for words.

Chapter Eight

Nineteen hundred, a new year, a new century. Snow fell in big, fat white flakes on New Year's Day. Dora Lottie busied herself making caramel popcorn balls. Asa and Ansel devoured them as fast as she could make them. "Mommy, make the boys stop," she pleaded.

Willa May looked up from her quilting -- she was still working on 'Lil Daniel's quilt. She had put it aside whenever she started a new baby quilt for her grandchildren and she was nearly finished with it. Daniel stirred the logs in the fire. He turned to Willa May and put his hand up for her to keep on quilting. He went over to the table and pulled both boys by their ears away from the popcorn balls. The twins took it as a chance to start a wrestling match with their pa. Soon the three of them were rolling around on the floor. Grunting and squealing, the twins sounded like the pigs out in the pen. Elroy sat by the fire, as always, and watched them, laughing and cheering them on.

Willa May looked up and watched them, too, for awhile. Then she looked toward Elroy and the fire beyond. She watched the flames leaping up the chimney and thought back on the century just past. She was forty-seven years old. It seemed like a century to her since she had been the scrawny little girl who had brought Daniel to her mama to have his arm stitched up. Three wars had come and gone, counting the Indian Wars out west that took 'Lil Daniel and the Spanish American War. Daniel was fond of saying that war lasted just long enough for those boys' coffee to get cold. Long enough to make a hero out of that Roosevelt fellow. Now the news was all about the automobile taking the place of the horse since a man up in Massachusetts built the first one seven years before. Walt Whitman still predicted that men would build a flying machine any day now. Brothers by the name of Wright were already working on gliders. So far, none of these new-fangled contraptions had made any difference to them up on their mountain.

It had been years since she last saw Josie. Walt Whitman told her that when he was working in Charleston for the governor, he had run

190

into Josie early on at a party. She had acted surprised to see him, but when she saw him dressed up and mixing with important politicians, she came up and introduced herself by her married name. Once they were alone, she asked Walt Whitman what on earth he was doing there. He told her how Willa May had used the money she had sent to put him through college and now he was working for the governor. All this came as further surprise to Josie, but she seemed pleased. After that, he saw Josie regularly, sometimes going to her house for lunch or tea. He said Josie asked him all kinds of questions about the family, wondering where everybody was and what they were doing. The last time he saw her was to tell her that Glenny had died in the mine. Josie looked sad and said to tell her folks that she was sorry to hear about the tragedy. But she didn't come to her brother's funeral. Willa May figured she was still too ashamed of them.

It had been five years since New River State College had opened its doors a few miles away in Montgomery. Walt Whitman got a job there teaching history after George Atkinson was elected governor. He was happy with teaching, it came naturally for him. He and Annie Catherine doted on their boy, Thomas Lee. Willa May was glad to see them so happy, even though she knew Walt Whitman worried for his brothers working in the coal fields. There wasn't a more bitter person than Walt Whitman when it came to the horrible way the mines were operated. He backed the miners in wanting to create a strong union and work for better working conditions. As worried as he was for his brothers, Walt Whitman was thrilled about Hattie Sue finding a job and then a husband in Young Doc. Young Doc hadn't sprung the question yet, but they all knew that he was in love with Hattie Sue. He was so good to her and no one was happier than Hattie Sue. After all the fear and humiliation she had suffered at the hands of 'Lil Luther, she thought Young Doc, kind and caring, was like an angel sent down from heaven.

Nobody had seen 'Lil Luther for years and folks had stopped talking about him. Sometimes Big Annie would sigh and say, "Wonder where that boy got himself off to." But Luther never mentioned 'Lil Luther. Willa May suspected that he knew deep down what had happened to his grandson, but he never said anything for fear of finding out that he was right. Both of them had set such a store by the boy, it was a shame they were so blind to his ugly side.

Asa and Ansel were like young bucks, strong and bursting to get out into the world. But Daniel and Willa May were too scared to let them go, having lost too many of their babies already. Dora Lottie was turning from a little girl into a young woman right before their eyes. She looked like Josie with blazing red hair down to her waist, but smaller than Josie had been. Where Josie had been selfish, wanting riches and a big fancy house, Dora Lottie had a heart of gold. She was always doing little things to brighten everyone's day and she wore a constant smile.

"Willa May? Are you there, Girl?"

She turned from the fire to find Daniel standing by her. The look on his face told her that he didn't know whether to be worried or amused by her dreamy expression. Picking up her quilting, she said, "Sure, I'm here. Where else would I be?"

Daniel grunted. Turning to the twins, he said, "How about a game of poker, boys?"

"Sure, Pa!"

"Deal me in," Elroy said, rolling across the floor to the table.

While the men played cards, Willa May quilted the last stitches on 'Lil Daniel's quilt. When she finished, she cut the thread, feeling as if she were cutting the last ties that bound her to 'Lil Daniel. She had done for him what she needed to do, paying tribute to his death -- something she hadn't been able to do when he died. It had taken her years, but now she had met her obligation, her final obligation.

She stood up, setting her scissors aside, and said, "It's done. 'Lil Daniel's quilt is all done."

The four men turned as one and Daniel stood up, motioning for Asa and Ansel to go and help her. "Hold it up so we can get a good look-see."

The twins, looking like spitting images of 'Lil Daniel, stood on each side of the quilt like bookends and held the quilt up for all to see. The others stood back, admiring it. Willa May was proud of all the intricate stitching she had labored so hard over month after month, year after year. She thought Daniel would praise her efforts, but his face took on a solemn expression as he gazed at the quilt. When he did speak, his voice came out in a hoarse whisper, "Well, I'll be. It's just like 'Lil Daniel."

Still sitting at the table, Elroy said, "Willa May, I'll bet 'Lil Daniel would be real proud of that there work. It's downright beauteeful."

"Where are you goin' to put it?" Asa asked.

"You ain't goin' to fold it away, are you, Mommy?" Dora Lottie asked. "It'd be a shame to store something so pretty."

"Dora Lottie's right," Daniel said. "Why don't you hang it up on the wall, like a big picture, so everybody can see it?"

"All right," Willa May agreed, thinking that would be the very thing to do. She would put it in a place of honor for 'Lil Daniel.

They hung the quilt that night. Daniel said it being the new year and the first day of the new century, it would only be right to hang it right then and there. He and the boys set to hanging up Willa May's Amish quilt while Dora Lottie helped her get supper on the table, a venison stew with some cornbread and rice pudding for dessert.

Once the quilt was hung, everybody kept looking at it through the evening. Each one said what a beautiful piece it was, like a regular work of art. Asa and Ansel carried Elroy home and saw him to bed. When they came back, they turned in for the night. So did Dora Lottie. Daniel poured himself a glass from a jug and sat down by the fire to admire the quilt. Willa May finished putting away all the kettles and pots from supper, then started up to bed. Turning, she said good night to Daniel. In place of his usual, "Be up directly" or "Get that there bed warmed up for me", he sat in rapt silence. Willa May wondered if he was feeling poorly from all the stew he had eaten at dinner. She started to ask if he wanted her to mix some soda water when she saw the sparkle of tears streaming down his whiskery face in the glow of the fire.

In all the years since 'Lil Daniel's death, Daniel had never said a word about missing his son. Seeing his tears, Willa May thought maybe he just couldn't bring himself to speak of it. Putting it into words would have caused his heart to burst open like a dam springing loose, flooding his soul with all the sorrow and longing he felt inside. The quilt had sprung that dam wide open and he couldn't contain all his pent up emotions any longer. Quietly, Willa May slipped upstairs, leaving Daniel to grieve in private. No sooner had her head hit the pillow when she heard Daniel's tears explode into shuddering sobs. She recalled what Elroy had said long ago when she was mad at Daniel for leaving her and going into the mountains for months at a time. He told her that she was the strong one and that was what had drawn Daniel to her. She tried to be strong that night, listening to Daniel's crying even though her own heart ached anew.

When Daniel came to bed, silent as the snow falling outside, he slid in beside her. She turned to him and put her arms around him, gently resting his head on her breast. He started crying again and she held him until he finally drifted off to sleep, his body still shuddering occasionally in his sleep.

She hoped that this one night would be the end of Daniel's mourning, and that he would let go everything he had stored inside his heart over the years. But he made it a habit to stare at the quilt awhile before turning in each night, as if by sitting with it, he was back with 'Lil Daniel again. It took some time before Willa May realized that the quilt no longer made Daniel sad. It brought him comfort to have this one last remnant of his son. Some folks visited graves to commune with their lost loved ones. For Daniel, the quilt was like 'Lil Daniel's grave.

In June of 1902, Hattie Sue and Young Doc were married. To hide the fact that 'Lil Luther was dead, Hattie Sue filed for divorce in Fayetteville, citing desertion as the cause. Two witnesses -- one of them was Luther -- stated they hadn't seen 'Lil Luther in over five years and had no idea where he was. The judge granted the divorce, freeing Hattie Sue to marry Young Doc the following month in the Page Baptist Church where Daniel and Willa May were married thirty-six years before. The family had a big outdoor celebration at Lizzy's, roasting chickens in the yard over an open fire with all the fixings that everyone brought. The only person missing was Josie. When Willa May sat down with her piece of the wedding cake, Walt Whitman came over and sat with her. She asked him if he had seen Josie since he left Charleston. He told her that he wrote to her and visited her whenever he could get to Charleston. Josie's rich husband was getting richer on the money he made from his mines. Walt Whitman said he had tried to talk to the man, trying to make him see how deplorable conditions were and how upset the miners were. He told Josie's husband that the miners were like a keg of gunpowder, just waiting for something to set them off. But Walt Whitman said that when he was finished, Josie's husband looked right back at him with a broad smile and said he was sure that Walt Whitman was exaggerating.

"The man's a fool, Mommy," Walt Whitman said, not a little disgusted. "The United Mine Workers have been trying to unionize miners across the state for over a decade now. You watch -- something is bound to happen. When it does, there won't be any way the mine owners can control them."

"You mean like a strike?" she asked.

Walt Whitman snorted. "More like all out war," he replied.

Lizzy died that fall just when the leaves were starting to blaze like a fire up in the mountains. Creedy said she had gone to church that morning and when they sat down to Sunday dinner with Hattie Sue, Young Doc, and the boys, she complained of feeling tired and said she thought she might turn in early that night. They no sooner got up from the table and were starting to wash the dishes when Lizzy grabbed her chest and turned white with pain. Hattie Sue helped her into a chair and called for Young Doc. He rushed into the kitchen and took one look at Lizzy, recognizing right away that it was her heart. He picked up her frail body and carried her to her room where he set her down on her bed. He told Creedy and Hattie Sue to stay there with Lizzy while he ran out to his wagon to fetch his bag. By the time Young Doc ran back into the house, Lizzy was gone.

Creedy broke down and didn't stop crying for days. Young Doc rode over to Paint Creek and told James Houston and Ethan Allen. James Houston volunteered to tell Willa May and Daniel if Young Doc would stop and pick up Walt Whitman on his way back through Montgomery. It was nearly dark when James Houston knocked at the door. Willa May and Daniel were just sitting down to supper when Daniel heard someone coming. When he opened the door, one look at James Houston told him there was bad news.

Daniel and James Houston drove Willa May over to Lizzy's that night. She and Hattie Sue laid Lizzy out in her best dress, the color of violets. They took turns sitting with Creedy, he was taking it so hard. Elroy said later he had never seen so many tears in one man before. Big Annie and Luther came, bearing food and jugs. Cousins and friends stopped by -- everyone but Josie. Funerals, to Willa May, seemed like a blur of faces and soft voices whisking past. She recalled going to a county fair once and riding on the carousel with Claude Daniel and Thomas Lee when they weren't any bigger than a minute. Looking out at the waiting crowd whirring past reminded her of the way she felt when death came to pay a call. Everything spun past like a dream and she wanted to reach out to grab hold of something, but it seemed she couldn't for all the spinning.

At the funeral, after the preacher read the Twenty-third Psalm,

Walt Whitman read from Emily Dickinson, "Because I could not stop for death, It kindly stopped for me..." It was Lizzy's favorite poem. Willa May thought it was surely true of Lizzy, always too busy, it seemed, even for dying. They buried Lizzy next to Pole, Big Jim, and Glenny.

Willa May wondered if word might have gotten to Augie and whether he might come to the funeral, but she reckoned he didn't hear since he wasn't there by the time Lawyer O'Neal read the will. She knew if there was something free to be gained, that her no-account brother would have been sitting there in the front row, telling the lawyer to get on with it. Lizzy left the house to Willa May and said that whatever she decided to do with it, it was to remain home for Creedy. After the funeral, Big Annie asked her if she would be willing to sell the house, that she and Luther had always fancied the place. Willa May told her about the will saying that the house was to remain home for Creedy. At first, Big Annie didn't like it much. She had never liked Creedy and always said he scared her because of how he looked with his hunchback and his deformed legs. But Luther spoke up and said that if that was the only way they could have the house, that it was fine if Creedy wanted to stay on. Creedy would have to earn his keep, though, like he had with Lizzy. Before she agreed, Willa May wanted to talk it over with Creedy.

When they finished supper that night, she asked Creedy if he would sit down so they could talk about his future. She told him that Big Annie and Luther had offered to buy the house and that he could stay on with them.

Creedy shook his head, still wiping tears, and said, "I never thought Big Annie liked me much."

"Oh Creedy, I think once she gets to know you better and she sees how much help you'll be to them, she'll like you just fine."

"Won't nobody ever be as good to me as Lizzy," he sobbed.

Willa May put her arm around his shoulder and said, "Aren't too many people in this old world like my mama, you're right, Creedy. But you have to put what's done behind you and start a new life for yourself. And remember if it doesn't work out with Big Annie, you can always come and stay with us."

"But this here's my home."

It broke Willa May's heart the way he said it. She never realized how deep Creedy's feelings were for Lizzy and the home he had come to look upon as his own. "I know that, Creedy. All I'm saying is that you can count on us if you ever need us."

Creedy nodded and said, "I thank you kindly, Willa May."

For a time, Creedy was content to stay put there. He worked hard in the garden and around the house for Big Annie and Luther. Three years later, Luther died. Willa May had begun to think that Big Annie had grown used to Creedy, but she was wrong. It didn't help, either, that Big Annie was getting on in years. Losing Luther had jumbled what pieces she had left of her mind. That winter was a cold, brutal one with lots of snowstorms and drifts so high, they covered the front door.

It was a bitterly cold night in February when the wind shrieked outside like a woman gone screaming mad. In the middle of the night, Willa May and Daniel woke to a pounding at their door. Thinking it was Elroy and he had crawled his way over to their place sick, Daniel got up. When he opened the door, Creedy was standing there. Barely more than skin and bone, he huddled on the stoop with just a moth eaten blanket wrapped around his thin shoulders. His whiskers were caked with ice crystals and he was white from the cold. Through chattering teeth, he asked, "Can I come in and get warm, D-Daniel?"

"Creedy, what in tarnation are you doing out on a night like this? Why, it's freezing cold out there. Where's your coat and hat? Your gloves and scarf?"

Daniel pulled Creedy inside and closed the door against the moaning wind. He led Creedy over to the fireplace where the last embers were glowing a faint red. Quickly, he stirred the embers and added logs to start a roaring blaze. Creedy stood close to the hearth, shaking so hard that his bones rattled. Daniel reached for the blanket Creedy had wrapped around his shoulders and looked at it closely in the firelight. "Why, Creedy, this old blanket's covered with lice."

Willa May had come down by then and was making her way across the room to where Daniel and Creedy were when Creedy looked from Daniel to her and shuddered. "Big Annie's been making me sleep out in the chicken coop. She won't let me in the house at all."

Willa May and Daniel were shocked. "You mean she's kicked you out?"

"No, she wants me to do the work and she feeds me. She just won't let me in the house."

"How long has this been goin' on, Creedy?" Daniel asked.

"Since Luther died. I don't think Big Annie's right in the head no more. She talks to herself and she told me that Luther's ghost is haunting her. Crazy talk. I couldn't leave her seeing as how she can't do much for herself. Her younguns only come around on Sundays for supper. But I just got so cold out in that coop tonight, I just couldn't stay no longer. I just couldn't.''

"Creedy, you don't have to stay there," Willa May said. "From now on, you're goin' to live here. Daniel will ride over to see Dessie and Shep as soon as the storm breaks and let them know what's happened. Meanwhile, I'm goin' to draw you a good hot bath and I want you to burn all those clothes you're wearing, you hear? The blanket, too. We'll get you some overalls and shirts to wear. Once you're moved in here, we'll get you a new coat and some new boots."

Willa May started to boil some water in her big kettles to fill the tub. Daniel poured Creedy a cup of hot coffee and found him some clothes to wear. Willa May went up to bed and let Daniel help Creedy burn his clothes -- they were crawling with lice -- and get bathed. Once Creedy was in a warm bed with plenty of quilts to keep him warm, he looked at Daniel and said, "I can't thank you enough for taking me in."

"Creedy, you're goin' to be just fine here. I just wish you had come to us sooner. You could've saved yourself a lot of suffering if you had."

Creedy shrugged, "I just couldn't bring myself to up and leave, knowing Big Annie needs somebody to watch over her."

Two days later when the storm broke and Daniel could get down off of the mountain, he rode over to Page to see Dessie and Shep. Shep hitched up his wagon and Dessie climbed in to go see about Big Annie. They found her up by the old tool shed, frozen to death. There was a plate of food frozen solid on the ground beside her. They figured she had gone out to take Creedy some breakfast. Not finding him, she had set down the plate and wandered around in circles over the property.

At the funeral, Dessie and Shep told Creedy that he had done the right thing by leaving. They didn't realize how far gone Big Annie's mind was and they said if Creedy had stayed that night, he would have surely frozen, too. Willa May felt that Creedy still believed that Big Annie would have been alive if he had only stayed on. She pitied Big Annie for never seeing past Creedy's deformity to the loyal heart beating inside him. He deserved better than he had received.

Once he moved in with Willa May and Daniel, he and Elroy took to each other like two old dogs. They were company for each other, sitting up and playing checkers at night, and talking over the old days. Elroy could never get Creedy to take a drop of whiskey. Creedy was too much of a church goer for that. Elroy told Willa May once when he caught Creedy working in the garden, "You know, Willa May, except for the fact that Creedy's never been a drinking man, I'd say he's one of the best old boys I ever done come across."

Willa May chuckled and replied, "Well, Elroy, I reckon it takes a good old boy to know one."

Elroy laughed and gave her a look that held all kinds of mischief. Between Elroy's orneriness and Creedy's deep sense of loyalty, they had more character than most folks Willa May had ever known. She supposed that what they lacked physically, they more than made up for in spirit. She smiled to herself, thinking they certainly were good old boys, the best she had ever known.

Asa and Ansel grew into fine men, still as close as two peas in a pod. When they were old enough, they started in the bootlegging business with Daniel and Elroy. They had heard enough from their folks about the dangers of mining that they never showed any inclination to go into the mines like their brothers. As young men, they looked much like Daniel the first time Willa May saw him, carrying the dead mountain lion. Like Daniel and 'Lil Daniel, they both loved the mountains. They often went off together for weeks at a time like Daniel and came home brimming with tales to tell. Daniel and Willa May knew they were wild as bucking broncos, but they could handle themselves if they had to. Sometimes they went off for a few days drinking in Charleston. Daniel wouldn't tell Willa May, but she knew that whiskey wasn't the only thing keeping their bellies warm when they went into town. She saw how the young girls at church smiled a little too much and too long whenever the twins were there, some of them asking coyly if they were coming to an upcoming picnic or social. She chuckled to herself at those times, thinking that those girls would turn every shade of crimson if they knew what her boys were up to with some less respectable gals in town. She caught Daniel smiling to himself once or twice, too.

Dora Lottie married a young man by the name of Wolerton and moved to Montgomery. He worked on the dam that was being built in Glen Ferris after a hydroelectric generating station opened in

Kanawha Falls. It was owned by a company in the metals business. The company wanted to build a tunnel under Daniel's mountain, from its southern face to their hydroelectric station three miles away. Over the years, several men from the company paid them a call, trying to either buy Daniel's land or lease the water and mineral rights to it. But Daniel saw what had happened to other folks who had sold off rights to big companies and he said he would see those men dead and in hell before he would let them carve up his mountain. It went that way for years, the company offering fool's gold and Daniel telling them to go to hell.

Willa May's greatest joy was in Claude Daniel and Thomas Lee. Both boys begged to come and spend time with their grandparents every summer. Daniel always pretended like he didn't recognize them just to vex them. Once, Thomas Lee asked, "Why, Grandpa, you mean to tell me you don't know who I am?"

With his blue eyes twinkling, Daniel acted as though he suddenly realized who the boys were and pointed to Walt Whitman and Hattie Sue, asking, "You mean to tell me that they've still got you after all these years?"

To Willa May, those boys were as cute as the day was long. Claude Daniel, with his coal black hair so like 'Lil Luther's and Thomas Lee with his deep set, chestnut brown eyes were the embodiment of pride to her. Daniel thrilled in showing the boys how to ride and hunt. Elroy told them war stories till their eyes grew big as saucers, all about the War Between the States, brother fighting brother. When they were big enough to read, Creedy took exceptional pleasure in having them read the Good Book to him. Even though Creedy never learned to read or write, he knew the Good Book by heart. If the boys missed one word, he let them know. As they grew into young men, Thomas Lee often spent many an hour with Creedy, talking over the olden days and reading scripture to Creedy. Creedy loved it. He thought the sun rose and set on Thomas Lee.

The summer when Thomas Lee was seven years old, Walt Whitman brought him to Willa May and Daniel for the entire summer, saying he was busy working on his doctoral degree and needed peace and quiet. Thomas Lee was happier with his grandparents in the summer anyway. There, he could track animals with his grandpa and run barefoot through the rows of corn in the garden, teasing Creedy with his nonsense -- and Creedy licked it all up like a bear cub after a honeycomb.

200

When Walt Whitman brought Thomas Lee late in May, he left off some books for them to read by a woman writer from England by the name of Beatrix Potter. The books were so tiny. When Thomas Lee showed them to Willa May, she held one of them in the palm of her hand, marveling over the pretty pictures -- Peter Rabbit in his little blue coat and that rascal, Jeremy Fisher, all set to go fishing. There was cute little Miss Tiggywinkle, plump and round with sparkling dark eyes so like Thomas Lee's. Thomas Lee insisted on reading all the books the first night. Even Daniel, Elroy, and Creedy carried on over them. From that night on, they read at least one Beatrix Potter book each night along with their scripture reading and a chapter from The Prince and the Pauper. Everyone went to bed with a light heart that summer. Willa May knew it was from their reading time. Throughout the summer, Thomas Lee searched all over the woods for a hedgehog like Miss Tiggywinkle. He wanted to catch one and keep it for a pet. No one had the heart to tell him that they had never seen any such varmint in their hills. One day when Thomas Lee and Daniel were up in the woods, they spotted a mole. Thomas Lee nearly burst with joy, saying, "Look, Grandpa. Miss Tiggywinkle!"

Daniel couldn't bring himself to tell the boy that what he had found was a common mole, so he pretended to go along and said in a voice filled with awe, "Well, I'll be."

Both Claude Daniel and Thomas Lee were bright, so bright Willa May couldn't keep up with them. Claude Daniel had a doctor's mind right from the start, watching closely whenever Daniel skinned a 'possum or a squirrel for dinner, wanting to know what each innard was called. Thomas Lee couldn't get enough of reading. He read sonnets from Shakespeare, the whole story of King Arthur, and Beowulf when he was only ten years old. He read everything he could get his hands on. What time he wasn't reading, he questioned Willa May endlessly about the history of her family and their home. He ate up stories about the Indian chief, Cornstalk, and Andrew Lewis's army. He listened again and again to stories about Ambrose Bierce, General Cox, and David Hunter Strother, the man who hurled a stone all the way across their gorge to win a bet during the Civil War. When Daniel told Thomas Lee that he had worked over at Hinton with John Henry who was already a legend, Thomas Lee's eyes bulged in astonishment.

Willa May knew the boys were way smarter than she had ever been, even smarter than Walt Whitman was at that age and she had never known anyone smarter than Walt Whitman. She watched the boys play and challenge each other as boys do, each wanting to be the cock of the walk. In her mind, she saw 'Lil Daniel and Walt Whitman when they were just boys. How she loved those grandsons.

One hot summer evening, Thomas Lee and Willa May sat out on the porch, snapping beans for supper, when a wagon pulled up in front of the cabin. For anyone to come calling during the week was unusual enough, but this wagon had two colored folks riding on it. The man driving the team of mules was small but strong, no stranger to heavy labor. He had wide shoulders, muscular arms, and a barrel chest. The woman -- a small, thin little thing -- looked prim in her blue flowered dress and pretty blue hat. She even had on white gloves, as hot as it was. She looked at Willa May a long time and Willa May started feeling plain under this nicely dressed woman's gaze. After a moment's pause, the woman asked, "Is this the home of one Daniel Shrewsbury what's married to a woman named Willa May?"

Willa May stood up and stepped down off the porch. "Yes...I'm Willa May. Just what is it I can do for you?"

The woman smiled, showing lots of white teeth against her dark skin. "Why, Miss Willa May, you already done plenty -- more than I can ever repay you for."

Willa May knew she had never seen this woman before. Squinting in the blazing sun, she asked, "Do I know you, Miss?"

"It's Mrs. -- Mrs. Leon Warren. Except them that knows me just calls me Dicey."

Willa May couldn't believe it. Little Dicey, just a skinny little girl when Daniel swept her up in his arms, wrapped in their wedding quilt so long ago. Now she was a grown woman. Willa May clutched at her heart. "Dicey? The same little Dicey that left here with her brother, Isaiah?"

Giggling, Dicey nodded. "That'd be me, all right."

"Well, Lord's sake! Get down off of that wagon and come on in. I can't believe it! After all these years." Willa May was nearly jumping with excitement.

Dicey and her husband climbed down and went inside. Willa May could see that her man was nervous about being in a white person's home, so she said, "Now you both just come on in and set yourselves down. I got a blackberry pie I made today and some fresh squeezed lemonade to cool you off. And I don't take no for an answer."

"That's the Willa May I remember," Dicey laughed.

They sat down and cut into the blackberry pie. "What in the world happened to you after Daniel took you two off that night?"

"Well," Dicey answered, wiping her mouth daintily, "Daniel took us to his friend, Eb, that big old mountain man?"

Willa May nodded, recalling Eb...and his ripe odor.

"Eb took us on to Pittsburgh to a family there that had helped runaways before the war. Their names were Parker. Mr. Parker took us on to some Quaker folks that lived on a farm, close to the state line. Then that Quaker family took us on to Buffalo up in New York State. From there, we rode across Lake Ontario to Canada. Isaiah's still there. He's a preacher now. But I never wanted to live there. I figured that I was rightly born here in the United States of America, and Lord willing, I was goin' to die here, too. So I came back by way of Buffalo -- that's where I met Leon, here. He was working on the Erie Canal up there. When he found out I came from around here, he said he had cousins living close by. We came here and settled down. It took me quite a few years, I reckon, but I'm back and I aim to stay."

Willa May took Dicey's hand in hers and said, "I'm mighty glad you made it, too."

"That reminds me," she said. Turning to Leon, she added, "Go fetch that surprise for me."

"Surprise? Why, Dicey, you didn't have to bring us anything. You know that."

"Oh, yes I did, too. And I think you're goin' to be mighty glad to get this here little surprise."

Leon came back in. When Willa May saw what he was carrying, she gasped. Folded over his big arm was her wedding quilt that Dicey had been wrapped in the night Daniel carried her off into the darkness with Isaiah. She rushed over to where Leon was holding the quilt. Through the blur of her tears, she could see that the quilt was clean and just like new.

"I took good care of that quilt all these years for you, Willa May. I figured I owed you that much after what you and Daniel did for us."

Willa May held the quilt to her, recalling the young girl she was when she pieced and sewed night after night with her mama, making a quilt for her hope chest. Nothing could have made her happier at that moment. She ran her hand over the colored pieces and thought about all the hopes and dreams that were stitched into that quilt. "Thank you, Dicey. Thank you for bringing something I cherished back to me."

Dicey smiled and hugged her. Then her face grew serious. "Them men came back here after Daniel took us away, didn't they?"

Willa May nodded. "Burned us out, they did. They beat me and made me lose the baby I was carrying. They left me knocked out cold with little Josie tied to me."

"Oh, no." Dicey shook her head sorrowfully. "I always knew deep in my heart that you and Daniel had risked everything for us that night, trying to save us from those men who killed our folks. We owe you our lives, Isaiah and me."

"Just seeing you alive and well and grown up into such a lady like you are is all that matters. I've wondered many a time whatever happened to you two. I'll tell you something else -- I can't let you leave before Daniel gets a chance to see you. He'll be so tickled, he just won't believe it. Little Dicey back after all this time."

Dicey and Leon stayed for supper. Daniel was as delighted as Willa May to see Dicey doing so well. They talked and talked, all squeals and laughter at first. As the evening wore on, their voices turned to soft sighs and quiet reflection. Dicey asked Daniel to show her where her folks were buried before she left. Daniel reminded her that the land her pa had bought years ago was still theirs, but Dicey shook her head, saying, "Too many bad memories, Daniel. Please, if you can ever sell it, go ahead. I don't ever want to see that place again. It'd only bring back the fear and the pain."

"Then let me pay you back what your pa gave me for the land. That's the least I can do."

"No," Dicey shook her head, refusing to hear such talk. "You gave me my life, Daniel. Ain't no money in the world can do that. You keep your land and the money Pa gave you. Whatever he gave you wasn't enough for the two lives you saved."

With big tears in her eyes, Dicey leaned over and hugged Daniel. Daniel and Leon both looked embarrassed at this show of feelings. They were men who never showed much of what they felt inside and neither knew what to do when a woman displayed such tenderness.

It was growing dark when Daniel took Leon and Dicey over to the gorge and showed them the two graves he had kept up over the years. Dicey picked some wildflowers and placed them on the graves. She cried as she offered a prayer for her folks. She asked Daniel if he ever found out who the men were wearing those hoods that night. Daniel scuffed his boot in the dirt and looked across the gorge. "Let's just say, Dicey, that them men learned a lesson from the Good Book, 'an eye for an eye and a tooth for a tooth'."

Dicey nodded, knowing that Daniel wasn't going to say more, but she knew that he had avenged her folks' deaths. Appeased, she and Leon rode off into the night. After that, Dicey came around once or twice a year, usually in summer and fall. Willa May felt it was a shame that they couldn't have been closer, but she knew there were folks who would readily don robes and hoods if they heard of any white folks befriending coloreds. It had been forty years and still folks weren't ready to accept people of color as equals. Didn't say much, Willa May thought, for humankind.

On a hot, muggy night in late July when the air felt moist and heavy, Willa May was in bed when she woke up to hear Asa talking in a whisper to Daniel. Daniel had been asleep next to her, but he leapt out of bed and headed downstairs.

"What is it? What's happened?" she asked, feeling groggy still.

Neither Daniel nor Asa answered her right away and that brought her around. Before she could ask Asa again what had happened, she heard a moan from downstairs. Nobody had to tell her it was Ansel. Asa wouldn't have woken his pa in the middle of the night unless it was an emergency and the twins were never far apart. "All right," she sighed, upset with Daniel and Asa for not speaking up. "What's happened to Ansel?"

Even in the dark, she could see Asa turn from her to Daniel and back again. He stood shifting back and forth on his feet like he had when he was little and had to get to the outhouse. Another moan drifted up from below. "Stop that hopping around and tell me what's goin' on," she snapped.

Asa's voice came out breathless and she could hear the fear in it. "Anse" -- Willa May was the only one who insisted on calling him by his full name -- "got himself cut up. Pretty bad, too."

Stalking out of the room, Daniel rushed for the stairs. Willa May pulled her shawl around her shoulders and hurried down behind him. In the light of a candle, she could see Ansel slumped over in a chair by the mahogany dining table. His shirt hung in shreds. Dark crimson splotches outlined each tear and spread in strange patterns over what was left of the shirt. His right arm hung limp and blood dripped from his fingertips, making a small pool on the cabin floor.

"I need more light!" Willa May cried, racing to where their boy lay moaning.

Daniel lit some coal oil lamps. As the light grew brighter, Willa May could see Ansel's chest and belly through the tears in his shirt. Blood seeped from a number of gashes and matted the golden hair that covered his chest. She started pulling off his shirt -- what was left of it -- taking care to pull as gently as she could where the blood soaked material stuck to his skin. Once she had the shirt off, she could see more surface cuts across his belly and one deep cut high on his right shoulder. Willa May didn't like the way that his arm dangled limply. The cut had gone through the muscle and possibly severed tendons. She worried that Ansel might lose the use of the arm, it looked so bad.

She turned to face Asa. "What in tarnation did you get yourself into?"

Asa's eyes were wide and showing a lot of white. He couldn't take his eyes off of Ansel. "Do you want me to go fetch Young Doc?"

"No. What I want is an answer. And sometime before your brother bleeds to death."

At that, even Daniel looked fretful. He always said that when she got riled, Willa May was meaner than a nest of copperheads. Elroy knocked on the door just then, hollering, "What's goin' on?"

Daniel crossed the room and opened the door. Asa still hadn't answered Willa May and she was growing angrier by the second. He shifted from one foot to the other, staring wide eyed at his brother. Elroy rolled in and Willa May heard his breath catch when he saw Ansel's bloody wounds. She threw herself at Asa, pounding his chest with her fists and yelling, "Are you goin' to give me an answer or do I have to beat it out of you?"

Asa wouldn't stop her. He just stood there and took every blow while he stared at Ansel, turning white from fear of losing his twin. Daniel pulled Willa May off of Asa, holding her arms so she couldn't move. She screamed, a long deep scream that came from deep in her gut, a scream of helplessness and frustration. Daniel held her to him. Her screams left her limp and crying. Through her tears, she heard Ansel's voice. Weak from loss of blood, he begged, "Mommy, don't be mad. I'm sorry to cause you so much trouble." Willa May shook Daniel's hands off and ran to Ansel. His eyes rolled in their sockets. She knew he could hear her, but he couldn't find her. She brushed his hair, wet from sweat, back from his forehead and said, "It's all right, Son. I'm goin' to fix you up good as new. You just hang on while

206

Mommy takes care of those cuts."

She thought she saw Ansel give a little nod, then his eyes closed and his head fell forward. Luckily, Thomas Lee and Claude Daniel were still with them. At first, Willa May didn't see the two boys watching from the steps. Her screams had woken them.

Claude Daniel came closer and studied Ansel's wounds. He turned to Thomas Lee and said, "Get some fresh water. Lots of it."

Willa May reached out and stopped Thomas Lee as he headed obediently toward the door. "You boys go back to bed and let us grown-ups handle this. It's not for little boys to see." Claude Daniel kept his eyes fixed on Ansel and said, "If you and I both work on him, I think we can sew him up before he loses much more blood."

It was as much his take-charge way of saying it as what he had said that made Willa May look at her grandson, all of twelve years and see the man he was to become standing before her. He glanced up at her long enough to say, "Grandma, get your quilting thread. Grandpa, we're goin' to need lots of whiskey for cleaning the wounds and the needles. Thomas Lee, I need that water. Now."

Thomas Lee sprang past Willa May and Daniel headed for the shed to fetch a keg of whiskey. Elroy rolled over and asked, "What can I do?"

Without turning around, Claude Daniel said, "Hold those needles over the fire for a couple of minutes, then bring them over here."

Willa May handed Elroy two of her quilting needles and he took his spot by the fire. Daniel came in with the whiskey. Claude Daniel and Willa May soaked some clean cloths and wiped down Ansel's wounds. Elroy rolled back over with the needles. Willa May threaded them, handing one to Claude Daniel and taking the other for herself. Thomas Lee came in with the first bucket of water. Seeing that they were trying to help Ansel, Asa poured the water into the biggest kettle and stoked the fire.

With only a moment's hesitation, Claude Daniel began stitching one of the wounds, telling Willa May to suture another one close by. He told Daniel to keep soaking the deep gash on Ansel's shoulder and to clean it thoroughly. Fortunately, Ansel was still passed out, as much from loss of blood as from his drinking earlier that night, Willa May suspected. But when Claude Daniel started sewing up the deep gash on Ansel's shoulder, Ansel twisted away in pain. "Asa, help me hold him down," Daniel said. Ansel moaned with every stitch. Claude Daniel set about sewing the torn tissue they could see inside

207

the wound, then the outer flesh.

When Willa May and Claude Daniel were finished, Daniel and Asa carried Ansel to his room. Then Claude Daniel said, "Better go get Pa and tell him what's happened. Tell him to come and see if he can keep Uncle Ansel from sinking into a fever. Maybe he can give Uncle Ansel something for his pain."

It was Daniel's turn to look surprised. "You reckon the boy's right?"

"Go on. Do as the boy says. He must have learned something from watching his pa all these years," Willa May replied.

Daniel hurried out the door. Willa May started to make biscuits and coffee, figuring everyone was hungry, but Elroy brushed her aside. "I can do that. Thomas Lee can help. You go on in with Ansel."

By the time Daniel came back with Young Doc and Hattie Sue -- she couldn't bear to hear that her baby brother was hurt -- Elroy and Thomas Lee had made a fine breakfast. Young Doc looked in on Ansel and gave him a shot, then he came back and joined everyone at the table. While they ate, Daniel bragged on how Claude Daniel had tended to Ansel. "Just like a real doctor." It made Young Doc happy. He was so proud of Claude Daniel, it was no wonder that everyone assumed the boy was really his son.

They finished eating and Willa May looked at Asa. He had been noticeably quiet through breakfast. "Asa, I reckon it's about time you tell us how Ansel got himself cut to pieces like he did."

All eyes turned to Asa. He squirmed in his chair. Daniel agreed with Willa May. "That's right. Speak up, Son. I want to hear it all."

Asa knew when Daniel said he wanted to hear it all, he meant everything. Looking down at the tabletop, Asa sighed and said, "We were just playing poker with some old boys over at the Stockton Tavern."

"And what old boys would that be?" Daniel inquired.

"Oley Hansford, Tiny Shinn, Red Hutchinson, and Dewey Braxton."

Daniel took in the names and nodded for Asa to continue.

"Anyway, Oley was losing real bad to Anse all night and getting drunk as a lord, to boot. He was down to his last dollar when Anse beat him with a royal flush. He jumped up, pulled out his hunting knife, saying Anse was cheating and called Anse a fucking sonofabitch -- sorry, Mommy, Hattie Sue."

"And what'd Anse do?"

"Anse stood up real slow, keeping his hands where Oley could see them and keeping his eyes right on Oley and that knife. Then he grinned real big and said, 'Did I hear you call me a fucking sonofabitch, Oley?' And Oley said, 'That's right'."

"Is that when he went for Anse?" Daniel asked.

"Not exactly, Pa." Asa squirmed some more in his chair.

"Well, what *exactly* did he do?" Willa May could hear Daniel getting exasperated.

"He looked right at Oley and said, 'Well now, Oley, I'll have you know I'm not just a fucking sonofabitch. I'm one *hell* of a fucking sonofabitch...according to your wife'."

Daniel rubbed the back of his neck and muttered, "Oh, shit."

"That's when Oley looked at Anse and said, 'Just what would you be knowing about my wife?' Anse grinned even bigger and said, 'I know she's got a pretty red birthmark on the inside of her left thigh the color of a ripe June strawberry'. That's when Oley started slashing that big old hunting knife at Anse, jumping clear across the poker table. Anse picked up the bottle we'd been drinking from, broke it over the table, and used it to fend off Oley. He got in a few good cuts, too."

"How bad was Oley hurt?"

Asa grinned sheepishly. "Lot worse than Anse, Pa."

Daniel looked at Asa reproachfully. "Well, when Anse is well enough, he's got some answering to do for himself. Neither one of you is too big yet for me to handle. You hear me?"

Asa sat up straight and put on a serious face. "Yessir."

Ansel's punishment was no more poker playing while he was under his folks' roof and to go to church every Sunday for the rest of that year, starting the following week. But that worked to his favor, too. Oley Hansford was there, his jaw bandaged up from where Ansel had cut him, and his left arm was in a sling. His pretty young wife, Louise, sat next to him, not daring to look left or right. She was sporting a shiner on her right eye. Ansel sat next to Willa May and she looked from him to Asa, to Young Doc, then to Daniel. Every one of them smiled all the way through the service. She figured folks must think that those Shrewsbury men were the happiest gallderned churchgoers that Baptist church had ever seen.

In the last days of August, Thomas Lee and Claude Daniel decided to go hunting for a twelve-pound bronze cannon that was said to be somewhere on the mountain. The Confederates had used it to blast General Lightburn's men in 1862. Rumor had it that it was up in a ravine where the boys in gray had left it in their rush to get down off Cotton Hill to claim the Yankees' left-over supplies. Many a yarn had grown up over the years about the cannon. Thomas Lee and Claude Daniel were determined to find it. They had planned quite an adventure, taking along a tent and some provisions for several days.

The boys were gone three days when close to suppertime, Thomas Lee came running into the cabin out of breath. He told Daniel to come quick. Willa May and Daniel feared that something terrible had happened to Claude Daniel.

"What's wrong? What's happened, Thomas Lee? Is Claude Daniel hurt?" Daniel asked.

Thomas Lee gulped in air and shook his head, holding onto his ribs. "No," he gasped, "he's fine. He sent me here to get you."

"Well, did you find that old cannon? Is that it?"

Again, Thomas Lee shook his head. "Something else. You'd better come see."

Daniel turned to Willa May. "I reckon I'd better go, then." Turning back to Thomas Lee, he said, "This had better not be some kind of fool trick. I ain't goin' to be real happy with you if that's what this is all about."

Thomas Lee shook his head harder. "It's no trick, Grandpa. Just come quick."

"I'll hold off on supper till you get back. And bring them younguns with you. They're probably hungry as little bears by now," Willa May said.

Creedy and Elroy were shucking corn on the porch. Willa May went out with them to watch Daniel and Thomas Lee disappear into the woods, heading toward the ridge that looked down over Gauley Bridge. "Wonder what in tarnation those younguns have found?" she sighed, sitting down in her rocker to help with the shucking.

Elroy shook his head and gave a snort, "Willa May, it's hard telling. You know what younguns are like. What ain't worth a hoot and a holler to us is like a gold mine to them. They probably found some old soldier's ring or something and they're figuring they done found some lost treasure that'll make us all rich."

"I wouldn't mind being rich," she replied. "Lord knows I've been poor long enough. Seems to me it'd only be fair to try being rich for awhile now."

Willa May was joking, but Creedy took her seriously. He looked up from the ripe, golden ear of corn he held and said, "Does that mean I can quit this here shucking for good?"

"Not if you want to eat," Willa May answered, winking at Elroy.

Elroy snickered and said, "Oh, hell. What good would it do to be rich anyhow? Probably, the government would take all of it anyway."

They laughed all evening, coming up with any number of things that the two boys could have found. It was way past nightfall when Daniel and the boys came wandering back to the cabin. Daniel looked grim as he walked inside to where they sat waiting. He carried a lady's hat box in his hands. It looked the worse for wear, dirty and crushed on one side. Gently, he set it down on the floor in front of where Creedy sat in his favorite rocker.

"Well, what'd you find, Daniel?" Elroy asked, leaning over for a good view.

Daniel didn't say a word. He waited until everyone was huddled over the hat box, craning their necks to see. All he said as he lifted the lid to the box was, "You ain't goin' to believe it."

It seemed like half a lifetime to Willa May until the lid was raised enough for them to peer inside. What they saw there made Creedy gasp, "Oh, my Lord!"

Elroy and Willa May both looked in wonderment at the tiny thing inside. "Who would do such a thing?" Willa May cried, wondering why Daniel had brought this into their home.

"That's what the law's goin' to have to figure out, I reckon," Daniel said as they all stared in horror at the small corpse inside the tattered box. It was a baby, newborn. The birthing cord was cut, but never tied. What was left of the cord dangled down across the baby's belly. An intricate hat pin rose out of the baby's chest, right where its heart was. It was obvious to them that somebody had killed the poor child and tried to cover their tracks by leaving it up in the woods inside the hat box.

"Where did you find it?" Willa May breathed, still taking in what she was seeing and wanting somehow to wake the slumbering baby and comfort it.

Claude Daniel spoke up. "We found it up in a cave. It was real dry in there. I reckon that's why it's stayed so well. It hasn't rotted much at all."

211

"Oh, my Lord!" Creedy cried again and limped out onto the porch for air.

Elroy, still looking at the baby, echoed Willa May's thoughts. "Who could've done such a thing? Killing a helpless little baby."

Daniel frowned. "I don't know, but I aim to find out. I'm goin' for the sheriff right now. He's goin' to want to ask the boys some questions, so I reckon you'd better feed them and get them cleaned up. Try and keep 'em awake till I can get back."

Willa May did as Daniel said, feeding the boys a supper of cold fried chicken, corn on the cob, pickled beets, turnips, and cornbread. They washed it all down with slices of the chess pie Willa May had baked that day. As they ate, Elroy pumped them with questions about how they had come across the box. They took turns explaining that they had climbed all over the hillside, searching for the ravine where the cannon was supposed to be. When they didn't find it, they started looking for a good place to hide a cannon. After two days, they found the cave. Its entrance was covered with branches. They had to drag the branches away before going inside to search for the cannon. Holding just a candle, they wandered deep into the cave to find only bear leavings and further back, the box. They figured that they had found something worthless -- photographs or letters -- then they opened the lid to find the dead baby inside.

Daniel came back with the sheriff and the boys told their story again. The sheriff said he recognized the hat box from a store down in Montgomery. Maybe he could find the killers if he could find out who their regular customers were. He thought he could trace the hat pin to its owner. It was a pretty pin, with elaborate scroll work in silver and a large oval stone that looked like a ruby. The stone was surrounded by tiny pearls. It was something folks would recall seeing.

Before he left, the sheriff thanked Daniel and the boys for their help. He asked if they would be willing to testify if there was a trial. Daniel said he guessed that if it came to that, that he and the boys would be there. As the sheriff turned to leave, Willa May asked, "What about that poor little baby? What's goin' to happen to him now?"

"Right now, the body is evidence. But once we've had a chance to examine it and photograph it for our investigation, it'll be buried, I guess. Why?"

"Oh, I reckon after birthing fifteen of my own, it just bothers me that somebody could have harmed something so helpless and fragile.

212

Seems to me that the least we can do is see to it that the little fellow gets a decent burial."

The sheriff smiled -- the only hint he had shown of a softer side -- and nodded in agreement. "I'll sure see to it that he gets buried right, with a preacher and all. Then I aim to find the cold-blooded killer that did this and see that he gets what he's got coming, too."

Willa May felt relieved to hear this. None of them could imagine what would bring a person to kill a baby and it nagged at them. For several nights, Willa May woke up thinking about the baby, shivering to think what kind of monster was responsible for his death. As for Elroy, he could talk of nothing else for days. Creedy couldn't bear to listen to Elroy. He was too shocked by such cold-hearted brutality.

It was mid-September when Daniel came home with the news that the sheriff had arrested a man and a woman for the murder. The man's name was Lavender. He worked in the mines and roomed at a boarding house in Montgomery. Lavender was having an affair with the woman whose husband owned the boarding house. Her name was Cynthia Skaggs. Her husband was a traveling salesman, on the road for months at a time. She knew that if her husband found out she was pregnant, he would know the baby wasn't his and kill her and the boarder, too. The couple kept it a secret that she was expecting. She starved herself during the pregnancy, cinching in her corset as tightly as she could until the last two months. The boarder told everyone she was feeling poorly and ran all her errands while she hid herself away inside the big house. When the baby was born, they killed it and hid the body. They used the fancy hat pin, a gift that Lavender had bought for her. Lots of folks had seen her wearing the hat pin and knew it belonged to her.

When the two were brought in, it didn't take long for the sheriff to get a confession out of them. They were still trying to keep their affair from the woman's husband. In the end, the pair pleaded guilty and each was sentenced to twenty-five years in prison. Willa May thought they got off easy at that.

Before the boys went home at the end of the summer, Willa May took them over to the gorge and pointed down to the New River below. "See that river yonder?"

Both boys nodded and peered down into the canyon.

213

"I'm goin' to tell you about that river. It's the oldest river on this continent. Did you know that? My school teacher, Mr. Shaw -- God rest his soul -- told me so. Only river older than this one is the Nile way over in Egypt land. The New River starts down in what they call the Smoky Mountains down in North Carolina and hooks up with the Greenbrier River after it cuts through Virginia and heads on up here into West Virginia. Just down the mountain in Gauley Bridge, it partners up with the Gauley River to make what's called the Great Kanawha. Now the Kanawha flows south to north. It's even older than the mountains surrounding it."

Claude Daniel and Thomas Lee gazed at the tops of the mountains spread out before them veiled in early morning mist with shafts of sunlight piercing through. Their eyes took in every slope of the dark green hills as Willa May spoke.

"This old river has seen every kind of human from the earliest on. The first folks were hunters, scouring the hillsides for varmints to feed on. Then came some Indian tribes who never really got settled in here. After them came the Cherokee and Shawnee. They lived here, claiming all this land as their own till the white man came from across the ocean and elbowed them out. Way back in the seventeen hundreds, a gal named Mary Draper Ingles was taken prisoner by the Shawnee right here on this very river. But that old gal must've had some spunk because she made her way back upstream to where her kinfolk had a cabin over in Blacksburg. When the railroad came, it brought more folks into these hills. My own folks came here way back when the Indians were still living here. They hailed from Scotland. They came by way of the north part of Ireland over yonder in Europe. There's been Kincaids here in these parts as long as there's been white settlers."

She paused for a moment, letting the boys digest all this. Thomas Lee spoke up and said, "Tell us more, Grandma."

Pointing to a cliff overlooking the gorge, she said, "See that rocky cliff?"

Two heads nodded as one.

"Indians say that two young folks, Little Fawn, who was Cherokee, and Running Deer, who was Shawnee, fell in love. When their folks wouldn't give them their blessing, they jumped from that cliff right there to their deaths on the rocks down yonder." She turned back to the boys looking at her with big eyes. "And that's why folks hereabouts call that cliff 'Lovers Leap'."

214

Willa May saw that the boys were eating this up. No sooner did she finish, when they asked, "What else, Grandma?"

"Well, down at Beards Fork, they tell me that some real smart scientists studied some carvings they found scraped into a big old rock. Some folks around those parts thought it was some kind of Indian writing, but these men said they thought it was some ancient Irish language. Something they called 'Ogham'. They figured that the drawings were some kind of message, maybe something from the Bible."

"You reckon," asked Thomas Lee, "that all these stories are true, Grandma?"

Willa May shrugged. "Only the bears and the wildcats and the other critters can say for sure. They've been here longer than anybody."

"Something I don't understand," Thomas Lee said. He squinted up at her.

"What's that?"

"Why would those two Indians want to kill themselves just because they couldn't marry up?"

Chuckling to herself, Willa May ruffled Thomas Lee's long brown hair and said, "Oh, someday -- and probably not that far off -- I think you'll know the answer to that."

Claude Daniel spoke up. "If your folks hadn't let you marry Grandpa, would you and Grandpa have killed yourselves?"

Willa May sighed. "I know I look like just an old woman to the two of you, but there was a time when I was young and pretty with bright red hair down my back. One day, I looked up to see this strapping young man walking toward me out of the mountains with a dead mountain lion slung across his back --"

"You mean Grandpa?" Thomas Lee asked, his big brown eyes nearly popping.

"Yessir. That was your grandpa, all right."

"Grandpa killed a mountain lion? For real?"

"Yep. But that's his story. You've got to ask him to tell that one."

"Did you know right then that you were goin' to marry Grandpa?"

"No, but he knew it. Told me so, too."

The boys giggled, elbowing each other. "And did you say 'yes' right then?"

"Not exactly. I didn't see him again for another five years."

"Five years! Where did he go?"

"Off to war."

"The war where Uncle Elroy lost his legs?"

"The very one."

"So what did you do?"

"Waited."

"For five whole years?"

Willa May nodded, smiling to herself and remembering that back then, it sounded like a long time to her, too.

"Gosh, Grandma. You must've loved Grandpa a lot to wait that long."

"Well, if you know that there's only one special someone in this whole world for you, then you do just about anything you have to for him."

Thomas Lee shook his head in doubt. "I don't know any old girl I'd ever wait five whole years for."

"You will. Take my word for it. You will."

Chapter Nine

James Houston and Ethan Allen were still working in the Paint Creek mines, both of them married and raising their families -- big families of six and seven children -- on pennies a day. Like all but the Cabin Creek mines, the Paint Creek mines had joined the United Mine Workers by then. James Houston was one of several miners who discovered that they were being paid two and a half cents less on the ton than other miners who had already unionized. As one of the union leaders, James Houston was among a group that met to settle on a new contract. The miners asked for the two and a half cents they felt they were rightly due. The increase amounted to fifteen cents more a day for each miner, but the mine operators stood firm. No raise, no matter what other miners were making. James Houston went back to his men. When he told the miners they had been turned down, they decided to strike.

In April of 1912, the miners in Cabin Creek heard about the strike over in Paint Creek. They went to their operators and demanded the right to join the union. Blacklisting was another thorn in their sides. If a miner was fired at one mine, his name was sent around to all the mines in the area, warning them not to hire him. But the worst offense was a practice the miners called "cribbing". Mine operators came up with the idea to attach what they called a "crib" to the cars. It was an extra piece that fit around the top of each coal car to make the car even deeper. With a crib, a coal car could hold an additional five hundred or even a thousand pounds, but the miners weren't paid for the surplus weight. Cribbing infuriated the miners, forcing them to do extra work with no additional pay. The Cabin Creek miners also wanted to have their own check-weighmen to verify what the company weighmen said they had mined. Under state law, mines had to hire check-weighmen, but coal operators disregarded the law. It was common knowledge that the coal operators cheated the miners. Everyone knew that some miners loaded as much as three thousand pounds, but the check-weighmen only marked off a fraction of that.

It came as no surprise to folks in the valley when the Cabin Creek miners joined with the Paint Creek miners and went out on strike, too.

With no intention of losing money, the mine owners hired mine guards. To keep the peace, they said. But everyone knew that these guards were brought in to break the strike and they had been instructed to use any means necessary. A hardened crew, the guards were employed by the Baldwin-Felts Detective Agency in Bluefield. Many had served time. They were common thugs, hoodlums looking for trouble. Train after train arrived in Montgomery, unloading hundreds of guards who patrolled the company property twenty miles into the hollows. They were itching for a fight. Smug and surly, they claimed they had broken many a strike before. Most of them weren't even from West Virginia.

Knowing trouble was brewing, Walt Whitman went to see Daniel and Willa May. He told them that James Houston and Ethan Allen had been thrown out of their homes, along with all the other striking miners. The guards had loaded up all their belongings and hauled them out of the coal camps, dumping everything over a hill once they were off company owned land. Other guards herded up the miners and their kin. Poking them with their rifles, they marched the miners and their families out of the camps in front of all their neighbors. The mine owners knew the miners had nowhere else to go. Walt Whitman said that some of them were finding shelter under cliffs and in caves. Lucky ones like James Houston and Ethan Allen put up tents along the banks of the Kanawha River. With no food and no money to buy any, they were slowly starving. Their children couldn't even go to school because the schools were on company property. The miners couldn't pick up their mail because the post offices were on land owned by the mines. Crossing onto company owned land was considered trespassing and the guards, hidden along the hillsides, were told to shoot all trespassers.

When Walt Whitman finished, Willa May asked, "What can we do? I'll be more than happy to send food and clothes, you know that. But what about the children? Are James Houston and Ethan Allen really goin' to force their younguns to live like that? Starving and homeless?"

"They're bitter men, Mommy. I already offered for the children to come and stay with Annie Catherine and me so they could at least go to school and have a roof over their heads and food to eat. But neither James Houston nor Ethan Allen would hear of it. They said that they were setting an example for so many others who are already worse off than they are. Besides, they feel that it's a lesson in life for their children to see what it means to be loyal to something, to sacrifice for that loyalty."

Daniel shook his head. "Hell of a lesson, I'd say."

Elroy spit a stream of tobacco juice into the open fire. "Just how far are those boys willing to carry this strike?"

"As far as they have to, I guess, Elroy. And that's what worries me. What with the murdering hearts of those mine guards they've brought in, it wouldn't surprise me to find all those miners massacred. Like the army used to do to the Indians. It wasn't right then and it isn't right now. But the mine owners have all the power. They run the schools, the stores, and the government. Those miners are facing a losing battle."

Daniel stood up and stretched. "They might have all the power, but they damn well better not touch a hair on the head of one of mine, by God!" That said, he stalked out the door and sat on the porch.

Walt Whitman looked at Willa May. "Mommy, I'm telling you this right now. Be prepared for anything. It's going to get a lot worse before it gets better...whether Pa likes it or not."

A few weeks later on a Saturday night, Asa stumbled in carrying Ansel over his shoulder. Bright red blood dripped across the floor as Asa made his way over to the same chair where Ansel had sat when Willa May sewed him up from the fight with Oley Hansford.

"Wh-- what happened?" Willa May gasped. Before Asa could answer, Daniel demanded, "Who shot him?"

Willa May bent over Ansel and saw a red splotch spreading in a wide circle from his back, up on his left shoulder. "Help me get him into bed. I'll need to get that bloody shirt off so I can see how bad the wound is. You might have to go fetch Young Doc."

This seemed to quiet Daniel for the time being. The two of them carried Ansel to his bed, Daniel holding Ansel's arms and Asa taking his feet. Before they laid Ansel down, Willa May unbuttoned his shirt and, with Daniel's help, got it off. Once they put Ansel face down on the bed, she examined the wound more closely. The bullet had gone through. It left a dark hole at the tip end of his collar bone, shattering that part of the bone. Still he was lucky. It seemed like Ansel was always lucky, always getting by. Elroy was fond of saying that Ansel could charm a snake...or charm the pants off a person. Willa May figured that he had probably charmed the pants off the wrong person this time. "The bullet's gone clean through. I'll stitch up that big hole in the front. Meanwhile, he'll need a poultice to keep it from festering."

Daniel made the poultices. He knew all the plants and herbs and where they grew. Willa May thought he would go out and start picking what he needed to make the poultice, but he didn't move. He asked Asa again, "Who shot him?"

Asa danced from one foot to the other. When he didn't answer right away, Daniel said, "I asked you who shot your brother and I want my answer. Now."

Asa took a long breath and said, "Emmet Petry."

"Petry? Ain't he the preacher down at that Baptist Church in Montgomery?"

"Yep."

Daniel looked Asa right in the eye and raised his eyebrows, waiting.

"Well, Pa, seems that Anse has been seeing the preacher's wife on the sly. Her name's Irene. You've probably seen her. She's a little old thing, about five feet high with dark brown hair and big brown eyes --"

"And your brother's been cavorting around with a married woman? A *preacher's wife*?"

Asa shifted back and forth. "Yessir."

"How long has this been goin' on?"

"Between Anse and Irene?"

Daniel looked harder at Asa. "You mean to say he's been seeing others, too?"

Asa drew another long breath. "Well...we are talking about Anse, Pa."

Daniel looked from Asa to Willa May. She shrugged. She didn't know what Daniel expected her to do about it. Ansel was a grown man. From the time he was no taller than the table, he and Asa had both done as they pleased. Wild as they were, she was surprised that Daniel found it difficult to understand how they got into such scrapes. They looked exactly alike, but Ansel was the leader. He reminded Willa May of Daniel when they were first married. He was reckless, a free spirit that nobody would ever tame. Ansel was always taking

220

chances while Asa showed a saner mind. Asa stood back and watched Ansel prove himself again and again. He was always there to pick Ansel up when he failed and got himself hurt. Nearing seventy, Daniel couldn't comprehend the recklessness of the son who was most like him in his youth. As he stood there looking at Willa May, he didn't say it, but she knew what he was thinking. *"Why would that boy do such a thing?"*

A part of her wanted to say, "Why would you try and tangle with a mountain lion when you didn't have anything but a hunting knife to defend yourself?" Before she could say it, Daniel turned and headed out the door. She knew he wouldn't be back for awhile. As he was going out the door, she heard him muttering to himself like he did these days, wondering what Ansel must have been thinking about.

"Is Ansel in love with this Petry woman?" she asked Asa, as she set about cleaning the bloody wound and sewing it.

"Anse?" Asa said it as if she didn't know who it was she was talking about.

"Asa," Willa May said, turning to look at him, "you've got to help me understand this. Why in the world would your brother go fooling around with some married woman -- married to a preacher, of all the gallderned things -- if he didn't care about the woman?"

Asa screwed up his face, deep in thought. "'Cause she was there?"

"Because she was there," Willa May repeated, frowning as she said it. "Well, do you mind telling me who else was there?"

Asa looked sheepish. "Anse is right popular with the womenfolk, I reckon you could say, Mommy."

"Oh, I'd say he's right popular, all right. But I'm telling you right now, Asa, the two of you should be married and raising families by now. Raising younguns of your own so your pa and me wouldn't have to worry ourselves sick about what kind of trouble you're up to every time you're out of our sight."

Asa was dumbstruck. It had never occurred to him that he could do anything that Ansel hadn't thought of first. "You reckon, Mommy?"

Willa May nodded. "I reckon, all right."

Two days later, Ansel was up and about, chopping firewood for them. Daniel tried to talk to him, but Ansel just said, "Oh, I've learned my lesson, all right, Pa. I won't be climbing through that preacher's window no more."

Daniel knew Ansel didn't catch the drift of what he was saying. Like Willa May said, Asa and Ansel were grown men. They were past

221

the point where their parents could tell either of them what to do. All Daniel and Willa May could do was hope that the boys would come to their senses and settle down before some jealous husband shot them both between the eyes.

Willa May and Daniel clung to every piece of news they could get about James Houston and Ethan Allen and the strike at Paint Creek. They began hearing more and more about a woman called Old Mother Jones. She was all that folks could talk about. James Houston described her as a glorious angel flown down from heaven. But Daniel heard some men say at the Stockton Tavern that she was nothing more than an agitator the union had brought in. He heard them say that she was a loudmouth, crude in her choice of words, a demon sent straight from hell, according to the mine owners. At eighty-two years old, she surprised everyone with the energy she showed in helping the miners in their struggle. When Walt Whitman stopped by to bring them up on the latest news, Daniel asked him what he thought of the spunky little woman. "Well, Pa, I saw her speak to the miners last week. I was with James Houston. You'd think she was on some holy mission, ready to march right into hell if need be, just to wage war with the mine operators. She says she's going to give a speech next week and claims that when Governor Glasscock hears what she has to say, that he'll be forced to step in and settle the strike. She's already invited the miners to come and hear what she has to say. I guess she plans to make the speech on the steps of the capitol building. I don't really see the governor showing up for this, though. He wouldn't dare show his face to those striking miners."

The next time Walt Whitman stopped by, he carried more news about the fiery little woman, saying that the governor had left town rather than face her. When Old Mother Jones heard this, she called him gutless and made off-colored puns about his name. "She warned that there's going to be plenty of bloodshed ahead -- blood flowing like rivers, I think is what she said -- if Glasscock keeps ignoring the desperation of the miners. When she finished, the miners went on a killing rampage, shooting every mine guard they could find. Then they started searching for scabs."

"Scabs?" Willa May asked, confused.

"They're the men who took the miners' jobs during the strike."

Daniel looked at Walt Whitman and asked, "And what did the mine operators do when they heard about all the killing?"

"They had squirreled away weapons of their own. Enough to equip a small army. Meanwhile, the governor grew afraid and finally stepped in to try and settle the strike. But he was too late. The mine owners feel that they have all the power. Besides, they have time on their hands. How much longer can the miners and their families exist on nothing?"

"So the fighting didn't stop?" Willa May asked.

Walt Whitman shook his head. "Two Baldwin-Felts guards were shot."

"Bad?" Daniel asked.

"One died. The other one staggered off toward Montgomery with a pack of angry strikers on his heels. Lucky for that fellow that when the miners went to the hospital, demanding to see him, the doctors there said that the man had died of the wounds he had suffered."

"Yep, he was lucky, all right," Daniel agreed.

"When the miners went back into the hills, they found the man's bloody jacket. Somehow it ended up in the hands of Mother Jones. She went to one of the union meetings and cut up the jacket in front of all the miners, handing out bloodstained pieces of it. The men pinned the pieces to their jackets, wearing them like a badge of honor."

Willa May shook her head. "Can't somebody do something to stop all this? What's goin' to happen now?"

For weeks, Daniel and Willa May heard about murders and bloody fighting. Even some of the wives joined with their men, battling for survival. Rumors had reached them that some of the women had to fight off the advances of the mine guards who felt they had the right to take any of the miners' women and have their way with them. It seemed they especially liked young, pretty ones who still had their looks.

The next time Walt Whitman stopped by, he told them that James Houston had been in a major skirmish over near Milburn where he lived. All the shooting left the houses chopped to pieces like meat on a butcher's block. "When the miners over in Cabin Creek heard what had happened, they joined forces with the men from Paint Creek. It looks like the bloodshed Mother Jones predicted is coming and there isn't any way to stop it."

Daniel and Willa May worried night and day, fretting for the safety of their boys and their families. Willa May sent food every week, but she despaired that it wasn't nearly enough.

Then Walt Whitman brought worse news. James Houston had been one of the first to realize that the mine operators had brought in more armed guards. In an open battle, the miners stormed the hills. Above them, the mine guards sat with machine guns. They opened fire on the miners, scattering them like squawking geese as they yelled to each other to take cover. James Houston's family hid from the guards, knowing that they would shoot anyone -- children included. He took his family to the safety of a cave up in the hills. Ethan Allen's wife and children escaped to Montgomery and slept on the riverbank with no shelter. Some of the church ladies took pity on them and brought them food and blankets to keep the little ones warm.

"Are they all right? Should we go and get them?" Willa May asked.

"No, just when everybody was set for another battle, the governor declared martial law. Now there's an army manning the hillsides around Montgomery, going all the way back into Milburn and across the river at Cabin Creek."

Walt Whitman told them that he was disgusted by the newspaper accounts that made it sound like the miners had gotten the fight they deserved. "They simply fail to understand that for too long, the miners have been cheated and roughed up by mine guards who even take liberties with their wives. The newspapers just don't want to admit that the mine guards are there to keep the miners too scared to open their mouths, too scared to fight for their own dignity. Everyone knows that they were hired to beat any miner who even mentioned better working conditions or better living conditions."

Daniel nodded. "All them newspaper folks need to do is take a look at them miners. Just look at their faces. All their pride is beaten out of them. They know they can't do no better by their kin and they know, too, that the companies've got 'em whupped, no matter what they do. It's all there in their faces. Just look at them sometime."

"I know, Pa. I've seen it, too. Mother Jones says the mine companies are like the feudal lords, owning everything and controlling everything in those men's lives. Why, they even own the graveyard where they dump the miners' bodies when they drop their picks, too exhausted to go on. Like Anse says, the coal companies have got the miners by the balls and they just keep squeezing."

Willa May cleared her throat to remind him that she was listening, too. She had to give Ansel credit, though. At least he knew to say such things in the company of other men.

"Sorry, Mommy," Walt Whitman blushed.

Two days later, Walt Whitman returned. James Houston and Ethan Allen had both been arrested under the new martial law. A makeshift court held in Pratt -- the miners nicknamed it the "Bull Pen" -- was convicting miners who had participated in the battle.

"What's goin' to happen to the boys?" Willa May asked.

"They'll stand trial," Walt Whitman said.

"Just how fair will this here trial be?" Daniel asked. Willa May could tell from his voice that he was ready to take up his gun, go over to Pratt, and show them justice, Daniel Shrewsbury style.

Walt Whitman shrugged. "I don't know, Pa. I'd like to think that they'll get a fair trial, but everything is just chaos over there right now. I think everybody is waiting for something explosive to happen, expecting it to happen. I wouldn't be surprised at anything those mine operators might do."

"Well, by God, I ain't about to let them throw my boys in the hoosegow for trying to fight for any scraps of respect they can get from them damned operators!" Daniel thundered, pounding his fist on the table where they were seated. Willa May could see the storm clouds gathering in Daniel's blue eyes.

"Just don't do anything rash, Pa." Walt Whitman knew how angry Daniel was and, like Willa May, he knew that Daniel might very well ride into Pratt with guns blazing and break his boys out of that prison. "It could backfire on you."

"What do you mean?"

Walt Whitman squirmed, knowing that this wasn't going to set very well with Daniel. "Anything you do could make it rougher on the boys in the long run. The court may see it as some kind of conspiracy, or at the very least, a ploy by the union to defy the order for martial law."

"Damn!" Daniel stood up and started pacing back and forth like he did when he was young. He had that trapped animal look about him and Willa May didn't like it. She squirmed a little herself, just watching him.

"Do you know when their trial will be?" she asked, hoping this would make Daniel stop pacing. It didn't.

"Who knows?" Walt Whitman shrugged. "If I can find out when their trials are, I might be able to persuade some lawyer friends to take their cases as a favor to me. I'll get word to you as soon as I know anything."

Daniel and Willa May found that justice, coal baron style, was swift, though. The day after the strikers were thrown in jail, they stood before the judge. No matter what they were charged with, every miner was sentenced to a prison term. When Walt Whitman's friends arrived, they argued with the judge that the strikers had a right to be tried in a civil court, that the military courts had no jurisdiction. Nothing they could say would sway the judge from his duty as he saw it. James Houston and Ethan Allen were both found guilty. James Houston was sentenced to fifteen years when the judge learned he was a union leader. The court claimed that he was one of the main instigators responsible for organizing the men. Ethan Allen received a year in prison for shooting at mine guards. The judge ignored the fact that he was shooting in self-defense. By the time Walt Whitman came to tell Willa May and Daniel about it, the boys were already on a train headed for prison.

"They what?" Daniel bellowed.

"They sent them to prison, Pa."

Daniel leapt up and started pacing, eyeing his gun rack. Asa and Ansel watched him, both ready to join Daniel in the blink of an eye if he chose to descend upon the mine operators and show them his wrath. Even Elroy and Creedy shook their heads, unable to believe what they were hearing.

"I reckon I need somebody to tell me I'm still living in the United States of America, by God," Elroy said. "'Cause I do believe I done ended up over in one of them foreign countries that's ruled by some king. 'King Coal'. Wouldn't surprise me none if they start beheading them miners."

"Never thought I'd live to see the day," Creedy agreed.

"What about the boys' families?" Willa May asked.

"Ethan Allen's family is back in the tent colony just outside of Paint Creek. They're really frightened. As for Nila Rae and James Houston's children, they took off for Ingram Branch the minute they heard James Houston was convicted. Her kinfolk took them in, so they're safe."

"Well, you tell Ethan Allen's wife we'll come down and fetch her and the children up here where they'll be safe and have a roof over their heads."

Walt Whitman frowned. "She won't come. Ethan Allen told her to stay put no matter what happened. That the union would see to it that they were cared for. She's trusting that he's right."

"She needs to think of those children," Willa May argued.

"I'd say she thinks she is."

By that fall, Daniel and Willa May were relieved that the fighting had been quelled and the governor lifted his order for martial law. A few weeks later, fighting erupted again and the troops were called back in. This time miners were arrested in droves. Grover Jenkins, the owner of the Stockton Tavern, told Daniel that even Mother Jones had been arrested. The judge gave her a twenty year sentence for her part in stirring the miners into fighting. The few strikers that remained faced a sentence worse than prison -- they had to watch their families starve while they lived like animals in their tents.

"How can they run the mines with all the miners locked up?" Daniel asked.

"Them mine operators done hired more men," Jenkins shrugged.

Living in flimsy tents, wearing rags and trying to keep warm when the snow was knee deep outside, the miners and their families were losing hope. Jenkins described how they stood by in grim silence as they watched their babies die of hunger, pneumonia, typhoid and smallpox. "Just one epidemic after another." He shook his head sorrowfully.

Willa May thought they had heard the worst, that nothing more could possibly happen. Then Walt Whitman and Annie Catherine brought Thomas Lee with them one Sunday early in February. All three wore dour faces, even Thomas Lee. What they said set Willa May's hair on end. Some mine owners and their hired thugs had taken a train ride late at night past some of the coal camps along Paint Creek. The miners were calling the train "The Death Train". After hearing what happened, Willa May said they should have called it "The Devil Train" for the evil purpose it carried. The men on the train had loaded a Gatling gun on it along with rifles and machine guns. As they rode past the shabby coal camps, the train slowed down and the men inside the train opened fire on the wooden shanties where the miners lived...defenseless men, women and children. "Obviously, they didn't care who their bullets hit," Walt Whitman reported.

Ansel, listening to the news, seethed, "To them rich mine owners, it wasn't nothing more than target practice."

"And that's not the worst of it," Walt Whitman added. "Josie's husband was one of the mine owners. He started the shooting. Bragged about it afterward."

227

Hearing this, Daniel stood up and started pacing. He had paced so much all fall and winter, that he had worn down the wood floor in front of the hearth. Willa May saw Ansel give Asa a look and she knew that they weren't going to let this rest. Not this time. They had been hankering to get into this mess for months now.

"Does Josie know?" she asked.

"I went to see her yesterday. When I told her, she looked pretty upset at first, but then she turned to me and asked me what I thought she could do about it."

Willa May stared dumbfounded at Walt Whitman. "Well, to start with, what she can do is to tell that murdering scoundrel she's married to that he was trying to kill her own people. That would do for starters."

"She'll never do that. She's grown very comfortable, living well like she does. And I think that by now even she believes her lies about her past. No, she won't do anything that would threaten her way of life."

"You didn't say how many folks were killed when the train went through," Ansel said.

"Only one man. It's hard to believe. I guess they were just lucky it wasn't daylight or there would've been even more dead. Those folks were just fortunate that those heartless murderers were too cowardly to come out in the daylight...like rats."

Ansel nodded in agreement, shooting Asa another look. This time Daniel saw the look. Willa May knew from the expression on Daniel's face at that very minute that he and the boys were going to do something to avenge this, but she didn't know just what. She did know it was useless to try and stop them, as useless as it would be to try to convince Josie she would be better off without the cold-blooded murderer she had married.

Sick of all the fighting, the people of the state elected a new governor. He was one of the Hatfields from the infamous family of feuders in Mingo County, Henry Hatfield. Daniel and Elroy chuckled, speculating that being kin to Devil Anse Hatfield, this new governor would set things straight...one way or another. Being a Hatfield, he didn't lose any time taking the bull by the horns. He had been a doctor before he was elected governor so when he visited the tent colony with its sick and dying families, he took his medical bag along and treated the sick. Ragged, skeletal children with distended bellies looked up at this stranger with eyes that begged for help, the newspapers reported. Some had fevers; others writhed in fits of delirium from typhoid and smallpox. Their mothers were too weak themselves to care for them. Willa May read to Daniel and Creedy how Hatfield treated as many of them as he could, staying several days in one of the tents. The newspaper story went on to say how surprised the miners were to discover that this kind man in their midst was their newly elected governor.

When she finished reading the story, Willa May sighed, "It's a sin and a shame that this Hatfield came too late for Ethan Allen's family." Smallpox and pneumonia had killed all their babies just five weeks before. Violet, Ethan Allen's wife, lost her mind. She had watched her children die, one by one. In her grief, she cut her wrists. Some neighbors found her before she could bleed to death, but she was committed to the hospital for the insane in Spencer. Walt Whitman took it upon himself to visit Ethan Allen in prison and told him. Ethan Allen looked lost and hopeless, a ghost of the man he had once been.

"It's a damn shame that Violet and them younguns couldn't hold on a little while longer," Elroy agreed.

For the next few months, the newspapers continued to cover the new governor's attempts to reconcile the miners and the mine owners. The mine owners didn't appreciate the favoritism that Hatfield showed to the miners by tending to their illnesses. They grew even angrier still when the new governor visited Mother Jones and finding her sick with pneumonia, ordered that she be sent to a hospital for proper care.

When Hatfield returned to the governor's mansion, he issued an ultimatum -- reach an agreement or suffer the consequences. James Houston's men won their two and a half cent raise and the right to hire their own check-weighmen. Miners no longer had to buy from the company owned stores. The Cabin Creek miners were allowed to join the UMW. While James Houston crowed over a victory, Willa May thought the miners had paid a mighty high price for such table scraps.

Through a pardon from the governor, James Houston and Ethan Allen were allowed to return home. James Houston went back to his waiting family and his job. Ethan Allen came back to no family and with no desire to go back into the mines. Daniel and the twins went to Montgomery to meet the train when the two of them arrived. James

Houston was all smiles, elated that his union had won. But none of them were prepared for how Ethan Allen looked. Gaunt and pale, he was stooped like a man twice his age. His hair had turned completely white. A nervous tick in his right eye caused him to blink constantly. He kept peering at Daniel and his brothers as if to make sure that he was with his own kin. His hands trembled so badly that Willa May didn't dare pour his cup to the brim when he drank coffee. His shaking made him spill most of it. He didn't say much; he just looked off in the distance and nodded vaguely, hardly understanding what was said to him. Sometimes, he just sat and cried. Silent tears streamed down his bony cheeks, covered with stubble. With Ethan Allen living at home, there were plenty of men to do all the hard work around the place: the plowing, the repairs, building, and keeping up with the bootlegging business. Willa May was afraid that Ethan Allen, being around all that whiskey, would take to the jug like Elroy, but he never did. She figured his soul was too lost to even take comfort in drink.

The twins saved up enough money to buy a truck for their deliveries, an old Ford. To them, it was a marvel. But to Willa May, it rattled and hissed like a snake. She claimed that riding in it was downright dangerous, the way it bounced her around. She had to hold on tight just to keep from being thrown out onto the dirt road. But Asa and Ansel thought they were something riding around in that truck.

They took it into their heads to build Willa May and Daniel a house that spring. Ethan Allen offered to help. They started in early spring, promising that this would be a real house -- not a cabin -- with a parlor for when company came calling. It had a separate dining room away from the kitchen and the cooking area. They moved the mahogany dining table in there. The twins went to a second hand furniture store and brought home eight chairs with matching dark red cushioned seats. There were seven of them now, counting Elroy who always took his meals with them. With so many mouths to feed, Willa May thought it was high time to have enough seating space for everyone.

The house had four bedrooms upstairs: one for Willa May and Daniel, one for the twins, one for Ethan Allen, and one for Creedy. The twins took special care to paint each room the color Willa May wanted. They used light yellow for the parlor and dining room, blue for their folks' room, green for their own room, beige for Creedy's room, and a pale peach color for Ethan Allen's room. It was late in

June when they moved in. The following Sunday, Walt Whitman drove up in a shiny black, brand new Model T. He parked it by the new house. Everyone stepped down off the porch to marvel at the new automobile. Walt Whitman walked up to Daniel and handed him the key, saying, "Happy Anniversary, Pa!"

Daniel looked from Walt Whitman to the big black car and back. He couldn't believe that Walt Whitman was really giving them the automobile. Daniel had just turned seventy that year and Willa May figured he probably thought he wasn't ever going to need an automobile, much less own one. It was a long time before he finally asked, "What are you talking about, Son?"

Grinning that familiar Shrewsbury grin, Walt Whitman clapped Daniel on the back and said, "I thought it was about time you stopped riding around in that wagon and gave those mules a well deserved rest, Pa. Do you like her?" This last he asked in a worried tone, wondering if maybe Daniel didn't care for such a new fangled contraption. The same big grin spread slowly across Daniel's face. He reached out and pulled Walt Whitman to him in a big bear hug, just like he had when Walt Whitman was just a little thing. Once they had hugged and clapped each other on the back, Daniel walked around the new Model T, shaking his head. He kept saying, "I can't believe it! I just can't believe it."

Daniel looked over at Elroy who was sitting on his little cart, all smiles himself and shaking his head like he didn't believe it, either. Suddenly, Daniel said, "Elroy, you recollect telling me nigh on a month ago that they were having that fiftieth reunion celebration for all them boys that fought at Gettysburg battlefield up there in Pennsylvania?"

Elroy squinted up at Daniel. "Yeah..."

"Well, start packing, Elroy, because we're goin'!"

Everyone stared in astonishment at Daniel. Ansel, scratching the back of his neck and grinning sheepishly, said, "Pa, you ain't never driven in your life. How are you aiming to drive all the way to Gettysburg, Pennsylvania?"

"I ain't," Daniel said. "Ethan Allen will drive the new automobile. Creedy and Elroy can trade off riding with you and Asa in the truck."

Elroy looked up at Ansel, afraid that Ansel might say, "Now, hold on there just a gallderned minute. How did I get hooked into this?"

But Ansel, like Daniel just minutes before, looked from Daniel to the fancy new car and back. "Can I drive the Model T some?"

Daniel's grin spread wider. "Reckon you can if you want to. Asa, too. That's if you can get your older brother to give up the driver's seat to you."

Asa and Ansel both turned to look at Ethan Allen, standing beside Walt Whitman, taking in the scene. Ethan Allen nodded, showing the briefest glimmer of a smile, the first one the family had seen since he had gotten back from prison. Willa May began to think that maybe Daniel had done all this not so much for Elroy as for Ethan Allen, to get him away for a while where maybe his troubles wouldn't follow him.

If that weren't enough, Walt Whitman looked at Annie Catherine and Thomas Lee. "In that case, maybe we'll come along, too."

"What?" everyone asked in unison.

"I figure that fiftieth reunion at Gettysburg is going to be history in the making. I'd like for Thomas Lee to see that and understand just what that battle meant for those men. Besides, I'm a history professor. Remember? How do you expect to keep a historian away from an event like that?"

Still grinning, Daniel put his arm around Walt Whitman's shoulder and said, "Well then, we'll make it a family trip, by God."

"Then I'm goin' to ask Walt Whitman to be in charge of getting us there," Willa May declared. "Daniel will take us over every mountain between here and there if he's in charge. And Ansel would have us stop at every tavern and sporting house we pass. So, if we're ever goin' to get Elroy there in time, I reckon Walt Whitman will have to lead us."

The men winked at each other and nudged each other in the ribs. Daniel said, "What do you mean, Girl, that I'd take you over every gallderned mountain?"

Before she could think of a smart enough answer, Ansel piped up, saying, "And what would I know about taverns and sporting houses?" He smiled angelically, but everyone spotted the devilish twinkle in his eyes.

Snickering, Elroy said, "Oh Anse, I do believe Willa May's got you on that one. You like the ladies too much for anybody to believe different on that."

Before Elroy could protest, Ansel scooped him up in his arms. Looking at Asa, he said, "I told you the next time this old coot got smart with me, I'd take him and throw him off of Lover's Leap."

Elroy wiggled and squirmed like a greased pig, yelling, "Anse, you blasted fool, set me down. Right now. You hear me? Set me down, I say!"

That only egged Ansel on. He pretended to turn around and head toward the gorge. Joining in the joke, Asa yelled, "Anse! Don't do it. He'll be good from now on. Just bring that poor old feller back!"

Elroy squawked and flailed his arms helplessly. Ansel pretended to get madder by the minute. When he had gotten fifty yards from the house, Elroy grew desperate and thought he had better get help before he met his Maker. He hollered, "Daniel! Daniel, come talk some sense into this youngun of yours. Don't let him throw me down in that gorge! Daniel? You hear me? Help!"

Hearing more than a hint of terror in Elroy's voice, Ansel couldn't hold his laughter any longer. He fell to his knees with Elroy still in his arms and laughed and laughed. Soon he and Elroy were both cackling like geese, rolling on the ground and wrestling like they did when Ansel was little. Elroy said, "Anse, I'll get you for this. If it's the last thing I do, I'll get you good."

The others watched, chuckling to themselves over Ansel and his antics. Even Ethan Allen had to smile at Ansel's tomfoolery. Walt Whitman shook his head, laughing to himself. Looking at Ansel, he said, "If my baby brother isn't the wildest thing in these mountains, I don't know what is."

When everyone calmed down, Annie Catherine and Willa May went into the house and started supper. Annie Catherine had brought some fresh strawberries, so Willa May sent Thomas Lee up to the ice house to get some cream. They sat down to a fine meal of chicken fried steak with gravy, mashed potatoes and peas, pickled beets, cole slaw, sweet potato muffins, and strawberry shortcake. During supper, Ansel kept asking Walt Whitman about the new automobile.

"She's a fine machine, Anse. Four cylinders. Twenty-horsepower. Henry Ford, when he developed the Model T five years ago, said he wanted it to be the kind of car every family could own. Now he's working on a theory that he can produce more cars by assembling them in steps and hiring more workers to operate each step of the process. Mass production, they call it. An excellent theory. It will make the Model T even more affordable."

"And that'll make Ford even richer," Ansel said.

"That, too," Walt Whitman nodded.

"I bet you that someday they'll make whiskey that way. In stills that will make hundreds of gallons at a time."

"Probably. But it'll have to be legalized first. Too many groups these days claim that alcohol is the root of all evil."

Ansel leaned back in his chair, tilting it back on its legs. He stretched his arms out on the back of Willa May's and Asa's chairs and said, "Root of all evil? Why, hell, brother, if you ask me, root of all fun is more like it." Willa May looked at Ansel, wearing that devilish grin of Daniel's. More and more, she could see just how reckless and wild he had become. Even though he and Asa were twins, Asa paled in looks compared to Ansel. Ansel's swaggering somehow made him more irresistible, more charming. Even men liked him, favoring his joking and bantering manner to Asa's quieter, shier ways. Like a banty rooster that pranced and preened for the hens, Ansel was the cock of the walk. He knew it. They all knew it. Just nobody held it against him.

All the menfolk laughed at Ansel's comment, their heads bobbing in agreement. Ansel looked at Walt Whitman and grew serious. "Folks are always goin' to be wanting whiskey, legal or not. I just hope I'm around to get rich off the stuff once they do legalize it. And rich I'd be, too."

"You've got a point, there," Walt Whitman agreed. "If a man could produce whiskey for sale using Ford's example of mass production, he could be mighty rich indeed."

At that, Ansel grew thoughtful. Everyone knew that Ansel could be the man to grow rich from such a venture. Ansel was a smart businessman. He was smart enough to make enough profit so Daniel didn't have to work anymore. Smart enough to support the whole family on the income he made from the few stills he and Asa had stashed back in the hills behind the house. He also managed to outsmart the revenuers that came poking around, trying to nail him.

On their way to Gettysburg, Daniel said they would stop in Wheeling for the semi-centennial festival, celebrating the first fifty years of statehood. Willa May wasn't really interested in it, but Daniel seemed set on it and so did the twins. Once they mentioned it to Walt Whitman, it was decided. Elroy pestered them constantly, afraid he would miss getting to Gettysburg on time. After the fiftieth time Elroy asked if they were going to get to Pennsylvania before July first, Daniel said, "Elroy, I said I'd get you there and by God, I will. But this here is important, too." It struck Willa May as strange that Daniel was being so patriotic of late, first Gettysburg and now this semi-centennial, but she chalked it up to old age.

There were lots of speeches at the celebration. Even the governor spoke about the progress the state had made since its conception during the War of Secession. Henry G. Davis served as the master of ceremonies and introduced a woman who turned out to be the daughter of the state's first governor. The woman seemed refined and somewhat soft spoken, but Willa May wondered if she was talking about the same state. She made a flowery speech about the wonderful feeling of brotherhood across the state and how well the people of the state were faring. Willa May decided that this lady had never seen the starving faces of the children down on Paint Creek. Certainly no one was getting rich in the state except the mine owners. Maybe the woman was too busy writing in her diary or some such important task, Willa May concluded. However foolish their words were, the crowd seemed to be eating them up, cheering on each speaker more than the one before.

Just before the fireworks that evening, Willa May spotted a familiar face among the important people making speeches on the podium. Walt Whitman watched her, knowing that she had seen Josie with those powerful people in their expensive clothes. Willa May's eyes turned to the man beside Josie. He was small, not much bigger than Willa May, but she could see that he was one dandy dresser. In a tail coat and top hat, sporting spats on his shiny black shoes, he was about the prissiest little thing Willa May had ever seen. A real peacock proud of his beautiful feathers. He was talking with the politicians, nodding and smiling at everything they said. Willa May wouldn't have been surprised if he had bent over and kissed the soles of their shoes. He seemed the type. She glanced over at Daniel who was eyeing the little man, too. Daniel wore a look like when he suffered from indigestion after a meal that hadn't agreed with him. She could tell that nothing would please him more than to pick up that little runt with his slicked back hair and send him sprawling on his face in the dirt.

There was such a throng of people surrounding them that Willa May lost track of some of their party. Daniel had all he could do to keep the people around them from pressing in on Elroy in his wheel chair. Creedy looked even more hunched over than usual, squashed between a fat woman licking the icing on a sweet roll and Elroy's wheel chair. Willa May could barely see over a tall man in front of her wearing a big white hat. Stretching to get a glimpse of Josie and her pip-squeak husband, she hardly noticed the fireworks that spewed showers of sparkling light from the heavens. The bursting and popping soon made such a racket, though, that she had to put her hands over her ears. With every new explosion, the crowd "oohed" and "ahed", pointing at all the beautiful colors.

Ten minutes into the fireworks, Willa May looked up at a huge spray of glittering diamonds that mushroomed against the black velvet sky. In the midst of the booming fireworks, she heard a scream. Not the excited squeals like she heard all around her, but a horrified shriek. Others must have heard it, too, because everyone turned away from the starry show up in the sky and looked back at the stage where the speakers were. A small cluster of politicians and businessmen were huddled over something. Even though the fireworks were still splintering the air, popping and crackling, the mob of people had grown hushed, looking up at the circle of people on the stage. Several moments elapsed before one of the men rushed to the edge of the platform and called out, "Is there a doctor in the crowd? A man's been shot!"

The crowd gasped, all eyes searching for a doctor. "Right here!" A man wormed his way through the swarm of bodies. As he climbed onto the stage, some of the group huddled over the wounded man stepped back to let the doctor pass. It was then that Willa May saw Josie down on her knees, cradling her husband's head. Even from where she stood, Willa May could see the bloodstains on Josie's pink flowered dress and the look of fear on her face. Then the doctor knelt down by the body and she lost sight of Josie. It wasn't long until some of the men picked up Josie's husband and carried him off the stage.

Walt Whitman leaned over and said, "I'll go see about Josie." He was gone before anyone could answer.

It gave Willa May a chance to look around for the rest of the family. Daniel was standing behind Elroy, his face like a stone statue, knowing that it was Josie's husband who had been shot. Elroy turned around in his wheel chair, asking what was going on. Creedy craned his neck, trying to get a good view so he could describe the scene for Elroy. Annie Catherine stood a few feet beyond Creedy and Willa May could just make out Thomas Lee's young profile on the other side of her. Turning around, she searched the crowd for Ethan Allen, Asa, and Ansel. Moments passed before she saw them moving toward her through an ocean of people. Ansel gave her one of his big grins, charming as ever, and asked, "What in tarnation's goin' on? Why is everybody so quiet all of a sudden?"

Daniel said, "Somebody done shot Josie's husband." He gave Ansel a look then -- just a quick glance -- but Willa May knew at that moment that Ansel had known all too well what was going on even before he asked. Daniel was only pretending to answer his question because he knew, too, that Ansel was already aware of what had taken place. She turned and looked at Asa and Ethan Allen. They stood stretching and gaping at the stage. There was a glow in Ethan Allen's eyes that hadn't been there since before he had gone to prison...and something more. Willa May was reminded of the old saying: "Curiosity killed the cat, but satisfaction brought him back." Her son, while appearing to be curious about the shooting, was glowing with profound satisfaction.

Walt Whitman rejoined them. "He's dead. Shot once through the head, once through the heart, and once...well, lower."

He didn't need to say anything more. Three shots. Dead on target. Fired during the fireworks so nobody would notice.

Ansel, still looking toward the stage, said, "Well, I reckon he won't be shooting at no more coal camps in the middle of the night and killing poor defenseless folks in their sleep."

They waited for Walt Whitman to go see about Josie at her hotel. He explained to her that the family was there and asked her if there was anything they could do to help. When she heard her family was there, she replied abruptly, "No. Tell them to go home and not to worry about me."

When Walt Whitman told them, Daniel grunted and walked away, getting the message loud and clear. Willa May shook her head, realizing that Josie hadn't changed in all their years apart. "I tried," Willa May said, shrugging her shoulders.

Walt Whitman tried to make up for what Josie had said and patted her hand. "I'm sure Josie appreciated the gesture, Mommy."

"Surer than me," she answered.

The next morning, they set off again for Gettysburg. The ride in the Model T was a little smoother than in the truck, but not much. The roads were pitted with ruts. They took their good time, taking in the countryside as they traveled further east. There was some pretty country in Pennsylvania. Acres and acres of good farmland. Driving south and east from Wheeling, they made it in plenty of time, several days before the celebration. Finally satisfied, Elroy stopped pestering them. He grew as giddy as a little boy buying candy when they pulled into town.

They checked into a hotel and Elroy wanted to go see the battlefield right away. It was a few hours before supper, so everyone went with Elroy to see the place where, fifty years before, he had lost his legs in battle. Willa May had never seen as solemn a place as Gettysburg battleground. She could almost see the spectral ghosts of the men who had died there roaming the field. Hearing Elroy talking about the battle -- "Now here's where old Longstreet attacked the bluebellies that second day -- See down yonder? That's where old Pickett himself led his men in the big charge. He lost about ten thousand men right here on this field that day. Push me over there. Right there is where I recollect I was standing when I heard this big 'Boom!' and everything went black. When I woke up, my legs were gone."

Memories came flooding back to Elroy across fifty years. Memories of seeing his friends lying wounded or dead, shot to pieces in the middle of that grassy field one hot day in July. Watching Elroy that afternoon, Willa May believed that he could still hear their dying cries. Cries for help, cries for Death to put an end to their suffering. More than once, she saw Elroy wipe away a stray tear as he looked out over that field, so quiet and peaceful now. She knew that when the reunion did commence, it was going to take its toll on him.

Over the next few days as they waited for the other men to arrive, they had time to explore the surrounding countryside. Heading east, they came to some good farming land around Lancaster. They passed black buggies with some of the Amish people that Willa May and Hattie Sue had seen at the fair years before. Willa May knew that where there were Amish women, there had to be quilts. They stopped at a store and Willa May asked the woman who was running it where she could see some Amish quilts. The woman took Willa May to her house where she looked at two dozen quilts, all hand pieced and hand stitched. They were some of the most beautiful quilts Willa May had ever seen. She struck up a friendship with the woman, describing all the quilts she had sewn over the years. Like Willa May, the woman had made over thirty quilts. Daniel grew tired of waiting for Willa May and came up to the house, knocking on the door and peering inside for any sign of her. As soon as he saw her sitting in the middle of all those quilts, he shook his head and muttered, "I might have known."

Willa May started to show him all the different patterns, naming each one. She had only gotten to the seventh or eighth quilt when Daniel said, "Which one's your favorite?"

Thinking that he was just making polite conversation, Willa May looked around her at each quilt. She pointed to a basket pattern in pinks and blues against a black background. Daniel took one glance and turned back to the store lady. "We'll take that one right there."

"What?" Willa May gasped. "You're goin' to buy it for me?"

"I figure it's the only way of getting you out of here."

Willa May was so shocked, she couldn't say a word. The store lady asked, "Now you're sure that's the one you want?" Willa May nodded. The woman wrapped up the quilt and Willa May walked back to the car with Daniel, holding the new quilt to her and cherishing it already. That night back at their hotel when they went to bed, Willa May felt Daniel's arm slip around her and she snuggled against him. He leaned over and kissed her, a long, sweet kiss, the way he used to kiss her when they were first married. Breathless, she pulled away and looked at him. "Now I know why you bought me that quilt. And here all this time, I thought it was out of the kindness of your heart," she teased.

Daniel chuckled softly. His eyes danced with merriment when he looked at her and said, "I thought I'd keep you warm tonight before that quilt gets a chance to...if that's all right with you."

"Why, Daniel Shrewsbury, in all the years we've been together, when wasn't it ever all right with me?"

"There's goin' to be an awful lot of men here the next few days. Maybe after seeing some of them, you might decide to throw me over for one of them."

She ran her hand down the side of Daniel's face, brushing back the silvery gray hair at his temple, feeling the bushy growth of his beard along his jaw. "There could be a thousand men out there on that battlefield, but not one of them would be my Daniel."

He laughed again and pulled her to him. "Willa May, have I ever told you that you're the prettiest thing I ever laid eyes on?"

"You know you don't have to go buttering me up like that. You got me here right where you want me. And besides, I'm sixty years old. I doubt that I'm all that pretty any more."

"To me, you are. To me, you're still that spunky little gal with hair brighter than any fire. To me, you're still my beautiful bride, all decked out in a white lace wedding gown."

"Daniel! What's gotten into you?"

He didn't answer. Instead, he leaned over and kissed her again, his strong arms holding her close. Then ever so softly, he whispered, "*You* got into me. You're like a fever inside of me, burning away, sapping my strength. I love you, Willa May. Always have and always will. Ain't nobody ever meant to me what you have."

While all this sounded beautiful, like music played on a violin, Willa May wondered what brought it on. "Daniel? Are you feeling all right? You're not sick or anything, are you?"

Another soft chuckle in the darkness. She could feel his warm breath against her ear as he whispered, "I'm better than I've been for many a year, darlin'. I plan to be here lying next to you for a good many more. It's just that seeing you sitting there in the middle of that floor today with all them quilts around you, you were a little girl again. The little girl that took me to her mama so I could get my arm sewed up. I just wanted to hold you to me once more, to know that you're still mine after all these years, I reckon."

With that, he kissed her once more. She could feel herself melting into him as she had so many times over the years, the two of them becoming one for just a fraction of time, holding each other, blending together while they blended in the darkness. Willa May decided she liked Gettysburg.

The next day was July first and all the men who had come there for the reunion gathered on the grassy field, many wearing their uniforms -- sagging uniforms with bullet holes in them; some with two sleeves, but only one arm to fill them; some, like Elroy, with no legs; and some with one. Fifty years before, they had been enemies, ready to kill each other for the color of the uniforms they wore. Now they were old men. White haired, shaky and stooped with age, they lined up: blue on one side, gray on the other. Then they walked across the field where Elroy had shown them that Pickett had made his charge. They faced each other -- some walking behind those in wheel chairs, some helping others with canes. In the middle of the field, the two lines met and shook hands. There were more than a few onlookers brushing tears from their eyes, watching these gallant men finally making peace. Willa May looked out over the line of men in gray, trying to find Elroy. When she caught sight of him, she noticed he was talking with the man beside him. It took her a second or two, looking at the man, before she said aloud, "Well, I'll be."

Daniel was standing beside her. "It's some sight, all right."

240

"No. Not that. Look who's standing next to Elroy."

Daniel shaded his eyes with his hand and scanned the pasture. The smile he had been wearing faded and his jaw clenched. "I won't have nothing to do with him," he said and turning, stalked away.

Walt Whitman was standing on the other side of Daniel and heard what they had said. He looked out now across the grassy green field where Elroy was smiling and nodding, happy as a lark in spring. "Who is that?"

"That," Willa May said, "is your no-account Uncle Augie."

Walt Whitman looked harder, then turning to Willa May, said, "No wonder Pa walked off in a huff. After what you've told me about him, I'm inclined to agree with Pa. If you want to see him, I'll understand. But don't expect any of us to speak to that no-good bastard." With that said, Walt Whitman walked off in search of his pa.

Willa May was bewildered by the sharpness in Walt Whitman's words. She couldn't remember him ever being so curt, like a scorching hot iron. Some things, she thought, were just instinctive, like knowing when something is rotten without having to be told, a trait that even the wildest animals possessed. It didn't take long for all the children to get the word that their Uncle Augie was out there with Elroy. Ethan Allen looked him up and down. Spitting at the ground, he walked off to join his pa and Walt Whitman. Asa, on the other hand, took one look and quickly turned away. Never one to walk away from trouble, Ansel stood a long time, sizing up his uncle whom he had heard stories about all his life. Willa May grew scared that maybe Augie would end up like Josie's husband. She said, "Why don't' you go and find your pa and your brothers?" As wild as he was, Ansel was always respectful of his parents, always doing as he was told. This time, he lingered, still appraising the paunchy, gray haired man in Confederate gray talking with Elroy. There was a cold gleam in Ansel's blue eyes. "Ansel? You hear me? Go on, now." Still reluctant, he slowly turned away and sauntered off as if he hadn't a care in the world. Willa May knew that he was calculating just what he would do to Augie if given the chance. She started to worry about folks reading the next day in the newspapers about one more death at Gettysburg, fifty years after the battle.

All this time, Creedy had been watching Ansel, just as worried as Willa May. Once she saw Ansel stroll over to Daniel and the other men, she turned her attention back to Elroy and Augie. Looking in the same direction, Creedy said, "I wouldn't go thinking about getting reacquainted if I was you, Willa May...especially if you don't want no more bloodshed."

She started nodding before she realized that Creedy had said no *more* bloodshed. She looked at him with his wispy white hair blowing in the soft breeze. A quick glance from him told her that she wasn't the only one who suspected what had gone on in Wheeling at the semi-centennial celebration. He was right. She forced herself to rein in her own feelings about Augie and the night they were burned out, the night the men in their feed sack hoods held a gun to her baby's head and killed the baby growing inside her. Just thinking back on it, she wanted to scratch Augie's eyes out.

The men out in the field started breaking off and going back to their waiting families. Elroy came back, all grins. "Did you see who I was talking to out there, Willa May? Did you see?"

"I saw," she nodded.

After a lifetime of living with her, Elroy knew by the tone of Willa May's voice that she didn't want any part of Augie, even after fifty years. He didn't say another word about it. Willa May was prepared to lay into him if he had. She wasn't the only one fired up. It was deadly quiet riding back to the hotel and the silence carried over through supper. Elroy was beginning to feel as low as a snake's belly, thinking he had ruined everyone's good time.

They were eating dessert -- apple pie with home-made ice cream -- when Augie came strutting up to their table. "Well, if it isn't my long lost little sister!" he announced in a booming voice. Trying to embarrass her, she knew.

Augie must not have looked too closely where he was standing or he would have made sure he was out of Daniel's reach. He no sooner said the word, "sister", when Daniel bolted up from his chair and swung his fist at Augie. He knocked him off his feet onto a nearby table where people were just starting to eat their supper. Knocked him out cold. Turning to Willa May, Daniel took her arm and politely escorted her out of the room of stunned onlookers. The rest of their group followed. Ansel came last, tossing some cash on Augie's limp body to pay for their meal. He wore a smile similar to the one Ethan Allen had worn in Wheeling. It showed a deep satisfaction.

Chapter Ten

For months after they got back from Gettysburg, it was all Elroy could talk about. Sometimes he got a charge out of looking back on all his buddies growing old and then, without warning, he would tear up over it. Daniel and Willa May never knew whether he would end up laughing or crying when he talked about it. One evening the following April, they were sitting out on the porch after supper and Willa May was just about to start reading for the evening. Some Scripture from Proverbs followed by a chapter from Miss Louisa May Alcott's <u>Little Women</u>. Reading about the war set Elroy to remembering again. Shaking his head, he said, "Remember how we all got lined up there on the field that day and marched toward each other? And how, once we met up, we shook hands?"

Everyone nodded. Daniel and Creedy sighed heavily, as if to say, "Here we go again."

"Well, I was thinking on it today," Elroy continued, oblivious to the heavy sighs around him, "and I can't get over how there we were, some of us facing each other fifty years before, looking each other in the eye down the barrels of the rifles we were carrying, ready to kill each other. Back then, of course, we weren't thinking about what the blue coats were like, whether they were family men or somebody's son or grandson. We just knew they were wearing blue. That meant they were the enemy, the very ones that was keeping us from our own homes and our own families. There we stood last summer, smiling at each other and patting each other on the backs, just like we was old friends. Who knows? Maybe one of them old boys I shook hands with was the one that fired the cannon that blew my legs off. Funny, ain't it?"

"Elroy," Daniel said, "you might be right about one of them soldiers you shook hands with being the very one that was the cause of your losing your legs. But you can't go on thinking about it, wondering all the time. It'll eat you up inside. Just be glad you lived through it and got yourself straightened out and led a good life."

243

Elroy was too lost in his wondering. With a faraway look in his eyes, he said dreamily, "Still, I would've liked having a wife and younguns of my own."

Willa May looked from Elroy to Creedy, sitting in his favorite rocker as he whittled on a piece of hickory wood. Creedy never said a word, but he nodded, like he knew all too well what Elroy meant. Her eyes met Daniel's and both of them wondered what they could say. Even Ethan Allen squirmed in his chair, nodding in agreement. Elroy's words struck a chord in his heart, too.

Willa May was relieved when she heard the Model T chugging its way up the road to their house. Asa and Ansel had left right after they got home from their deliveries that afternoon. She was surprised to see them coming back so soon. They usually came home in the middle of the night, staggering and giggling from drinking. The big black car pulled up and she could see that there was a girl in the front seat next to Ansel. Asa was in the back seat by himself. When they got out, they were all smiles except for the girl, who looked embarrassed, her eyes inspecting the tops of her shoes. She looked awfully young. Willa May wondered what she was doing out with two men at least twelve years older than she was. Her thoughts must have registered on her face because Ansel winked at her as he came around the front of the Model T. Pulling the girl with him, he stepped up on the porch, announcing, "Mommy. Pa. I'd like you to meet your new daughter-in-law."

Daniel and Willa May were speechless, looking first at Ansel, then at the girl, and finally at each other. Willa May found her voice first. "What are you talking about, Ansel?" She was sure she hadn't heard right.

Ansel shook his head, grinning and giggling nervously. "This here is my wife, Corey. We tied the knot just this afternoon over in Fayetteville at the Justice of the Peace." Pulling Asa over to join them, he wrapped his arm around Asa's shoulder and said, "Asa, here, was my best man. Witnessed the deed, you could say."

Daniel and Willa May looked from Ansel, dressed in his Sunday suit and tie, to the small girl next to him. She couldn't have been more than fifteen and shy as a rabbit. The poor thing couldn't bring herself to look either Daniel or Willa May in the eye. From what Willa May could see of her, she was pretty with blonde hair in curls down her back, green eyes -- when she finally caught a glimpse of them -- and dimples that nearly jumped off her milky white skin.

244

Ethan Allen recovered first. "Seems to me this calls for a drink. C'mon, Pa. What do you say? Let's break out some of that home brew we've got stashed away up in the ice house and toast the newlyweds."

It was the most anyone had heard Ethan Allen say at one time since he had come back home. Hearing that a drink was to be had, Elroy spoke up. "Why, I never thought I'd live to see the day! Ansel Shrewsbury tying the knot. It's goin' to bring on a storm, for sure." Ansel was too excited to notice that Willa May and Daniel were still thunderstruck. He beamed at his new bride like he had found a treasure. Leaning over, he pulled Elroy to him and squeezed so hard that Elroy cried, "You're goin' to break my gallderned ribs, Anse. What's got into you, anyway?"

Ansel clapped Elroy on the back and said, "Why, Elroy, love's got into me! Now tell the truth, Elroy, ain't my Corey just about the prettiest little thing you ever laid eyes on?"

Corey looked like she might just shrink to the size of one of the gnats flying around the yard. Willa May felt sorry for her, remembering how nervous she was the first time she met Daniel's folks. She said, "Hush now, Ansel, you're goin' to embarrass the girl to death before she even sets foot in her new home." She stood up and took Corey by the hand, saying, "Why don't we go on inside, honey, and set out some vittles while the menfolk get their jugs?"

A glimmer of a smile turned Corey's mouth up at the corners, but only for a second. Still too shy to speak, she nodded and let Willa May take her hand. Inside, she watched Willa May, daring every now and then to take a peek at her surroundings. She looked like she needed something to do so Willa May had her set the table, thinking that it was a good thing that Asa and Ansel had found eight chairs to go with the dining table. Now there would be one more sharing meals with them. No sooner did they get the food on -- some cold leftover chicken, pickles, cheese, and a loaf of bread -- when the men came in with some home brew that Ethan Allen had made. Frothy and cold, everyone agreed it hit the spot.

They drank to the bride and groom. The bride blushed a deep crimson, but the groom was too excited to notice. Once they sat down and started eating and talking, Ansel told them that Corey's name was Corrine Jarrett and her pa was a miner over on Paint Creek.

Ethan Allen nodded. "I knew old Tiny. Good man."

"But Ansel, why didn't you tell us you were getting married? I'd

245

have like to have been there. After all, I am your mama," Willa May said.

Ansel cast a furtive glance at Asa. Asa saw Willa May watching all this and looked away. At that moment, Willa May knew something was up. She started wondering if Ansel had been in the woodpile with this little girl and maybe had gotten her pregnant. Something just wasn't right about all this and she didn't know what. At least, not yet. Knowing Ansel, she would find out sooner rather than later.

Ansel took his bride over to the cabin that had been Daniel's and Willa May's for so many years. He was set on raising a family in it like his ma and pa had. Asa moved in with Creedy, not wanting to be a bother to Ethan Allen. Creedy was tickled to share his room with one of the boys. It gave him somebody to talk to after the lights were out and he hadn't fallen asleep yet.

Daniel came to bed after he saw Elroy home, still too stunned to know exactly what to say about Ansel's marriage. He climbed into bed next to Willa May and, as always, put his arm around her and pulled her to him. She rested her head on his chest and waited for him to say something. Anything. Instead, he heaved a deep sigh, his chest rising so high that Willa May's head nearly rolled off.

"He's old enough to get married if he wants to. You know that. We both know that."

Daniel stayed silent for a minute. Then, he sighed again, "Yeah, but she ain't. She ain't much more than a girl."

"She's older than I was when we got married."

"That was different," Daniel argued, not wanting her to bring up that point.

"How was it different? Age is age. Just numbers."

"It was different, that's all."

"Just because you want it to be different doesn't make it different."

"You'll see," Daniel said and turned over on his side, marking an end to the conversation. Over the years, Willa May had come to learn that when a man didn't want to admit he was wrong, he simply ended the conversation, one way or another. To her way of thinking, a man would never come right out and admit he was wrong. It just wasn't in him. She turned over, her back to Daniel's, smiling in the darkness at the foolishness of men.

...*BOOM!* Daniel and Willa May sprang out of bed. Daniel ran to the open window where the April sun was already pouring in. Willa May raced to the hallway. She saw Ethan Allen's back as he ran down the hall toward the stairs. He was pulling the straps of his overalls up over his bare shoulders with one hand and toting a pistol in the other. Asa burst out of Creedy's room, pulling up his Sunday trousers he had worn the night before. He rushed to Willa May, put his hands on her shoulders, and asked, "You all right, Mommy?" She nodded. He whisked past her to where Daniel was standing by the window. Creedy came out into the hallway with his scrawny, twisted legs dangling out from the hem of his nightshirt and his white wispy hair standing on end. "What in tarnation?" he squawked.

Seeing that Creedy was all right -- scared out of his wits, but unharmed -- Willa May rushed back into her room where Asa and Daniel were peeking out the window. From downstairs, she could hear Ethan Allen lifting down one of Daniel's shotguns and loading it. Then she heard footsteps crossing the floor to the front door.

Suddenly, another blast split the still morning air. It sounded like it came from right under their room, in front of the house. Peering around Daniel's shoulder, Willa May saw a huge man with blonde curly hair. Wearing a yellow coat, he was the biggest man she could remember seeing since Joe Turner. He had his back to them and from that angle, he looked like a big yellow bear. He must have been nearly seven feet tall and well over three hundred pounds. He was walking toward the cabin, his double-barreled shotgun raised like he was ready to blast away anyone that dared to stick his head out the cabin door...and that would be Ansel.

"Who is that man?" Daniel asked, wondering like Willa May what had possessed this huge monster to come shooting at them.

"Oh, Lord," Asa sighed, rolling his big blue eyes.

Daniel turned away from the stranger in their yard and looked at Asa. "You know that man?"

Asa nodded. "That's Corey's pa. Tiny."

"They call *him* Tiny!" Willa May cried. "He doesn't look so tiny to me."

Tiny Jarrett fired another shot at the cabin, sending a chunk of one log flying up over the roof. Daniel spun around. "That does it, by God." He stalked out into the hallway past where Creedy stood trying to cover up his nightshirt with both hands. Seeing his pa rushing off, Asa followed. From his spot at the doorway, Creedy was torn between rushing back to his room and getting properly dressed and missing all the commotion, or risking what was left of his modesty and watching from Willa May's perch at the window. Curiosity won out. Still trying unsuccessfully to cover himself up, Creedy came over and peeked past Willa May to where the giant named Tiny was loading his shotgun and walking determinedly toward the cabin.

Willa May heard the door swing open below and Tiny Jarrett whirled around, his shotgun raised and ready. A second later she could hear triggers cocked from the open windows below her. She knew Ethan Allen and Asa were looking down the long, black barrels of their shotguns right back at Tiny Jarrett. Before either side could fire, Daniel walked out to where Jarrett was standing. When Willa May saw Daniel didn't have a gun, she caught her breath, her hand over her mouth. Daniel was so mad, he would have taken on an army of Tiny Jarretts, gun or no gun. It took Daniel three long strides to get to where Tiny Jarrett stood, holding his gun aimed directly at Daniel. But Daniel merely reached out and pushed the barrel of the shotgun aside. He looked up into Jarrett's face and said, "I want to know just what the hell you think you're doing shooting up my place, Mister!"

For a second, Willa May could see Jarrett peering around Daniel at the two guns aimed at him from the house. Looking back at Daniel, he said, "I came to kill that low-down sonofabitch named Ansel Shrewsbury. That's what I'm doing here."

Daniel stepped even closer to Jarrett who stood almost a whole head taller. "You do that and I'm telling you right now, you won't live to tell about it."

"You that good-for-nothin' pup's pa?"

By this time, Daniel was right up in the man's face, standing as tall as he could stretch. "I'm Daniel Shrewsbury and Ansel's my son. I'll thank you to stop talking about him like he wasn't no better than a mangy old dog."

It was hard to tell whose face was redder, Daniel's or Tiny Jarrett's. "Well, he ain't no better than a dog, far as I can see."

"What'd he ever do to you?" Daniel challenged. Willa May wondered what Daniel was thinking of when he asked this. He was talking about Ansel and that meant Daniel had left himself open for almost any kind of answer.

"That bastard ran off with my baby girl! That's what he done."

"I told you once, I won't stand for you calling my boy names. Besides, he married that little gal, legal and all."

Tiny Jarrett grunted. "About time, I'd say."

"What do you mean by that?" Willa May shook her head, knowing that her suspicions about Ansel and his bride were right. *Daniel, this is Ansel we're talking about. You don't want to know.*

For a moment, even Tiny Jarrett looked at Daniel like he must be blind or a fool, maybe both. "He dee-filed my little girl. That's what I mean. He come slinking around and got my baby knocked up with his bastard. Why, she's been having the morning sickness for nigh on a month, now. All the while, that son --"

Here, Daniel almost touched noses with Jarrett, showing him he wouldn't tolerate any more name calling.

"-- that son of...yours has been chasing everything in skirts up and down the valley, married or not. Your boy just can't seem to keep his horse in the barn!"

From behind Willa May, Creedy said, "I reckon he's got Daniel on that one."

It seemed he did. Daniel, at a loss for anything better to say, finally said, "Well, they're married now, ain't they?"

Somehow it worked. Willa May thought the angels must have been smiling down on Daniel because Tiny Jarrett looked like a balloon with all its air let out. Grudgingly, he mumbled, "Yeah. Reckon they are, at that."

A glimmer of the part of Daniel she always saw in Ansel came shining through when Daniel clapped Tiny on the shoulder. "Well, hell, I reckon we ought to break out a jug and drink to our forthcoming grandchild then."

Tiny lowered his shotgun and a slow grin spread across his broad face. "By God, I reckon you're right, Shrewsbury."

In no time, the two men were drinking and slapping each other on the backs like they had been kin all their lives, making bets on whether Corey's baby would be a girl or a boy. Tiny insisted he would like a grandson, but Daniel said he had a hankering for some more girls around the place. Meanwhile, the only sane male in the house as far as Willa May could see was Ethan Allen. He came in and sat with her, drinking his morning coffee, strong and black, sipping it right out of the saucer like he always did. Listening to the father of the groom and the father of the bride, he looked at Willa May and shook his head. "Who would have thought they'd end up the best of friends?"

Willa May sighed. "Men."

But she knew, too, that once Daniel had seen Tiny off, he would have himself a talk with Ansel, a heart to heart. With any luck at all, Ansel might just learn to keep his horse on home pastures. With any luck at all.

249

It was to her, though, that Daniel first said anything about it. That night in bed, she no sooner rested her head on his chest, running her hand through the mat of silver hair covering it, when Daniel said, "You recollect last night when we were talking about Anse's new wife being so young and all? You said that you were younger than she is when we got married."

"Uh-huh."

"You recollect I said how that had been different?"

"Mm-hmm."

"You asked me *how* it had been different?"

She stopped rubbing his chest. "What's your point?"

"Corey's pregnant. You weren't. That's my point."

With that said, Daniel turned over, leaving Willa May with her thoughts. *Men! You can't live with them and you can't wait for them to get back when they're gone. A mighty strange breed, men.*

For two days, they didn't see any sign of Ansel or his new wife. When they did show their faces, they were always touching each other, holding hands and rubbing each other's backs. Ansel looked like he thought he was the first man to do such a thing, grinning and winking at Corey whenever she got up the nerve to look at him. Corey knew all too well that everyone was aware of what they were up to and mortified that they did know. Daniel was uneasy, too, looking off into the distance whenever he spoke to Ansel. It was like he was afraid that Ansel might catch on to the idea that his ma and pa had been up to the very same thing for the last fifty years. For some reason, it was more than Daniel could handle so he just kept on looking off over the tops of the cornstalks or at the stand of trees on either side of the house -- anywhere, but into his son's eyes. The very son who was so much like him. Willa May found it curious that Daniel was going through such a painful time, watching the two young people heated up over each other and looking like they were Adam and Eve in the Garden, naked in each other's eyes, and enjoying the view.

Willa May couldn't stand it any longer and decided to find out once and for all just what it was that was bothering Daniel. He climbed into bed that night, a hot night in late May with a full moon so bright that their room looked lit up inside. She could see Daniel plainly in the silvery light. She no sooner put her head against his bare chest when she asked, almost bursting from wondering, "Daniel, what is it about Ansel and Corey that makes you look away when you talk to them?"

"What are you talking about? I do no such thing."

"Sure you do," she insisted. "Just today, when Ansel came over before leaving on his deliveries, he was talking to you about setting up some more stills. You looked everywhere but in his eyes."

"No, I didn't."

"Oh, yes you did, Daniel Shrewsbury. Ever since they got married, you've been looking off, looking at anything but Ansel's eyes when you have to speak to him. What's gotten into you, anyhow?"

"You've been reading too many books, Girl."

"What's that supposed to mean?"

"You got a big imagination, that's what it means."

"Was it my imagination tonight at the supper table when Ansel put his hand on Corey's belly, feeling the baby kicking, and you got up and went out onto the porch?"

"I was done eating, that's all."

Willa May raised herself up onto her elbows and looked at Daniel. He looked away, his eyes roaming the ceiling. "And you're doing it again now."

At first he didn't say anything, just lay there in silence. Then Daniel's chest heaved with a long sigh. He mumbled something she couldn't quite make out, still looking away.

"What?" she asked, only catching a word or two.

Turning to her, Daniel ran his hand down her back, leaving it rest against the curve of her hip. She could feel his warm hand raising her nightgown, then the soft pressure of his fingertips against her skin as they traced little circles. Another sigh. "They remind me of the way we were, back when we were young."

The words hung there, hovering above them like a soft, dark cloud. She tried to understand what Daniel meant, but for the life of her, she couldn't grasp what it was. Finally, she lay down, resting her head on his chest again. "What's wrong with that?"

Another long sigh. Just when she thought he wasn't going to answer, he said, "I'm getting old."

"I know that. So am I."

"But I don't want to get old. I want us to stay the same as we were."

What she was hearing pierced Willa May's heart. "I know. But I'm getting old. And so are you. It can't be helped. It's just a fact of life. Now we've got to find joy in our aging and joy in the blooming life that our younguns have given us."

For a long while, Daniel didn't answer. He just lay there, tracing circles on the soft flesh of her hip. "When I was young and we were first married, I thought nothing would ever change. That we were always goin' to be so young and full of juice. Now I look into the mirror every morning and I see this old man looking back. Sometimes it's such a surprise, I wonder who in tarnation that old man is."

Willa May chuckled softly, knowing exactly what Daniel was saying. Too many times she had looked into the mirror and wondered who that gray haired woman was with the crinkly lines around her eyes, eyes that used to be so clear. Now they were clouded over like the sky got sometimes when the sun refused to peek out all day. "I've seen this old woman in that mirror, too," she offered, hoping that might lift Daniel out of his sadness.

"That's just it. When I look at you, I still see the little girl in you. But when I look at me, I see my white hair all shaggy like an old dog's, my beard gone white, too. I feel a soreness in my joints that I never had when I was young. I get to thinking that it's all goin' to be over with and all too soon. There's so much more that I wanted to see to and the clock is ticking faster than I can keep up with, seems like."

"Maybe that clock is trying to tell you it's time to slow down a little and take some pleasure in the time we've got left here on this earth," she suggested.

Daniel nodded. "That's what my head tells me, but my heart wants to run free up in them mountains some more, explore all the places I never got to and tend to our land and our livestock better."

Willa May was getting exasperated, hearing Daniel saying he should have done better by their place. Sitting up in the middle of the bed, she pulled her nightgown back down, bringing her knees up to her chin. "Daniel Shrewsbury, don't you go talking about doing better by us. You did as good -- and some better -- than most. You never hear your folks complaining, do you?"

"No..." Daniel looked at her, knowing she wasn't going to let him get away with blaming himself for things left undone.

"And you haven't got some terrible disease or pain that you're not telling me about, do you?"

He looked at her like maybe she was the one that was starting to talk crazy. "No..."

"Well, since you're not dying on me and you can't do work in the middle of the night, then hush up your fool talk and put your silly notions out of your head once and for all. Help me off with this nightgown so you can do what you started a few minutes ago."

Daniel's troubled frown turned into his familiar devilish grin, the same one that Ansel could flash at the drop of a pin. "You telling me to do my husbandly duty, Girl?"

"Just because Ansel and Corey are younger doesn't mean we can't enjoy some frolicking ourselves."

Daniel sat up on one elbow. He helped her shed her nightgown and pulled her to him. With both arms wrapped around her, he lay back against his pillow. She could see his eyes grinning at her just like they had a thousand times before. She thought maybe their little talk had done some good. She could have sworn the next morning that she had been sleeping with the Daniel she had married so many years before.

Near the end of June, Ansel came home with the news that some archduke had been killed over in Europe, causing a big stink. Willa May just shrugged, figuring it was someone else's troubles, not theirs. By August, Germany had invaded Belgium. The following month, fighting erupted in France, a battle in a place they called the Marne. The war was spreading quickly and everybody in Europe seemed to be caught up in it. Willa May kept praying that America would be able to stay out of this one. For a while, it looked like her prayers had been answered.

In November, Corey gave birth to a nine pound baby boy. They decided to name him Clarence Mackenzie, Clarence for Corey's pa -- Tiny was just a nickname -- and Mackenzie for Corey's mama's family. Corey wanted everyone to call the baby Clarence, but he was labeled "Mack" right from the cradle. He was a burly little thing, barrel chested like his giant grandpa, with curly blonde hair and Corey's green eyes. It wasn't long until they saw that he was Ansel's son, full of devilment and not afraid of anybody or anything. Elroy often grinned and shook his head watching Mack charge across the yard after the hens, hardly bigger than they were. "Just like his pa, that youngun."

To Willa May, the best thing about that baby was the change he created in his pa. Ansel was so proud of him and he adored Corey for giving him such a fine son. It finally occurred to Ansel that there was no place like home. He stopped his carousing and stayed put, much to the disappointment of every woman in the valley between the ages of fourteen and forty. Women still smiled sweetly at Ansel, twirling their hair and batting long lashes, but if it affected Ansel at all, he didn't show it. He only had eyes for Corey. It certainly lifted a weight off Willa May's shoulders.

While she was happy for Ansel and Corey, she couldn't help but worry about Walt Whitman. He was upset over the war, fretting that President Wilson would give in to the Allied countries, and start sending men over there to fight. Thomas Lee, off at the university in Morgantown, was their only child. He planned to become a lawyer. A smart boy, Willa May thought he was even smarter than Walt Whitman. He wasn't alone at the university. Claude Daniel was there as well. Young Doc was so proud that Claude Daniel had decided to go into medicine. He was already planning for Claude Daniel to come into practice with him. With the fighting getting worse, Walt Whitman feared that the two boys would never finish their schooling.

"This war is different than any one we've ever fought before," he told Daniel one Sunday in July of nineteen sixteen.

"War's war," Elroy said, listening in.

"Not this time, Elroy," Walt Whitman insisted. "For one thing, there are so many countries involved. And the way they're fighting this war is different, too. Why, those trenches along the Western Front stretch for over four hundred miles and they haven't changed position much in close to three years now. They're not fighting out in the open like they did at Gettysburg, charging across a field. It's hard to win a war with both sides dug in and not able to make any significant gains. And the weapons they're using -- airplanes dropping bombs, submarines blowing up ships, machine guns drilling down men faster than any rifles they used before."

"So what are you saying, Son?" Daniel asked, taking in everything that Walt Whitman had been telling him.

"I think the only hope the Allies have is to get the United States into the fighting. With the high casualties they're suffering, they need more manpower. Russia alone has fed thousands of their men to the Eastern Front. I don't even know how they can continue after such heavy losses. I read the other day that Russia has lost nearly a million men, trying to keep the Austro-Hungarian army at bay." Walt Whitman paused, sighing deeply. "Like I said, they need men to win.

254

Our men."

Ansel was holding Mack on his lap, feeding him a biscuit with honey. Hearing this, he looked up, "Well, all I can say is if we get into it, I'm goin'. Like you say, they need help and if we're it, then so be it."

Corey, seven months along with their second baby, looked away. Willa May understood. No woman wants to hear her man say he's going off to war, especially when she has a part of him growing inside her.

"They say," Creedy put in, "that the old German Kaiser is Satan himself!"

Walt Whitman nodded. "And if they lose this war, there will be plenty of his own countrymen who will wonder what ever possessed them to follow him into war. Same with the Czar. Those people have had it mighty tough. We can only imagine what it's like for the common person over there."

The newspaper was full of reports on the war. Willa May and Daniel followed it closely. The Allies fought a bitter battle that month that the newspaper called the Battle of the Somme. France was staggering from all the fighting and the French army relinquished command to the British. When the battle was over in November, almost a million men had died and all they had to show for those deaths was a gain of less than ten miles. Like Walt Whitman said, they were running out of men.

The Kaiser ordered his submarines to fire on any ship they spotted, whether it was a battle ship or not. When the Germans started sinking ships, it came as no surprise to Willa May and Daniel that President Wilson said that the United States must go over there and help out. Congress agreed and on April sixth, America joined the Allied forces.

Ansel and Asa enlisted that day. Daniel and Willa May knew they would. Corey cried and begged Ansel not to go, but he told her that he had to do his part. He felt that in war, every able bodied American male was duty bound to join the fight. Wiping her tears, Corey nodded, knowing that Ansel was set on it and there wasn't anything she could do about it but pray for his safe return.

The following Saturday, Willa May asked Ethan Allen to drive her into Montgomery to see Walt Whitman and Annie Catherine. She found them both in tears, Annie Catherine too upset to get out of bed. Thomas Lee and Claude Daniel had signed up, too. They were assigned to the same company as Asa and Ansel. Willa May made

Annie Catherine a hot toddy, spiked with some of the brandy she had kept over the years from Mr. Shaw. Sitting next to her bed, Willa May waited while Annie Catherine sipped the hot brew. Dark circles lined Annie Catherine's eyes streaked with red lines. "Willa May, what am I going to do?" she sobbed, her chest heaving.

Willa May put her arm around her and held her tight. "Just the same as I'm goin' to do. We're goin' to pray that our boys come home safe and sound. We're goin' to go on living our lives day by day till they do come back to us."

"But it's easier for you. You've got other children. And you know what it's like to lose one of your own."

"Easier? Losing somebody you love is never easy. And yes, I do have other children. But something I learned long ago is that each one is special in his or her own way. When one dies, none of the others can take that one's place. When we lost 'Lil Daniel, I thought I'd die from the pain of it. But while it was a struggle for me, it nearly killed Daniel. That's why you have to be strong, Annie Catherine. For Walt Whitman's sake. He loves that boy so, he's goin' to need your strength to get him through this...till Thomas Lee gets back."

"If he gets back."

"Now don't even think that way. Put your faith in the good Lord above and believe with all your heart that he will come home to you."

Annie Catherine just looked out the window at the leaves blowing on the maple tree outside. At first, Willa May thought she wasn't going to answer, but she said, "You're right. I'm being a ninny. And Thomas Lee wouldn't want that. He wants so much to make us proud. Now I've got to be strong so he'll be proud of me, too."

By the time they left, Annie Catherine had dressed and come downstairs to start supper. As Willa May was leaving, Annie Catherine gave her some blackberry preserves, Daniel's favorite. Willa May hugged her, thanking her for the preserves. When Annie Catherine pulled away from her, Willa May looked her in the eye and said, "Now don't forget what we talked about. And anytime you feel you need some extra help, you just let us know. We're never too busy to help out."

Annie Catherine managed a smile. "I'll do my best. It's what Thomas Lee deserves." She put her arm around Walt Whitman and added, "From both of us."

They left Montgomery by way of Deepwater Mountain. Willa May wanted to stop in on Young Doc and Hattie Sue. When they arrived, it was the same scene. Hattie Sue was dragging herself around the kitchen, wiping her tears on the hem of her apron. Both Ernest Roy and Claude Daniel had enlisted. Ernest Roy had finished college and was living in Roanoke, Virginia, teaching school. He was going into the Navy there. Willa May knew it frightened Hattie Sue to think about her eldest boy being on a ship with the German submarines causing such a problem. "At least Claude Daniel will have his uncles to look out for him, and his cousin to keep him company. But...but Ernest Roy --" She burst into fresh tears.

It threw Young Doc into turmoil to see Hattie Sue in such a state. She had been so strong through the years. Being a doctor, he wanted to make it better, but Willa May knew that this wasn't an aching he could treat with pills or an injection. This was a heartache and there wasn't anything in Young Doc's medical bag for that. He pulled Hattie Sue to him and patted her gently on her back. Looking at Willa May, he shook his head, lost for words. Willa May glanced at Ethan Allen, but he was no longer equipped to deal with such sadness. Gesturing to Willa May, he moseyed out onto the porch. Moments later, Willa May heard the steady creak of the porch swing.

"Now look here," Willa May said, "I want you both to come over here and sit down with me. I'm goin' to tell you just what I told Annie Catherine."

When she left, Young Doc walked Willa May out to the Model T where Ethan Allen was already seated behind the wheel, anxious to get going and put all these sad faces behind him. "Thank you, Willa May. Hattie Sue needed to hear that."

"You can't mend a broken heart," she reminded him.

"Well, it's my professional opinion, you might say, that you're just what the doctor ordered. Hattie Sue has been crying for days and nothing I said seemed to help. I didn't know what to do. But I think that she'll bear up now and do just what you said -- take each day one at a time and send up prayers every day."

"Doc, when you've been around as long as I have, you'll see that -- and this is *my* professional opinion -- the power of the human spirit is a mighty awesome thing."

Young Doc nodded. "You've made a believer out of me."

She waved goodbye as they pulled away and started back toward home. In her upset state, Hattie Sue had baked up a storm, trying to keep busy so she wouldn't think about her boys. When her tears had dried, she saw that she had baked enough to feed a small army. She gave Willa May a custard pie and a few dozen sweet potato muffins still warm from the oven, and a chocolate layer cake to take home. When Daniel met them, his eyes grew round, looking at all the food Willa May brought back. He sat down right away and had a slice of the custard pie and a muffin spread with the blackberry preserves. Washing it down with a cup of coffee, he wiped his mouth, saying, "If the war is goin' to mean all this good cooking, then maybe we should've gotten into the fight sooner."

Their sons were shipped overseas in September of nineteen seventeen. From that point on, the family hungered for any word of how they were doing, sharing their letters -- except the ones from Ansel to Corey. They were always about how he missed her and the babies, filled with longing. Corey treated each of the letters like it might be her last, clutching it to her and even pinning each new one inside her brassiere. "So it'll be close to my heart," she said. Seeing how lovesick the girl was, Willa May remembered how hard it was waiting the five long years for Daniel to return from the war. She prayed that this war -- "The Great War" -- as people were calling it, would be over soon.

It was from Thomas Lee that they received the most news. His letters to Walt Whitman and Annie Catherine were always filled with where they were fighting and how the other boys were holding up. One said that they had gotten close to Paris and the boys had gone into the city one night to see the sights. They ended up in a burlesque house and the French girls tried their best to impress Ansel, flirting so openly that it had brought a blush, the first one any of them had ever witnessed, to Ansel's face. Willa May watched Corey as Walt Whitman read the letter aloud to them. A dark cloud came over her young face, hearing about the French girls throwing themselves at her man. Then Thomas Lee said, "But tell Corey that Anse told all those pretty gals that he already had a beautiful wife and nobody could take her place." Daniel looked at Willa May and she could see him breathing a sigh of relief, knowing like her, that he had figured Ansel would take on the whole bunch. Corey breathed a long sigh, too. She smiled and said, "That's my Anse," just like she had known all along that Ansel would be strong, even so far from home. Willa May wished she could have said she felt the same confidence in her son, but she remembered all too well what he had been like before he married Corey.

The weeks went on and the letters kept coming, the war bringing them all closer. With the four boys fighting together, they shared the same fears, listening for word...any word at all. They prayed the boys would be okay, knowing that whatever befell one would probably befall all. That spring, the Germans thought they could finally defeat the Allies once the fighting ended on the Eastern Front. The war was concentrated now on the Western Front. The first fighting broke out in a small town called St. Quentin. Walt Whitman showed Willa May and Daniel on the map that the town was in a valley by a river called "Somme". Seeming invincible, the Germans pushed the British army back thirty miles. The Kaiser's forces planned to take Paris and battered the city with what the newspapers called "Big Berthas". A few weeks later, they marched toward Belgium, getting as far as the Lys River. The Allies were devastated with losses. Everyone worried that this time the Germans would finish the Allies off for good. Near the end of May, fighting raged again along the Marne River where they had already fought one battle.

Willa May and Daniel were just sitting down to supper one evening when Young Doc and Hattie Sue stopped by, excited about the news. The Americans were pitching in to help the French stop the Germans at a place called Chateau-Thierry, close to Paris.

"Well if them Germans thought they'd done had a fight already, they're in for it now, all right!" Elroy declared. "They ain't never come up against the Shrewsbury boys, by God."

All that June, the family received letters from the boys saying that they were in the middle of some heavy fighting. They were pushing the Germans back, moving them out of the Belleau Wood. The Second Battle of the Marne turned the war around for the Allies. By September, Walt Whitman received a letter from Thomas Lee saying that the Allies had taken back all the land they had lost since that spring.

In September, just a year after the boys had shipped out, they started fighting in the Argonne Forest. No one had gotten a letter in a few days when Daniel was sitting out on the porch helping Elroy and Creedy peel apples to make applebutter the next day. Two servicemen pulled up in front of the house. When Willa May saw them, her heart sank. Corey was helping Willa May fold some wash and she saw them, too. She started sobbing, saying, "Oh, Lord, no. Don't let it be Anse! Please, Lord!" Willa May put her arm around Corey and pulled her to the door. She could see Daniel's back as he stepped off the porch and shook hands with the two men, nodding to them.

Creedy got up, too, knowing that it wasn't going to be good news. He stood on the edge of the porch, leaning against his cane. Willa May could hear one of the men talking to Daniel. Daniel nodded and shook the man's hand again. Then the two men got back into their automobile and drove off, leaving Daniel standing there in the dust. He watched their car as it disappeared down the dirt road, past the trees. It seemed to Willa May that Daniel stood there for a lifetime, looking out over the dying cornstalks yellowing in the early fall sun. Creedy must have heard what the serviceman had said because he stood shaking his head and wiping his eyes with his shirt sleeve. Willa May thought that even the birds had stopped chirping and the flies had stopped buzzing around the barrel of peeled apples. Everything came to a stop as if the world had stopped turning. Daniel turned around and looked up at her. Tears sparkled against his cheeks in the late afternoon sunlight, shining as bright as any star she had ever seen. Daniel's eyes went from her to Corey. When Corey cried out, Daniel shook his head and looked away for a minute, frowning. Willa May was dying inside, dying from the knowledge that one or more of the boys was gone, dying from the misery of not knowing which one.

Daniel heaved a long sigh. He shook his head as if to clear it from the overwhelming sadness the servicemen had placed on him. Taking a deep breath, he came up onto the porch and looked at her through the black mesh of the screen door. "There was...there was heavy fighting," he started, swallowing hard to keep his voice steady. "Asa was killed.

Willa May gasped, then her lungs deflated as she leaned into Corey. She could feel the air going out of Corey's body, too, a deep sigh of relief. Daniel turned to Corey. "That's not all." Another cry -- a whimper, really -- worked its way up out of Corey's throat.

"The whole gallderned unit was hit bad. Claude Daniel and Thomas Lee were both wounded. Anse, too."

"No!" Corey shrieked.

Daniel swallowed again, looking away. "Looks like Claude Daniel and Thomas Lee will be all right. Coming home soon, I expect."

The silence that fell between them then separated the two women from Daniel like a steel door. Seeing that Corey couldn't work up the courage to ask, Willa May managed, "And Ansel?"

"He's in real bad shape. Seems he took on a whole company of them Germans, shooting at them with a Hotchkiss eight-millimeter machine gun that he grabbed out of some Frenchmen's hands when he saw Asa fall. Wiped out the whole bunch. They're saying he'll be a hero...if he lives."

Corey broke into sobs. The two women held onto each other. Numb, Willa May felt a fog settle around her as she clung to Corey. She didn't remember Young Doc and Hattie Sue arriving. Nor when Walt Whitman came. Seeing the state the two women were in, Young Doc gave Corey an injection to calm her down. Through her fog, Willa May heard Young Doc say something to her, but she couldn't make out what it was.

Ethan Allen had been up at the stills with Elroy when the word came. He and Daniel set off into the mountains together the next day. When Willa May came back to the world, she could hear Elroy sniffling from a corner of her room and Creedy blowing his nose outside on the porch. She was in her bed. Hattie Sue and Young Doc were sitting next to the bed. Hattie Sue held her hand as tears streamed down her face. It was most of a week before Willa May felt up to getting out of bed and getting dressed. Daniel still wasn't home. Downstairs, Annie Catherine was cooking a pork roast and Willa May smelled the odor of meat.

When they sat down to supper, she felt everyone watching her, glancing at her when they thought she wouldn't see. Willa May knew they were all fretting over her. She wanted to tell them she would be all right, but the words just didn't come. Everyone tried their best to fill the silence with talk about the Indian summer they were having, what they had been canning and how they wanted to plant more tomatoes next summer. She let them go on, figuring that it was probably helping them just as much as they thought it was helping her to hear them chattering about such trivial matters. After some carrot cake and coffee, the womenfolk cleared away the last of the dishes. Walt Whitman sat down beside Willa May and took her hand. "Mommy, I've got something I'd like to talk over with you. Are you up to it?"

She looked at him and saw him as if she were looking at him through an early morning mist. She nodded slowly.

"They're sending Asa's body back. It should be here in the next couple of days. I'd like to request that he be buried at Arlington National Cemetery, if it's all right with you and Pa. Pa's not here and he may not be back in time to decide. So I'm asking you if it will be all right to give Asa a military burial and see him buried a hero who

261

died for his country."

She tried to understand just what Walt Whitman was asking of her, but it seemed to Willa May that he might have asked her if he could go out and play with 'Lil Daniel. "Is 'Lil Daniel here?" she asked, standing up to look out the door and see if she could find him. It seemed to her that he had been gone a good long time and she was going to get after him for worrying them so.

"No, Mommy," Walt Whitman said, "'Lil Daniel's gone. Remember?"

Nodding, she said, "Asa's gone too, isn't he?"

"Yes, Mommy."

"Ansel?"

She heard Walt Whitman sigh deeply and braced herself, more out of instinct than anything she could really feel. "We don't know yet."

Like the sun coming out from behind gray storm clouds, Willa May saw Walt Whitman's face come into focus. He looked so worried. "This Arlington -- is it a pretty place?" she asked.

Walt Whitman smiled, patting her hand. "Yes. A beautiful place."

"I reckon it'll be all right, then," she shrugged. Then the fog returned, settling over her again.

Asa's body came home a few days later. Nobody had seen Daniel or Ethan Allen in that time. "I'm telling you," Elroy said to nobody in particular, "Daniel will come back when he's good and ready and not before. I know him too well. Just you all go on and give Asa a good send-off. I'll just sit here and wait for Daniel. Ain't no use doing nothing else now."

Walt Whitman and James Houston saw Willa May to the church. The preacher gave a good eulogy, talking about how there wasn't a nobler death than dying for one's country. Willa May wanted to tell him she would rather have Asa alive than noble. Then Walt Whitman read, "When Lilacs Last In The Dooryard Bloomed", Asa's favorite poem. They carried the coffin out and loaded it onto the back of a horse drawn wagon. Everyone followed it down Deepwater Mountain to Montgomery to the train depot there. The trees were ablaze, fiery reds and burnt golds. Willa May thought how Asa would love to see those colors one more time and how he died looking out on woods like these, somewhere in a place she would never see. A man took pictures of them loading Asa's coffin onto the train. The picture appeared in the newspaper the next day with a caption that read: "Local War Hero To Be Buried At Arlington". Walt Whitman and Annie Catherine accompanied Asa's body to Washington, D.C. They saw Asa buried with full honors in Arlington Cemetery.

Thomas Lee was the first of the boys to get back, just after the armistice. He had been wounded in the knee and walked on crutches. Doctors told him he would probably walk with a limp the rest of his life. As soon as he arrived home, he went to visit his grandparents. The following week would be Thanksgiving and he knew it was going to be tough on Willa May and Daniel. When he got to his grandparents' place, he found that Daniel and Ethan Allen were still holed up on the mountain. None of the family had seen or heard from them. Elroy had taken up a post, sitting day after day on the front porch and watching the trees, now almost bare, searching for any sign of them. It was almost lunch time, so Willa May asked Thomas Lee to sit down with them. He hugged and kissed everybody, telling Corey that it wouldn't be much longer till Ansel would be coming home, too, now that he was in the clear. Holding little Mack on his good knee, Thomas Lee ate two bowls of beans and four slices of cornbread, crumbling the last slice into his buttermilk like he had when he was no bigger than Mack. Aside from his knee, he didn't look bad, just older. War did that, Willa May thought. Shaking his head, he said, "Grandma, nobody makes beans and cornbread like you. I haven't eaten this well since I left here."

Taking time for lunch, Elroy grinned as though he had been the one to cook the beans and bake the cornbread. "Ain't nothing like good old home cooking."

Thomas Lee hefted Mack off his knee and stood up, loosening his belt. Elroy chuckled, slapping Creedy on the back. "What'd I tell you? Why, I bet Thomas Lee ain't eaten so high on the hog in a 'coon's age."

"You've got that right, Uncle Elroy."

"Well, save some room for dessert," Willa May reminded. "Corey's baked you a homemade apple pie."

"My favorite."

"Yessir. She remembered. And she baked an extra one for you to take back home with you when you leave."

"Why, thank you, Corey," Thomas Lee smiled. Willa May thought she could see the ghost of the boy who had gone off to fight the war, his dark brown eyes still so smart and snappy.

"I'll cut you a slice right now, Thomas Lee," Corey offered, "but first tell me about Anse. Is he really goin' to be all right?"

His glistening brown eyes grew dark. Willa May could see it was hard for Thomas Lee to talk about this yet. But seeing how fretful Corey was, he felt obliged to let her know just what had gone on. "Anse is going to be okay, Corey, but I can tell you, it was touch and go for awhile. As soon as I could move, I had them wheel me down to his room. The nurses must've gotten tired of having to haul me down there because the doctors finally asked if I'd like to be moved into Anse's room, knowing I was his nephew."

Willa May reached over and closed her hand around Thomas Lee's big strong hand. Giving it a squeeze, she said, "I'm mighty glad he had you there with him."

"Me, too," Corey murmured.

"Anse was hooked up to a lot of tubes and they had him in a little tent for awhile."

"In a tent?" Elroy repeated, not understanding why the doctors would put Ansel in a tent.

Thomas Lee nodded, "To help him breathe better. He'd taken one shot in his right lung and it had filled up with fluid and then pneumonia set in. He was having a tough time breathing."

"You say he took one shot in his lung? How many places was he shot?" Willa May asked.

Thomas Lee looked at Corey and then at his grandmother. "Altogether, Anse took eight shots."

"Eight!" Elroy cried. "Lord Amighty!"

Thomas Lee nodded, watching Corey and Willa May carefully. "The one in the lung, one in his hip, three in his left leg, one in his left arm, one in his shoulder and one just above that -- more on his neck, I guess you'd say."

Elroy blew a long, low whistle, shaking his head. "Eight shots. I can't believe it."

"You saw it when he got shot?" Willa May asked.

"I was already wounded, lying on my side and holding my knee. Asa saw me and started over toward me and that's when the Germans shot him. I saw Asa fall and next thing I knew, there was Anse, bending over Asa. His face was toward me and I could see him crying, screaming for Asa to get up. Bullets were whizzing past him all the while. I don't know how he didn't get killed right then. I guess Anse saw that Asa was dead. He turned around and charged right at the Germans, not even bothering to take cover behind the trees. He hadn't gone too far when he came upon some French soldiers fighting with us. They'd just set up this machine gun and Anse grabbed them and shoved them aside. Then he took that machine gun and started spraying those Germans with fire. The bullets kept coming at him, too. When one would hit him, he'd flinch, but he just kept on firing. Looking back, I don't think he felt any of those shots, he was in such a rage. I've never seen anything like it," Thomas Lee said. "And I hope I never do again."

In her mind, Willa May could see Ansel, see that wild, savage side of Daniel coming out in him when he saw his twin brother lying there dead. It didn't surprise her to hear what Thomas Lee had described. It was just what Daniel would have done. She squeezed Thomas Lee's hand again and said in a solemn voice, "Lord willing, you'll never have to witness something like that ever again, Son."

"Amen," Elroy and Creedy chimed in.

They sat in silence for a few moments, each of them thinking about the suffering their boys had endured and praying that they would be able to put it behind them so they could get on with their lives now. Willa May hoped that this would be the last time any of her kin would have to go off to war.

Corey stood up. "I'll get you that pie now, Thomas Lee."

He smiled. "Thank you, Corey."

For Thanksgiving, Thomas Lee brought them something special, or so he said. He came in, carrying a bucket filled to the brim with what looked to Willa May like seashells. Elroy picked one up, and seeing that it was hard as a rock, he asked, "How do folks eat these gallderned shells, Thomas Lee?"

"They're clams, Uncle Elroy. And you have to steam them open, then eat the meat inside."

"Don't appear to have much meat, being such little old things," Elroy grumbled, still turning over the gray colored shell in his hands and inspecting it like a geologist examining a fossil.

"Just a bite, but it's really good. Dip it in melted butter. You'll see."

Thomas Lee took over the stove, pulling down one of Willa May's

265

big stewing pots and filling it with water from the pump outside. He sprinkled some salt into the pot and stoked up the stove. She watched him, seeing how tickled he was to be sharing this new eating experience with them. "So where on earth did you eat clams, Son?" she asked while the water started to bubble and steam.

"Friend of mine lives in Massachusetts. A little town called Chatham, on Cape Cod. It's right on the water. They eat a lot of shellfish up there, those people. He was on his way through to some relatives in Virginia and dropped these off for me. One of the things I liked best was a chowder they made with these clams. It had bits of potatoes in it, something like our potato soup, but the clams add a salty zest to it."

Thomas Lee picked up the bucket and poured the clams into the steaming water. He picked up the mound of butter that was setting on the table, put it in another, smaller pot, and set it on the stove, too. "You're going to love this, Grandma," he said, watching over the two pots like a mother hen watching over her eggs.

A few minutes later, he emptied the clams out into the sink, letting the steaming hot water run over them. Willa May could see that each little shell had popped open, reminding her of a bunch of hungry mouths waiting to be fed. Quickly, Thomas Lee put the clams on a platter and poured the melted butter into a bowl. Grinning like an elf, he said, "C'mon, Grandma. We're about to start our feast."

The clams were right tasty to Willa May's way of thinking. Salty, but tasty. She liked the melted butter on them. She could feel it running down her chin a couple of times as she dug at the open shells for the bite of meat inside.

Elroy wasn't quite as taken. He scrunched up his nose and said, "Right gritty 'lil fellers, ain't they?"

Creedy and Corey wouldn't even taste the clams, being wary of something so strange and new. But Walt Whitman, Annie Catherine, Thomas Lee, and Willa May ate their fill, licking their buttery lips and dabbing at their chins with their napkins. "Next time your friend sends you some of these clams, Thomas Lee, we'll make some of that soup you were telling me about."

"Do you like them, Grandma?"

"Sure do," she agreed, digging at another one.

Elroy looked at them like they had lost their minds. Willa May guessed that clams were one of those things that a person either loved or hated, with no in-between. She could see that Thomas Lee was overjoyed that she had taken to them so well. He and Walt Whitman put away most of the bucket, smacking their lips for a half hour or more.

They no sooner cleared the table when Corey brought out the turkey. Walt Whitman started carving the bird while everyone took deep whiffs of the chestnut stuffing that Corey had made. Before they could serve the turkey, Daniel and Ethan Allen came through the door. Everyone rushed to them, hugging them and welcoming them back. When Daniel came to Thomas Lee, he shook Thomas Lee's hand and then pulled Thomas Lee to him, holding him close extra long. Thomas Lee had tears in his eyes when he said, "Grandpa, I'm sorry about Asa. We all are."

Daniel nodded and pulled Thomas Lee back for another hug. Ethan Allen, looking wearier than usual, shook Thomas Lee's hand and hugged him, too. Daniel looked at Willa May. She nodded to him, knowing that he was back now and everything would be all right. Somehow, she was finding it easier as she grew older to forgive Daniel's need to be alone in times of crisis. Maybe she just knew him better. Maybe she knew herself better. She was just glad that he was back and happy that they hadn't started the meal without him.

Everyone went back to the dining room. They were saying thanks for all their blessings when they heard a noise outside, an automobile pulling up. Willa May rushed to the door, hoping it was Ansel, but it was Young Doc and Hattie Sue. They had Claude Daniel and Ernest Roy with them. After more hugging and crying, they pulled in extra tables and chairs and ate their Thanksgiving meal together. Willa May couldn't remember a Thanksgiving as special as this one. It was such a relief to have the boys back, even though she missed Ansel and Asa. She knew that Daniel did, too, but for that one evening, it was good to have their grandsons back and to take part in their parents' joy at having them home safe and sound.

The men ate second helpings of everything, heaping on ladles of giblet gravy over their mashed potatoes and turkey. The women cleared the dishes and started coffee. Then they heard another knock on the door. "Oh, no," Willa May said, thinking that they must be getting company and wanting to keep the day just for family. She wiped her hands and took off her apron. Turning around, she didn't realize that Daniel had already answered the door. Then she saw a tall, young man with golden hair dressed in uniform. He grinned at her and said, "Happy Thanksgiving, Mommy." Before she could speak, she heard the clang of the knife Corey was holding as it fell to the floor. Both women gave a small cry of surprise. Ansel pulled them both to him and held them close. When he finally let go, Willa May saw tears streaming down Ansel's face. Her own eyes blurred with tears as she noticed that Corey, too, was crying. When the two of them finally let go of him, Ansel went through all the same hugging and crying that the other boys had suffered that day. He came to Daniel and held onto his pa an extra long time. Daniel patted Ansel's back like he had when Ansel was little and came running to him over some hurt, both of them knowing that this time the hurt was more than his pa could fix. Stepping back, Ansel looked deep into Daniel's eyes and vowed, "I ain't never leaving this place again, Pa, as long as I live." Daniel nodded, hugging Ansel to him once more, his eyes fixed on Willa May's. They both understood. He wanted nothing more than to live out his days on their mountain, far from the madness of the world. Neither Willa May nor Daniel blamed him.

Chapter Eleven

No sooner were the boys home when more trouble erupted in the coal mines. Ansel came home from one of his deliveries telling the family about a sheriff in a little town over in Mingo County who openly supported the miner's union. One of the infamous Hatfields was caught up in the trouble, a man Ansel called "Two-Gun" Hatfield. Willa May read in the newspaper a few days later that his real name was Syd Hatfield. This Hatfield and some of the leading citizens said that if the miners wanted to go out on strike, they'd stand by them. Taking the men at their word, miners from a camp called Red Jacket threw down their picks and walked out.

James Houston stopped by that Sunday and told them that he had been in touch with some of the miners and from what they had told him, the mine operators were recreating the mine war at Paint Creek. They brought in Baldwin-Felts men and evicted entire families just as they had evicted James Houston and Ethan Allen. Thinking that the miners were going peacefully, the hired thugs threw out all the strikers' families and went back to the Matewan train depot.

"Now them boys didn't know it," James Houston continued, "but they made a big mistake. While they were standing there, waiting for the train, old Two-Gun himself walked up and shot that no-good Albert Felts right in the head. Then they told me that all hell broke loose. Them Baldwin-Felts men had bullets raining down on them from every window on the street. Five of them dropped where they stood. A few of them pulled out their guns and fired back, giving the others cover while they made a run for it."

"How many people got hurt?" Daniel asked.

"When it was all said and done, a dozen were dead. Seven of them were mine guards. Another four were winged."

"Too bad they didn't get them all," Ansel sighed, leaning back in his chair and clasping his hands behind his head.

"Oh, that ain't all," James Houston said. "Here's the best part. When the train pulled in, folks on board looked out at all the dead bodies and them folks over in Matewan was dancing and singing all around them. They said that it looked like some drunken brawl. Some of the men spat streams of tobacco juice on the corpses. One woman on the train got upset and said them people singing and dancing were the Devil's disciples. She said it loud enough for everyone in the train car to hear and another passenger set her straight, saying that the ones lying dead in the street had been the ones doing the Devil's work."

The following week James Houston stopped by again. This time Walt Whitman was there. "So tell me, is it true what I heard about that Hatfield fellow over in Matewan marrying the mayor's wife just a week after they put him in his grave?" Walt Whitman asked.

James Houston nodded. "Yep. Some folks are finding it pretty strange that the mayor was one of them that was found dead when the smoke cleared last week. More than a few of them are wondering just who fired the shot that killed the poor bastard."

Two-Gun Hatfield became a local sensation. The newspaper was full of reports about him. Willa May read each one aloud to the rest of the family. They could hardly believe it when she read about a motion picture show being made about him, making him out to be a hero. The article went on to say that it was a popular show in the mining camps. But soon they read that Two-Gun had been arrested along with twenty other men on charges of murder. Before they could bring the men to trial, several of the eyewitnesses who were scheduled to testify were shot. One of them was Devil Anse Hatfield, one of Two-Gun's kin. After that everyone in the state felt that the trial was nothing but a sham. Nobody in their right mind would testify against the men, knowing it would seal their own doom if they did.

Once the trial started, Ansel brought a newspaper home every day. Elroy would roll himself over, away from his post by the fireplace, to listen as Willa May read all about it. The trial was being held in Williamson, but the newspaper said that folks there were too afraid to show their faces on the streets, knowing there was bound to be more bloodshed. On the third day, the judge was forced to halt the proceedings when an angry mob of miners threatened to storm into the courtroom. Creedy gasped when Willa May read that the mob numbered close to a thousand. When the judge had settled everyone down, fifty Baldwin-Felts men marched into the courtroom. The courtroom was like the nitroglycerin used in the mines, deadly and unpredictable.

270

The trial dragged on for over two months. Even though the newspaper said that some witnesses testified that they had seen Two-Gun kill Albert Felts, the jury returned a verdict of "not guilty". Hearing this, Daniel chuckled, "That's because every one of them jurors knew that to vote 'guilty' was like signing his own death certificate."

When the trial ended, Ansel came home one day telling them about a shooting in McDowell County. He said that nobody was very clear about who did the shooting. Rumors circulated that it was the Baldwin-Felts men, trying to frame Two-Gun Hatfield and his friend, Ed Chambers. "Them old Baldwin-Felts boys would like nothing more than to see Two-Gun stand trial in their territory," Ansel added.

It wasn't long until Ansel came home bearing another, more startling report. Two-Gun and Chambers had been arrested and the law was taking them to Welch to stand trial. But as the police led the accused men and their wives into the courthouse, some Baldwin-Felts men opened fire on them. Ansel sighed, "It was a regular massacre what them boys walked into." Again the newspapers were full of reports about the shooting, but no one was arrested. People were too terrified to offer testimony. Listening to the reports, Elroy reminded Willa May and Daniel of what he had said years before. "We're living in a country ruled by a tyrant king. King Coal."

Soon Ansel told them about another mine war brewing in Logan County. When James Houston stopped by, he told them about a sheriff there by the name of Chafin. He said that this Chafin controlled everything and he wouldn't stand for any union men entering his jurisdiction. "We've tried time and again to send some of our men over there, but Chafin always sees to it that the men leave town, whether they're willing or not. He likes to brag about how he owns the miners in his county. But we showed him. He tried to enter our headquarters in another county, saying that he was there to arrest one of our men. Well, Chafin didn't have any right to arrest anybody there and our men knew it. One of our boys shot him. Of course, Chafin had to have the last laugh, bragging about how the union would never break him. He's one low-down sonofabitch."

Willa May and Daniel didn't realize how much this Chafin's blustering infuriated James Houston until they heard that he was one of five thousand miners who decided to storm the king's castle. They met on Lens Creek. Packing guns, they aimed to climb Blair Mountain. The mountain was a huge wall that separated the

Guyandotte and Coal Rivers. It was the outer wall of Chafin's fortress. When the governor heard what the miners were up to, he called on the President to lend help. He warned the miners that he would call in troops unless they gave up their cause and went home. After so many arrests during the Paint Creek strike still vivid in their minds, the miners scattered like mice from a prowling cat.

But Chafin kept challenging the miners, unable to stop swaggering. Finally the miners couldn't tolerate any more. They prepared to storm Blair Mountain again. Mother Jones arrived, calling the mine operators names and hailing the miners as gallant heroes like knights of the Middle Ages. James Houston told them that she might as well have stayed home. As soon as she had stirred the miners into action, she begged them not to go, warning that if the governor called in federal troops, it could be the end of the union. Like the others, James Houston was too disgusted to turn back. They grew disgusted with Mother Jones as well. Listening to James Houston's account, Willa May pictured Mother Jones as an angel with broken wings, fallen from grace in the eyes of all who had believed in her.

Armed with a machine gun, rifles, and pistols, James Houston, along with six thousand other miners, started up the mountain. The President sent a general to tell the miners that they were committing an act of treason. Moved by his words, the miners surrendered their weapons. But Chafin couldn't let the miners go without a fight. He sent some of his men to arrest the last of the miners. As soon as the miners heard, they headed back, prepared to fight.

James Houston and his men tied red neckerchiefs around their necks and Chafin's men bore white arm bands. James Houston led a group who took over the railroad and ransacked a store for some supplies. Chafin put out a call for help. War veterans and Baldwin-Felts men descended on Logan County in droves. Chafin's men positioned themselves on the top of the mountain for miles. In an effort to help, mine operators hired airplanes to drop bombs on the miners.

Willa May and Daniel fretted over James Houston, hearing that Chafin had ordered his men to use tear gas. Some of Ansel's friends who had fought in Europe with him told him that the fighting on Blair Mountain was every bit as bloody as it had been on the front.

When federal troops arrived, they launched an assault against the miners and Chafin. A cease-fire was called. James Houston and his men were relieved. But the mine operators weren't about to let

272

something like this go. They hired lawyers to charge nearly five hundred miners with murder and treason. They accused James Houston of being one of the union leaders. His trial was scheduled to take place in Jefferson County, away from Chafin and his iron-fisted grasp. Soon the trial was moved to Fayette County, just a few short miles from Willa May and Daniel.

Daniel and Ansel went to the courthouse every day. Daniel meant to make sure that nobody threw James Houston into prison again. A few of the men who stood trial with James Houston received prison sentences, but James Houston was acquitted. He testified under oath that he was with one of the union organizers over in Paint Creek on the day he was charged with killing men on Blair Mountain. It was a lie and everybody in the courtroom knew it. But history had shown them that honesty was foolhardy when it came to dealing with the mine operators.

For months after the march on Blair Mountain, James Houston regretted what they had done. It was far from the brilliant achievement he had hoped it would be. The trials that followed depleted the union's funds. Local newspapers turned public opinion against the union, claiming that it was the coal operators who had been victims in this bloody battle. They even quoted John L. Lewis as saying that the union had been wrong in how they had handled the problem.

James Houston did take heart in the knowledge that Sheriff Chafin was sentenced to two years in prison. His fiefdom, like old Pharaoh's Egypt, had toppled at last. With it, the vise like grip of the coal operators crumbled. After a long, bitter war, the miners of Logan County were free to unionize.

Early in the spring of 'twenty-one, before the buds had started popping through, the family set out for church on a Sunday morning. It was still cold and they had to put quilts over their laps as they bumped along in the Model T. By then, Elroy wasn't getting around much, always fussing about every ache and pain. He was just content to stay home and wait for them. Ethan Allen was tending the stills up behind the house. He hadn't gone to church since he had come home from prison. The rest of them waved goodbye to Elroy and Ethan

Allen helped him roll into the house where he fried some bacon and eggs for him. Seeing that Elroy was satisfied to sit by the fire, Ethan Allen went up to the stills.

While everyone was gone, Elroy dozed off, sitting by the fire. He found that he did that more and more. Willa May took it as a sign that he was just getting old. Ethan Allen was headed for home when he heard screaming and shrieking coming from the house about a quarter of a mile away. Running as fast as he could, the screaming grew louder the closer he came to the house. Ethan Allen burst through the front door and found Elroy in flames, rolling on the floor and screaming in agony. Ethan Allen grabbed a quilt and wrapped Elroy in it, trying to pat out the flames. All the while, Elroy shrieked in terror, burnt all over. Once the flames were out, Ethan Allen tried to pull the quilt off of Elroy, but he stopped when he saw pieces of Elroy's charred flesh peeling away with the quilt.

"I'm goin' for help, Elroy. You hear me? I'm goin' to get you help!" Ethan Allen was never sure if Elroy understood, but he ran for the door and saddled up Daniel's mare. He took off for Page, knowing that Young Doc would be at church with his folks. The family was climbing into the Model T when they heard shouting coming from a distance and the faint thunder of hooves. Everyone looked up to see Ethan Allen bearing down hard on them. He was yelling for Young Doc as he raced up. The mare was in a lather and Ethan Allen was out of breath as he said, "You gotta come quick, Doc. It's Elroy -- he -- he fell into the f-- fire and near burnt himself to death."

Everyone gasped, but Young Doc said, "I'm right behind you, Ethan Allen."

It seemed to Willa May like the twisting road stretched out before them longer than it had ever been before. All of them were so worried, trying their best to reach Elroy and save him. Ansel drove as fast as he could, swinging them from side to side as they rounded the curves up to their place. They pulled up behind Young Doc and Hattie Sue. Ethan Allen had already swung down from his horse and told Mack to see to her. Daniel hopped down and helped Creedy out. Corey had ridden back with Young Doc and Hattie Sue. She stood back holding their youngest, Robert, in her arms, not wanting to go in the house for fear of what she would see. Daniel helped Willa May out of the car and said, "Stay out here with Corey till we see what's to be done." With that, he turned and followed Ansel and Ethan Allen inside.

274

It was then that Willa May noticed how quiet everything had gotten. An ominous silence that reminded her of the day they received word that Asa had died. Elroy had been with them for years now, a part of the family, closer to her than her own brother had ever been. Tears filled her eyes as she stood there, wondering what Daniel would tell her when he came out of the house. They waited for more than twenty minutes in utter silence. Neither Willa May nor Corey said a word. Creedy walked up onto the porch and stood, waiting like them, leaning heavier on his cane than Willa May had noticed in a while. If it was going to be hard on her and Daniel to lose Elroy, she knew it would be even harder on Creedy. They had kept each other company over the years. Elroy carried on his foolishness and Creedy, watching out for Elroy, became Elroy's legs. He fetched everything for Elroy. It was going to be sad to see them parted. The silence dragged on and with each passing minute, Willa May grew more frightened that Elroy was inside dying, suffering beyond anything she could imagine. It didn't seem fair to her that someone who had suffered the loss of his legs should have to die such a terrifying and painful death. She couldn't help wondering how such a thing could happen on so peaceful a Sunday morning.

After what seemed forever, Daniel came out onto the porch. He saw Creedy standing there, but he didn't have the heart to tell him that his best friend was gone. He looked toward Willa May, his face grave. His eyes, like hers, filled with tears. He just shook his head. Creedy sat down on the porch, deflated, like all the stuffing had come out of him. Hanging his head, he started to cry, looking more like the helpless little boy that Lizzy had taken in than the old man he had become. Willa May went up and put her arms around him. She stroked his hair, the same way she used to stroke away her children's tears. After a while, he calmed down and said, "I've known some mighty good folks and some mighty low-down mean ones, too. But for the life of me, I can't understand why this had to happen to one of the best ones I ever knew when there are plenty of them mean ones walking about here on God's green earth, just bringing misery to everybody around them."

Willa May was swept back in time to the day when Creedy first came to live with Lizzy and Pole. She recalled her mama telling her how cruel Creedy's own pa had been, how his pa had just tossed him off of the wagon like he was throwing out garbage. Holding Creedy to her now, she said, "I reckon you have known your share of mean folks, at that, Creedy, but I think we all have to count ourselves lucky to have known such a fine man as Elroy and just be thankful that he shared a part of our lives."

Creedy nodded. Out of the corner of her eye, Willa May saw Daniel walking away, headed for the gorge. It wouldn't have surprised her to see him take off into the mountains. But when he came back an hour later, he said, "I've been looking for a good place to bury Elroy. I think he would've liked looking out over the gorge, enjoying the view of the water and the mountains. Then I got to thinking that Elroy's just as much a hero as Asa, having lost his legs, fighting for what he thought was right. Maybe we should give him a military burying and ask all the old boys who are still living to show up in their uniforms and see Elroy off."

Willa May agreed. "Elroy would have liked it just that way."

All the old soldiers in the valley showed up, some not much better off than Creedy, walking on canes or sitting in wheel chairs. Miss Lively, the church pianist, played "Dixie" followed by "The Battle Hymn Of The Republic". Elroy's coffin was draped in both flags. They buried him beside Big Jim, next to Willa May's folks, Big Annie, and Luther. Creedy had always said when his time came, that he wanted to be buried on the other side of Lizzy. Now Elroy would be there, too. He and Creedy would be together in death as they had been in life, both part of Willa May's and Daniel's family forever.

When the boys got home from the war, they each were given the Purple Heart for having been wounded in the fighting. Ansel was given the Medal of Honor for taking out an entire company of Germans single-handedly. It surprised Ansel that anyone would think to honor him for doing what had come naturally to him. Willa May thought that he grew sad whenever he had to talk about the medal. It reminded him of losing Asa. He had become a local hero without knowing it. Folks were always coming up to him and shaking his hand, saying how proud they were to know somebody so brave. Ansel nodded to each one, bearing the painful reminder of Asa in silence. Some folks took his silence for humility, figuring that the swaggering young man that went off to war had come back a fine, upstanding citizen. Willa May figured it must have been that kind of thinking that brought a group of the county leaders over to their place that spring soon after Elroy died.

They came riding up in their automobiles, chugging like wheezing horses gasping for air. They climbed down out of their cars and shook hands with Daniel and Ansel, nodding to Ethan Allen who was content to stand back and watch from the barn where he was feeding the livestock. "What can we do for you?" Daniel asked. From the surprise in his voice, Willa May knew Daniel was just as bewildered as she was to see these uppity old coots on his land.

"Well, sir, it's Anse here that we've really come to see," said Clayton Blankenship, the president of the bank over in Fayetteville.

Daniel looked at Ansel. Willa May was sure he must have thought for one quick moment that Ansel had done something awfully bad to have brought all these leading citizens to their doorstep. She almost expected Daniel to haul off and punch one of the men, thinking to protect Ansel from them for whatever wrongdoing he had committed. But Blankenship was finished talking with Daniel. He turned to Ansel, tipping his hat and saying, "Anse, I'm sure you're aware that there's goin' to be an election come this November for a new county sheriff. We'd like to see you put your hat in the ring, so to speak, and run for office."

Ansel scratched the back of his neck and grinned sheepishly. "Why me?"

The men looked at each other, surprised at Ansel's question. "Why, don't you know that you're the biggest hero these parts have ever seen?" said Royal MacMillan, the mayor. "Right up there with Stonewall himself."

Now it was Ansel's turn to look surprised. "But I don't know nothing about being a sheriff. Truth be known, I've sort of been on the opposite side of the law in some respects."

Clayton Blankenship grinned and elbowed one of the others. "Anse, everybody in the valley knows you're a 'shiner. There's no shame in that. A man's got to earn a living the best way he knows how. And we're handing you a new way. That's all. Running a moonshine business doesn't befit a war hero like yourself. And as for not knowing how to be a sheriff, why all you do is uphold the law. With all the trouble over in Matewan and Logan County, we want to see somebody in charge of our county who isn't goin' to let such things happen here. We need someone whose name is known, respected, and feared. Nobody's goin' to want to challenge the law while you're the law in Fayette County...nobody."

Ansel listened to what they were saying, looking at his pa every now and then for some kind of sign as to what he should do. When Clayton finally stopped his chatter, Ansel shook his head, not knowing quite what to say. "I don't know," he said doubtfully. "Could I have a week or so to think about it? To talk it over with my folks and my wife?"

"Why, sure. Take your time. But remember, it's a fine job -- a job that could open other doors in the future if you do well. It pays pretty good, too. We hear that your lovely wife is expecting your third. A man with a family has got to make a good living. So think about it all you need. Just let us know what you decide."

Royal MacMillan added, "With your war record and your popularity in these parts, the election will be a snap."

Ansel nodded. "I'll think on it. I promise."

When it appeared that the men had run out of words, they shook hands all around again. The county leaders said their good-byes and take cares and got into their shiny automobiles. They chugged back down the road, leaving a cloud of dust in their wake. Daniel and Ansel stood watching them until they disappeared around the bend. Then Daniel said with a grunt, "Well, I'll be damned!" and clapped Ansel on the back.

Both Daniel and Willa May thought Ansel would charge right in and say yes to the men. But, like his word, he talked it over with all the family. He especially wanted to hear what Walt Whitman and Young Doc had to say. All of them thought it seemed like a good thing, everyone except Ethan Allen who asked, "Does this mean you're goin' to arrest me for breaking the law next time I go out on deliveries?"

Ansel grinned. "Like old Clayton Blankenship said, 'A man's got to earn a living the best way he knows how.' So I reckon you'll be the one 'shiner the law will have to look the other way for."

With that settled, Ansel drove over to Fayetteville the following Friday, just before the bank closed and asked to see Mr. Blankenship. When Ansel told him he had decided to run in the election, Blankenship smiled broadly. He pulled Ansel by the arm and told his head teller he was leaving for the day. Together, they collected the other men who had come out to Daniel's place. They held a "strategy session" as they called it, planning Ansel's campaign over a bottle of fine Kentucky bourbon.

In the spring of 'twenty-three, Thomas Lee graduated from law school at the University of Virginia. When he came back from the war, he went right back to school and finished his undergraduate degree with honors, finishing first in his class. When the University of Virginia wrote that they had accepted him into their law school, Walt Whitman and Annie Catherine were ever so proud. The three of them acted like the university had done Thomas Lee a favor in accepting him. But Willa May told them they weren't looking at it in the right way. The way she saw it, Thomas Lee was so smart that the law school down in Virginia was lucky to get a fine, intelligent boy like their Thomas Lee. Thomas Lee set off for Charlottesville at the same time that Claude Daniel returned to Morgantown to enter medical school. They both made excellent grades, which didn't surprise Willa May either.

One frosty morning early that spring, she and Ethan Allen were making soap. They could buy soap at the store over in Fayetteville, but it always smelled so much like perfume that Willa May never felt quite clean. The men didn't appreciate smelling like a bunch of flowers, either, so Willa May made soap when they needed it, using up the winter's ashes from the fireplace and making her own lye. They sat down to rest after they poured the lye into the tallow to allow it to harden before Willa May cut it into bars. Ethan Allen sat back in his chair, his legs crossed as usual, sipping his black coffee from his saucer. "You reckon you and Pa will be goin' to see Thomas Lee graduate come May?"

"Lord willing and the creek don't rise," Willa May grinned.

"We're all mighty proud of Thomas Lee and Claude Daniel. They're real smart and everybody knows they're goin' to do real good once they're out on their own."

"I could've told everybody that when those two boys were no bigger than that mahogany table over there."

"Walt Whitman and Young Doc did all right by them two younguns," Ethan Allen went on.

Willa May began to wonder where Ethan Allen was leading with this conversation. It was unusual, to say the least, when Ethan Allen said more than two or three words at one time. "As good as they could, I reckon. Just what is it you're saying, Son?"

"I've just been thinking, that's all. You know, even if my boys had lived, they'd never have been no more than coal miners like me. Or maybe 'shiners. I would've liked to have seen them go to fine schools and all, but I couldn't afford it. Not on a miner's pay. They would've been lucky to get through high school. Probably would've had to quit before that just to help out at home and put food on the table."

Ethan Allen had a faraway look in his eyes that he got sometimes. Willa May's heart ached for him, knowing that he was missing his wife and family. He would look so sad at those times, like it had only been days instead of years since he had lost them. She wondered if he would ever get over being robbed of his kinfolk or if the scars on his heart would ever heal. Looking at him then, she reckoned not.

"Your boys were good boys," she said, not knowing what else there was to say. "They would have made fine men. Maybe they would've been coal miners, like you say. But the main thing is they would have been good men. Like their pa."

A ghost of a smile passed across Ethan Allen's face so quickly that if she hadn't been looking at him, Willa May would have missed it. From living with him, it certainly seemed like he was just a ghost of the man he had been. A wispy spirit, thinner than air, haunted by his past. He nodded. "They would've been good men. Maybe they could've been sheriffs like Anse. Who knows? Maybe they *could've* gotten out of the mines. Maybe."

The changes that Walt Whitman had predicted years before were starting to reshape the way folks lived. Everyday there was a new invention that everyone just had to have -- telephones, victrolas, radios, newer and bigger automobiles. But the biggest change came with Prohibition. There had been a crusade for making liquor illegal since the War Between The States. Some dubbed it "The Woman's War". Certain fine upstanding citizens declared that liquor was evil and anyone who sold it might just as well be consorting with Satan himself. It was people like these who believed liquor turned anyone who drank it into violent, lawless criminals. Together, they raised such an outcry that Congressman Volstead from Minnesota pleaded with his fellow Congressmen to create a law condemning the sale of what he called "evil brew". Volstead wanted to shut down all the saloons so nobody could buy liquor. New Year's of nineteen twenty ushered in a new law prohibiting the sale of spirits throughout the nation.

At the time, everyone laughed, thinking such a law ridiculous.

As Ansel was fond of saying, folks were going to find whiskey if they wanted it badly enough, law or no law. The theory that drinking whiskey led to violence backfired. Prohibition became the catalyst for a whole new crimewave. Headlines warned of a new kind of saloon called a "speakeasy" and a new kind of bootlegger called "gangsters". Along with his drink, a man could buy a woman for the night or gamble away all his earnings for that week in these places. Names appeared in the news that Willa May and Daniel had never heard before. Names like Johnny Torrio, Dutch Schultz, and the most famous of all, Al Capone. Dubbed the king of the gangsters after killing off his enemies in gang wars, he kept the Chicago police busy until the infamous St. Valentine's Day Massacre. It made for exciting reading. Daniel and Creedy couldn't wait for Ethan Allen to get back from his deliveries with a newspaper so Willa May could read to them about the FBI war against these gangsters.

Prohibition made it more difficult for Ethan Allen as well. He had to be so careful. It seemed that revenuers lurked behind every tree. Ansel was still sheriff over the county and he kept his word, looking the other way, but he couldn't do anything about the revenuers. A federal marshal showed up, asking Ansel about the bootleggers in his county. He demanded a list of names so he could assign his men to watch the bootleggers and catch them in the act. Ansel didn't like it. He knew almost every man in the county who was selling whiskey. Many of them were his former drinking buddies. He also knew the men who were buying the illegal whiskey. It didn't set well with Ansel to have to name names for this stranger. On the other hand, he knew he had sworn to uphold the law. Clayton Blankenship was the one who had called for the marshal to come and "clean up the valley".

Against his better judgment, Ansel made out a list of names for the marshal. When he handed it over, the marshal studied the list for a long time, not saying a word. Rubbing his chin, deep in thought, he seemed to be setting the names to memory. He looked up at Ansel and said, "Why, I don't believe you're being completely truthful here, Sheriff, with this list you've handed me."

Ansel drew himself up and stared the marshal dead in the eye. "What do you mean I ain't been truthful? I've given you all the names I know."

The marshal glanced down again at the piece of paper in his hand and looked back at Ansel. "But you've left off your brother. One Ethan Shrewsbury. I've been informed that the law has been after him for years. Before him, they were after you. Now I suggest that you reconsider the names you've listed here and see if maybe you've left off any other names."

"If you think I'm goin' to turn in my own kin, you'd better think again," Ansel said.

"Oh, I know all about your kin, Sheriff. I'm asking you for any other names you've conveniently forgotten. That's if you still want to be sheriff of this county."

Hearing this, Ansel looked away, still not wanting to turn in his friends and neighbors. He felt cornered into it all the same. Sighing, he snatched the paper out of the marshal's hand and scribbled down some more names. Then, pushing past the marshal, he stalked out of the jailhouse and went home.

That night, when the rest of his family had already been sleeping for hours, Ansel was still up pacing back and forth, unable to shake off the feeling of being trapped. He heard a sudden knock on the door. Wondering who it could be at that time of the night, Ansel swung the door open to find Hattie Sue. She was out of breath and crying. "Anse, you'd better come quick!"

"What is it? What's wrong?"

"It's Ethan Allen. He's been shot. Doc's working on him, but it doesn't look good."

When Ansel heard this, his eyes got a steely cold look in them. When he spoke, Hattie Sue wasn't sure she was hearing her own brother. "Who did it?" he asked, clenching his jaw.

Hattie Sue shrugged. "We don't know. Lilmer Robbins from over at Agnes' Place brought him to us. He's lost a lot of blood. We'd better hurry."

Agnes' was a tavern before Prohibition. Now it was supposed to be a restaurant, but everybody knew that a man could wet his whistle in the back room. It was one of Ethan Allen's regular stops. Ansel figured that Ethan Allen must have been ambushed when he pulled up outside of Agnes' and unloaded the barrels from his truck. When Ansel got to Young Doc's, he saw Young Doc pull the sheet up over Ethan Allen as he rushed in the door behind Hattie Sue. Hattie Sue screamed. Young Doc put his arms around her while Ansel went over to where Ethan Allen lay covered up and pulled back the sheet, already splotched with Ethan Allen's blood. Ansel saw that Ethan Allen had been shot in the back...more than once. He turned around and stalked out of the house. Young Doc had to run to catch up with him. "Anse,

282

where are you goin'?"

The look on Ansel's face scared Young Doc. He was thinking that Ansel was going off to find who had done this to Ethan Allen and gun him down in cold blood.

Ansel didn't even stop. He just called over his shoulder, "I'm goin' to tell Mommy and Pa."

Willa May was up reading that night, more an excuse to make sure Ethan Allen got home all right than anything. Around midnight, she dozed off in her rocker. The copy of Miss Edith Wharton's <u>Ethan Frome</u> that Walt Whitman had lent her fell open in her lap. She woke with a start when she heard someone pounding at the front door. Instinct told her that something was wrong and like a mother hen counting her chicks, she remembered Ethan Allen. Rushing to the door, she yelled, "Who's there?"

Ansel's voice on the other side of the door called, "It's me, Mommy. Anse. Let me in."

She could hear Daniel's footsteps on the floor upstairs as she opened the door to find Ansel standing in the blackness. From the lamplight, she could read Ansel's face and she knew trouble was at hand. Just as she was about to ask Ansel what was wrong, Daniel came downstairs. Taking one look at Ansel, Daniel asked sharply, "What is it? What's happened?"

Ansel moved past Willa May. Looking at his pa, he answered, "I was home around midnight when Hattie Sue came to the door --"

Daniel, still half asleep, waved his hand and said, "I don't want a story. Just tell me what's happened."

"Somebody's shot Ethan Allen. He's dead."

The words brought Daniel around quicker than Willa May would have thought at his age. His blue eyes pierced Ansel right where he stood. "Who done it?"

Ansel shrugged. "Nobody knows. He was shot in the back. I counted five bullet wounds."

Daniel's breath came out in a big whoosh, like somebody had driven his fist into Daniel's gut. When he caught his breath again, he looked up at Ansel and said, "Who do you *think* done it?"

For a minute or two, Willa May didn't think Ansel was going to answer. Then he raised his head up from his chest and said, "Only person that's been asking around about Ethan Allen and some of the other 'shiners is this federal marshal that came in to see me this week. He's supposed to be here to stop all the bootlegging. He knew that

I'd been selling before the war. It had to be him."

Daniel thought on this a while before he asked, "What does this here marshal look like?"

"He's six foot, maybe a little more. Black hair slicked straight back and a big handlebar mustache. Been staying over at the Conley Hotel in Fayetteville."

"He still there?"

"Far as I know, he is."

Daniel chewed on this a little more. Then he asked, "Where's Ethan Allen's body now?"

"At Doc's."

"You got your automobile out there?"

Ansel nodded.

"Take me to my boy, then."

Ansel started to say something, but Daniel held up his hand, stopping him before he could even get the words out. "Don't you do nothing about this. You hear?"

Ansel nodded again, knowing that Daniel was deadly serious.

"I don't want you flying off the handle here and doing something that could ruin your life in the long run. Just sit tight and do what you would naturally do. You've got a good job and the respect of the folks in this here valley. Don't give them folks the idea that you're goin' to go off on a killing spree just because your brother's been shot. It'll cost you your job and it'll land you in prison."

Ansel looked pained, but after a minute or two, he nodded once more.

"I want your word on it," Daniel insisted.

Reluctantly, Ansel said, "You've got it, Pa."

All the family gathered for the funeral. Effie Lee and Dora Lottie brought their girls over. They cooked and cleaned for days. Hattie Sue baked a dozen pies and ten cakes and brought them with her. They sat up with Ethan Allen's body for a full day and night. Folks came by to pay their respects from all around: Ansted, Fayetteville, Oak Hill, Mossy, Paint Creek, Cabin Creek, Gauley Bridge, Kanawha Falls, Montgomery, Page, and all the hollows. Many of the miners that Ethan Allen and James Houston had worked with gathered in the yard, all of them shaking their heads and wondering why, after all the tragedy he had suffered, Ethan Allen would come to such a violent death. Willa May and Daniel wondered, too. Willa May felt like she was getting too old to try and make sense out of the mysteries of life. She had accepted the fact that she had to swallow whatever dish Fate served up and choke it down no matter how bitter it tasted. "Fair" was something children argued about, not something grown people like her could believe in. She put on her black Sunday church dress and her black hat that hot August morning and let Daniel lead her down the aisle of the church to where her dead son lay in his coffin. Before they closed the lid, she bent over and kissed her boy goodbye for the last time, noting how cold and waxy his jaw felt to her lips. Then she went home to a house that seemed emptier, even though Ethan Allen had never enlivened it when he was living. Still, his absence filled the house like his presence never had.

During the wake, they discovered that four other men had been shot and killed that same week. Three were 'shiners like Ethan Allen, all of them trying to eke out a living to put food on the table for their families the only way they knew. The other one was Claude Jenkins. He owned a tavern over in Mossy. All of them had been on Ansel's list. If that weren't enough, the federal marshal and his men had arrested ten others on the list and thrown them in jail in Charleston where they sat awaiting trial.

Ansel brooded. "They got everybody I gave them on that list. It's all my fault! I should've quit before I handed over them names."

Daniel and Walt Whitman watched Ansel stewing. Walt Whitman said, "Don't be so hard on yourself, Anse. You did what you had to do and nobody is going to fault you for it. We all expected that, at some point, Ethan Allen would get arrested and have to serve a little time. I'm sure that's as far as you thought this would go, too."

"Still, I'd like just one clean shot at that low-down sonofabitch!" Ansel hissed, slamming his fist on the table.

"Now you gave me your word you wouldn't go off and do something reckless that could cost you more than what you've suffered already," Daniel reminded. "I'm counting on you to keep your word."

Willa May could see Ansel warring with himself, his heart telling him to avenge his brother's murder and his mind telling him to do what his pa was saying. "All right," he muttered, not liking it at all that he felt so helpless, trapped by the vow he had made. For Willa May, it was like watching Daniel so many years before as he paced on her mama's porch, wanting revenge against the men who had burned them out. She couldn't be sure if Ansel would stick by his word, knowing he was so much like Daniel.

Ansel kept his word, though. The following Tuesday he was in a meeting with the city leaders when the federal marshal was killed while he was lighting a fat cigar in front of the hotel where he boarded. He was shot in broad daylight, more than once. The doctor who pronounced him dead said that the shots must have come from several different directions from the way they entered his body. Eyewitnesses said they heard firing and saw smoke coming from six or seven windows across the street. By the time the law arrived at the scene, there wasn't a trace of the men who had done the shooting. Nobody from any of the establishments where the shots were fired had seen anyone coming in or leaving with a gun. Some federal investigators showed up to look into it. The governor, Ephraim F. Morgan, called it a "scar on the face of the good people of the state" that such a thing had happened. In the end, the case was dropped since there was no evidence and no witnesses. Through it all, Ansel stayed above suspicion, with his airtight alibi. The Charleston Gazette called it "Mountain Justice" in bold lettering across the front page. One newspaper ran an editorial, asking when the people of West Virginia would stop their "eye for an eye" style of justice and become more "civilized". When Willa May read it, she wanted to spit. There wasn't anything civilized about the way her boy had been gunned down in cold blood, nor the other four that were murdered. She knew it wasn't Christian, but she never felt a speck of sorrow when she heard that marshal had been killed. She just felt relief, knowing that Ansel, for once, had listened to his pa.

Ansel's third child was another boy, named Emmanuel, but the family just called him Manny for short. Corey was expecting her fourth and she and Ansel were both hoping for a little girl. When her time came that fall, Corey gave birth to a beautiful girl with blond, curly hair that lay in ringlets around her pretty little face. She looked so angelic that Corey wanted to name her Mary, for the mother of Jesus. So they settled on Mary Ellen. Since Manny couldn't say her name, he called her "Nellie" for short and the name stuck.

Corey had a hard time giving birth. She bled heavily for several days afterward. When Ansel went back to work, she made the mistake of bringing in some wood. She started bleeding badly, the blood gushing down her legs. Seeing the bright red pool spreading around her feet, she screamed. Mack, their oldest, came running in. Frightened at the sight of all that blood, he telephoned his pa at the sheriff's office and told Ansel that his mommy was bleeding all over the place and wouldn't stop screaming. Ansel slammed down the phone and flew out the door, not even telling his deputies where he was going or what had happened. He and Corey had moved to Fayetteville after he was elected sheriff. Now he made for home as fast as he could. By the time he got Corey to Young Doc's, she had lost a lot of blood. Young Doc told Ansel if he wanted to save her, he must get Corey to Montgomery, to the hospital there as quickly as possible. Ansel jumped in his car and headed down Deepwater Mountain for Montgomery, swinging around curves on two wheels and taking both sides of the road.

Once Corey was in the hospital, the doctors tried desperately to stop her bleeding, but she died early the next morning. Hattie Sue had gone to Ansel's to care for the children. Ansel called her, waking her up around three-thirty to tell her that Corey was dead. "Come on home, Anse," Hattie Sue said. "Your babies need you now."

Ansel grieved sorely for Corey. He thought the sun rose and set on her. Not since Creedy grieved for her mama had Willa May seen a grown man cry like Ansel did, crying for days. Daniel tried to get him to take a drink, thinking that maybe he might be able to drown his sorrows in a jug, anything to help him through the suffering that tortured him. But Ansel shook his head, saying his children needed him sober.

At the cemetery, once they saw Corey lowered into the ground and everybody started walking away, Ansel just stood there. He looked down at the coffin with tears streaming down his face. Willa May put her arms around him and said, "Why don't you come on home for awhile and let us help you with your younguns?"

Ansel couldn't speak. He tried, but he fell to his knees in sobs. He didn't want his babies to see him like that and Willa May knew it. She led the children away, leaving Ansel with his grief.

Willa May knew she was too old to be raising more children, but the four babies brought a life back into their home that had been absent for a long time. With Elroy and Ethan Allen dead, there was just Daniel and Creedy and herself. Three old people, each with his own set of aches and pains, just waiting for the good Lord to call them home. All that changed when Ansel came home, bringing his children. Daniel showed Mack and Robert how to hunt and care for the livestock. Creedy took little Manny on walks up in the woods, picking berries and watching the squirrels, the birds, and all the small woodland creatures. Willa May spent her days caring for the new baby, taking delight in every new event in her life -- her first tooth, her first word ("Nana"), when she started to sit up, when she started to crawl, and her first awkward steps. Nellie was the apple of her eye. Willa May knew that all four children were getting spoiled from all the attention, but she could see, too, that it was a relief to Ansel to see them so happy and carefree. It lightened his load.

Once Corey died, women started eyeing Ansel again just like they had before he married Corey. Ansel was in his thirties and Willa May knew she wasn't being partial by thinking that he was the finest looking man living in the county at that time. The way the women flirted and sashayed around, trying to catch his eye, was proof that he was handsome. With the sadness he carried after Corey's death, Willa May thought that females saw a tenderness in Ansel that he hadn't had when he was cavorting around in his younger days. This made him all the more irresistible. One Sunday, as Ansel was walking out of church with Willa May, Florie Thompson, fresh out of high school and full of the devil, came up to Ansel winking and smiling. "Good morning, Sheriff," she said, pressing a piece of paper into Ansel's hand. When they got in the car, Willa May watched Ansel as he unfolded the paper. He took one look at it and wadded it up, sighing in disgust as he tossed it out the window.

"What was that? A love note from a secret admirer?" she teased.

"I suppose you could call it that," was all that Ansel said.

The ladies were soon disappointed if they thought that Ansel was going to pick up where he left off, courting two and three at a time. He didn't court at all. He stayed at home what time he wasn't working, taking care of his children and helping around the place. He would fix things that were broken or build new when they were beyond hope. He seemed content enough, just quieter than Willa May had ever known him to be. Daniel worried about him, too, wondering where the old Ansel was that they had always known. In his day, Ansel had been a rake and a rogue, but the man he had grown into was content to keep peace with himself and provide for his family.

288

Another mine war erupted in 1925. Willa May was grateful that it was up north of them. Still, James Houston kept them informed about the bloody and fierce fighting. "Them mine operators ain't learned much in the way of strategy over the years. They still throw families out onto the road to starve to death. You'd think that they'd figure out that them kind of tactics won't beat us. The union's goin' to win in the end."

"Just what are the miners doing to fight back?" Ansel asked.

"Oh, some railroads and coal tipples have been blown up."

"But I heard that these incidents backfired on you boys," Walt Whitman argued.

"You mean those three mines that blew up?"

Walt Whitman nodded. "I hear the death count is over a hundred men."

"We have to keep hitting back. If we don't, we might as well lie down in the middle of the road and let them mine operators run right over us."

The mine war dragged on for four more years. The victory that James Houston had hoped for dwindled with each mine that was mined out. Hundreds of miners found themselves out of work. Just when folks thought that things couldn't get worse, in October of 'twenty-nine, the world turned upside down.

Clayton Blankenship, in his office at the bank in Fayetteville, heard the news of the big crash and ordered the bank closed. The rest of the bank personnel suspected that he feared a run on the bank, that folks would be running scared and wanting to take their money out. They closed early, pulling down the dark green shades and leaving Blankenship alone in his office. It wasn't until the next day that Ansel got a call from Esther Blankenship, fretting that her husband hadn't come home from work the night before. Ansel tried to calm Mrs. Blankenship down. He told her he would send his men out looking for Clayton. Thinking that maybe Clayton had gotten drunk after word came about the crash and remembering that he always kept a bottle of Kentucky bourbon in his bottom drawer, Ansel drove over to the bank and had Blankenship's secretary unlock it for him.

When Ansel found Clayton, he wasn't drunk, he was simply dead. He had blown out the back of his head, sitting at his desk, the bottle of bourbon open with an empty shot glass next to it. The wall behind Clayton was splattered with blood and bits of Blankenship's brains. Ansel realized, looking at Blankenship's bloody corpse, that things were going to get much worse for everyone. If Clayton Blankenship, a successful man -- a powerful force in the county and the state -- had come to such an end, then where did that leave the common man?

News of Blankenship's suicide jolted the entire valley. People's heads spun from the wallop of that gunshot; it had blown a hole into the fabric of the community with the same deadly certainty that it had bored a hole in Blankenship's head. When Ansel told Esther Blankenship that her husband was dead, she fainted in his arms. He sent for Young Doc and waited while Doc saw Esther, giving her some pills to help her sleep. When Young Doc came back out into the hall where Ansel was, he shook his head in disbelief. "Have you heard the news?" he asked Ansel.

When Ansel said he hadn't, Doc said, "This kind of thing is happening everywhere. Millions of dollars were lost, entire fortunes. Some of those wealthy men, like Clayton, couldn't deal with it, I guess."

"How long will this slump last?"

Doc shrugged. "Who can say? Nobody seemed prepared for it. Now, nobody seems to know how to get us out of it."

Clayton Blankenship was buried in Oak Hill Cemetery in a concrete tomb with elaborate lettering that spelled out his name. Even the governor came to the funeral and the news of Blankenship's death made the front page of The Gazette. After the funeral, the mourners went back to their homes and prepared themselves for more hard times.

Willa May was seventy-seven years old and feeling every bit of those years. But it was Daniel she worried about. Ten years older, he was looking on to ninety. Gone was the golden haired boy of her youth, the fine strapping man of her middle years, and the silver-haired man of her later years. Now she saw a skeleton of the man she had once known. What little hair he had left lay in white wisps across the top of his head. His shoulders, once so wide and strong, were stooped and frail now. His devilish blue eyes that had danced with merriment were clouded over and, more often that not, closed in sleep. It got so that Daniel could drift off as he was talking, losing the gist of whatever it was he was trying to say. Willa May wasn't the only one who saw the decline in Daniel. Creedy, old as he

290

was, was still younger than either of them. He would often look at Daniel with a worried frown, knowing like Willa May that Daniel's time was winding down. But like Willa May, Creedy couldn't bring himself to face that end. They went on each day, doing the things that had become so familiar to them and listening to Daniel say that he wanted to go hunting that fall, yet knowing that he wasn't able any more. Neither Willa May nor Creedy had the heart to tell him, though.

Chapter Twelve

Since the turn of the century, companies had been trying to buy timber rights and mineral rights to Daniel's land. Daniel ran off each one, sometimes with the barrel end of his shotgun pointed at their backs. In the fall of nineteen thirty, he got an offer from a chemical company that wanted to dig a tunnel under his mountain and across the double horseshoe in the river to bring water down from his property. At first, like the rest of the offers, Daniel was prepared to say no and chase the men off his land. But Thomas Lee happened to be visiting them that day and he said, "Grandpa, I think maybe you should listen to these men. Hear what they have to say before you turn them away. It might mean a lot to the people in the valley."

Daniel reluctantly consented. The company's representatives sat and talked with him, pulling out papers with graphs and maps on them and showing Daniel their plans. They needed electricity to help run their metals and chemical plants. They pointed out that building the tunnel would create jobs for some of the impoverished men in the county who had lost jobs in the mine wars. According to their plans, it was going to take over four years to dig the tunnel and set up what they called their "power facilities". Daniel listened to the two men, not saying a word while he examined all their papers. By then, he had a reputation as being hostile from having run off so many others offering propositions to use his land. The two men began to grow nervous, taking Daniel's stony silence for the quiet before the storm. When they were finished dickering, both men were mopping their foreheads and their voices had grown tight and squeaky.

Daniel looked at Thomas Lee when the men finished their sales pitch and asked, "So you think this here tunnel will do some good for folks around here?"

Thomas Lee nodded. "It could give hundreds of families food to eat these next few years."

Daniel turned back to the two men. "This won't tear up my farm, will it? I don't want a lot of machines coming onto my land and ruining my garden and my woods."

"No, sir," one of them gulped. "All the heavy machinery will be down at the base of the mountain and nobody should have to disturb your farm or your woods beyond what we've shown you."

"Good," Daniel grunted. "You can start your digging."

"Well," the other man laughed nervously, "that's not quite how it works, Mr. Shrewsbury. You see, we have a contract that we want you to read --"

"I can't read."

"Well then, you'll want a lawyer present to read it and discuss it with you before you sign it."

"I can't write, either."

"Then you'll definitely want a lawyer to go over all this with you."

"Who do you think you've been talking to all this time? This here's my lawyer." Daniel clapped Thomas Lee on the back, grinning with pride. "I done all the discussing I want to do. From what you've told me, you're goin' to pay me for the use of my land, and then you're never setting foot up here again. Meanwhile, you're goin' to hire a lot of men to dig your tunnel and then you'll leave me be once and for all."

The man grinned sheepishly. "That's just about it. You're right, sir."

"Fine. When do I make my mark on this here contract, then?"

Letting his grandpa have his say first, Thomas Lee spoke up. "We can meet and finalize our negotiations next week in my office in Montgomery, if you like, gentlemen."

A look of relief came over the two men's faces. "That will be fine."

Hawk's Nest Tunnel was begun, but the workers soon ran into a problem. Silica dust. The men digging the tunnel didn't know it, but with every breath they drew, they were killing themselves as surely as if they had taken a gun to their heads like Clayton Blankenship. The dust filled their lungs, making it impossible for the men to breathe. Some of them died quickly, while others hung on for years, dying a slow death. The silicon under Daniel's mountain was almost one hundred per cent pure. By 'thirty-three, several hundred of the workers had brought a law suit against the company and won a huge sum of money. Willa May and Daniel heard through Thomas Lee that over half of the money went to pay the lawyers the men had hired to represent them. With so many men dying from silicosis, Gauley Bridge earned the name, "the town of the living dead". It gave the

293

town a reputation that none of the civic leaders appreciated. To their dismay, the name stuck.

In the autumn, Daniel's health started failing. Willa May heard him coughing more and more each day. She told him he should have Young Doc take a look at him, but Daniel had never been sick a day in his life and wasn't about to admit that he was sick now. The coughing grew worse. Willa May watched him get up and go outside to spit out what he brought up from his lungs. His color turned bad, too. He looked peaked. One night, Daniel came to bed and couldn't get to sleep for all his coughing. He got up and went outside to spit. Willa May wondered if he had gotten sick from his supper, he was spitting up so much.

When Daniel climbed into bed, he was drenched with sweat. Yet Willa May felt his body trembling next to her. The following morning, she decided to persuade Daniel to go see Doc, even if she had to tie him down to get him there. As always, he refused. "I ain't goin' to see no doctor, Girl."

"Why not?" she argued. "You were up half the night coughing and spitting. He can give you something to help."

"No, he can't."

"How do you know he can't help if you don't go?"

"Ain't no doctor that can help."

He said it so matter of factly that Willa May took it for just more of his stubbornness. Later that morning when she had finished hanging out the wash, she went to set the washtub against the house. She saw a pool of sticky, partly dried blood spattered on the ground next to the house. Her breath caught in her throat. The longer she stood there looking at the pool of blood, the harder it got for her to breathe. Like some giant hand had reached down, squeezing her throat, Willa May felt like she was strangling. Everything started whirling around her, growing dark. Her only thought was, "Please, Lord, don't let it be so. We've had a long time together, but I'm not ready for this. I'm not ready at all! Please, Lord, don't let it be true."

She wasn't sure how long she stood there staring at all the blood. It could have been twenty minutes or it could have been two hours. When she was finally able to move, she made her way slowly back into the house. Numb, she looked at Creedy who was sitting at the table, playing a game of cards with Ansel's three boys. Little Nellie was playing over in a corner with one of her dolls. She sat down in her rocker, gripping the arms of the chair for support.

Creedy looked up and said, "Willa May, you don't look so good. You're not coming down with something, too, are you?"

She shook her head, still too stunned to speak. Daniel came in from the barn. Seeing them playing cards, he bent over Manny and told him, "Play them." He watched the game for a few more minutes before he noticed Willa May. The minute he looked at her, Daniel knew that Willa May knew. They looked across the room at each other, across all their years together, knowing that for the first time in seventy years, they were going to be separated; one of them going on, the other staying behind. Willa May couldn't bear it. Tears stung her eyes as she got up and went up to their room where she sat down and cried harder than she had cried in years.

When she came back downstairs, Daniel was gone. The kids were still playing and Creedy was fixing them some cookies and milk.

"Where's Daniel?" she asked.

"Said to tell you he's gone hunting," Creedy said.

"What?" Willa May gasped, turning around.

Creedy shrugged. "I told him he ain't got no business goin' up in them hills, sick as he's been, but he said he was bound to go."

Willa May stood frozen to the wood floor. Creedy looked at her and said, "Daniel said something else. Just as he was leaving."

"What was that?"

"That you'd understand."

By nightfall, all their children and some of the older grandchildren were gathered at the house. Young Doc asked Willa May how long Daniel had been coughing and looking poorly. She told him it had been a good six weeks or more, then she took him outside and showed him the bloody mess -- congealed now -- that Daniel had spit up the night before. Young Doc didn't say a word. From the look on his face, Willa May knew that her first desperate thoughts had been correct. Daniel was dying. A cancer, Young Doc said, probably in his lungs, maybe his throat. In any case, it was probably in its last stages.

"There's nothing you can do?" she pleaded.

Young Doc shook his head sorrowfully. "The only thing I could do for him now is to give him something for the pain."

Hearing the word "pain", Willa May asked, "How bad will it get?" She knew that Daniel couldn't tolerate anything that would keep him down.

Young Doc fixed her with a long look. "Do you really want to know?"

She felt that tightening in her throat again and she couldn't get her breath. That same spinning sensation started and everything around her grew blurred. She felt Ansel's arms around her, strong like Daniel's once were. She leaned against him, letting him lead her back into the house. Inside, Creedy and Walt Whitman looked so forlorn that she wanted to say, "Nobody's died yet." But her throat was still too tight to speak. Ansel must have seen how she was looking at them, though, because he said to Walt Whitman, "Why don't you take Mommy on up to her room for a while?" Turning to Young Doc, he asked, "Can you give her something to help her rest? This has taken its toll on her." Young Doc nodded. He and Walt Whitman placed themselves on either side of her and led her upstairs. Young Doc gave her a shot and she started feeling woozy, but she recalled later that Ansel was sitting on the edge of her bed, saying, "I'm goin' up into the woods now, Mommy, and see if I can find Pa tonight. I'll try and get him to come on home, but if I can't, I'll see to it that he's all right. You know Pa. He ain't goin' to want all of us fussing over him."

She tried to nod. Then Ansel's face became Daniel's face and she was fourteen again, walking up the aisle at the Page Baptist Church on her pa's arm. She could see Daniel looking down the aisle at her, grinning his devilish grin and beaming with pride. For some reason, the aisle began to stretch out before her, pulling Daniel farther and farther away from her. She kept walking faster and faster, but she couldn't get any closer. Daniel was calling to her, but he couldn't get down the long aisle to her. She ran toward him, crying as she watched him grow smaller and smaller, then he disappeared altogether. Everything went black.

Hattie Sue told her months later that she had called out in her sleep for Daniel and that they could hear her all the way downstairs. She said that Walt Whitman couldn't bear it and rushed out of the house. Creedy just sat in Willa May's reading chair, rocking and crying. James Houston took it as long as he could, then he went outside with Walt Whitman. The girls -- Hattie Sue, Effie Lee, and Dora Lottie -- started to come upstairs to sit with Willa May. But Thomas Lee said, "You ladies get your rest. This could go on for weeks. I'll sit with her tonight. Go on, now. I'll call you if she wakes up." Thomas Lee sat with his grandmother all night, reading her ancient copy of <u>Great</u>

Expectations. It was one of the books that she had read to him and Claude Daniel one summer so many years before. Willa May started to come to once during the night, calling for Daniel again. Thomas Lee took her hand and held it in his own, rubbing it gently, then she drifted off again.

Ansel searched all that night and the next day. Finally, he found Daniel just as it grew dark. Daniel had built a fire and was cooking a squirrel he had killed. When Ansel came up on him, he just looked up and said, "I figured you'd be here. Set yourself down and get warm. Supper's almost ready."

They had finished their supper when Daniel spoke again. "How's your mama?"

"She's taking it pretty hard."

Daniel nodded, knowing that would be the case. "I ain't goin' back with you. You know that, don't you?"

"Yeah, I figured you'd want to stay up here. But I'm goin' to ask you to stay put up here and when you want to come on back, just tell me."

"How am I supposed to do that? Send up smoke signals?"

"I'll be coming up here and looking in on you every couple days or so. If you need anything or want to come back, you can let me know."

"I don't need no nursemaid checking on me. I ain't no baby."

Ansel sighed. "Listen, Pa, Young Doc says that near the end, you're goin' to be in a lot of pain. You'll probably want something to take the edge off. If it gets more than you can bear --"

"More than I can bear? Hell's fire, what do you think it's been like already? My lungs feel like they're filled up with a hundred bleeding sores that bust open every time I start in with that gallderned coughing. So what do you know about what I can bear?"

Ansel tried to answer, but Daniel had gotten so upset that he started in one of his coughing seizures. He hacked and wheezed, hardly able to draw breath. Standing up, he staggered a few feet away and brought up blood. Ansel went to him and tried to help, but Daniel shook him off. When he was finally able to speak, his face was dotted with perspiration and he was shaking like a leaf in a high wind. "I know what you're trying to do. You want to help me, but Son, you can't help me die. A man's got to do that himself. I choose to die up here, in the place I love."

"What am I supposed to tell Mommy and the others?"

"Hell, tell them what I just said," Daniel grumbled. Then in a softer voice, he added, "Tell your mama I love her. Now leave me be."

Ansel left, looking back over his shoulder as his pa took up his place next to his fire. He reported the whole thing to his brothers, Young Doc, and Thomas Lee. All of them tried to figure out what to do, whether to go up and try to talk sense to their pa or to just keep a close watch on him from a distance. Willa May was inside, sipping some sassafras tea when she spotted all of them headed for the barn for their talk. She knew that Ansel must have brought back news that he figured would be upsetting, so he wanted to ask the other men what to do. She stood up and headed for the door, wanting to hear for herself what Ansel had to say. Hattie Sue tried to stop her, but she pulled away, saying, "I want to hear what Ansel is telling them. Don't any of you try and stop me!" The girls looked at each other, not knowing whether to defy her or let her have her way. While they stood wondering, Willa May walked outside. It didn't take her long to get the gist of what Ansel was telling the others. Listening to them hemming and hawing over what to do, she stood it as long as she could. She marched inside and said, "If your pa told you to leave him be, then that's just what you're goin' to do. He's still your pa and if he says he wants to be alone, then you'll leave him be. All of you."

They dropped their heads, unable to face her. Young Doc spoke up. "Willa May, there's goin' to come a time -- and I don't know how soon -- when Daniel won't be able to take care of himself up there, let alone defend himself if some wild animal should come upon him. We're trying to decide how to honor his and your wishes, letting him die with as much dignity as possible. But we're also concerned that he could, in the end, become frightened or disabled in some way. We don't want to think of him up there needing help and not getting it."

"You're not thinking of Daniel. You're just thinking of yourselves, trying to leave yourselves free of blame if he dies up there. But what none of you realizes is that Daniel wants to die up there, up in that wilderness where he feels closest to what he loves. He doesn't want to die coughing his life up, lying in a bed, not able to see the sun rise or watch a cardinal on the wing or hear the gurgling of the water flowing down off the mountainside. That's how he wants to die...and that's how we're goin' to let him die."

Hearing her words, the men looked at each other. Walt Whitman broke the silence. "All right, Mommy. If this is the way you and Pa want it."

Willa May nodded emphatically. "That's how we want it."

Over the next four weeks, the house was always filled with kinfolk. Ansel worked in Fayetteville at his office as usual during the day, but he came home and set off into the hills at least three or four nights out of the week. He made sure that Daniel was still alive, but never bothered him. Walt Whitman, Young Doc, and Thomas Lee took turns staying up at the house overnight while Ansel was up in the woods. The girls were always there, baking, cooking, cleaning, and washing. Creedy kept Ansel's children busy, playing games with them and taking them for long walks. Then, one Saturday morning in early December, Ansel came home. He walked straight over to where Willa May sat in her reading chair with a quilt across her lap. She was reading Leaves of Grass, remembering how it had always been Daniel's favorite. Ansel knelt in front of her and took her hands. Tears formed in his red rimmed eyes. "Pa's gone, Mommy."

Hearing Ansel, the girls gasped and started crying. Willa May swallowed hard and looked at Ansel. "Was it the cancer?"

Ansel shook his head. The words came hard for him, but after a minute or so, he said, "No, a critter got him."

"Bear?" she asked, her voice tight.

Ansel shook his head. "From the looks of it, I'd say a mountain lion." No sooner were the words out of his mouth when Ansel broke into sobs, burying his head in her lap. She set her book aside and ran her fingers through Ansel's blonde hair, so like Daniel's. She quoted: "So Daniel was taken up out of the den, and no kind of hurt was found upon him, because he had trusted in his God."

When he was calm, Ansel gathered everyone in the house and told them he had buried Daniel up in the hills where he had fallen. He wanted to spare the rest of them from having to see what the mountain lion had done. In her heart, Willa May knew that the mountain lion had done Daniel a favor. Daniel had died like he would have wanted to die, a courageous and noble death, not a suffering one.

There was a memorial service at the church. Folks they had known all their lives came to pay their respects, saying they had always admired and respected Daniel. Some quoted Thoreau, saying that Daniel had lived life in his own way, "marching to the beat of a different drummer". Willa May nodded, adding, "And that had made all the difference."

A few minutes into the service, the door to the church creaked open. Willa May turned around to see who had come late. She saw a woman, almost her age with gray hair pulled back into a sleek bun under the wide brim of a big black hat. She was slender and dressed in a black suit that looked like it must have cost a pretty penny. In that instant, Willa May realized the woman was Josie. Their eyes met for only a second, then Willa May turned back toward the preacher. Walt Whitman and Ansel, sitting on either side of her, had turned and looked, too. Ansel didn't seem to recognize his sister, but Willa May knew that Walt Whitman had kept seeing Josie over the years and, of course would know her.

Willa May asked the preacher to read the sixth chapter of the Book of Daniel from the Good Book, the story telling how Daniel had been sent down into the lion's den and was delivered. Walt Whitman, in a shaky voice, read her favorite poem, "Annabel Lee". She nodded her head when he read the part about the angels in heaven being jealous of their love and taking that love away forever. She knew just how Mr. Poe had felt, losing the love of his life. She felt she had lost everything.

Walt Whitman barely made it through the reading. He came back and sat down next to Willa May, bursting into tears. She took his hand and rubbed it gently. When the service was over, Ansel and Walt Whitman led her down the aisle where they walked past Josie. Willa May could see Josie as she looked out of the corner of her eye, but she acted like she didn't notice the stranger and just kept walking. Once they were outside, Willa May had Ansel help her into the car and told him to take her home. They rode in silence, Willa May lost in her memories and Ansel not knowing what to say to be of comfort. He knew all too well after losing Corey what she was going through.

At home, the girls put together a buffet supper with chicken and dumplings, candied squash, mashed potatoes, green beans, cranberries, cornbread and hot rolls. There was also a whole table of sweets for dessert, with two of Hattie Sue's fruitcakes soaked in whiskey. All that food, but nobody except the youngsters had much appetite. In the middle of supper, they heard a knock at the door. Walt Whitman was sitting at the head of the table where Daniel had always sat. He got up and answered the door, speaking in a soft voice to whoever was there. Slowly, as if he weren't very sure he should be doing it, he led Josie inside.

Hattie Sue and Effie Lee sprang to their feet and rushed over to hug Josie, saying, "Look here, Mommy! Look who's come to see you."

They must have thought Willa May was going to think of having Josie back as somehow filling the emptiness in her heart now that

300

Daniel was gone. But it was too late for that. Josie came in, hugging her brothers and sisters, kissing Annie Catherine and Thomas Lee on the cheek. When she came to Willa May, tears filled her eyes as she said, "I wanted to let you know how sorry I am about Pa. Is there anything you need? Anything at all I can do for you?"

Willa May pulled back from her, disgusted. "Why would you think I'd want anything from you after all these years? As for your pa, you as good as told him he was dead the day you ran off and broke his heart. He went off into the hills for months after you left, he was so hurt. If you think you can come back here and be accepted into my home -- into my heart -- after all this time when all you ever did was send us your money, with nary a letter nor a note telling us how you were, then you're mightily mistaken. I can't forgive all the years and forget they ever happened. I just won't do it." Willa May saw the look of hurt and surprise registered on Josie's face. Looking to Walt Whitman behind her, Willa May saw him hang his head. Unable to take any more, she turned and went up to her room, leaving the rest of the family staring after her in silence.

Josie turned to leave, but Walt Whitman stopped her, trying to persuade her to stay and let him talk to Willa May. Josie shook her head and said, "Mommy's right. It's too late. I've been a fool, thinking that I didn't need anyone and that money could replace the people in my life. I suppose I've been an even bigger fool coming here and thinking that I could be welcomed here once more. No, Mommy's right. It's just too late." She left, allowing her driver to help her into her car.

The following spring Willa May was coming out of church when she noticed a tall monument close to where her folks were buried. She asked Ansel to walk her over to see it, picking their way across the ground still soggy from the melted snow. When they drew close, Willa May caught her breath. It was very tall, almost as tall as the church itself. On the top stood a mountain man dressed in hunting clothes and carrying a gun. Large lettering on the base read:

DANIEL SHREWSBURY
NOV. 23, 1843 - DEC. 5, 1930
"HOME IS THE HUNTER
HOME FROM THE HILL".

Willa May knew in an instant that the monument had been Josie's doing. She knew it was Josie's way of saying she was sorry for all the torment she had caused them. Using the quote from Robert Louis Stevenson's "Requeim" was another futile attempt on Josie's part to appease her, she reckoned.

Ansel whistled through his teeth. "That's some statue," he breathed, admiring its beauty. Before she could say anything, he added, "Pa sure would be proud to be remembered like that by his family."

"How do you know it was one of us who did this?" Willa May asked, wondering just how much Ansel did know about it.

Ansel shrugged. "It just looks like something Walt Whitman would think of, that's all."

Willa May grunted. So it was Walt Whitman's sentiments and Josie's money. How convenient for her.

With Daniel gone, Willa May wandered around their place like a lost kitten looking for its mama. For months, she simply sat and pined her life away, wishing she had gone on, too. She figured she would be better off dead than without Daniel. In her life, it was the hardest loss yet. If she hadn't had Ansel, Creedy, and Ansel's children, she thought she might have died that first winter out of sheer emptiness.

In July of 'thirty-two, they had some horrible rains with thunder and lightning like the world was coming to an end. The storms raged on for days, pouring rain by the buckets. Ansel brought Willa May over to Dora Lottie's to help her get ready for her daughter Beulah's wedding. They all hoped the rains would end before the happy day. Beulah was marrying a young man who worked at the hydroelectric generating station in Glen Ferris. His name was Dewey Pearce. He was a nice boy, always bringing Beulah and Dora Lottie some fresh apples, pears, or peaches that his folks grew on their farm. The whole family was happy for Beulah.

The women were up to their elbows in powdered sugar, making icing for the cakes they planned to serve. Although it was daytime, they had lights on throughout the house. Outside, the sky was pitch black. Around four o'clock that afternoon, Dora Lottie was standing over the sink, washing the icing off of her hands and peering out at the rain coming down in slashing silver streaks against the darkness. Suddenly, a strange look came over her face. Her eyes grew wide, focused on something faraway. Willa May remembered that look from when 'Lil Luther stabbed Glenny. A chill scurried up her spine as she watched Dora Lottie now, knowing that she was seeing something that none of the rest of them saw. Dora Lottie broke the silence in the room with a loud gasp and clutched her throat. "Oh my Lord! It's Nila Rae." The hair on the back of Willa May's neck bristled. She knew without a doubt that something was wrong at James Houston's place.

"What is it? What's wrong with Nila Rae?" she asked. "Are James Houston and the younguns all right?"

Dora Lottie swallowed hard and said, "Mommy, I don't mean to upset you, but I think we'd better send Anse over to Milburn and check on them."

Dora Lottie lived in Montgomery, only a few miles from Milburn. "Well, sure," Willa May agreed. "Send him right now if it'll make you feel better, honey."

Dora Lottie rushed past her to the parlor where Ansel was sitting and talking with Dewey. When he saw how upset Dora Lottie was, Ansel stood up and said, "Don't worry about a thing. I'll just run over there with Dewey, here. We need a breath of fresh air, anyway, don't we, Dewey?"

Dewey nodded, "I reckon we do at that." He looked scared out of his wits from the urgent look on Dora Lottie's face. The two men left, carrying a lantern to see the big Chevrolet that Ansel had parked across the street. Willa May watched from the window in the parlor, standing beside Dora Lottie. She breathed a sigh of relief when she saw the light from Ansel's headlights move down the road.

"Let's go back and finish the cakes now," Willa May suggested, trying to keep Dora Lottie from fretting any more.

They worked another two hours, baking and frosting applesauce cakes made from apples that Dewey's folks had canned the previous fall. The kitchen smelled spicy from the dozen cakes they had made.

When Ansel came back, his clothes were soaked and clinging to his wet, glistening skin. He didn't have to say a word -- Willa May knew he had brought bad news. She handed him a towel and as he wiped his face, he said, "Creek's flooded. Flash flood is the word we got. We never made it down to Milburn. Creek's too high. Can't get through by car."

"But what about James Houston?" Willa May asked, more worried than ever.

Ansel shrugged. "I came back here so we can call Walt Whitman, Thomas Lee, and Young Doc. We might need all of them to help once we get to them."

"It's that bad?" Beulah asked, a look of fear lining her pretty, young face.

Ansel nodded. "Dewey and me saw whole houses being swept down the creek. I just hope they made it to high ground before it was too late."

Dora Lottie ran over to the telephone and started calling all the menfolk. By nine that night, they had gathered at her house, preparing to go on foot to Milburn. Claude Daniel was there, too, just home from his residency in Morgantown. Ansel hugged Willa May before he left. "Don't you worry now, you hear?"

"I won't, she replied, trying to sound like she really meant it. But neither of them believed it. "Just don't try to be a hero and do something foolish." Ansel promised he would be careful. Neither of them believed that, either.

The women watched as the men, grim faced, set off into the blackness of the night, wearing rain slickers and carrying lanterns and supplies. The women kept a coffee pot going all night, taking turns sitting up and waiting.

It was late the next evening when Dewey came back, bringing word. "James Houston, his younguns, and grandkids are all okay. But they're mighty worried about Nila Rae. She had made it up onto the hill above the water, but she remembered that she had left all their money sewed up inside their mattress, so she ran back down there to see if she could get it out in time." Here, he stopped and looked down at his feet. He shook his head. "She never made it back. James Houston saw the house being washed away and yelled for her, but even before they lost sight of it, the house started to bust up and fall apart."

"Did anybody see her? You sure she didn't scramble out to safety on the other side of the creek?" Willa May asked.

"No, ma'am. They ain't been able to find a single sign to show that she got out. So now Anse is leading them on a search."

"You tell him we're all praying for them, you hear?"

Dewey nodded like a good boy and was all set to turn and leave when Dora Lottie said, "Here, Dewey, take some food back with you. If the creek washed everything away, they're goin' to need something to eat till more help can come." She loaded up a big box with fried chicken left over from supper, cold beans, and four of the applesauce cakes. "Now go on and bring us back word when you can. And be careful -- all of you!"

304

It was the next day, around the same time, when Dewey came back. This time, he looked pale and haggard, so Willa May knew he was bearing bad news. He looked like he didn't want to have to tell them. Finally, Willa May spoke up. "They found Nila Rae, didn't they?"

"Yes, ma'am. Found her down by the schoolhouse. She was wedged in behind the building," he replied.

Willa May could see that he simply couldn't find the words to come right out and say it, so she said it for him. "And she was dead."

Dewey nodded. "She was all cut up. Stomach tore wide open and both...well, you know...were missing, too," he said, blushing from having to mention female body parts to a room full of women.

Hattie Sue and Annie Catherine started crying. Dora Lottie and Beulah tried to comfort them. "The rest of the family is okay, though?" Willa May asked.

Dewey nodded. "James Houston was awful shook up, though. Anse is with him, but James Houston screamed like a wild man when we found her."

"Where are they staying if the house is gone?"

"Everybody headed up to the houses on the hillside. The store got flooded, too, but they were able to pull canned goods out. They're passing out them cans, but it's not goin' to be nearly enough to feed all the folks up there that don't have a home no more."

That set the women in motion. Rushing about, they pulled down canned goods and packed them in boxes with the rest of the cakes. When they were finished, Annie Catherine said, "Take me over to our place and I'll throw in all our canned food, too."

Dewey had to get Thomas Lee and Claude Daniel to help him carry all the food over to Milburn. Willa May could tell from the looks on Thomas Lee's and Claude Daniel's faces that things were worse than they had imagined. Her heart went out to those families, but especially to James Houston and his family.

A week later, all the bodies had been gathered for one mass funeral service with preachers from the Baptist and Methodist churches delivering eulogies. The rains hadn't let up all week and during the funeral, another storm erupted. Snake Couch, a neighbor of James Houston's, raced into the church as though he was being chased there by a pack of demons, his eyes as big as cue balls, shouting, "Flood! Flood! Creek's flooding again!" Everyone hurried out of the church, trying to get home before the flood hit to salvage what few belongings they could, leaving all the coffins lined up in the empty church.

Willa May's family loaded into their cars and drove to Dora Lottie's. James Houston and his family joined them, too exhausted from the first flood to hole up through another. They spent the rest of the summer rooming with Dora Lottie and Walt Whitman, sleeping on pallets on the floor. By Thanksgiving, they were able to get back to Milburn, but the creek was still so high, they couldn't cross it until the following summer.

It was a hard time for everyone. Whenever they picked up a newspaper or saw a news reel at the movie house, there were people standing in endless soup lines. Entire families with no home, no job, no way to feed their babies. People turned to the government for aid, but there was none to be had under Herbert Hoover's leadership. Willa May told Ansel that folks needed a change, someone in government who had enough vision to bring the nation out of its hopelessness.

Late in September, Ansel took Willa May into Gauley Bridge to buy the sugar for the applebutter they planned to make the following day. It was a sunny day, one of those days when the sky was bright blue and the grass couldn't get any greener. Willa May was drinking in all that golden sunshine, too busy to notice a small group of people standing outside the bank. When Ansel pointed to them, she figured it was just another run on the bank. They had certainly seen enough of that. As they drew closer, Ansel said, "Well, I'll be!"

Willa May's eyes followed Ansel's to where a woman, her hair graying and pulled back under a large hat, stood on the back of a wagon in front of the bank. The woman looked like she was preparing to speak to the crowd gathered there and Willa May wondered who she was. No women had made speeches since the days of Mother Jones. "Who is that?" she asked Ansel, nodding toward the woman.

"That's Mrs. Roosevelt. I'd heard she was campaigning for her husband here in the state, but I never got word that she was goin' to show up here."

"Let's go hear what she has to say," Willa May suggested.

It wasn't as much what Mrs. Roosevelt said, though, as how she said it, taking time to listen to people and asking questions when she didn't understand what they were trying to say. Looking at her, Willa May could see she was smart. But it wasn't her intelligence that made everybody take notice of her. It was more the way she treated them. Showing a genuine interest in folks and their problems, their health and their working conditions, she offered the first ray of hope in a long, long time. For the first time in her memory, Willa May saw somebody who could make a difference in people's lives treating them with respect and dignity even though they were poor and jobless. Dignity was something Willa May knew that mountain people and coal miners had, but outsiders -- people who had it better -- didn't see it. Outsiders couldn't seem to find the honor in the sweat and grit that covered the faces and hands of mountaineers. But there, standing in front of her was somebody who seemed to do just that.

After she finished talking, Mrs. Roosevelt moved through the small, shabby crowd, shaking their hands, asking how they were and what she could do to help. Willa May had read stories in her childhood about Joan of Arc being a saint, an angel soldier sent to help the French. Whereas Joan of Arc had been a peasant herself, one of the commoners, here was a lady born into wealth and educated in the best schools moving through a throng of people who had never been outside the state. Some hadn't even been outside the county. A few of them couldn't read or write. Yet she was treating them like equals with an ease and grace that struck Willa May as being sincere. She had a soothing effect on those troubled souls gathered around her.

Even though women had gotten the right to vote back in nineteen and nineteen, Willa May had never voted, figuring that one politician was just as good -- or bad -- as another. Watching Mrs. Roosevelt, Willa May made up her mind to vote that November. A vote for F.D.R. was a vote for Eleanor, she thought.

Willa May wasn't the only person there that day to be charmed by Mrs. Roosevelt. In November, she had Ansel drive her over to the polls and she placed her vote along with millions of others. By the next morning, it was announced on the radio that the rich man from New York would be the next president. Willa May sent up a prayer that the new president would find some way to bring the country around and get folks back to work and out of soup lines. What no one in the valley realized was that politics were changing in Europe, too. More and more, the newspaper bore headlines about the Nazi Party in Germany and a little man with a brush over his upper lip named Hitler. Since the Big War, nobody thought another world war could happen. But the stage was being set even as Willa May and Ansel listened to the President's voice on the radio saying, "We have nothing to fear, but fear itself."

After he finished his residency, Claude Daniel decided to join Young Doc's practice. Willa May was glad to have Claude Daniel and Thomas Lee back for good. Thomas Lee was busy setting up his law office in Montgomery. Over six feet tall, with a powerful speaking voice and blazing brown eyes, Thomas Lee cut quite a figure in the courtroom. He made a name for himself when he won a case for some miners' widows, winning a huge settlement for them and their children from the mine owners. Their husbands had been working in a room inside the mine when a loud rumbling erupted followed by a slate fall. For days prior to the cave-in, the miners had tried to convince the bosses that it wasn't safe in that room. The bosses laughed it off, calling the miners yellow bellied cowards. When the dust settled, the miners were buried alive under tons of slate. As president of the local UMW, James Houston advised the widows to go see Thomas Lee. He told the grieving women that he was sure they could sue the mine operators. Thomas Lee won their case in front of a courtroom full of miners who had given testimony against the bosses, showing they were to blame for the accident by forcing the miners to work under unsafe conditions. The widows were awarded a hundred thousand dollars each. Crying and praising the Lord, they hugged each other and Thomas Lee, too. In addition to his fee, Thomas Lee received baked goods every week. Every fall, the widows sent him a hog they had slaughtered. The family always had a fine smoked ham for Christmas dinner, thanks to those widows.

Claude Daniel was finding his work far less rewarding. He was a good doctor, but he discovered that many of the people in the hollows distrusted doctors, still believing in home remedies. One day, a young mother brought in her baby boy with a raging fever and an earache. When Claude Daniel examined the baby, he asked the mother how long her baby had been sick. She told Claude Daniel that the baby had been feverish for four days.

"What your baby needs is something to fight this infection in his ear. That's what's causing the fever. Has he been able to keep down liquids?"

The mother shook her head. "Not for two days now. But I've been treating his earache, so that can't be what's the matter with him," she argued.

"What have you been giving him for it?"

Expecting to hear that she had given the baby aspirin, Claude

Daniel turned around when she said, "I've been pouring a little of my pee in his ear."

"You *what*?" He couldn't believe what he was hearing.

It was the mother's turn to look shocked. She repeated, "I've been pouring some of my pee into his ear. Just a few drops is all it takes."

Clenching his fists, Claude Daniel took a deep breath and said, "Now you listen to me, your baby needs medicine for his ear infection. Not home remedies. I'm going to give you some pills for him and I'll give him a shot before you leave. I want to see this child back here in this office two days from now. Do you understand?"

The mother gave him a wary look, then nodded reluctantly. When Claude Daniel told Willa May about it, he said he knew that she wasn't going to do what he had told her. The woman was sure that the remedies her folks had used on her were reliable and she didn't pay any heed to this young doctor and his newfangled ways. A week later, when she hadn't brought the baby back, Claude Daniel asked some of his patients where the family lived. He found them over on Loup Creek in a shack not much bigger than an outhouse. The husband, in dirty long johns and baggy overalls, stood on the front porch, blocking the door. Claude Daniel tried to explain that he was the baby's doctor and that he had come all the way over there to see if he could be of any help.

The man shook his head and mumbled, "Nope. Don't need none of your help. Don't need nobody's goddamn help."

Claude Daniel could see that the man wasn't going to let him past, so peering over the man's shoulder, he squinted to see inside the dark little shack. "So your son is better then?"

The man jutted his chin out and stared coldly at Claude Daniel. At first, Claude Daniel didn't think the man was going to answer. Finally, he said in a defiant tone, "Lonnie done died yesterday."

"He died? But why didn't you bring him back to me if he wasn't getting better? What's wrong with you people?"

"We do things our way. We don't need no doctor and we don't need your goddamn meddling, neither. So if you don't want to end up needing a doctor yourself, you best be getting off my land!" He shoved Claude Daniel backward off the porch onto the dusty ground. Claude Daniel picked himself up, brushing off his clothes. He picked up his medical bag. Shaking a finger at the man, he said, "You should be shot for letting that baby die!"

"Only shooting around here's goin' to be when I fetch my shotgun and blow you clean open."

The man turned and strode inside. Claude Daniel decided it was best not to stay and see if he was getting that shotgun. When Claude Daniel returned to the office, he told Young Doc what had happened. He wanted to bring charges against the man and his wife, but Young Doc shook his head. "Wouldn't be any use. No jury in this county would find them guilty of any wrongdoing. Just be glad you got out alive."

"But that baby died needlessly," Claude Daniel argued, still filled with bitterness and anger.

Young Doc nodded. "You're going to see a lot of things that are going to make you mad enough to strangle some of these people with your bare hands, but I'll give you a piece of advice right now. Change what you can and learn to live with what you can't change."

Claude Daniel looked at Young Doc like he was seeing a stranger. Finally, he said in a low voice, "I don't think I can do that."

A few weeks later, Big Earl Lilly brought in his youngest daughter, Carleen. The girl was only twelve years old and it didn't take Claude Daniel long to discover that she was pregnant, about four months along. The poor girl could hardly lift her face, she was so ashamed. When Claude Daniel told Big Earl that Carleen was pregnant, Big Earl exploded. "Hell's fire! I know she's knocked up, you danged fool. Who do you think got her that way?"

The truth hit Claude Daniel like a bolt of lightning. "Well, what do you want me to do about it?"

"I want you to get rid of the baby. Why else would I bring her here?" Big Earl thundered.

Claude Daniel fixed Big Earl with a steely gaze. "Why would you think that I would commit murder for the likes of a disgusting child molester like you?"

"Carleen ain't the first one of my gals I done brung here," Big Earl spat, offended at this kind of treatment. "Besides," he whined, "I promise it won't happen again. Just do what you have to do, Doc. For little Carleen's sake."

Claude Daniel had swallowed all he could stomach. He thought of Carleen's four older sisters and wondered how many abortions Young Doc had performed to cover their shame and prevent their public disgrace from wagging tongues. Grabbing Big Earl by the front of his shirt, Claude Daniel yanked Big Earl's face to within an inch of his own and through gritted teeth, he said, "You've come to the wrong

310

doctor this time. If I cut on anybody in your family, it's going to be you. Now unless you want to lose what little manhood you have, you'd better get out of my sight right now." With that, he shoved Big Earl back against the wall, rattling all the little bottles and pill jars in the room.

"But Doc," Big Earl choked, "think about poor little Carleen. How's she goin' to face all her little friends?"

Claude Daniel started to say, "You should have thought of that before you messed around with your daughter." He caught himself and sighing heavily, said, "All right. For Carleen's sake, I'll take care of it this time."

Big Earl started to smile, a smug, knowing kind of smile. Seeing that smirk on Big Earl's lips, Claude Daniel gave him one final blow...a knee to his crotch. Big Earl's smile disappeared as his eyes threatened to burst out of their sockets. Groaning, he grabbed his privates. In a voice hoarse from pain, he promised Claude Daniel, "I'll never touch her again. I swear it, Doc! Never again."

That night, Claude Daniel packed his things and moved to Charleston where he got a job in the hospital. A few months later, he opened his own office. He still saw things that turned him sour on his fellow human beings, but nothing as bad as he had experienced working with Young Doc. He vowed to turn over any child molesters to the law and help place the victims in homes where they would receive better care. With that vow, he began a one man crusade in the name of the helpless.

Ansel started taking Willa May to the movie house in Gauley Bridge twice a week. The children usually went with them. Ansel said he liked going, that it helped to put his problems out of his thoughts. All the women in the county still begged for any scrap of attention that Ansel would give them, but he didn't seem to notice. Or so Willa May thought.

Every Sunday afternoon and every Wednesday night, like clockwork, they all went to the movies. Willa May enjoyed most of the movies, like "It Happened One Night" with Clark Gable. She especially liked Claudette Colbert, commenting, "Now that little gal's got spunk." The movies she liked best were Tarzan movies. Whenever she saw one, she found herself wishing that Daniel was there to see it with her. Daniel would have liked Johnny Weissmuller, she thought. Ansel had caught her on more than one occasion mesmerized while Tarzan swam down a river with crocodiles right on his heels or faced down a lion, like Daniel. On their way home, she told Ansel she just knew that his pa would have been all wrapped up in those Tarzan movies and how she wished she could tell Daniel all about them.

Willa May didn't realize that Ansel had a different reason for going to see all those movies. A different reason altogether. There was a girl who sat in the ticket booth -- Leanne Toliver -- always chewing gum and looking so bored that Willa May wondered if she didn't fall asleep in that booth once everybody bought their tickets. Leanne had a past; it was well documented throughout the valley. She had given birth out of wedlock to a little girl with red curly hair the same shade as her own two years before. Nobody knew who the father was, but there had been a lot of speculation on the matter. Some said it was the owner of the movie house, Walter Sampson, who always reminded Willa May of a greased pig. Others said the father was a young, married preacher at the snake handling church Leanne attended up in Scrabble Creek, one Zebulon Prescott. He was known to breathe fire and brimstone while holding a bunch of copperheads in one hand and trying to reach up the women's skirts with his other. Still others said that Leanne had looked the wrong way at the moon one night when it was full and a traveling salesman had his way with her up in the balcony of the movie house, an area where many a baby had been conceived by local reckoning. The Tolivers were a closed-mouth bunch and never hinted at who the father was. Willa May figured they didn't know either. Leanne was a working mother now, trying to bring home enough pay to put food on the table for her and her baby so her folks wouldn't throw her out.

Ansel appeared to be set on going to movies twice a week, come hell or high water. They saw many a movie together in those years, but Willa May never guessed what he was really doing until one Sunday evening when Ansel told her he was thinking of marrying again.

"Well, Ansel, I'd love to see you marry again. You're long overdue, the way I see it. But you haven't brought anybody home. Just who did you have in mind?"

He looked a bit sheepish and cleared his throat. "Mommy, I reckon this'll come as news to you, but I've been seeing somebody right

312

regular goin' on three years now."

He was right. It certainly was news to Willa May. If anyone was regular in his hours, it was Ansel. She began to wonder how on earth he had been finding the time to court this woman, since he was always home at the same time every night and never went out once he was home, except to take her and the youngsters somewhere. "You want to tell me who it is you've been seeing all this time?" she asked.

He scuffed the toe of his shoe across the floor and kept his head lowered. "Leanne Toliver."

"That gal down at the movie house?"

Ansel nodded. Looking up at Willa May, he said in a rush, "I know what you're thinking. That she's done had a baby by some other man and never bothered to get a wedding ring on her finger first. But she ain't that way, Mommy. I've come to know her real well and she's awful shy. She knows what folks have been saying about her behind her back, calling her a whore and all. But she ain't like that. Not at all."

It touched Willa May's heart to see how fiercely Ansel was defending the honor of the girl he loved. To think he could have had any girl in the valley and he landed on the one everybody would have least suspected. "You don't have to convince me, Son. If you love her and you think she'll make you a good wife, then that's all that matters. It's nobody else's business what's gone on before."

A grin spread across Ansel's face. His eyes showed her how grateful he was for her approval. "Thank you, Mommy, but..."

He stopped short and looked at her like there was more. She started to wonder if maybe he had put another baby in Leanne's belly and was trying to find the words to tell her. Bracing herself, Willa May asked, "Ansel, what is it?"

He stood up and started pacing back and forth like Daniel used to do. Watching him, Willa May was swept back forty years. He looked so much like his pa, it took her breath away. Finally, he came over and knelt down in front of her. Taking her bent and gnarled hands in his, he said, "I've saved up a little bit of money over the years and I've bought a place of my own. For Leanne and me."

Willa May wanted to clasp her hands over her ears so she wouldn't have to hear what was coming. With Ansel gone, there was no way that she and Creedy could keep up the place. She knew it and Ansel knew it. The house and the land it was on were all she had left of her and Daniel. How could she bear to leave it?

313

"Mommy, I need a place to start all over. A place that I've built up for my new family. It ain't that I don't want to be here with you. I'd like nothing more than to keep up this place and my new place. But we both know that can't be. I'm still sheriff and I've got to put in my time there, too." He paused and looked at Willa May. He knew how much it was hurting her, like a knife cutting into her heart, to hear these words. "Mommy, this here's been my home all my life. When I was over there fighting in the war with Asa, Thomas Lee, and Claude Daniel, all I wanted was to get back here and stay put for the rest of my life. But a lot has happened since then. We both lost the one person in the world we loved most. After Cory died, I never thought I'd find anyone again. Why, it took me over a year to even screw up the courage to ask Leanne to have a cup of coffee with me. That's how afraid I am that I'll lose everything again. But Mommy, I have to try and live again. I ain't old yet. I can still raise more kids and still have a chance at a life for myself. I want that life to be brand new, a fresh start for me and a fresh start for Leanne."

Willa May saw the pain in her boy's eyes, trying his best to tell her it was time to let go, time to move on once and for all. After what seemed like a season in eternity, she said, "What do I do with this place? You know how your pa was about not letting anybody tear up his land."

"I was talking with Thomas Lee about all this. He's got some ties in the statehouse now and he said he thought maybe the state might be interested in buying up the land and making a park out of it. That way, nobody will ever be able to destroy pa's mountain. It'll always be just like he left it."

"They won't go tearing down the trees to build some fancy new buildings?"

Ansel shook his head. "No. Thomas Lee says it'll be just like it's always been. Wild and untouched, just like Pa liked it."

"All right, I reckon. So long as they stick to their word that they won't so much as lay a hand on Daniel's woods."

"You can come and move in with Leanne and me. We picked out a pretty little place over at Poe."

"No, Son, I don't think so."

Ansel looked at her, not knowing what to do about her disagreeing with him. "But why not? There will be plenty of room. Leanne and me can see to it that you have everything you need."

Willa May shook her head and shrugged her bony shoulders. "I can't go that far away from here. Why, that's over by Carnifax Ferry. Nope, it's just too far. I have to be closer than that to the home I've always known."

This put a hitch in Ansel's plans. For a minute, he didn't know what to say. She knew he meant well, but he just didn't understand. She could never be that far away from the place she loved, the place that still kept Daniel alive in her memory. She needed to at least be able to see it, even if she couldn't be on the mountain. She could see that it created a problem for Ansel.

He patted her hands and said, "Don't worry, Mommy. We'll figure something out. I'll talk it over with Thomas Lee and see what he says."

Like his own pa, Thomas Lee was able to come up with just the right solution. Beulah and Dewey were living in the upper end of Glen Ferris, less than a mile away once they traveled off the mountain. They didn't have children, so there was more than enough room in their cozy little house. Thomas Lee and Ansel paid them a call. Before Beulah could say a word, Dewey, who had been listening over by the kitchen sink, said, "Anse, go home and tell Willa May she's living with us now."

In 1935, Willa May signed over Daniel's land to the state, with the agreement that they would never sell his land or destroy his mountain in any way. The state government made it into a park called Hawk's Nest. Willa May knew that Daniel would have liked the name. While Creedy went to live with Ansel and his family, Willa May moved to Glen Ferris.

It was different living under someone else's roof. Beulah and Dewey tried their best to make Willa May feel at home, but other than her room with her wedding quilt and 'Lil Daniel's quilt folded on the bed she had shared all those years with Daniel, nothing was her own any more. She tried to help around the kitchen as best she could, baking biscuits, cakes, and cobblers that made Dewey lick his lips. It was homey at night, sitting in their parlor as the sun sank below the mountains and listening to the radio or Dewey sawing on his fiddle. Beulah and Dewey found that Willa May was a big help, especially once their babies, Willie Joe and Roy arrived. It was comforting to know that Willa May was there to advise them whenever one of the

315

boys was sick.

Creedy, on the other hand, loved every minute on Ansel's farm. Leanne turned out to be a hard worker, doing most of the chores around the place while Ansel was at work. As old and slow as he was, Creedy fed the chickens, milked the cows, slopped the hogs, and brought in fresh food from the garden for dinner every evening. He sat in his favorite rocker on the front porch peeling, slicing, and shucking the vegetables for Leanne to cook. Ansel's boys were getting big and helped Leanne with the plowing, planting, and the handiwork. They kept busy building pens and painting the house and the barn. Nellie was always up in the hayloft reading a book. She loved to read. At the end of the road leading up to the farm was a schoolhouse and a church. Ansel saw to it that Nellie started school in that little one room schoolhouse. He was proud when she proved to be the smartest pupil in the school.

Ansel was happier than Willa May had seen him in years with a new wife and a new place all his own. He felt a strong duty to his job, but his heart would always be tied to the earth, like his pa. Ansel wasn't as much of a loner, a true mountain man, like Daniel, but he took joy in watching seedlings grow from the rich, tilled soil or in bringing a new calf into the world. Important as his sheriffing was, he was always there when it came time to buy a new bull or decide what was to be planted in that year's garden. More than happy, he was at peace with his world.

In November of nineteen thirty-seven, Ansel and Leanne planned to have the entire family over to their farm for a big family Thanksgiving. They had cleaned and cooked for a week, getting ready for the celebration. On Monday, Ansel got a call from his office around four in the morning, waking up the whole house. His face showed his concern as he listened to what his deputy was saying. When he hung up, he turned to Leanne and said, "I've got to go in to work."

"Now?" Leanne asked. "But it's the middle of the night. Can't it wait?"

"Not this." Ansel was already making his way back up the stairs to their room to change.

Leanne looked at Creedy who watched from his bedroom door, wondering what could have happened that could be so urgent. Most of the time, Ansel's job only required him to haul in some drunk to sleep it off in the jail. Everybody was so poor, it wasn't worth it to try to steal anything. Leanne turned back toward Ansel, "What's happened?"

"There's been a murder," Ansel said. But on his way out the door, he told Leanne, "You'd better keep all the doors locked good and tight for a while. Till we can solve this thing."

Leanne had to read about it in The Gazette to find out what had taken place. The newspaper said that a body had been found by some deer hunters. Drunk, they had stumbled over a cloth sack that had been thrown over the hillside from the road above. It was a large, lumpy sack. Wondering what they had found, the men opened it. Inside, they discovered a body, chopped into pieces. Terrified and staggering from all the alcohol flowing through their veins, it took them the better part of the night to walk down off the mountain and get to the sheriff's office.

Ansel and his deputies drove up the mountain with the hunters and followed them down the hillside to where they had found the body. They took pictures of the scene, then took the sack over to the county coroner's and photographed the remains. They were able to keep it hushed up for a day while the coroner performed the autopsy, but what he discovered was too shocking to keep out of the news for long. The body was that of a man in his twenties. He had been shot through the head at close range, then the killer had chopped the body into pieces like a butcher slaughtering a hog, then boiled them. There were also signs of frostbite so they knew that the body had been stored in a freezer. It was so gruesome that nobody wanted to believe that someone living in the valley could have done such a thing. It was up to Ansel and his men to find the killer before anyone else fell victim.

The story appeared in the paper the day before Thanksgiving. It caused a scare among all the people living along Route 60, the road where the body had been found. It was a well traveled route, used by everyone. Folks started taking a long look at any stranger who happened to stop for gasoline or to have an order of meatloaf and gravy at the Gauley Diner. Doors and windows were locked up tight, even in the daytime when folks were used to just running out to the store or going to the doctor's office without locking their doors. It was such a grisly murder that some believed it must have been committed by a stranger driving through, certainly not by anyone living among them. Other, more suspicious minds began looking more closely at the men working behind the butcher counters at the A & P, wondering if they might spot a glint of madness in those familiar smiling eyes.

317

On Thursday, the family came together. All of Willa May's children, their children, and grandchildren were there. With the murder on everyone's minds, the menfolk gathered in the parlor. They shut the door so they could talk freely without worrying that one of the little ones would overhear the gruesome details of their conversation. The women gathered in the kitchen where the turkey was roasting and the cornbread stuffing was baking. They shooed the youngsters outside to play in the yard. Speaking in low voices as well, they glanced now and then at the door where the children came rushing in every so often to ask when supper would be ready.

Willa May moseyed into the parlor just as Thomas Lee asked Ansel, "Have you been able to identify the victim yet?"

Ansel nodded. "Call came in last night that some old boy who swept and cleaned the schoolhouse over in Mossy was missing. Boy by the name of Axle Lively. The principal called to report him missing from his work since last week. Said the boys used to like to hitchhike down to Montgomery to go to the movies. Said, too, that he wasn't right in the head. Real slow. Wouldn't know he was in danger till somebody put a gun to his head, which was just how it happened."

"Have you got any evidence yet that could help you catch the killer?" Walt Whitman asked, leaning against the cane he used now.

"Only that the killer showed a good knowledge of butchering meat, which means it could've been any of the butchers hereabouts. But think about how many farmers in these parts slaughter their own meat and would have their own private property where they could process the body and keep it all secret. Nobody would be the wiser."

Young Doc spoke up, peering over his wire-rimmed glasses. "You're right, Anse, there are hundreds of farms where the whole thing could have been done, out of sight of unsuspecting neighbors."

Ansel looked at Young Doc and after a minute, added, "Coroner said it could've been somebody with a medical background and sharp surgical tools, too."

Claude Daniel spoke up, "Oh, c'mon now, Anse. No doctor in his right mind would be able to commit such an act against people he's taken an oath to heal."

"Who said the killer was in his right mind?" Dewey piped up.

As the others nodded solemnly, Thomas Lee said, "Anse, I heard through some lawyers yesterday in Charleston that the governor wants the killer found before he can kill again...and to put an end to the terror that's spread throughout the valley."

"Yep," Anse affirmed, "I had a call yesterday around noon. He wanted to know what we'd found out so far. At that time, I didn't even know the identity of the victim. But like we've been saying here today, the killer could be just about anybody. Don't forget where the body was found. Thrown over the hillside from a main road. Maybe it was someone just passing through."

Thomas Lee shook his head. "I don't think so, Anse. If the victim wasn't local, I could agree with you. But seeing as how you've identified him as somebody from around here, known by all to be mentally handicapped, it's more likely that the killer knew this Lively boy. It could be that the boy knew his killer, too. Maybe that's why the gunshot was fired at such close range."

"Makes sense," Ansel agreed.

Walt Whitman nodded. "Picture this. The Lively boy wasn't hitching *into* town to go see a show. He'd already been to the movie and was on his way home. The killer -- someone Lively would know -- had spotted the kid in town, follows him a ways out of Montgomery and pulls up, knowing the kid would be thumbing. The killer picks up Lively, drives a few miles, talking and putting the boy at ease in hopes of catching him completely off guard. And while he's driving along, he pulls the gun out, reaching across the seat and placing the gun right up to the boy's head and shoots. It's dark and late, so nobody has seen or heard anything. He takes the body to where he can process it -- a butcher shop or a barn, like you said --"

"Or his office, if he was a doctor," Young Doc amended.

"Or his office." Walt Whitman nodded. "I think if I wanted to find a starting point, I'd find out who the kid knew well. Right now, he's the only clue you've got. Maybe, by finding out who he knew, you can pick up something that seems not quite right, something the killer has overlooked."

Ansel grinned at his brother. "If you ever want to come out of retirement and work for me, you've got a job, big brother!"

Ansel's deputies started piecing together bits and pieces of Axle Lively's life: who his friends and neighbors were, where he had worked before, and who his doctor was. For the next year, Ansel kept a running watch on as many of the Lively boy's close friends as possible. Day after day, he prayed that the something Walt Whitman said wouldn't be quite right would turn up. It proved to be a dead end. Slowly, like an old horse getting up in the morning, people in the valley started breathing sighs of relief, thinking that maybe the killer had been a stranger, someone just passing through. Little by little, people left their houses, remembering at the last minute that they had forgotten to lock up. Most shrugged and continued on their way.

The following November, almost a year to the day, another body was found. On the Monday before Thanksgiving, a farmer by the name of Vernon came to Ansel's office. He was upset that his wife hadn't come home from town where she had gone to a beauty parlor appointment on Saturday. Thinking that maybe his wife had run off or was with another man, he went out to look for her. He hitched a ride into Montgomery, but halfway there, he spotted his car, empty and parked on the side of the road. He looked into the car and saw a bag of groceries on the passenger side. The woman and her purse were missing. When he tried to start the car, he found that the clutch was gone. Figuring that she had waved down help, he went on into Montgomery. But nobody had seen his wife. Her name was Jewel.

Ansel told the farmer he would put out an all points bulletin and have his deputies make some calls. When he asked the farmer to take him to the broken down car, the farmer rubbed the back of his neck and said, "Sorry, Sheriff, but I had the boys down at the filling station tow her into town. They fixed the clutch and shined her up like new." He thought a minute and asked, "Why did you want to see the car?"

Ansel looked at the man and sighed. "I wanted to see if maybe there was something that would help us find your missus."

"I done told you. There wasn't nothing there but a bag of groceries."

Ansel thought of what fingerprints might have been left on the car and shook his head again. "If you think of anything else that might help, call me."

"Sure will, Sheriff. I just want to find my Jewel, that's all. Sure hope she didn't run into any trouble."

When the call came on Tuesday from a hysterical woman sputtering about her boy finding a sack with a body in it, Ansel knew without being told that he had found Jewel Vernon. The boy was around fourteen. He had been out squirrel hunting when he came across the body. Beyond that, he wasn't much help. He kept saying, "Sheriff, I didn't do nothing wrong. Swear to God, Sheriff!"

The coroner's report came back almost a twin to the one he had handed Ansel the year before. A bullet to the brain, fired at close range. The body, cut up and processed like a hog at slaughtering time, was boiled, then frozen. By Thanksgiving Day, when the family met

320

again, the newspaper had proclaimed that there was a crazed killer in the valley, comparing him to Lizzie Borden and Jack the Ripper. Seeing what a stew Ansel was in, Walt Whitman said, "What you do now is find out who the Vernon woman knew well -- well enough to trust to pick her up on a lonely mountain road. Then compare that to the list you've got from last year's investigation. If your men have been thorough, there will be at least one name that's on both lists."

Trying hard to act like he wasn't beaten yet, Ansel asked, "Where in the world did you learn to figure out a puzzle like this? You been reading some of Mommy's mysteries?"

"Truth be told, yes. I've read my share of Sir Arthur Conan Doyle."

"Maybe I'll read some, too, if it'll help me see things so clear." Turning serious, he asked, "What else should I be reading about?"

Walt Whitman recognized the earnest tone in Ansel's voice and said, "I'd be reading everything I could get my hands on about famous killers, particularly those who cut up their victims. And I'd be asking myself why the killer chooses only to kill at this time of the year. Just what is it about this time of the year that sets off the spark inside his mind to kill again?"

Ansel nodded. "I'll go to the library over in Fayetteville tomorrow. Thomas Lee, I'd be obliged if you could check out some books when you're down in Charleston, too."

Ansel started searching for the one person that both the Lively boy and the Vernon woman knew. He didn't turn up a single name. In the meantime, he read everything he could get his hands on about famous killers, what made them tick and what made them kill. He also read every detective story he came across, saying it might help him think of something he might have overlooked. He knew deep in his gut that there was a missing piece to the puzzle, something that had escaped his attention. It gnawed at him constantly.

Months passed. By Halloween, people started getting nervous, putting extra locks on their doors and telling their older children to stay indoors at night. The first two weeks of November that year, Ansel was so wound up, he couldn't stop fidgeting. He spilled every cup of coffee he picked up. Leanne said he tossed and tumbled at night, that she couldn't understand why he even bothered to come to bed since she knew he didn't sleep. By Armistice Day, Ansel's eyes were two dark circles. If Willa May hadn't known better, she would have guessed that somebody had given Ansel matching shiners; he looked that bad. Night and day, he studied and restudied all the files on the Lively case and the Vernon case, looking for that missing piece of the puzzle. He came home, weary and fretful that soon he would have a third case on his hands. For a break, he and Leanne brought Creedy and the children by to see Willa May on Sunday. Walt Whitman and Annie Catherine were there, too. One look at Ansel and Walt Whitman asked, "You're expecting another killing, aren't you?"

"Wouldn't you?" Ansel asked in a clipped tone. His helplessness was eating away at him.

Walt Whitman sighed. "I suppose I would at that. Still no leads?"

Ansel ran his fingers through his blonde hair. "There never were." He sounded utterly hopeless.

"He's got to slip up sometime."

"Yeah, but by then somebody else will be dead."

Dewey shook his head, sympathizing with Ansel's situation. "And nobody knows who could be next. It's downright scary, ain't it? Why, I won't let Beulah go up to Gauley Bridge alone and that's just a stone's throw away."

"You've got a right to be antsy," Ansel agreed. Looking at his niece, he added, "You listen to what Dewey's saying now, you hear? I sure don't want nothing to happen to you just because you might be thinking that your husband's being too protective."

Beulah nodded. So did everyone in the room.

A week later on Friday afternoon, Ansel got a call. This time from home. Creedy, who hardly knew how to place a call, was on the other end. "Anse? Anse? You there, Anse?" he hollered into the phone.

Ansel knew that Creedy would never go near a telephone. He was too afraid of "the blasted contraption" as he called it. Right away, Ansel guessed that something was amiss. "What's wrong, Creedy? Are the kids okay?"

"Anse," Creedy shouted, "I think you'd better come home. I'm mighty worried."

"We're awful busy here, Creedy. Can't Leanne help you?"

"That's just it. Leanne took Faith down to Beulah's to pick up her big white tablecloth for dinner on Thursday. She ain't got back yet."

Ansel started to worry about his wife and her little girl. "When did she go?"

"It's been five or six hours by now, Anse. It don't take no six hours to pick up a tablecloth."

Grinning, Ansel said, "Oh, Creedy, I wouldn't worry none. Her and Beulah probably started talking and just lost track of the time, that's all. I'll give Beulah a call. Meanwhile, don't you fret none. Leanne and Faith will probably pull up outside as soon as you hang up."

"If you say so," Creedy yelled, the doubt in his voice coming through the phone line loud and clear.

"I'm sure she'll be home real soon, Creedy. Maybe all this talk about that killer has got you all stirred up."

"I reckon," Creedy grumbled.

"Sit tight and I'll get back to you after I talk with Beulah."

When Ansel called Beulah, he grew alarmed when she told him that Leanne and Faith had left three hours before. "Do you know if they were goin' to make any other stops?" he asked.

"I don't think so, Anse. Leanne said she needed to get right back to the farm and start baking pies she promised Mom she'd bring for Thanksgiving."

Ansel was silent on the other end. Growing worried, too, Beulah asked, "You don't reckon something happened to them, do you?"

His mind racing, Ansel searched for a reason -- any reason -- why Leanne and Faith weren't home yet. After a long silence, Beulah thought perhaps he hadn't been listening to her. Choking back the panic he felt, Ansel finally said, "I don't know." He hung up without saying good-bye.

Ansel sent three of his deputies out in their police cars and called the sheriff in Nicholas County. He asked him if he would send a car out on the route leading from his house over to the Fayette County line. Then he set off himself, down the mountain toward Gauley Bridge, but he didn't make it that far. At a bend in the road, just below where he had grown up, he spotted his car...empty, just like Jewel Vernon's. The terror that had been creeping under his skin since he had spoken with Beulah came lurching up into his throat, making it hard to breathe. He pulled up alongside his car and got out. Peering into the back seat, he found the white tablecloth Leanne had picked up at Beulah's folded neatly. Nothing else.

Right away, he put out an all points bulletin for Leanne and Faith, but deep in his heart, he knew it was futile. By Monday morning, when the call came into his office that a man thumbing a ride into Gauley Bridge had stumbled onto a sack lying by the side of the road, Ansel knew who it was inside the sack. Thomas Lee and Claude Daniel were with Ansel, wanting to be there when word came.

Thomas Lee told Willa May that when word did come, Ansel put his head down on his desk and cried. Knowing how these investigations went, Thomas Lee stepped in and told the deputies what to do. Seeing Ansel so distraught, the deputies followed Thomas Lee's orders without any questions.

The coroner's report showed that only one body had been inside the sack: a female between the ages of thirty and thirty-five, shot once in the head, then cut into pieces, boiled, and frozen. Ansel couldn't function. Numb, he merely nodded to Thomas Lee whenever he was asked a question. Out of routine, he got up in the morning, dressed, and went to work. If someone had asked him his name, Thomas Lee didn't think Ansel could have replied.

Claude Daniel insisted on seeing the remains. He wanted to help, but he was left just as mystified as everyone else. Mostly, he had hoped to find some clue that would help Ansel. He told Willa May that with Anse so deep into shock, he didn't know how anyone could help.

"That's okay," she replied. "There'll come a time when Ansel will be able to put this behind him. Maybe years from now. But he'll always know that you and Thomas Lee were there in his time of need. That's what matters. Always remember that. Blood is all that matters. You might think I'm a tottering old woman, but I've seen my share of grief and bad times. It all boils down to one thing...family. My Uncle Luther -- that'd be your great, great uncle -- once said that family is all we've got. He was right, you know. Those words have stuck in my mind ever since. So always remember: nothing matters more than family."

Claude Daniel's eyes looked into hers. She could see a twinkle in them, a twinkling that reminded her of Daniel and how he used to look surprised and pleased when she came out with some deeply personal remark, baring her heart.

"I'll remember, Grandma," Claude Daniel vowed.

It was at that moment Willa May felt that she knew why the good Lord had let her keep going after Daniel had passed on. It was to let the young ones, the ones who still had to make their stand in the world, know why -- why they were there, why they had to decide what their stand would be, and that it was all for family. That was her legacy she could pass on to them.

She knew, too, that if she had spoken these thoughts to Ansel, they would have been lost on him. Like a man adrift at sea, he was in a place too far removed from the rest of them. All the family could do was be there for him, offer their support and see to his welfare, taking care of his children, making decisions he wasn't capable of making.

Creedy saw Willa May on Thanksgiving Day at Dora Lottie's. Shaking his head, he said, "I knew. I just knew something was wrong. I only wish it hadn't been up to me to break it to Anse."

Willa May took Creedy's withered hand in hers and patted it. "Now, Creedy, you did what you had to do. Nobody can fault you. Ansel will have to come to grips with this as best he can. We've both seen enough of this old world to know that. Besides, Ansel is strong. He'll see his way through this."

Creedy nodded, a lost soul himself.

That Thanksgiving was even quieter than the two before. Ansel reminded Willa May of Ethan Allen, just a shadow of the man he had always been, a ghostly figure wandering through the house, hollow inside. It pained her to see her boy suffering so. She wanted to take all his grief and soak it up so he wouldn't have to go through it himself. But she knew she couldn't do his grieving for him. It was his loss, his pain. So everyone -- Willa May included -- simply gave him his freedom to do what he had to do to get over yet another loss.

Willa May was sure that Ansel would quit his job, being so upset over Leanne's death. But once the burial was over, he set his mind to catching her killer. He was a man driven by one purpose and one purpose only. That winter he worked night and day, going over and over everything he knew about the three murders. In the meantime, everyone wondered what had happened to Faith. Her body was still missing.

In the spring, Ansel was no closer than he had been to finding the butcher killer. On Easter Sunday, Dora Lottie had planned a family dinner to try and cheer everyone up and take Ansel's mind off his problems. Since his farm was so big, they decided to hold their reunion at his place. They painted eggs to hide and made Divinity in pretty pastel colors. They made Easter baskets for all the little ones. Beulah had made Willa May's favorite dessert, coconut custard cake, made with angel food cake cut into cubes and surrounded by creamy custard then frosted with whipped cream and topped with coconut flakes. "Lord," Willa May declared, sampling some of the cake, "but that cake is downright sinful!"

The main dinner was a juicy ham that one of Ansel's deputies had brought over, something he did every spring. Dora Lottie baked the ham, topping it with slices of pineapple and ruby red cherries halved and pitted. She basted it in pure maple syrup that Creedy had tapped from the maple trees on Ansel's farm.

The family gathered around the table, their noses filled with the sweet aroma of that ham. Their mouths watered for the first tender slice. Walt Whitman did the honors and sliced the ham, a rosy pink and flowing with juice. No sooner had they tasted it, when Annie Catherine remarked, "I don't think I've ever tasted a sweeter ham. Anse, where on earth did you get it?"

Looking haggard from his investigation, Ansel said, "Oh, Billy Bob Noble, my deputy gave it to me. He gives me one every spring. Slaughters one of his hogs every fall --"

Ansel stopped short. His mouth was open as though he intended to add more, but his eyes were focused on something distant.

"What is it, Anse?" Walt Whitman asked.

Breathing hard, Ansel pushed himself back from the table. His eyes grew wide with the sudden shock of realization. "Oh, my God! Oh, my God!" His voice rose almost to a shout. Without another word, he turned away from the table and headed for the door.

Thomas Lee stood up and said, "I'm going with you, Anse."

"I'm going, too," Claude Daniel said.

Then Dewey said, "Count me in."

Willa May watched as Ansel rushed to the door, followed by the others. She turned back to Walt Whitman. "You thinking what I'm thinking?"

Walt Whitman nodded. "I think Anse is finally onto something. And it's been right under his nose all this time. Who would ever suspect a police officer? Everybody trusts an officer to help them. It all fits. I just hope Anse is right and they can catch him."

Ansel knew that Billy Bob would be at his farm on Easter Sunday. He handed each of the boys a rifle from the trunk of his car. "Circle around back. See if you can get inside the barn and the house without him seeing you. But be careful. This ain't no ordinary killer we're dealing with and I don't want him to slip between our fingers now."

"What are you goin' to do?" Dewey asked.

"I'll drive up to his house like I'm paying a friendly call," Ansel explained. "Thank him for the ham and jaw a while. See if I can't distract him. But if anything goes wrong, fire a shot. We'll all know to come running."

He gave the boys time to get close to the house and the barn, then he drove up and found Billy Bob walking toward him from the barn, carrying a fresh pail of milk in his hand. Ansel got out of his car and shook Billy Bob's free hand, thanking him again for the ham. He started chatting about the weather and what crops he was going to plant that spring. Twenty minutes had passed when Ansel spied Thomas Lee coming toward them, his rifle raised and aimed at Billy Bob Noble's back. When Thomas Lee was too close to miss, Ansel said, "So tell me, Billy Bob, what made you kill my wife?"

Billy Bob's face turned from a friendly smile to a look of shocked surprise then red with anger in a matter of seconds. Dropping the milk bucket, he let out a fierce, wild scream and threw himself at Ansel. Having grown up in the mountains, Ansel was used to surprise attacks and jumped aside. At the same moment, Thomas Lee fired three shots, dead center into Billy Bob's back, blowing three big holes through his lungs.

Ansel bent over Billy Bob's lifeless body. Looking up at Thomas Lee, he asked, "So how did you know?"

"I think you'd better come see what I found."

Billy Bob had an ice box in his barn. Inside it, Thomas Lee found little Faith. There were saws and butcher knives with blood dried on them which Ansel sent to the police lab in Charleston. Two days later, word came that confirmed that some of the blood matched Leanne's and Faith's. The only clue they could find as to why Billy Bob had committed the bloody murders was a yellowed newspaper clipping tucked inside the family Bible. Dated November of nineteen and ten, it told how ten year old Billy Bob Noble had come home from deer hunting to find his mama, his only living kin, shot through the head and cut up like a hog, then left hanging from meat hooks on a line in the kitchen. Billy Bob had grown up in Virginia, near Roanoke, so nobody in the valley had known about his past. When Ansel telephoned the sheriff's office in Roanoke, the sheriff found the files on Billy Bob's mother. The killer had never been caught and the sheriff at the time of the murder had always suspected that Billy Bob had been lying about being out hunting. Yet nobody could explain what had set Billy Bob off so many years later.

With no further reason now to be sheriff and sickened beyond understanding, Ansel quit his job. For no reason that anyone except Willa May could fathom, he set off into the hills. Nobody saw him again until the following fall.

Chapter Thirteen

By nineteen thirty-nine, Willa May thought she had seen all that life could throw her way, that nothing worse could befall them. With the Depression, the butcher killings, and all the loved ones she had lost, the family had somehow managed to survive them all. On September first, she braced herself again when Dewey read the morning headlines to her. Germany had built up an army under Nazi rule and invaded Poland. Before long, the Germans took over most of the countries surrounding them.

In July of nineteen forty, the only power left to challenge Hitler was England. Under a new leader, Winston Churchill, it became apparent that England would go to war. Churchill was always pictured chomping on a big stogie and looking too wide to get through the doorway. He reminded Willa May of a bulldog with its jowls flapping. What he lacked in being fit and trim, he more than made up for in spirit. "That old codger is downright foxy. I like him," she declared.

Like the rest of the family, Willa May held her breath, hoping and praying that the nation wouldn't have to get into this war, but the more she heard, the more it seemed that they were bound to get into it. Italy had shaken hands with Germany and the fighting spread into Greece and Africa. The biggest shock came from a small island in the Pacific, though. On December seventh of 'forty-one, as they sat in Beulah's parlor listening to the radio, reports broke in saying that Japan had attacked Pearl Harbor in Hawaii.

"Lord have mercy!" Dewey exclaimed, jumping up from the sofa and rushing into the kitchen to the telephone.

"Who are you calling?" Beulah called after him.

"Walt Whitman. I want to see what he makes of this."

Dewey spoke to Walt Whitman in a low, serious voice while Beulah and Willa May listened intently for more news. Minutes later, Dewey came back, shaking his head.

"What did Walt Whitman have to say?" Beulah asked.

For a minute, Dewey didn't seem inclined to answer, looking first at the women, then his two little boys playing on the floor, then out the window at the mountains and the river across the road. He turned back to his wife and finally found the words to reply. "He figures it's goin' to mean war for sure."

Willa May could see the worry on Beulah's and Dewey's faces. She wondered how the country could pull together with the Depression lingering on. Seemed like this was the worst time the country could have picked to get into a fight, but they didn't have much choice now. If the Japanese could bomb Hawaii, then who was to say that California and the west coast wouldn't be next? It had been a long time since any foreigners had tried to invade the country. Now with airplanes and submarines, it didn't seem much of a stretch to imagine it could happen.

Ansel's boys signed up right away. Mack went into the Navy while Robert and Manny became Marines. Ansel took Willa May with him each time he saw one of them off at the train depot in Montgomery. As each train pulled away, she saw Ansel wiping a stray tear. He had already suffered so much loss, she just prayed that the Lord would bring his sons back to him whole and healthy.

Soon she was receiving letters and cards from far away places like Camp Lejeune, Quantico, and a place called the Great Lakes Naval Base. It was always the same message -- they were faring well, eating well, but missing the good home cooking they loved so well. Once they shipped out, the letters and cards arrived less often.

Ansel was doing all he could to keep up with his big farm while the boys were away. Nellie was in high school, a full-blossomed girl with a pageboy hairdo like Katherine Hepburn wore, making straight A's on her report cards. Ernest Roy, Hattie Sue's boy, was a principal at one of the schools in the valley by then. He told Ansel that it would be a shame for such a bright girl like Nellie to miss going on to college. Ansel started setting back money from the hogs and cows he sold and the extra crops he grew to put Nellie through school.

The family began using the ration stamps that the government distributed. They used every contact they had to trade for what they needed -- gasoline stamps for sugar or chocolates, a pair of nylons for a case of Coca-Cola. They always figured out some way to get the things they needed. Once, late in the war when Mack was stationed in the Pacific, he wrote that he sold two cartons of cigarettes for three hundred dollars apiece on the black market. It became a game to see just how they were going to get whatever they wanted from the bartering. Sometimes they had to trade two or three times to finally get the item they had their hearts set on.

In the evenings, they sat by the radio, listening for the latest word on what Hitler was doing and how the boys overseas were holding up. One minute they were singing along with the Andrews Sisters and their song about the apple tree, next thing they knew, they would be hanging onto every word that Edward R. Murrow was saying. Ernie Pyle was another journalist Willa May liked. She couldn't wait for Dewey to read his articles to her. But her favorite newsman was young Eric Sevareid. Willa May loved to listen to him talking about the latest happenings in the war. Walt Whitman preferred Walter Cronkite and Dewey started listening to his reports, too.

Month after month, year after year, they heard about blackouts, invasions, and battles. Words like "kamikaze" and U-boat" fell off their tongues as if they had always used them.

Beulah's and Dewey's boy, Roy, kept a map up on the wall in his room. Every time they heard about a new battle, Roy put a pin in the map to show where the heavy fighting was so they could keep track of Ansel's boys. In the spring of 'forty-two, Manny was in the thick of the fighting on the Bataan Peninsula. Under General MacArthur, they had stayed there after being beaten back from Manila. It was a bad time for the boys, battling starvation, disease, and the Japanese. Manny wrote to Willa May that he was heartsick when the general told his company that he was ordered to leave for Australia. The men lined up to see MacArthur off. Before he left, he saluted the men, telling them, "I shall return." The man standing next to Manny sneered, "What for? We'll all be dead by then." A fight broke out among the men as soon as they were dismissed. Some of Manny's friends didn't take kindly to what the man had said, but it was his misfortune to have been right. A few weeks later, Manny's company, exhausted and unable to continue, surrendered to the Japanese. Already starved and sick, they were forced to march sixty miles with the Japanese pushing them past all endurance until they dropped in their tracks. Manny was one of the ones who slumped to his knees one day, carrying a raging fever and too exhausted to go on...until a Japanese soldier blew off two of his toes.

Ansel told Willa May a week later that he had been notified that Manny was captured by the Japanese and was officially considered a prisoner of war. Little by little, the news divulged the horrors and degradation suffered by Allied troops under the tyrannical hands of the Japanese. Newspapers were calling the march that Manny had been forced to make "The Bataan Death March". Hearing about it, Willa May was reminded of the stories she had heard about a war prison called Andersonville during the War Between the States. Even now, she couldn't believe that human beings could show such a lack of mercy for their fellow man. She prayed that Manny would survive and return home to his family. Ansel, though, couldn't bear not knowing if his son was dead or alive. The wondering weighed heavily on him.

On June sixth of 'forty-four, Roy placed a pin on a place in France right on the water, a place called Normandy. Robert was among the men under General Eisenhower who landed that day at Omaha Beach. Most of them died trying to take the beach. On the radio, the family heard that the boys were having a rough time. By the end of July, the Allies had moved past the Nazi lines and into the French countryside.

Mack was on a PT-boat in the Pacific at the time. Willa May was always afraid he might come upon a Japanese submarine and get blown right out of the ocean. He wrote and told her once that he was worried about some of his buddies who had been missing on one of the PT-boats, PT-109. Later, he found out that his friends had died when their boat was cut in two by a Japanese destroyer, but some of the men had managed to survive.

In the spring of 1945, they tuned in every day, leaving the radio on for most of the day, while the Russians surrounded Berlin. Beulah and Dewey took Willa May to visit Ansel on his farm one sunny Sunday early in April, hoping to bring some cheer to the too quiet farm. They roasted chickens and Beulah made her special sweet potatoes with brown sugar and walnut topping. After dinner, they cleared the dishes and cleaned up the kitchen. They were all out on the porch when Creedy, barely able to get about, came back from the pig pen after slopping the pigs. On his heels was a duck, quacking and nipping at Creedy's trouser leg. Ansel pointed and said, "See that old duck? He follows Creedy all over. He's meaner than a rattlesnake. For some reason, he's decided to pick on poor Creedy. Creedy can't abide that duck -- says he'd like to cut him up for Sunday dinner, so he's named him Hitler, telling that duck that he's been named for the worst sonofabitch that's ever lived."

At that moment, Hitler grabbed Creedy's pant leg and nipped again. Everyone chuckled as they watched Creedy trying to shake off the duck. "Truth be told," Ansel went on, "I think Creedy likes all the attention he gets from the little varmint."

Creedy came up to the porch, still shaking his leg and grumbling under his breath at the duck.

"Creedy," Willa May asked, "you remember that old hog Daniel had? Hannibal was his name."

Creedy nodded, giving the duck an extra nudge with his foot.

"Recollect how old Hannibal just loved Elroy?"

"Even I remember Hannibal!" Ansel laughed.

"Well, I think that this duck has the same feelings for you that Hannibal had for Elroy," she chuckled.

Creedy shook his head, watching the duck as it quacked and chattered at him, making a racket. Looking up at Willa May, he said, "Well, I know now how Elroy must have felt, that's for sure. This gallderned duck is like that albatross you read us about once in that poem about the sailor. A regular curse, all right." Hitler nipped at Creedy again as if he knew what Creedy had said. Everyone laughed harder while Creedy jumped away, grumbling more.

Never a healthy person, Creedy was more stooped with age and arthritis. He barely managed to totter along, sometimes using a cane when his arthritis was acting up. But he always tried to give back what he got, determined to keep working around Ansel's place as old as he was. The following week, Ansel was out plowing. Creedy insisted on getting out there with a hoe and working with him. Ansel tried to talk him out of it, but Creedy wouldn't hear of it. They had been working for a couple of hours when Ansel pulled his mules to a halt. Turning around, he spotted Creedy on the ground. Ansel raced over to him and lifted Creedy's head, dotted with sweat and dirt. Seeing how red Creedy's face was, Ansel fanned him with the straw hat he always wore when he worked out in the fields. Creedy managed to raise his hand, letting Ansel know it was no use. Then he pulled Ansel close. Tugging on his shirt collar, he begged, "See to it they bury me by Lizzy. Then I'll be home. You hear?"

With tears trickling down his face, Ansel nodded. "I promise, Creedy."

All the breath seemed to gush out of Creedy's twisted and frail body as he went limp. Ansel knew he was dead.

Dressed in his sweat soaked work clothes, Ansel knocked at Beulah's kitchen door, holding his straw work hat in both hands.

"What's happened?" Willa May asked, knowing it was bad news from the grave look on her son's face. "It's not one of the boys, is it?"

Ansel shook his head, fighting tears. "No," he choked, "it's

Creedy."

Feeling a need to sit down, Willa May nearly collapsed into the nearest chair. Tears sprang to her eyes as she thought of how Creedy had come to be closer to her than her own brother. Once more, she felt like everybody that ever meant something to her was going off and leaving her behind: her babies, her folks, Elroy, Daniel, and now Creedy. All of them gone.

Ansel came over to her and took her hand, rubbing it gently. He told her what had happened. When he finished, he said, "I'm sorry, Mommy."

Willa May wrapped her hands around his and gave them a squeeze. "Somebody will have to tell Thomas Lee. Ever since he was a little thing, he dearly loved Creedy. He'll be heartbroken."

The family had agreed long ago that if two people could share a soul, they were Creedy and Thomas Lee. They loved to talk scripture, history, nature, and old times. They were kindred spirits. When Ansel drove down to Montgomery to Thomas Lee's law office, he knew he was facing a far more difficult task than when he broke the news to Willa May. Ansel told him as gently as he could, but Thomas Lee wheeled around in his chair behind his big desk, turning his back to Ansel. After a few minutes, he said in a tight voice, "Anse, there's a bottle of bourbon over there in that cabinet. Would you pour us some?"

For the next three hours, Thomas Lee sat with Ansel, not taking any calls or seeing any of his appointments, just sitting with Ansel and the bottle, drowning his grief.

Thomas Lee insisted on making all the funeral arrangements, buying the finest mahogany casket he could find, decorated with sprays of white roses with lilies of the valley cascading down each side. He gave the eulogy, reading from Leaves of Grass. He followed with a poem by John Keats, "When I Have Fears That I May Cease To Be". He told how Creedy, unable to read and write, was always eager to hear what Thomas Lee was learning in school. Creedy would always comment, saying things like, "Wouldn't it be something to see that?" or "Someday maybe you can go there and tell me all about it." Hearing this, Willa May realized that she had never known what a thirst Creedy had for knowledge. She thought it must have been a side of Creedy that he only let Thomas Lee see. Everyone joined in singing "When The Roll Is Called Up Yonder" and "Bringing In The Sheaves". Then Thomas Lee had a bagpipe player play "Loch

Lomond". Creedy had once told him that was the one song he recalled his mama singing to him.

They buried Creedy between Lizzy and Glenny in Page. Watching the casket being lowered into the ground, Willa May knew in her heart that Creedy, up in heaven, was happy to spend the rest of Time next to Lizzy. After the services, she went over to Thomas Lee and patted him on the back. "Creedy would be real proud of the way you saw him off."

With tears brimming in his dark brown eyes, Thomas Lee nodded. "Thank you, Grandma. I meant for it to be special. Like he always was to me.

A week later, they received news about another death. Word came over the radio in the middle of the weather report that Hitler had killed himself. Everyone breathed a sigh of relief, knowing that the Germans could never keep the war going now. News came the first week of May that Germany had surrendered to Ike over in France. The next day, May eighth, was proclaimed V-E Day. The family rejoiced in knowing that Robert would be coming home soon. Then came something that made them all catch their breath. On August sixth, a bomb, hundreds of times worse than any they had ever known, was dropped on a city in Japan called Hiroshima. A few days later, another bomb was dropped on Nagasaki. As horrible as the bombs were, people knew that President Truman felt he had to give the orders to use this new weapon. He knew that out of honor and devotion to their emperor, Hirohito, the Japanese would never surrender until they were completely beaten. Willa May knew it was a difficult decision. Just five days after the second bomb, Japan surrendered. By September second, when they signed the surrender on board the U.S.S. Missouri, Ansel hadn't had any word from Manny in over three years. All he had to go on was the letter from Washington, saying that Manny had been taken prisoner. For three years, the family had prayed that Manny was somehow still alive. With the war over, they would know for sure.

Willa May opened the newspaper the next morning to see the headlines, "Victory in Japan!" in bold print. A picture showed a sailor kissing a girl in the streets of New York City. Behind them a sign in Times Square flashed the news that Japan had surrendered. The kiss was one to remember. Willa May smiled to herself, looking at it.

Robert arrived home first, just in time for the holidays. The family was gathered at Ansel's. They were in the middle of singing carols beside Nellie's piano on Christmas Eve. During the second verse of "Silent Night", they heard a knock at the door. Ansel went to answer it, leaving everyone in the parlor. For the longest time, no one heard a sound. Everyone wondered what was taking Ansel so long. Willa May had begun to think that it was bad news about Manny when in walked Robert. Squeals of joy filled the room and Robert started passing through all the hugs around the room. He came up to Willa May, dressed in his uniform and sporting sergeant's stripes. He lifted her up off her feet and whirled her around, hugging her to him for the longest time. Just when she thought her ribs would crack, he set her down and gave her a big kiss on her cheek. "I missed you, Grandma. And I missed your homemade custard so much, I knew I just had to get home before it was all gone!"

Everyone laughed and Willa May pointed to a big glass punch bowl that had belonged to her mama. It was sitting on the sideboard next to the Christmas tree. "Yonder's the bowl," she said. "Better go get some while it lasts."

Robert made tracks for the punch bowl and poured himself some of the icy cold custard Willa May made every Christmas. The custard tasted like eggnog, but frothier. Every year, somebody -- Willa May figured it was Ansel -- laced the custard with a bottle of bourbon. Some years when Ansel got carried away, the custard was strong enough to sprout hair on a man's chest.

Willa May watched as Robert drank two cups of the creamy drink, licking the froth from his upper lip. When he went to pour a third cup, Willa May warned, "Better watch how much of that Christmas spirit you drink there, Robert. You probably aren't used to that much whiskey at one time!"

Shaking his head, Robert grinned. "That's okay, Grandma. I plan to get used to it this very night."

Laughing, the family gathered around the piano again and sang, "God Rest Ye Merry Gentlermen". The next day, as they sat down to Christmas dinner, Willa May saw two kinds of meat on the table, a fat turkey and a smaller bird. "Why did you kill one of your chickens, Ansel? There's plenty of meat on that turkey."

"That ain't no chicken," Ansel chuckled. "I've been saving that bird for a special occasion." At this, he winked slyly at Willa May.

It took her a second or two, then she chuckled, too. "You mean to tell me you took the ax to Hitler?"

Listening to this, Robert asked, "Who?"

They told him about Creedy and Hitler. Ansel added, "I figured it was only fitting to kill Hitler off once and for all, now that we've won the war."

Everyone agreed, raising their glasses. Ansel gave a toast: "To loved ones not with us, to loved ones soon to be with us, and to our Robert -- welcome home, Son." They tapped glasses and said together, "To Robert!" Robert and Ansel clapped each other on the back, both of them happy and relieved. In her heart, Willa May knew what Ansel was thinking: "Please, Lord, bring Mack and Manny home safe and sound, too."

Then Thomas Lee stood up and announced, "Now I know this is going to come as quite a shock to some of you, especially those of you who thought that Claude Daniel and I were going to live out our days as confirmed bachelors, but I want you to mark your calendars for February fifteenth because you're all invited to my wedding!"

"What?" everyone cried.

Looking from Thomas Lee to Walt Whitman and Annie Catherine, Willa May asked, "Did you two know this was coming?"

Smiling, they nodded. Walt Whitman said, "But let Thomas Lee tell you all about it, Mommy."

"I'm listening," she said.

Looking more embarrassed than Willa May had ever seen him, Thomas Lee said, "Most of you know Nola Shively, my secretary?" Everyone nodded, waiting for him to continue. "Well, we've sort of...I guess you could say we --"

"Fell in love?" Willa May asked, supplying the words that somehow Thomas Lee couldn't bring himself to say. It was the first time she had ever seen him at a total loss for words, so unlike the lawyer he was.

His face turned a flaming red as he said, "I guess that's the best way to put it. Yes, ma'am."

"Why didn't you bring her with you so we could congratulate you both?" she asked.

"Oh, I was going to, but her little brother just got home a couple of days ago from the service and she wanted to spend Christmas Day with her folks."

"Well, congratulations to you, anyway," she offered. "And you were right. It's about time you settled down and started a family. I'd just about given up hope of ever seeing a grandchild with your dark brown eyes. And as for you, Claude Daniel," she added, turning to

336

face him, "I wouldn't mind seeing you raise another doctor in the family, either."

Claude Daniel laughed and shook his head. Still blushing, Thomas Lee sat back down and said, "Thanks, Grandma, for your good wishes. And I'll tell Nola you said congratulations."

Everyone in the family knew Nola. She had worked for Thomas Lee since the war started. Tall and slender, she had short curly brown hair and pretty blue eyes. But she was only twenty-six, some twenty years younger than Thomas Lee. Willa May never gave any thought to any kind of romance blossoming between the two. It made her happy, though, to think that Thomas Lee was finally going to know the joys of having a family. Nothing he could have said would have made her happier.

In February, there still wasn't any word about Manny and Willa May could see it was wearing harder on Ansel. He looked almost as haggard as he did after losing Leanne and Faith. He had dark half-moons under his eyes and he had lost some weight, too. In his late fifties, Ansel was still handsome, just starting to show a little gray blended with the golden streaked hair at his temples. Working on the farm had kept him fit with a body more like a man twenty years younger. But now all his fretting had worn at him, making his shoulders appear slightly stooped and deepening the lines across his forehead. Every time she looked at him, Willa May still saw Daniel. Ansel tried to put on a happy face that snowy Saturday when he gathered with the rest of the family to see Thomas Lee get married.

The wedding took place at the Methodist Church in Glen Ferris. Nola had it decorated in red roses and white carnations to add to the Valentine's Day date they had chosen. When Thomas Lee came out with his best man, Claude Daniel, dressed in a black tuxedo, still trim and standing over six feet with dark eyes that sparkled like black diamonds, Willa May beamed with pride. It was the first time she had really looked at her grandson as a fully grown man. He cut a fine figure. Nola's sister was the maid-of-honor and she wore a red velvet dress with tiny white pearls sewn onto the top. Nola had made the dresses for the wedding. Now in her second year of college in Montgomery, Nellie played "The Wedding March" and the guests stood as Nola stepped through the arched door. She was dressed in a white satin wedding gown that bore the same tiny white pearls sewn into the bodice. She wore a long lace veil that reached all the way to the floor. Willa May stole a glance at Thomas Lee as Nola walked up the aisle toward him and saw that same look of pride and joy in his eyes that had shone in Daniel's eyes when her own pa walked her up the aisle so many years before. She knew at that moment that they were going to be happy together.

Thomas Lee placed the ring on Nola's finger and said his vows. The preacher was asking if there was anyone present who could say that Thomas Lee and Nola shouldn't be joined in holy matrimony when the door in back burst open, a blustery cold wind sweeping in with it. Everyone jumped and turned around. There stood Mack in his sailor uniform, grinning from ear to ear. Ansel raced down the aisle. He grabbed Mack and hugged him in a rib crushing bear hug. Robert joined them and the three of them held onto each other, hugging and clapping each other on the back. Then Nellie ran to them and Mack picked her up, whirling her around until she let out a squeal. All the guests were so caught up in their reunion that they had forgotten about the bride and groom. Clearing his throat, the preacher said, "Ahem. Can we get back to the proceedings here?"

Laughing, Mack hollered, "Sure, Preacher. I just didn't want to miss seeing my cousin get hitched after all these years!"

That set everyone to laughing. The preacher didn't appear to appreciate it, though. He frowned and cleared his throat again before he continued. Ansel and Robert led Mack over to the pew where Willa May was sitting and she hugged Mack just as the preacher said, "I hereby pronounce Thomas Lee and Nola husband and wife." Then looking at Thomas Lee, he added, "You may kiss the bride."

Never one to be outdone, Thomas Lee picked Nola up off her feet and gave her a kiss that was one for the storybooks. Ansel and his boys let out a whoop that rattled the rafters. Nellie started playing the organ as Thomas Lee swept Nola up in his arms and carried her down the aisle. All the Shrewsburys cheered Thomas Lee on. Looking over at Nola's kin, Willa May noticed they all looked like they had swallowed a sour lemon, their lips were so tightly pressed together. At first, Willa May thought maybe they should try and calm down a bit, but then seeing Ansel's joy in having another one of his boys home safe and sound, she figured the Shivelys could just stew in their own juices. This was one of the happiest days her family had seen in many a year. If Nola's family didn't like it, they knew where the door was.

Their party mood carried over through the cake and punch in the church basement. Dewey and his boy, Willie Joe, hauled out their fiddles and played some good old foot stomping music while Mack, Robert, and Ansel called on every female there for a dance, swinging them around and tossing them up in the air. One of Nola's cousins, a girl from Paint Creek, came over to Willa May panting for breath after dancing with Mack. Fanning herself, she exclaimed, "I've never been to a wedding party that was this much fun!"

Thomas Lee and Nola honeymooned in White Sulphur Springs. When they returned, they moved into a big white house next to the school in Glen Ferris. Willa May was happy to have Thomas Lee living so close. He often came by to see her on his way home from work, always bringing her a box of chocolates or a bottle of her favorite blackberry wine. Just before Easter, Nola shyly announced that she was in the family way. Willa May was tickled for the two of them, knowing that Thomas Lee had waited so long before settling down and starting a family.

They rose that Easter Sunday to find a raging snowstorm outside. "Old Man Winter's last hurrah", Willa May called it. By the time Ansel arrived to take her to church, it was really whipping up with snow blowing in whirling gusts, making the trees look like they were coated with whipped cream. The road was a slippery sheet of ice. They slid in every direction trying to get down the hill behind Beulah's. At one point, Willa May thought they were going to pitch head first toward the railroad tracks some fifteen feet below. Pumping the brakes, Ansel was able to swerve away from the edge of the narrow little road just in the nick of time. Everyone breathed a sigh of relief as the car straightened back onto the road. "Ansel," Willa May said, "I'd just as soon stick around and see my hundredth birthday so maybe I should just get out right here and walk."

"Mommy, you'd fall before you took your second step on this icy mess," Ansel argued.

Willa May sat back and started praying early that Sunday, praying that they would be able to get to church in one piece. It took a while, but Ansel finally saw her into the church. Mack and Robert were on either side of her, holding her so she wouldn't fall down the ice caked steps. Once the service ended, Willa May said to Ansel, "Son, I know you were all set to take me down to Walt Whitman's for dinner, but I don't think you ought to risk it in this storm."

Squinting against the gusty wind swooping and swirling around them, Ansel said, "Tell you what. Let's go a little ways and just see if maybe we can drive out of this. I hate to disappoint Walt Whitman and all the family."

They inched their way across the treacherous road and got into the car. Ansel had a Plymouth, a big boxy thing. Even backing onto the road, it swerved and whipped back and forth on the ice. "Fishtailing" was what Ansel called it. Once he came to a stop and started forward, he got it under control and they headed out of Glen Ferris, creeping along at a snail's pace. The swirling snow made it hard to see. Willa May kept thinking that Ansel would give up and turn around, but an hour later as they passed Smithers and headed toward the Silver Bridge that would take them over the river into Montgomery, she realized that he had meant to get to Walt Whitman's no matter how difficult it proved to be. She shook her head, thinking to herself that he was getting more like his pa every day he lived...and just as willful.

Before they could reach the bridge, they hit a white-out. All they could see was a wall of white encircling the car. As they drove out of it, Mack leaned forward and asked, "Why, is that a man standing there by the road?"

Ansel took his eyes off the road for a second and glanced over at his side of the road. "I can't see nothing in all this snow."

"Up there," Mack pointed. "See that black shadow?"

"Let me get closer. I'll slow down. Keep your eyes on it and see if you can tell what it is. If it's a man, he'll need a ride in this storm."

"But we're goin' the wrong way for him," Robert pointed out.

"Doesn't matter. Whoever it is, he'll probably be glad for the lift. Can you see him yet."

They slowed down, hardly moving at all. Mack peered through the windshield. "Yeah. I think it is a man. Pull over. I'll run across the road and see."

Ansel pulled off the road. Tugging his coat collar up around his ears, Mack jumped out of the car. Robert was sitting behind Ansel. He squinted against the blowing snow, saying, "I can't even see Mack now."

Everyone leaned forward, peering for any sign of Mack or the hitchhiker. Moments passed as they strained to see through the thick sheet of snow. Suddenly, the car door swung open and Mack hopped back in. He didn't shut the door and snow blew onto the front seat, scattering on the wind.

"Well?" Ansel asked. "Was there a man or not?"

"Sure was," Mack smiled.

"Where in tarnation is he? Doesn't he want a ride?"

Before Mack could answer, the man poked his head into the open door and said, "I sure do!"

Even covered in snow and red faced from the wind, Willa May knew in a second it was Manny. She clapped her hands together and squawked, "Praise the Lord!" Then, wondering what was taking Ansel so long to respond, she looked at him. His mouth was working, but he couldn't utter a sound. Tears streamed down his face. His shoulders gave a shudder as he burst into sobs. Everyone climbed out of the car. Huddled against the storm, they hugged, kissed, and hugged some more. Ansel was so shaken, he couldn't drive. Mack got behind the wheel as they climbed back into the car, brushing layers of snow off their coats. Manny sat up front between his brother and Ansel. Willa May watched with a knowing smile as Ansel wrapped his arm around Manny's shoulder, holding onto him like he would never let go again. She remembered feeling the same way when Ansel came home after the first Big War. As old as she was, she would never understand why men had to create wars that tore families apart and separated them from the ones they loved most in the world, sometimes forever.

When they arrived at Walt Whitman's, Manny was passed around the room like a new puppy. The menfolk ruffled his hair and the women hugged him and exclaimed how happy they were to see him home. He looked awfully thin when he took off his coat and they got a good look at him, thinner than Willa May liked. He explained that he had been in a hospital for six months after he was liberated from his Japanese captors. It had taken him that long to get his strength back and fight off the malaria he had contracted. Thin and peaked, he was still a welcome sight. Ansel didn't take his eyes off his boy all day.

They sat down to a big ham dinner and Claude Daniel brought some champagne. Everyone toasted Manny and welcomed him home. Just before they touched glasses, Willa May added, "And may we never see our loved ones go off to another war again."

"I'll drink to that," Manny said.

"Amen," Ansel agreed.

By evening, the storm had let up and the roads weren't nearly as treacherous as they had been that morning. Even so, Ansel left the chains on and the men were forced to take off their coats and spread them under the tires to get up the hill at Beulah's. Exhausted, Ansel was relieved when Beulah insisted that his family spend the night at her house.

The next morning, Beulah, good-hearted like her mama, got up and made a huge breakfast for them with pancakes, eggs, bacon, sausage, biscuits and gravy. She brought out her last jar of apricot preserves that she had been keeping back for a special occasion. Manny ate half a dozen biscuits and preserves, saying over and over, "Beulah, this here is the best eating I've had in years!"

Beulah smiled and said, "We've been saving them preserves for something special. I reckon seeing you back home again is special enough."

"Thank you, Beulah. I'm mighty glad to be home, too."

"Now that you're back, what do you think you want to do?" Willa May asked.

Manny shrugged. "When we left, things were still real tight, with nary a job to be had. I reckon I'll see if I can get hired on somewhere. If I can't, then maybe I'll just buy me some land with the money I've got coming to me from Uncle Sam and raise me some dairy cows. Folks always need milk, as long as they keep making babies. I figure that with all them boys back from the war now, there'll be a lot of babies coming into this old world for sure."

Ansel perked up. "I never thought of it that way, but you're right, Son. Maybe I'll take some of my money and buy some good milk cows, too."

Together, Ansel and Manny bought dairy cows. Manny bought a piece of land adjacent to Ansel's farm. They began a small dairy business, making deliveries all over the valley just as Ansel and Asa had back in their bootlegging days.

In the fall of nineteen forty-seven, Nellie was fresh out of college. She was hired as the new school teacher at the elementary school in Glen Ferris. Just a two room schoolhouse, it held six grades. It was so small that it only served the folks there in the village, Kanawha Falls, and a little hollow named Boonesboro. Faced with teaching three grade levels at once, Nellie wasn't the least bit worried. She had an air of confidence about her that Willa May was sure would see her through the low times when she wondered why she ever thought she wanted to be a teacher. But she was never one to stick her nose up in the air. Folks saw this right away and they knew that she would be good to their children and see that they received a proper education.

Education was a word that was being used more and more after the war ended. Soldiers came back home to finish their schooling, knowing after seeing some of the world, that they were going to need an education to get ahead. It was a good time to be a teacher.

Ernest Roy was superintendent of Fayette County schools when he hired Nellie. He let her know right away that it wasn't because she was kin that he had hired her. With a stern expression, he looked at Nellie and said, "You were one of five people we interviewed for this job. And it's no mistake, nor a show of partiality on my part that you were hired over the others. Your credentials were outstanding. In fact, your supervisor praised you, saying that you were the best in your graduating class."

"Thank you," Nellie replied, more than a little nervous by Ernest Roy's stern manner. "I promise you I'll do my best to live up to that."

"That's exactly what I expect, young lady. Just because you landed this job and just because we're related doesn't mean you'll continue in this job if you don't perform to our standards."

"Yes, sir."

"Now the first thing you should do is find a place close by to live. Maybe you can board with a family in the village."

"I can't live at home?"

"You're expected to be ready to receive those children by eight o'clock every morning which means you should be there shortly after seven to set up for the day. Living up in Poe, you'd have to leave home no later than six-fifteen...and that's in good weather. You could make it, but once you begin teaching, I think you're going to find that kind of a drive a waste of precious time and an unnecessary annoyance in the winter. No, take my word for it, you'll be better off rooming in the village. And the sooner you locate a room, the better."

"Whatever you say," Nellie agreed, not really wanting to move away from home and leave Ansel and her brothers to fend for themselves. But she could see that Ernest Roy wasn't going to rest until she was in Glen Ferris.

She left his office in Fayetteville, in the same building where Ansel's office had been, and drove down to Glen Ferris. It was almost noon and Nellie started feeling twinges of hunger. She stopped by Beulah's and had lunch with her and Willa May. They were excited for Nellie, getting her first teaching job, but they could see that something was troubling her. Finally, Willa May asked what was wrong.

"Oh, Grandma, I am happy about my job, I really am. But..."

"But what, darlin'?" Beulah asked.

"Well, Ernest Roy said that he expects me to live here in Glen Ferris now that I have this job. I'm worried about Pa and the boys -- what'll they do without me to cook for them and mend their clothes? And besides, I don't really know anybody here except you and Thomas Lee. How do I go about finding a room for rent?"

Beulah looked at Willa May and they both smiled. "First off," Willa May answered, "your pa and your brothers are so plum proud of you that they would never stand in your way. They're grown men and they can manage. Who knows? Maybe it'll put the urge in Ansel to find himself a new wife. These women hereabouts still swoon over him."

"As for looking for a place to stay," Beulah added, "you've found it."

"What?"

"You can stay right here. With all of us."

"Oh, Beulah, I couldn't move in on you like that!"

"Why, we'd love to have you. And I won't take no for an answer. You're moving in tomorrow and that's that. Besides, maybe it'll give my boys an extra reason to get their homework done with a teacher under our roof."

The next morning, Ansel drove Nellie down from the farm with all her things and she took the room across the hall from Willa May. Rooming at Beulah's, Nellie still felt like she could come home at night to family. Beulah and Dewey used the rent money she paid them to buy Willie Joe a guitar and get him lessons. Listening to Nellie, it brought back the burning desire to teach that Willa May had felt when she was a young girl. Often, Willa May helped Nellie grade spelling tests or arithmetic problems. She ate it up and she knew Nellie could see that she did. Nellie always came to Willa May for advice, spewing with ideas for decorating her classroom for each holiday. Once, she decided to make angels out of folded magazines, spray painting them and attaching wings tipped with glitter. For their heads, she used styrofoam balls and colored in their features then glued yarn on for their hair. Out of wire coat hangers, she made halos and covered them with sparkling gold ribbon. Willa May thought they were the cutest little things she had ever seen. Each child took one home for a

Christmas gift that year for their folks.

There was no hot lunch program at the school, so Nellie signed up parent volunteers to come in on Thursdays to make hot dogs or homemade soup for the children at a price they could afford. She used those lunches to teach the children their table manners. The first few weeks, Nellie could hear loud belches and slurping with their soup, but after a month, their food wasn't nearly as noisy going down.

Besides helping Nellie with planning and grading, Willa May was happy to spend time with her granddaughter and get to know her as the young woman she had become. Nellie knew how much Willa May had always loved to read and when she discovered that her grandmother could no longer see well enough to read fine print, she started reading a chapter each night to her. Together, they went through Fitzgerald, Hemingway, and Faulkner that year. Nellie was partial to Faulkner, but Willa May liked Scott Fitzgerald. Her favorite was The Great Gatsby, such a sad love story, she mused. Nellie drew everyone in Beulah's household into their readings. She assigned everyone parts in the plays she borrowed from Walt Whitman and Thomas Lee. Willa May favored "Our Town" and wondered if maybe that was how death really was, looking down on loved ones every day and talking it over with the rest of the dead. But Willa May's favorite playwright was Tennessee Williams. She could hardly make it to the movie house when "Cat On A Hot Tin Roof" was playing, featuring young Paul Newman and that dark haired beauty, Elizabeth Taylor. She cackled with glee when Sister Woman sassed Brick about which bowl game he had played in and looking her dead in the eye, he set her straight.

In the spring of 'forty-nine, the family planned a Sunday dinner together at Ansel's farm. It was Decoration Day weekend and Beulah and Dewey took Willa May over to Page for Sunday services. After church, Willa May decorated the graves of her kinfolk, then they set off for Poe. Dora Lottie wanted to get a head start on dinner, so she had gotten to Ansel's early. Putting on her apron and fetching a butcher knife, she set off for the barn to kill a couple of chickens. Ansel and his brother-in-law sat down at the kitchen table, drinking coffee and talking. They were so caught up in their men talk that they didn't realize how long Dora Lottie had been gone until nearly an hour later.

Ansel said, "Wonder what could be keeping my baby sister so long?" Checking the clock on the kitchen wall, he added, "Maybe I'll go up and see what's keeping her."

When he got to the barn, the door was ajar. After being out in the bright May sunshine, it was a while before his eyes focused in the sudden darkness of the barn. He heard Dora Lottie before he could see her. Hearing a weak moan, Ansel called, "Dora Lottie, is that you?"

Ansel's eyes slowly adjusted to the darkness and squinting into each corner of the barn, he found Dora Lottie lying on the ground face down. He rushed over to her and saw that her hair was matted with blood. When he tried to turn her over, he found the butcher knife she had carried with her driven into her stomach. "Sis? Sis, it's me, Anse. Can you hear me? Dora Lottie, can you hear me?"

Dora Lottie's eyelids fluttered, then closed again. She went limp in Ansel's arms. Ansel ran back to the house for help. By the time Willa May arrived with Beulah, Dewey, and Nellie, emergency attendants were loading Dora Lottie into an ambulance, ready to rush her to the hospital in Oak Hill.

"What on earth happened?" Willa May gasped, clutching Nellie's hand for support.

"Best we can figure it" Ansel replied, "was that she had gone up into the loft after a chicken. She must have stepped on some rotted boards and fell through. When she fell, she hit the back of her head on the stone wall of the barn, then landed on the knife."

"How bad is she?" Dewey asked.

Ansel didn't answer, he just shook his head. Willa May could see that Ansel felt somehow responsible, berating himself for not replacing the rotted boards in the loft before this. "Ansel," she said, taking hold of his arm, "this was an accident. You couldn't have known that somebody would get hurt on those old rotten boards. So don't go blaming yourself for this, you hear?"

Unable to look at her, he said, "If Dora Lottie dies, Mommy, I'll never forgive myself." To Willa May, he sounded like he was already lost in grief.

Everyone followed the ambulance over to Oak Hill, pulling up just in time to see Dora Lottie's husband go inside with her. It seemed like days instead of hours until they finally saw a doctor. From the grave look on the doctor's face, Willa May knew that they had lost Dora Lottie. He stepped inside the door to the waiting area where the family was seated. Looking around the room, he asked, "Is there a Walt Shrewsbury here?"

Leaning heavily on his cane, Walt Whitman stood up with Thomas Lee and Claude Daniel on either side. He started toward the doctor. "I'm Walt Shrewsbury."

The doctor spoke only a few words in too low a voice for the rest to hear, then he left. Walt Whitman collected himself then he turned to look at Willa May sitting next to Ansel. He limped over to them. Beulah and Dewey made room for him to sit down on the other side of Willa May. Ansel still looked like he would give anything if he could take Dora Lottie's place. "It's bad, ain't it?" he asked.

Walt Whitman nodded. Words were coming hard for him as he fought back tears. "She's bleeding inside her head. Doctor said he's never seen a worse concussion, the whole back of her head was split wide open."

"Can't they do anything?" Willa May asked.

"All they can do now is make her comfortable."

"Can we see her?"

"Mommy," Walt Whitman patted her hand, "she won't even know you were there."

"Yes, she will, too!" Willa May answered sharply, perhaps a little too sharply, she thought, when she saw a flicker of pain in Walt Whitman's eyes.

"She needs her rest. Please try and understand, Mommy."

"I want to see my little girl," Willa May insisted.

"I'll take you in," Ansel said. Ansel never could deny his mother anything. Willa May knew that, like his pa, Ansel would fight anyone who tried to keep her from doing what she wanted.

"Then let's go," she answered.

Ansel helped her up and they made their way to Dora Lottie's bed. There was a nurse sitting beside the bed. She apologized, saying she had orders to stay with her patient. "That's all right," Willa May said. "I just want to be here with her." Taking Dora Lottie's hand, she sat down in a chair that Ansel pulled over for her. With the nurse, Ansel, and Dora Lottie's husband, Willa May stayed with Dora Lottie until the last. She died around ten o'clock that night. Willa May never got to talk to her, to beg her not to go, but she believed that with the extra sense that Dora Lottie had always had, she somehow knew they were there. She knew they loved her and didn't want to lose her. They buried her close to Glenny in the churchyard in Page.

Ansel no sooner got home from the funeral when he set fire to his barn. He sat up all night watching it until the last board was nothing but smoldering ashes. That Sunday, Dewey and Beulah took Willa May and Nellie up to the farm. The women caught their breath when they pulled in the yard and saw the big black square burnt into the hillside where the barn had stood. Willa May asked his boys where Ansel was. Manny told her that Ansel had gone up into the hills after he watched the barn burn down, adding that Mack had gone into the woods to see if he could find their pa after Ansel didn't come home the first night.

"He'll be home when he's of a mind to be," Willa May said. "Remember when they cornered that Billy Bob after he killed Leanne and little Faith?"

Ansel's three sons nodded.

"Your pa went off then, too, if you recollect. Remember, too, that poem by that Englishman, the one that talks about when the world is too much with us?"

Again, they nodded.

"Well, that's just the way it is for your pa right now. Once he thinks he can face the world again, he'll come back. Meanwhile, you just have to carry on without him and keep this place goin' while he's gone. Matter of fact, I think it'd be a mighty fine surprise for him if you were to build another barn while he's gone. A fine new barn with some more milking cows. Something for him to do when he gets back."

Manny got up and came over to her and gave her a big hug. "Grandma, if I live to be as old as you, I only hope I'm near as smart."

Willa May laughed to herself and said, "Darlin', when you've seen as much of this world as I have and lived through it all with a Shrewsbury, then you get a little wise to the workings of the world and the men in it."

Manny gave her another hug and promised they would start on a new barn the following day. Hearing about it, Thomas Lee and Claude Daniel took the week off from their busy schedules and brought all the grandsons and great-grandsons -- all that were old enough to hold a hammer -- and helped put up the new barn. By the second day, all the women heard about the barn raising and they went up to cook for the men. It was a wonderful sight for Willa May, watching all the men in the family raise up entire wall frames on ropes. She sat under a big, shady maple tree and watched while they

348

worked. She only wished that Daniel could have been there to see his grandsons and great-grandsons pitching in together, knowing that he would have loved every second of it. It was a special joy, too, in knowing that Ansel would be so proud and pleased when he got home and saw the fine new barn, the family's gift to him.

When the first frost in November coated the ground like powdered sugar, Ansel came down out of the mountains. Manny said that when he first spotted him, Ansel was circling around the new barn, looking at it in total amazement as if he was looking at one of the pyramids over in Egypt. He went inside and came out again, then circled it once more. He shook his head and such a big grin spread over his face that Manny could see it from the kitchen window. All that mattered to the family was that Ansel was home again, ready to go on living. That Sunday, he came to take Willa May to church as though nothing had happened. When he walked her up the aisle of the Methodist church, heads turned and Willa May could hear folks whispering. She knew they were all talking about Ansel, but she didn't give a hoot in hell what they were saying. Her boy was home again.

Chapter Fourteen

In June of nineteen fifty, President Truman announced that the United States was at war with North Korea. This time James Houston's youngest boys and Beulah's and Dewey's boys enlisted. Fighting centered around Korea's thirty-eighth parallel. Early on, the capital city of South Korea fell into the hands of the communists. General MacArthur was put in charge of the troops, but it was the air war that played a big role in this new war. For the first time, they were fighting with jets, Sabres against Russian MiG's. A year later, Truman relieved MacArthur of his command, fearing that his plan to aggressively pursue the Red Chinese Army which was backing the North Koreans, would lead to nuclear annihilation. Ridgeway followed MacArthur, letting the troops fight it out on the battlefront with help from jet fighters.

James Houston lost his youngest son, Riley, at Pork Chop Hill. Beulah's son, Roy, was wounded when he took a bullet in his chest at Heartbreak Ridge. For days, the family didn't know if he would live. It was decided in the end that the communists would stay north of the thirty-eighth parallel. Korean citizens who weren't willing to follow the communist rule would stay south of that line. Being such a small country, Korea lost so many men that it never regained its strength.

Back home, Thomas Lee and Nola had already had four babies and one more was on the way. Their three little boys -- Lawrence, Thomas Lee, Jr., and Claude Daniel -- were a handful. All rough and tumble, they were spirited little boys. Sometimes Willa May thought Thomas Lee was amazed at so much life surrounding him as the boys tackled him to the floor when he came home each evening. But he was a good father, always tossing a football with them or swinging them on the swing set in the back yard. Even from the start, Willa May could see that Lawrence had inherited that same alert and smart manner that Thomas Lee had about him as a boy. He told her one day that he wanted to grow up to be a great writer. He said he wanted to write books even better than <u>Treasure Island</u> and <u>Kidnapped</u>, his two

350

favorites. Thomas Lee told her that the boy always had a book in front of his face, reading way into the night up in his bedroom.

In the fall of 'fifty-two, just after school started, Nola called Thomas Lee at his office in Montgomery. Little Thomas Lee had been out playing with a neighbor boy and hadn't come home for supper. When she called the neighbor's house, their boy said he didn't know where little Thomas Lee was. He had come home and left his friend playing over by the river. When Nola heard this, she asked, "What were they doing by the river? Thomas Lee isn't allowed over there." The neighbors only apologized, saying that they didn't allow their boy near the river, either. They said they would come right over to help search for little Thomas Lee, Jr.

With Thomas Lee driving home from work, taking the curves on two wheels, Nola and the neighbors began their search of the river bank. They walked the entire length of the village from where Beulah lived, but they never found a trace of the little boy. By the time Thomas Lee drove up, the neighbors had gone back and brought their own son over to show them where he had left little Thomas Lee. The boy led them up the river bank almost to the church where there was a small dock with a row boat tied to it. There was still no sign of little Thomas Lee.

Nola burst into tears, screaming for her little boy. Thomas Lee had to carry her back to their house where he called the police. Then he called Dewey and Beulah.

Within an hour, Dewey, Ansel and his sons were walking the river bank, too, helping in the search. Willa May, Nellie, and Beulah went to Thomas Lee's house to be with Nola. They could hear Nola upstairs crying when they arrived. Nellie took a glass of wine up to her to help settle her nerves. Beulah kept the other children quiet, holding their baby girl, Jolene, and rocking her to sleep in their big oak rocker.

An hour later, Claude Daniel came in, out of breath, carrying his black medical bag. Without a word, he headed upstairs and gave Nola a shot to help her sleep. When he came back to the kitchen, he gave Willa May a hug and a kiss. "I'm sorry I didn't say hello before, Grandma."

She waved him off. "You did just what you had to do. Nola needed you more than me. But I have to tell you, I'm awful worried."

Claude Daniel sighed heavily. "It doesn't look good, does it?"

"No, not good at all."

Ansel and his boys came in. Grabbing a cup of hot coffee, they all asked if they had received any news of little Thomas Lee from any of the others in the search party. Willa May shook her head. Kissing her on the cheek, they each took their coffee and headed out the door to rejoin the search. Claude Daniel followed them. Willa May thought they were already gone when Ansel stuck his head back in the door. "Are you goin' to be all right, Mommy? I'll stay here with you if you need me."

"Don't worry about me. Just find that little boy and bring him home safe," she said.

"You sure?" Ansel asked.

"Just go. Thomas Lee will feel better knowing you're there with him. He's the one that matters now."

The men were only gone a few minutes when Walt Whitman and Annie Catherine arrived. Thomas Lee had called them before leaving his office, but Annie Catherine was at a meeting of her church ladies. They apologized repeatedly for taking so long to get there. Both of them looked frightened, unable to face the idea that little Thomas Lee might be gone. Walt Whitman went back and forth from the house to the search team, bringing them news, checking on Annie Catherine and Nola. Annie Catherine insisted on staying with Nola in case she came around, saying she didn't want Nola to wake up all alone.

The police searched all night, going door to door through the village and asking if anyone had seen little Thomas Lee. No one had. It reminded Willa May of the story of the little boy who had put on wings made out of wax. When he flew too close to the sun, he fell to earth, but nobody saw him; they just went on about their daily business. By morning, she was worried about Thomas Lee. He had been out all night, pacing up and down by the river and calling for his boy until he lost his voice. Dewey came in around daybreak and offered to take Willa May home so she could rest, but she wouldn't hear of it. How could she rest with all this happening? Her heart broken, she just knew she couldn't rest until they found little Thomas Lee.

The police began dragging the river the following day. When Nola came to, they told her that they were still searching. She started screaming uncontrollably so Willa May sent for Claude Daniel to come and see to her. He gave Nola another shot and she slept through the day. That night when she came to, she begged them not to put her out again. She promised she would try to get hold of herself. Try as she might, though, Nola was a bundle of nerves, pacing back and forth, wringing her hands and jumping every time someone came in the door. Beulah, Nellie, and Willa May tried to take her mind off little Thomas Lee, but no matter what they talked about or what small task they gave her to perform in the kitchen, the three women knew that her mind was never off of her little boy.

For three days, the search team dragged the river, edging closer and closer to the falls at the lower end of the village. When they didn't find anything, they started dragging past the falls where the currents were swifter. On the fourth day, they found little Thomas Lee's body, bloated from being underwater for so long. Thomas Lee took one look at his son and fell to his knees, screaming amid sobs. It took Ansel and Claude Daniel both to get Thomas Lee to his car. When Thomas Lee came through the door, Willa May thought he had aged twenty years. His shoulders sagged and his eyes were red and swollen. He took one look at Nola who was holding her breath, hoping against hope, and said, "Our boy's gone." Nola jumped up from her chair and ran out of the room. "No! No, I don't believe you," she screamed. "Give me my boy back!" Racing upstairs, she ran to Thomas Lee's room and called his name again and again. Thomas Lee collapsed onto a chair in the kitchen. Leaning his arms on the table, he put his head down and wept. Ansel looked at Claude Daniel and said, "You see to Nola. I'll stay here with Thomas Lee."

Walt Whitman wrapped his thin, bony arms around his son, wanting to give Thomas Lee some comfort, but knowing there was little anybody could do for him. Annie Catherine followed Claude Daniel upstairs, saying she would watch the children and keep them busy. Beulah, Nellie, and Willa May were crying, too upset to offer support. None of them could believe that such a tragedy could befall a family that had been so happy. It was too painful for any of them to grasp. When Dewey came in, Beulah and Nellie set about collecting their things and getting ready to leave. Willa May couldn't bear to leave Thomas Lee as upset as he was and she said so. Ansel got up and took her hands in his. "Maybe it's best if you do go, Mommy. I'm sure that Thomas Lee is goin' to need some time to himself. I'll stay here with Walt Whitman and Claude Daniel till I see that Thomas Lee and Nola are all right. You just go on. I'm sure this has taken its toll on you, too. You're goin' to need your rest."

Willa May nodded, still looking at Thomas Lee slumped over the kitchen table, crying inconsolably. She kept thinking, if only there was some way to erase what had happened. But she knew that tragedy

353

didn't work that way. "We all have our crosses to bear," she told herself. She knew this burden was going to be one that Thomas Lee and Nola would carry for a good long while. If there had been some way to soak up all their pain, she gladly would have.

Ansel stopped at Beulah's the next day, his face covered with a five-day stubble. He looked almost as bad as Thomas Lee had, his eyes just as bloodshot and red rimmed. He sat down and Dewey started to pour him a shot of whiskey, but Ansel waved it away, "No thanks, Dewey. I've had enough whiskey in the last twelve hours to float that river out there." He gestured toward the big dining room window and the river beyond. "If it's all the same to you, I'd just as soon have a cup of coffee."

Dewey gave him an understanding smile and put a pot of coffee on to brew. Willa May reached across the table where they were seated and took hold of Ansel's hands. They were trembling. "How are they?" she asked.

Ansel looked up at her, grasping her hands in his and holding tightly. "I don't know, Mommy. I don't know. I think maybe Nola will make it, knowing that she's got the other three younguns to care for and one more on the way. But I don't know about Thomas Lee. Walt Whitman's awful worried, too. We sat up all night, drinking and talking, trying to keep Thomas Lee from goin' completely out of his mind with grief. But I don't know." Ansel looked off, his voice dropping with his last words. His eyes drifted to the window again and to the river. After a minute, he added, "Just ain't' right to lose a baby like that. Ain't right at all."

She knew that Ansel was thinking back to when he waited day after day for word of Manny, wondering if he was dead or alive. If anybody knew Thomas Lee's pain, it was Ansel. She was glad that Thomas Lee had his pa, his uncle, and his cousin with him.

Dewey brought Ansel's coffee over. "Is it all right with you and Beulah if I stay here some over the next few days?" Ansel asked.

Dewey nodded, sitting down with them. "Sure, Anse. Anything you need, you just say so and it's yours."

"Thanks. Claude Daniel and me decided to take shifts staying with Thomas Lee and keeping him...keeping him from doing anything crazy."

None of them had to ask what that "anything crazy" might be. "It's that bad?" Willa May asked.

Ansel rubbed the back of her hands with his thumbs. "Yeah. I'd say it's that bad."

For the next week, either Ansel or Claude Daniel was always asleep upstairs in the boys' old room, the other staying down at Thomas Lee's and helping out. It was three days after they found little Thomas Lee's body when they held the funeral at the church. Willa May couldn't remember a sadder funeral in all her life. Just looking down at the small coffin, she couldn't believe that it was meant to hold a child who had been so full of life. But Thomas Lee was still too deep in shock to accept what had happened. She watched him sobbing in Walt Whitman's arms, feeling utterly helpless.

It took most of a year for Thomas Lee to start acting like himself again. For months, he went off to work, but everyone wondered how he managed to keep up. He didn't seem aware that there was anybody around him most of the time; he was lost in a place far removed from the rest of them.

Two weeks later, Walt Whitman phoned, saying that Josie had died. Everyone was surprised that she asked to be buried at Page as close to her kin as possible. Willa May supposed that in death, she was finally able to claim them as kin. Walt Whitman and Thomas Lee were called in by her lawyers to be present at the reading of her will. She left her mansion on the boulevard in Charleston and her summer home in White Sulphur Springs to Walt Whitman. She requested that her money go to pay for a college education for any of the children in the family. Never having children of her own, she died a lonely woman. There was a letter addressed to Willa May that her lawyers gave to Walt Whitman. He delivered it to her that day.

When he opened it, he read:

> "Dear Mommy,
>
> By the time you read this, I will have gone on. I only hope that somehow you will find it in your heart to forgive me after all these years. I know you never approved of what I did, but please believe me when I tell you that I could no longer endure the way of life in which I believed you to be trapped. Now that I'm older, I know that you were never trapped, that you actually loved Pa and the life you had with him. By far, it was more than anything I ever had in my marriage, although it has taken me a lifetime to realize that. By the time I did realize what I had sacrificed, it was far

too late for me. Pa was dead and I knew that you
could never forgive me in this life for the heartache I
had brought upon the two of you. Please know
that I am sorry -- sorry for everything.

> Your loving daughter,
> Josie Shrewsbury"

Willa May listened as Walt Whitman finished reading. Then he
looked up at her and asked, "Are you all right, Mommy? This didn't
upset you, did it?"

"Yes, it does upset me, Son. It riles me to think that she spent her
life separated from us, not even claiming to be kin to us. And for
what? In the end, she didn't have anything but big old empty houses.
More like prisons than homes, if you ask me. What was it all for?
Can you tell me? I sure can't figure it out."

Walt Whitman shook his head. "I don't know. Shame? A need to
feel some sort of dignity? A desire to feel important? Maybe it was all
that. In the end, she did regret it."

"Yes. In the end."

Four weeks later, Walt Whitman keeled over in his living room
with a stroke. He died five hours later. When Thomas Lee came to
Beulah's door at four in the morning, Willa May knew he brought
more bad news. She wasn't sure who took it worse, Thomas Lee or
herself. After Walt Whitman died, Willa May took to her bed and
stayed there for six months, praying every day for the Lord to take her,
too. She wanted to put an end to all her loss.

In the spring, Claude Daniel called Beulah to ask her to tell Willa
May that Hattie Sue was in the hospital in Charleston where he
worked. Willa May got up out of bed, knowing that Claude Daniel
wouldn't have called unless it was serious. They climbed into
Dewey's car and he drove them to the hospital.

"What's wrong with Hattie Sue?" she asked when Claude Daniel
came to take them to her room.

Claude Daniel stopped and looked down at the floor for several
seconds before answering. Looking up at her with tears in his eyes, he
said, "It's cancer, Grandma."

The word hovered in the air like a bad odor. Willa May could feel
that familiar choking sensation in her throat like some huge hand
holding her, squeezing tighter and tighter. When she could manage to

get the words out, she asked, "How long?"

"A month...two, at the most."

She felt herself weaving like she was going to faint. Claude Daniel caught her and led her to a chair. "Maybe this is going to be too much for you, Grandma. I'll have Dewey drive you back home."

"No!" she said sharply, still feeling dizzy and wishing she could catch her breath. "I'm not leaving. Hattie Sue needs me."

"Grandma, I can't ask you to stay. Look at you. Why, you're just too weak for all this," Claude Daniel argued.

She sat up as straight as she could and looked Claude Daniel in the eye. "I'm not goin' anywhere. I'm staying right here and that's that."

Seeing how determined she was, Beulah said, "Claude Daniel, I think maybe Grandma knows what she can handle and what she can't. If she needs to go home and rest, she knows we're right here."

Claude Daniel was still doubtful. Finally, he relented. Showing them to Hattie Sue's room, Willa May stopped him outside the door and asked, "Can't they operate and take the cancer out?"

"We opened her up this morning. I assisted. Grandma, the cancer's too far gone. All we could do was sew her back up."

"Is she in much pain?"

"We can keep her comfortable, at least until the end. And then even the morphine we're giving her won't help much."

For the next six weeks, they spent their days and nights between Glen Ferris and Charleston. The last night, Hattie Sue was in terrible pain, begging for something -- anything -- to put her out of her misery. At one point, she grew clear in her head and looked at Ernest Roy and Claude Daniel. "I don't mind dying so much. It's leaving all of you -- all my family -- that I can't bear." Ernest Roy had to leave the room, he was too overcome to stay another minute. But Claude Daniel and Willa May were there when Hattie Sue breathed her last, each of them holding her hand and praying that the Lord would have mercy on her and end her suffering. She died at three thirty-five in the morning on July seventh, 1953.

That September, for her hundredth birthday, Willa May's family had a picnic at Hawk's Nest. The state had torn down their house, the cabin, Elroy's place, and the barn. Where they had been a long open shelter made out of stone now stood. Inside, there were places to barbecue with tables and benches. It was pretty enough, but Willa May couldn't help but miss their place as it had once been. Everyone brought food. They ate and ate, devouring hot dogs, baked beans, and homemade pickles. It might not have been considered such a feast by some, but hot dogs, West Virginia style, with spicy chili sauce, creamy cole slaw, onions and mustard, were Willa May's favorite. All the family knew how much she loved them. Afterward, while the little ones roasted marshmallows over the dying fire, Nola and Beulah brought out a long birthday cake with exactly one hundred flaming candles on top. Everyone joined in singing "Happy Birthday" to Willa May and Nola told her to make a wish and blow out the candles.

"Why, I can't blow out all those candles!" she protested.

Thomas Lee, smiling for the first time in ages, said, "C'mon Grandma, we'll all help."

Everyone gathered around close and blew at the candles with Willa May. The cake was delicious -- chocolate inside with a creamy chocolate filling and white frosting. It was a good thing they had made such a huge cake because everybody ate two helpings, shaking their heads as if they had never tasted anything so good before. Willa May thought they were probably right.

In 1956, James Houston came down with a bad condition that his doctors at first thought was tuberculosis. He coughed constantly and had difficulty breathing. When he took Willa May's advice and went to see Claude Daniel, he found out he had the dreaded black lung disease. After working in the mines all his life, breathing in coal dust day after day, he was told that he was dying from all that black dust that had accumulated in his lungs. It was eating away at the inner lining of his lungs, turning his lung tissue black.

Claude Daniel came to see Willa May the following Sunday, bringing her a copy of a new novel by a writer named Grace Metallius called Peyton Place. He had asked the store clerk to wrap it in pretty paper for her. After he read the summary on the inside of the cover to her, Willa May thanked him for the present, then asked him about James Houston.

He seemed reluctant to talk about it at first, then he said, "James Houston's x-rays showed he has what we call 'complicated black lung'. Both lungs have been almost completely destroyed. He has all the typical signs -- chest pain and severe shortness of breath."

"Can he do anything for it?" Beulah asked.

Claude Daniel shook his head. "There's no cure." Standing up, he paced up and down the front porch. Willa May could see that he was having trouble accepting this. Finally he said, "I can't tell you how many miners I see who are in the same boat as James Houston. Hundreds of them. It's not right. Here they've worked hard all their lives for the few dollars they've earned and now they're dying for it. It's just not right."

"Can't the union get them any help?" Dewey asked.

"All they can do is help with some of the medical expenses. If I had my way, there would be some sort of compensation for those men and their families, a part of it payable while they're ill and the rest paid to their families when they die. The coal companies owe the miners that much."

"Sounds fair to me," Willa May agreed. "So why don't some of the politicians in the statehouse do something about it? You'd think that they'd know that these miners need their help."

"Oh, they know all right, but we're a poor state. It would take the federal government to pitch in and supply funding for that kind of measure."

"So if some of you doctors who have treated those miners for black lung could get some of those old boys in the statehouse to make a big stink, do you think you could get the federal government to chip in?" she asked.

Claude Daniel raised his dark eyebrows and said, "That's a mighty big 'if', Grandma." Still, Willa May could see that she had planted a seed in his head because he looked thoughtful and preoccupied through the rest of his visit.

The seed Willa May planted that day grew and grew until it finally took root and became law. That fall, Cecil Underwood ran for governor and won. When he took office, he appointed Thomas Lee as his attorney general. By that time, Thomas Lee had become popular among the people in the southern part of the state, winning cases for many of them. He spoke out on issues where the rights of the common man were concerned, always defending the miners and farmers. Willa May told him that he should run for governor himself, but he just laughed and shook his head. "Trying to help people while you're battling the legislature is like trying to win a Monday night boxing match on TV with one arm tied behind your back." Willa May thought that he would make a fine governor, all the same. Thomas Lee said that he was surprised when the phone call came from

Underwood's campaign headquarters the day after the election, asking if he would take the job of attorney general.

As soon as Claude Daniel heard of the appointment, he threw a party for Thomas Lee. He had a home on the boulevard, close to where Annie Catherine lived now, in the house that had belonged to Josie. Nellie told Willa May that over a hundred people attended the party. Willa May had been invited, but she told Beulah, Dewey, and Nellie to go without her. At a hundred and two, she wasn't up to partying late. From what Nellie said, Claude Daniel made it an elegant occasion with champagne poured all evening by waiters in black suits and a long table filled with food. Nellie brought home a plate of food for Willa May and a bottle of champagne that Claude Daniel had insisted she take as well. The next evening, Thomas Lee and Nola stopped by. Willa May asked Thomas Lee to open the bottle of champagne so she could toast him properly. Everyone squealed with delight when the cork came out, making a loud pop. Willa May decided she liked champagne, even if it did tickle her nose with its fizzing and bubbling.

Most of all, she was proud of Thomas Lee. He and Claude Daniel had always been smart as tacks. Now all that smartness had paid off for them. One was the attorney general and the other a doctor. They had made the entire family proud. Her only wish was that Walt Whitman, Hattie Sue and Daniel could have been there to see them. They would have all been so proud.

While Thomas Lee was in Charleston working for the state, he and Claude Daniel got together and started the ball rolling, trying to get black lung legislation passed to help the miners. By the time it came into being, it was too late to help James Houston, though. He had passed on in 'fifty-six. But the law helped many miners and their families. It made the mine owners responsible for part of the funding, something Willa May never thought she would live to see. It did her heart good to see the mine owners forced to pay their fair share. In her years, she saw too many good men doing backbreaking labor day after day and year after year, getting nothing but a hard time in return. Now they had won back a small compensation for all the years of hard work.

In the fall of nineteen fifty-nine, folks took notice of a young

Catholic Congressman from Massachusetts who wanted to be the next President. Mostly, they laughed it off, saying there would never be a Catholic in the White House.

That same fall Nellie came home late from school one evening looking troubled. Willa May asked her what was wrong and she said she would tell her after she spoke with Ernest Roy. Willa May knew that it was Ernest Roy's supper time and she wondered what could have happened that Nellie would interrupt his supper. Nellie talked in a low voice over the phone for a few minutes and then hung up. When she came into the parlor with the others, she dropped into the nearest chair, slumped over as though she was too disheartened to go on. Willa May, Beulah, and Dewey looked at each other, wondering if they should ask what was wrong or just wait for her to talk when she was good and ready. While they were trying to decide, Nellie said, "I thought I'd seen about everything, but you'll never believe what I saw today." She shook her head like she wasn't sure even now that she believed it herself.

"Well, honey, what on earth was it?" Beulah asked.

Nellie heaved a deep sigh and said, "When we started school a few weeks ago, I saw that we had a new family from across the river. They had five children -- and that's just the ones that were school age. Three more are home as I found out today. The family's name is Blake." She stopped and looked at Beulah and Dewey to see if they recognized the name. But Beulah and Dewey shook their heads and shrugged.

"I knew from the ragged way the children were dressed that they must not have much. The children came to school without any lunches, dirty and just reeking from needing a bath. The three oldest ones have black, rotting teeth, so I could see they haven't had much care over the years, either. Why, some days they look like they've not only slept in mud puddles, but they've eaten dirt, too. Now I think I might not have been far from wrong."

"Did you say something to them to try and find out what was goin' on?" Willa May asked.

"Oh, sure. I've asked them almost every day, but they just hang their heads without a word. It's just pitiful the filthy condition they're in. I knew they were hungry, so I started bringing extra food with me, knowing that they wouldn't have anything to eat all day. So today I decided to find out once and for all what was goin' on over at their place. I rode the bus up to the bridge and got off with the children and

361

walked all the way back into that hollow up there on the hill. While nobody over there has much, at least the houses are clean and well kept, for the most part. But when these Blake children showed me their home, I couldn't believe my eyes. I've known some mighty poor people growing up, but this was far worse than anything I've ever seen. Just a shack with no insulation. The floors were so dirty, I couldn't see them for all the filth. There was dried food splattered here and there and a big dog was roaming around. I guess the leavings on the floor were his -- I can't be sure, though. The mother looks to be in need of medical attention. I don't think she has all her faculties from what I could see. There were two babies, lying in their own foul mess, screaming for someone to come and take care of them and the mother didn't seem to even hear them. As I was turning to go back outside to get some fresh air, the father, reeling drunk, staggered into the house and started shouting at me to get out and leave them alone, calling me a 'nosy old bitch'. Then he actually swung at me, so I rushed outside. The other five children were under the porch, huddled together in the dirt and obviously terrified of the father. It made me wonder if he's beaten them before in one of his drunken stupors. One of my other students who lives close by -- the Knight boy -- brought his mother over to talk with me. She says that they've lived like that ever since they moved there this summer. She knows that those children have spent every night right there under the porch. Some of the neighbors offered to take the children in, but the children are too afraid of the father, so they just stay there and suffer. She did say that they bring food to the children and I guess that's all the food they ever get, other than what I've brought into school with me."

"What are you goin' to do?" Dewey asked.

"I called Ernest Roy just now and told him what I saw there today. He said he would come tomorrow with the sheriff and have all eight of the children put into the county home for their protection. He promised he would do his best to have the father brought up on charges of abuse and take those children out of his custody once and for all. As for the mother, if she's as far gone as she appears to be, I guess that they'll have to commit her for treatment. Maybe they can get her into the hospital over in Spencer. I hear that they're doing good work over there."

"You did the right thing, honey," Beulah offered. Willa May and Dewey nodded in agreement.

"Just be glad that you can get those younguns some help," Willa

May said.

"I just hated leaving them there after what I saw. I've seen squalor, but I never thought I'd see -- or smell -- anything like what I did today. It just turned my stomach. And I'd like to take Pa's belt to that father for mistreating helpless children that way. It just burns me up!"

"Why don't I pour you a drink?" Dewey asked, getting up from the sofa. "You look like you could use one."

"Thanks, Dewey," Nellie sighed, running her fingers through her hair. "I think I'll run up and take a quick bath first, though. I still feel covered in that dirt and filth I saw over there."

The following day, Ernest Roy and the sheriff paid a call on the Blakes while the oldest five were at school. Like Nellie had said, they found what Ernest Roy termed "inhuman conditions" and the sheriff hauled the father off to jail. The children were all sent to the county home. Later, Nellie found out that they had been put in foster homes with good families. She worried about the memories that the oldest ones would carry with them.

Nellie found herself disillusioned from what she had witnessed. She thought of the children she taught as her own, teaching them right from wrong and giving them the best she could with what little she had to work with. The parents knew that and respected her for it. This incident shook her belief in her fellow man and left her wondering about what some people did to their children. It was a hard lesson. Willa May was glad that Nellie was able to get the children the help they needed. She told Nellie that they were lucky to have had her to stand up for them. She knew that the oldest ones would always be grateful to Nellie.

Willa May received word that Effie Lee had passed on late in nineteen fifty-nine. She had moved out to the coal fields in Indiana when her husband was laid off years before. Her oldest daughter wrote that Effie Lee had suffered a heart attack and just didn't make it. The mother in Willa May wanted her baby back home to rest through eternity with her own kin, but it had been some time since she had last seen Effie Lee and she reckoned that time and distance had taken its toll on how close they once were. Still, she wished that she could have seen Effie Lee one last time.

Ansel was the only child she had left and he was busy with his dairy business which was doing very well. His three boys had married and started raising families of their own. Nobody could have been happier about it than Ansel. He was just about the proudest grandpa Willa May had ever seen. Every time a new baby came into his family, he took her to the hospital so she could see her newest great-grandchild. Standing there looking through that glass at those little babies, it was hard sometimes to think she had ever been a wee baby like that, nursing at her mama's breast. But she could remember like it was yesterday what each one of her babies had looked like, how sweet each one had been. Looking at Ansel's grandchildren, she saw a lot of Daniel and Ansel in them. She chuckled to herself that some of the boys would grow up just as wild and reckless as their grandpa had been.

Once some of the little ones in the family got old enough, Ansel made a game of taking them up to the barn to help milk the cows whenever they visited. More than once, the rest of the family watched Ansel walking up the hill, an empty bucket in one hand and a child's hand in his other. Each time, Willa May knew just what Ansel was saying. He would take them up on the hill, dotted with cow droppings and feeling ornery as ever, he would say, "Watch where you're stepping here, now. I sure wouldn't want you to step in some of that delicious chocolate pudding laying here on the ground."

Then the child -- whichever one it happened to be -- would always look up, surprised at Ansel and say, "Uncle Anse, don't you know that's not chocolate pudding?"

"Sure it is," Ansel would answer. "My cows just leave piles of chocolate pudding everywhere, that's how good they are!"

The child would either give Ansel a doubtful look or if he felt particularly brave, he would point out that those big brown piles weren't chocolate pudding at all. Thomas Lee's youngest boy, Claude Daniel, came back from milking the cows once and pulling his pa aside, he asked Thoams Lee if Uncle Anse was a little touched. When Thomas Lee heard this, he laughed until tears streamed down his cheeks. Then he said to Willa May, "You know, Grandma, I believe Anse gets more like Grandpa every day he lives. I can still remember when I was just seven or eight, how I'd come to visit you two and Grandpa would always say to me right off, 'You mean to tell me they still got you?', as if I was going anywhere else at that age!"

Willa May laughed, remembering what a charge Daniel and Elroy got when Thomas Lee looked at Daniel, a puzzled expression on his face. Of course, both of them knew just what Thomas Lee had been thinking back then; nothing much got past the two of them. Thomas Lee was right, though -- Ansel was Daniel all over again, taking such joy in his grandchildren and all the Shrewsbury children. Often, looking at a room full of Shrewsburys, he patted Willa May on the shoulder and asked, "Did you ever think that you'd be bringing so many younguns into the world when you had us?" Willa May had to agree that she never had reckoned on having so many offspring.

In 1960, Willa May made up her mind to vote for the young Catholic boy running for president. He came courting the state of West Virginia, sparking all the folks with his talk of financial aid to their poor state and programs like preschool for children who had never had the chance at early learning. Kennedy was dazzling to those impoverished mountaineers who had never gotten anything but a hard time from every other politician...that was, when any of them paid West Virginians any attention at all. It paid off well for the young Congressman -- all that courting, shaking hands, and making promises -- quoting Robert Frost and saying he had "promises to keep" and a long way to go before he slept. When the Democrats held their national convention, the young candidate ran his family ragged, trying to gain enough electoral votes to put him over the top and guarantee him as their choice. Then the representative from West Virginia stood up and proudly proclaimed to the entire assembly on national television that all its electoral votes would go for Kennedy, handing him the nomination for his party. The announcement was met with thunderous applause, people cheering and chanting the name Kennedy.

Some folks in the state still worried that Kennedy might try to use his religion to change the country over to Catholics, but Willa May knew that was just hogwash. She told everyone that boy from Massachusetts was way too smart for that kind of nonsense. The kind of change he was promising was more like a wake-up call, like the rooster crowing out in the barnyard in the morning, letting folks know a new day was upon them. To Willa May, living over a hundred years and seeing more politicians come and go than she cared to remember, this man stood out like a bright shining star up in the night sky, more brilliant than any of the others, a signal lighting the way. She just

365

knew in her bones that he was meant to be President. Even though it didn't set well with Thomas Lee and all his Republican friends trying to stay in power in the statehouse, she decided like thousands of other voters in the state to cast her vote that November for the Kennedy boy.

The election was nip and tuck all the way. She grew tired, but Willa May stayed up and watched the TV returns that night until Walter Cronkite came on and announced that Kennedy had won. Usually, the only television she watched was "Bonanza" because Little Joe Cartwright reminded her so much of Ansel when he was young. But wild horses couldn't drag her away from the TV set on election night. She knew she wouldn't rest until she saw that young man who had charmed her fellow mountaineers assured of being the President. When the word came, Willa May, Nellie, and Dewey let out such whoops that the windows rattled, they were so happy.

The first thing Kennedy did once he was elected was to name his Cabinet members. For Attorney General, he called on his brother. Right away, the news people accused Kennedy of favoritism. But as Willa May always told her children and grandchildren, the only thing that mattered was family. She could see that Kennedy, coming from a big family, had learned that lesson already. To her way of thinking, it just showed how wise the man was. She couldn't understand why it was so hard for everybody else to understand this. Didn't they know there wasn't anyone a person he could trust like his own blood? In the end, Kennedy had his way and his younger brother -- the one with all the children -- was sworn in. Soon the new President was faced with the Cuban Missile Crisis, a sobering new experience in the nuclear age. Willa May felt that the President had certainly done the right thing in appointing his brother as his Attorney General. Who else could have given him support through such a dark hour?

On the day Kennedy was sworn into office, Annie Catherine passed away. She died in her sleep, just didn't wake up that morning. She left the two homes in Charleston and White Sulphur Springs to Thomas Lee. By then, Thomas Lee had made a name for himself across the state. There was talk among the Republicans that come election time, they planned to back Thomas Lee Shrewsbury for governor of the state. When Willa May heard this, she shook her head, wishing that Walt Whitman and Annie Catherine could have lived to see their only child sitting in the governor's mansion. She knew that Thomas Lee still had to get elected, but rumors of the crooked administration Wally Barron was running were on everyone's tongues. Folks wanted a man they could trust running the state, a name they knew and felt comfortable with. That was Thomas Lee. She only hoped she lived to see the day. Her own grandson a governor! It took her breath away just to think about it.

In May of nineteen sixty-three, Beulah told Willa May she had a phone call from a man named Bill Foster who said he wrote for The Charleston Gazette. He was interested in interviewing Willa May. Beulah took the man's name and telephone number and promised she would get back to him after she spoke with Willa May. Beulah explained to the reporter that, at one hundred and ten years old, Willa May was very frail and she might not be up to seeing visitors. But Willa May told her to call the fellow back and have him stop by that Thursday.

When Foster arrived, dressed in a seersucker suit and straw hat, Willa May was seated on a rocking chair on the front porch. She had on her favorite dress, the color of violets, dappled with small flowers of periwinkle and rose. As she rocked slowly back and forth, she gazed at the mountain across the river. She spent much of her time looking at the mountain where she and Daniel had settled, reminiscing about old times.

After he introduced himself, Foster said he was interested in interviewing Willa May for a series of articles he was writing for the upcoming centennial celebration. "As I explained to your granddaughter over the phone, there are a lot of events planned for the celebration. But I thought I would focus more on the memories of some of our elderly citizens. What they remember about our state -- the wars, the mines, the UMW and how it got started. A sort of collage in words and stories from the people who were there." Here, he paused as if to make sure that Willa May understood what he was saying. "Anyway," he continued, "when I began my research, I discovered that you're the oldest living native of West Virginia, Mrs. Shrewsbury, and I thought you would be the main focus of my articles."

"Willa May," she grunted.

A look of confusion came over Foster's face. "I beg your pardon?"

"It's 'Willa May', not 'Mrs. Shrewsbury'. None of my friends will know who you mean. Just call me 'Willa May'. Got that?"

"Yes, ma'am."

"Well, when do we start?" Her voice, raspy in old age, grew gravelly when she lost her patience.

"I want as much as you can remember," Foster pressed.

"Son," Willa May replied, "I won't leave out a thing."

Hearing that, Foster plugged in his portable tape recorder and placed it beside Willa May, handing her the microphone. "How far back do you remember, Mrs. -- er, Willa May?"

"Back to when the mountain laurel bloomed."

Foster looked hopelessly to Beulah, who sat next to Willa May in another rocker. She smiled and nodded to Willa May like a teacher nods encouragement to a student who has given part of an answer correctly and searches for the rest.

"When the mountain laurel bloomed?" he asked.

"You got a hearing problem, Son?"

"No, ma'am, I just don't understand."

"Mountain laurel. You know, what city-fied folks like yourself call rhododendron."

Foster looked even more perplexed. He shook his head and gave a slight shrug.

"The mountain laurel bloomed the summer when I was eight, back in 'sixty-one -- that's *eighteen and sixty-one* -- like the hand of God had come down out of the heavens and painted the mountains pink and purple. It was downright spellbinding, it was. And it was the summer that my Daniel first came walking out of the mountains, a dead mountain lion slung across the back of his neck..."

Willa May talked for nearly two hours into the microphone. By the time she finished, she had told Bill Foster all about the night the men had burned them out, killing her unborn baby. After an hour, the young reporter had removed his jacket, loosened his tie, and sat wide eyed as Willa May continued her story. When she finished telling him about Daniel's revenge, he begged her to continue, but all her talking had sapped her strength. She asked him to come by again the following week, same time, same day, and she would tell him more. So began a story that drew Foster back to that shady porch week after week throughout that hot, hazy summer. He realized after his third visit that Willa May's story was going to be far too long to use in its entirety in the newspaper so he decided to try his hand at a full-length book. He settled on <u>Mountain Memories</u> for its title. He planned to tell Willa May's story, "not leaving out a word".

During his calls on Willa May, he met several members of her family. Each time she introduced him to one of her grandchildren or great-grandchildren, he noticed the look of pride in Willa May's eyes as she described that relative's accomplishments. He already knew that her son, Ansel, owned a multimillion dollar dairy business that covered three states. After meeting Claude Daniel, Thomas Lee, and Nellie, Foster had to agree that Willa May did have a remarkable family. Foster recalled meeting Thomas Lee a few years before when he was writing an article on the former governor and he was aware of the rumors circulating around the state that Thomas Lee was going to be the next governor. When he mentioned the rumors, Thomas Lee started to reply, but Willa May broke in. "Why, my grandson is goin' to be the finest governor this state has ever seen! You just wait and see."

Epilogue

Willa May didn't see her grandson elected governor. I had spent all summer and most of the fall of 'sixty-three taping her memoirs for my book, recording the trials she had faced and the simple joys she had shared with her husband, Daniel. On November eighteenth, I received a call at work. It was Willa May's granddaughter, Beulah Pearce. She informed me that her grandmother had passed on that morning. The doctor said her heart had simply given out. Somehow, I found that disturbing. Over the course of my visits, I had grown quite fond of this frail silver haired lady. I had never known anyone who had more heart than Willa May.

As I drove to Page for the funeral, I noticed the hills around me -- the hills where Willa May had been a little girl. Stark bare branches stripped of their fall foliage lined the hills and I recalled that during my last visit, I asked Willa May how she was. She answered with, "I reckon I'll live to see the mountain laurels bloom come spring, Lord willing." I found myself wishing that she could have lived just long enough to see the mountains speckled with the bright pinks, purples, and reds of the rhododendron that she so dearly loved. I knew that with their return each spring, her memories always turned to her Daniel.

Her funeral was held at the Baptist church where she had been married some ninety-seven years before. She was buried next to the monument erected in her husband's honor. I watched them lower her coffin into the dark earth and felt a deep sense of loss, not only for the friend I had come to know, but for the courageous and noble woman I had discovered. I thought to myself how fitting it was when Thomas Lee, her beloved grandson, had quoted in his eulogy from the book of Proverbs, describing the woman of valor: "She is more precious than rubies." Willa May had indeed been a rare and precious gem.

The service took place on a sunny November day, Friday the twenty-second. No sooner did I arrive back at work that day when the teletype machine burst into life, printing the news that President

Kennedy had been shot in Dallas with no word about his condition. Less than an hour later, we were all thrown into shock when again the teletype printed out the message that Kennedy, the young promising President, was dead.

During the aftermath of the next few days -- Oswald's arrest, his assassination, the funeral procession with the riderless horse and young John F. Kennedy's farewell salute to his father -- I forgot all about a book that Thomas Lee Shrewsbury had handed me as we had walked back to our cars following the service. It was a well worn, first edition of Walt Whitman's Leaves of Grass.

Unable to watch any further coverage of the president's funeral, I turned off the television and climbed the stairs to my study. On my desk lay the book Willa May had left for me. Feeling shell-shocked from such overwhelming loss, I opened the book and sifted through the yellowed, brittle pages. I hoped to find some ageless words of wisdom, some message of hope in the lines of the great American poet. What I found was an aged photograph in sepia tones that dated back to the late eighteen hundreds. It showed a young soldier, sandy haired and grinning from an eternally youthful face. Turning it over, I discovered a name, written in flowing penmanship: "Daniel Shrewsbury, Jr.". Surprised, I turned the picture over again and examined the handsome smiling face more closely. So this was the young man who had died trying to capture Geronimo, the son who had gone off in search of adventure and his manhood. I recalled how often Willa May had said that her 'Lil Daniel had been the "spitting image" of his father. As she had said, he was remarkably handsome. There was a ruggedness, something so solid it seemed almost tangible, emanating from that reckless grin. Something that must have been the side of Daniel that had so charmed Willa May right from the start. Looking at it, I recalled an older man at the funeral service. A man with the same features, the same rugged appeal. I realized he must have been Willa May's only surviving son, Ansel.

I was about to tuck the photograph back in its resting place inside the book when I noticed something else held between the pages of the book. A faded blue ribbon, almost white with age. I knew instantly that this was the ribbon Daniel had sent Willa May during the Civil War when Eb suddenly appeared on her family's doorstep that blustery Thanksgiving Day.

The ribbon was frayed along the outer edges, much the worse for wear, but I felt deeply honored that Willa May had requested that something she held so precious be given to me. Over the last few months, she had shared the story of her life with me. Now she was sharing all that remained in her life that she cherished -- her book, her photograph, and her ribbon. All that she held sacred.

THE END

Rebecca Cale Camhi grew up in Glen Ferris, West Virginia. She received a B.A. in English from Marietta College, Marietta, Ohio, and an M.L.S. from the State University of New York at Buffalo. She is the author of two short stories for children as well as a collection of poems entitled <u>Still Lifes</u>. Mrs. Camhi has been named to <u>Who's Who In American Education</u> and <u>2,000 Notable American Women</u>. A member of Phi Delta Kappa and the American Library Association, she serves on the Steering Committee of the Western New York Writing Project at Canisius College. Her hobbies include horseback riding, snowshoeing, reading, quilting, and travel. She lives with her husband and two children in Buffalo, New York, where she works as a Library Media Specialist.